# THE FALLEN AND THE ELECT

## BOOK III - AURORA'S CHILD

Jerry J. K. Rogers

# Copyright Page

The Fallen and the Elect – Aurora's Child

Published by JJKR
http://www.jjkr-writings.info

Edited by Bradley Ray King
Copyedit by Cheresse Graves
Proofed by Moonlight Proofreading (Kristin Masbaum)

ISBN 13:  979-8-6360021-4-7

# Table of Contents

# Dedication


## The Book

*In memory of Minnie Medesta*


## The Series

*To Cesar, Cynthia, Vickie, Michael, Monika, and all members of the 163d Communications Flight, during my twenty-six years in the organization, you were the most dedicated and professional co-workers I've had the enjoyment of serving with in the California Air National Guard. And to the late Colonel David Bandini and late Major Hal Byers who led us through many challenges and successes.*

*God gives to each man his own destiny, and each decision is a brick laid upon that path.*

Dr. Ashere Vasquez

# Chapter 1 – An Unexpected Visit

"How did you get in here?" Cardinal Millhouse asked, his aged and brittle voice undermining the forcefulness he had intended to convey. He focused his question towards two men sitting on the brown leather couch in the office parlor of his personal residence. One, with dark skin, a well-groomed short afro and small mustache, had a thin build and wore a custom tailor-made pinstripe suit. He sat back relaxed with his arms up on the backside of the couch. The other man, portly, pockmarked face with short jet-black hair laced with light brown, olive skin and Mediterranean features, dressed similarly to the first, except for a poorly implemented tie. The tip reached halfway down over his potbelly.

Neither man responded to the Cardinal's inquiry.

"Who are you and what are you doing here?" the old, thin, and frail Cardinal asked with indignation that his previous question went unanswered. "I'm going to call the police," he said, rushing over to his desk to make the call.

"Why does everyone say they're gonna call the police, when you'll be dead in a few minutes before the police can get here to do anything?" the stocky man replied as he stood. "Of course, if you tell us what we want to know, we may let you live. I doubt it, but we'll at least think about it."

Cardinal Millhouse stopped. The threat seized his muscles, each rapid beat of his heart punched inside his chest. A pasty complexion washed upon his face. "Who are you?" he asked again, his weak voice was barely able to expel the question.

"You know who we are. We represent several of the nations and organizations who've donated heavily in what was supposed to help in eradicating a common pest seen by some as a thorn in our side and disease upon the earth. They learned that a good chunk of the monies given to the Church as a charitable donation to help with the special vaccine, were used to fund some sort of mysterious project, and the point man at Everest, who was responsible for our representatives' endeavors, seems to have disappeared. We need for you to tell us where he's at."

Again, Cardinal Millhouse attempted to make his way over to his desk as the pockmark faced man stepped over to intercept him.

"We've done our homework. We know about the personal security team that was outside and your duress alarm," the stout man stated, now standing next to the Cardinal and putting his arm around the frail cleric's shoulder, guiding him to the couch. "Come over and join my friend."

The dark-skinned man shifted on the couch over to the side. "Yes, come over and join me," he said while patting the empty center cushion next to him.

Cardinal Millhouse acquiesced to the stout man's physical coercion, sitting on the couch in the middle of the two. Droplets of sweat formed on his forehead.

The pockmarked man stood back up and strolled to the Cardinal's polished cherry wood desk and sat on the front leading edge. "So, Cardinal, are you going to tell us what we want to know?"

"What is it you want to know?"

"We want to know about what happened to the monies for the Aurora project. It seems Everest may have spent a good portion for something apart from the virus."

"I don't know what you're talki…"

The stout man interrupted; a wry grin flashed on his face. "Don't play games. Yes, you do."

"I was kept in the dark under the direction of the Church, they didn't tell me." Cardinal Millhouse didn't want to disclose anything concerning the child in case they weren't aware. He was thankful elements of the Society of the Holy Order of the Child managed the exodus of the child and Gary Applethorpe to Rome via confidential transportation methods and a convoluted route. This allowed him to maintain limited plausible deniability.

"Do you expect us to believe that?" the stout man asked. "You and the Church were the conduit in taking our donations. You know all aspects of what's going on, especially since you were the primary coordinator."

The overweight man presented Cardinal Millhouse with a puckish grin. "You're all knowing, aren't you, so you have to know more than that."

"Yeah, you do," The man next to Cardinal Millhouse said, as he put his arm around his shoulder and squeezed. "Come on, you can do better than that."

"What happened with the virus and the money? You promised your donors that they could keep their hands off as not to get in trouble with International laws. There was

3

another secret project, wasn't there? Or did Gary Applethorpe steal the money and run off knowing he couldn't produce the virus as promised? And be truthful, we'll know if you're lying. Was that little incident at the Everest labs several weeks back just a ruse?"

Hearing that the men did not seem to know about the child relieved Cardinal Millhouse. "The Aurora program was interrupted by two individuals, Father Jose Hernandez and Sister Justine Gates. The Church commissioned the two to find out why an angel killed everybody at a funeral at Thomson and Thomson. They ended up searching and finding out things we didn't anticipate. We thought they would've come up with some miscellaneous trite we could peddle, but that wasn't the case. They disrupted the Aurora project at Everest." Cardinal Millhouse regretted informing on the two members of his clergy in the Diocese. If the two unknown assailants went to go and question them, they could reveal information concerning the child.

"Wow, you threw them under the bus quickly. I mean our employers believed you when things slowed down early on with the death of the team members in Aguascalientes eleven and a half years ago, and the loss of that one doctor, I think her name was Doctor Valdez. Then for something like that to happen again late last year, and another doctor supposedly went missing – come on, are we gonna sit here and believe this? And do you expect us to believe that story about a priest and nun?"

"It's true. They believe that an angel was involved in attempting to try and hinder the project," Cardinal Millhouse said, stress and nervousness reducing his ability to project his aged voice. "I've excommunicated them, unofficially anyway. I was having my staff work on

4

the paperwork, though it's hard to do without revealing too much of the project. As far as I'm concerned, they're no longer representatives of God and the Church."

Both men stared at each other and remained quiet, Cardinal Millhouse not sure if he should continue with saying anything else.

"As God is my witness, that's the truth," Cardinal Millhouse said, breaking the awkward silence. "You know that a special order of angels has been directing all of this, just as with those whom you represent. And they foretold there would be those who would be against our work."

"It was an angel that recommended we talk to you. And as for those whom we represent, they placed a lot of financial resources in working with you in seeing Aurora through for years. You failed them, regardless of what the angels said."

"There's nothing else I could possibly tell you – I can tell you more after I find out more. We're still trying to analyze the full impact of what happened at the Everest lab in Eagle Rock."

"We know the impact, you failed. And you never did tell us where Gary Applethorpe is," the portly man stated.

"I don't know where he is."

"Are we supposed to believe that? We know that you and Everest have been working close together. You need to tell us where he is."

Cardinal Millhouse didn't want to risk divulging any more information than necessary, in turn, information concerning the child. His heart continued to race. "I think you should go, there's nothing else I could tell you."

"You're right, it's time for us to go," the stout man said as he nodded his head, focusing on his partner sitting on the couch. His colleague reached in his pocket pulling out a hypodermic and removed the orange needle cover.

"What's that for?" Cardinal Millhouse asked, attempting to rise off the couch, but the strength of the man sitting next to him overpowered his aged and feeble body, preventing him from getting up. "We want to make sure you're telling us the truth before we leave."

The dark-complexioned man inserted the needle into the side of the Cardinal's wrinkled neck made taut by his assailant pulling on his skin while subduing him.

"Now, you're gonna tell me all that you know about Gary Applethorpe, where he's at, and the monies for the virus?" the dark-complexioned man whispered.

Cardinal Millhouse's head began to swirl, his stomach became nauseous. "I've told you what you need to know; I don't know where Gary Applethorpe is. I wasn't told...he and the child left...they think the virus was destro...Angel Falls...they went through Chica...down to South Americ...I don't feel well...I feel..."

The Cardinal's eyelids fluttered before closing shut. His body became flaccid.

The dark-complexioned man slapped the Cardinal's cheek. "Stay with me, old man. They went through where? Down to where? What child?" He placed his middle and index finger on the Cardinal's neck to check for a pulse. It weakened, then ceased. "Crap, I told the chemist we should have used a lighter dose or different compound. I don't think the old man's body handled the new truth serum formula."

"It still shouldn't have killed him."

"Maybe because he was already stressed, his blood pressure may have been elevated and his heart or something couldn't take it."

"Leave him then, we'll find something," the large man said, walking around to the backside of the Cardinal's desk.

The dark-complexioned man stood while lowering the Cardinal's limp and lifeless body onto the couch, pulling up the legs and crossing the arms across the cleric's chest.

"What the...why are you doing that? They're gonna know that he didn't die of natural causes if he looks like he's been propped on the couch like that."

"I think it's the right thing to do, that's all. I mean he is a holy man and all," the dark-skinned man responded, now rearranging the Cardinal's body back to its original position.

"From what I've been briefed, our sponsors should've been more hands on early in the game with the project. If they had been, we more than likely wouldn't be here doing this right now."

"That may be true, but I thought the countries wanted to keep as much distance as possible. When we get back, we need to get in touch with Xavier to see if he wants us to start searching for that priest and nun the Cardinal mentioned."

"Maybe, but let's see if we can find anything else the old man might have been keeping from our employers. You think it's true about what one of the company's employees mentioned, thinkin' there was another secret project?"

"Dunno, the Cardinal did ramble something about a child. Keep looking, it's our best lead. Not sure what the Cardinal meant by that though. That angel said we should find what we're looking for. Let's just do like it told us."

The two men scavenged through the Cardinal's hand-crafted expansive cherry wood desk, rummaging through the top drawer, sifting through papers, pens, pencils, paperclips, rubber stamps, and other miscellaneous office supplies. They searched the side drawers scanning through notepads and writing tablets. For ten minutes, in the file drawers of the credenza behind the desk, they parsed through the file folders of each of the churches and parishes in the Diocese.

The dark-complexioned man went over to the built-in wall credenza, opening the doors to reveal a luminous LCD computer display screen, and keyboard atop a pull-out shelf. "Well, I don't have to worry about trying to use my cracking tools to sign into his account. The booger is logged on." He rolled the Cardinal's high-back leather office chair from the desk over to the computer terminal and sat. He pulled a USB stick from his pocket and plugged it into the USB port on the side of the display unit. "I'll copy all the relevant files and directories. There's gotta be something in here about what happened to the money our bosses invested."

"Maybe, if he was open about it," the overweight man responded, returning to searching through the books on the built-in shelving units next to the credenza. "But I doubt the Cardinal would've kept the information we're looking for on their church wide network system. I wouldn't."

Another ten minutes passed as both men circumnavigated the room making sure to return everything to its proper place.

"I'm going to go make a copy of the security video to show proof of the job," the dark-complexioned man commented. "Then I'll zap the video recorder and do one

8

more look on their network, then I'll verify the injection of the trojan logic bomb so we can crack into the network later if need be."

"Do you smell something?"

"I smell a dead lying Cardinal…wait…I do smell it – it's like rainwater or how the air smells before a thunderstorm."

A radiant and shimmering figure wearing white raiment with a vibrant blue sash and belt, stood in the middle of the room. "It is done, I see," the angelic figure stated.

"Yeah," the portly man answered. "But he died before we could fully question him. We did find out there may have been two persons who may know something about the destruction of the virus."

"There are three," the angelic creature said. "They're watched over by those antagonistic to my brethren and those who are against Aurora. Your job is now done."

"What did you want us to do?"

"There's nothing else here linking the Cardinal and the virus project at Everest?" the angel asked.

"Nothing we could find so far concerning Aurora; it's a bust for us," the portly man answered. "We managed to copy some information from the church's network, but the files look encrypted. When we get back, we'll try to decrypt them if they are, and then analyze them. Maybe there's some information in there."

"And he mentioned something about a child being associated with the project," the black man added.

"A child?" the angel responded. "You found out about a child?"

"Yes, before we got here, there was rumor of a child, and the Cardinal kinda confirmed it."

The figure darted over to the portly man and grabbed his head, twisting with such force that it caused a loud cracking sound. The portly man's lifeless body collapsed to the floor. Before the black man realized what had happened, the angelic figure was upon him and snapped his neck. His body fell to the floor seconds after the first.

# Chapter 2 – Investigation

Detectives Green and Matthews of the Los Angeles police department negotiated through the small crowd of spectators and news media congregating on the semi-circle driveway entrance leading to Cardinal Millhouse's ranch style personal residence. Initially, they were confused as to why they had been the ones called out to the scene. Initial reports stated the Cardinal died of natural causes, so why call in homicide detectives, more so for a high-profile case outside of their normal precinct. They deduced there was more to the initial reports.

Once inside, they navigated through the house as several Crime Scene Unit specialists dusted for prints and took evidentiary pictures in the foyer and adjoining hallway. Their guide directed the two detectives to the parlor office. A body lay covered with a white sheet on the couch. Extensive evidence collection was underway in every area of the room.

"Who found the Cardinal?" Detective Matthews asked while examining the deceased body of Cardinal Millhouse.

"Father Yancy, his aide. He had come over to close out some administration tasks with the Cardinal and to help him settle in for the evening," Lieutenant Wilson, the detectives' commanding officer, answered as he entered the room from the entrance leading to the dining area.

"Lieutenant, what are we doing here?" Detective Matthews asked, scratching his scalp through his short afro. "This isn't even in our assigned precinct."

"This is considered a high-profile case when you have a dead Cardinal with special circumstances," the lieutenant answered.

"Still not our precinct," Detective Matthews said as he rolled his light brown eyes.

"What are we looking at?" Detective Green queried while accomplishing a preliminary scan of the room. On the hardwood floor was what resembled the shape of two human bodies burned into the hardwood floor slats, each form etched in different positions and layered with grayish-black soot. Both spots had the remnants of a charred key set, a charred belt buckle, and blackened remains of a nine-inch melted piece of metal and plastic, assumed to be an expensive writing utensil. One contained a long needle and tiny melted blob of burnt orange and black plastic. A young priest with lightly curled hair and ebony skin tone was kneeling next to one of the anomalies scorched into the floor, administering the last rites. Lieutenant Scott Wilson went and stood next to the father, waving for the detectives to join him.

"Is he giving last rites to whatever that is on the floor?" Detective Green asked.

Lieutenant Wilson put his finger to his lips displaying the gesture for his two men to keep quiet.

"I'm done, Lieutenant," the kneeling priest said as he stood still clenching a rosary in his hand. He reached out with his right hand to shake the hands of the new arrivals.

"I'm Father Yancy, and yes, I'm giving last rites to these two departed souls."

Detective Green raised an eyebrow. "These were bodies?" he questioned in a skeptical manner.

"We have a strong reason to believe so. Look at some of the objects in the soot," the lieutenant directed. "This is part of your special circumstances."

Both men knelt with Detective Matthews pulling out a pen that he used to poke and probe the articles on the floor, ensuring not to move them too far from their original location. The one of most interest was a small melted blob of plastic wrapped around a presumed thin, inch long metal sliver etched with multiple lines.

"What is that?" Detective Matthews asked. "Looks like some sort of burned circuit thingy."

Lieutenant Wilson and Detective Green knelt to garner a closer look. None of the three recognized the mysterious object.

"It's what's left of a USB drive," a nearby Crime Scene investigator said.

The Lieutenant and Detectives Matthews and Green all curled their eyebrows giving the investigator a quizzical stare.

"How in the heck do you know that?" Detective Matthews asked.

"We see something like that all the time at fire investigations depending on how bad they're damaged." The investigator stooped next to the men. "Notice the charred electronics and the tiny little square patterns cut in the metal, that's one of the clues. They're found in all types of objects, keychains, pens, ends of flashlights, you name it."

"Were pictures taken of this?" Detective Green asked.

"Yep," the Crime Scene investigator answered as he stood and resumed his duties of examining objects in the room.

"So how do we know for sure this use to be a person? There's no natural way something like this could happen to someone," Detective Matthews said.

"You're right," Father Yancy whispered. "Nothing natural could cause this."

The detectives suspected Father Yancy's tone was implying something else.

Father Yancy continued. "We're telling the media and those in the church that Cardinal Millhouse appears to have died of yet unknown causes at this time. We're not mentioning anything of these two suspected bodies. We're being realists and know trying to keep something like this quiet will last all of about five minutes, but we're working to keep this under the lid."

"A natural cause story wouldn't last for long," the Lieutenant interjected.

"Follow me," Father Yancy requested.

Both detectives glanced towards the lieutenant, who nodded his head in agreement. Father Yancy took lead guiding the two detectives down the hallway and turning into the kitchen, where they passed through a laundry room and into a large walk-in utility closet towards the rear of the house. Several display monitors and the electronic equipment of the security system rested inside on a set of shelves. Multiple thin blue cables entered through an access sleeve in the wall below the ceiling appearing as a waterfall that flowed down to a large black electronic unit connected to a computer workstation.

A short Latino police officer in jeans, collared shirt, and lightweight blue vinyl jacket labeled "Police Crime Scene" stood inside the door in front of two display units and a keyboard. "About time someone got here. I was getting tired of waiting. I have it cued up."

"I take it this is the security system?" Detective Matthews asked.

"Yes," Father Yancy replied. "Watch what happens before and during the time of Cardinal Millhouse's demise."

The video replay displayed the two strangers entering the Cardinal's office parlor a couple of minutes before the Cardinal walked in. The sequence of events played out showing the three occupants in the room talking and leading up to the death of Cardinal Millhouse. Next, the two mysterious men rummaged through the room.

After a couple of minutes, Detective Matthews got bored. "Okay, so they're going through everything in the room, after they killed the Cardinal; it makes sense they were looking for something."

"Let me advance it," the crime scene investigator said. He fast forwarded the video to a later time stamp showing the two men looking as if to be talking to someone. Less than a minute later, their heads turned and snapped. Their bodies dropped down onto the floor. The digital video blanked for less than three seconds. Once the image returned, the dark silhouette of two men smoldered on the wood floor at the same location where the two had laid.

"What the hell?" Detective Green said, attempting to ignore the sensation of insects crawling on his skin. "That's too freaky."

Detective Matthews moved closer to the screen wanting to obtain a closer look at the image. "It's strange, though, you have two men who appear to be talking to thin air, then drop to the ground and then somehow go poof. Crap like that just doesn't happen. How do you know they didn't jack with this video, deleting where they somehow made it look like they were the same bodies of the two men who killed the Cardinal? Maybe that's why the screen blanked out. It was to cover their tracks."

"Watch this," the crime scene investigator said as he skipped back several seconds on the video and slowed down the playback speed to the point before where the men dropped to the ground. The stout man's head twisted to the left by what looked like large spectral hands that momentarily appeared and disappeared, followed by the body dropping to the floor. His partner experienced the same condition. The time stamp for the blank video displayed 2.75 seconds had elapsed.

"You see that?" the crime scene investigator asked. "It looks like something or someone grabbed the side of their faces, twisting their heads and snapped their necks, killing them before they fell to the floor."

With narrowed eyes and pursed lips, Detective Green stared at the crime scene investigator with disbelief.

"That's what you want to think," Detective Matthews responded still peering into the monitor. "I think you're seeing things."

The crime scene investigator rewound the video and replayed it, slowing the frame rate by one half. The same actions occurred on the playback, the ethereal hands a bit more prominent.

16

"I don't know," Detective Matthews said. He didn't want to admit the hands were more pronounced. "I still think the video has been jacked."

"We're gonna run it through digital analysis to make sure it hasn't been tampered with. If not, then we got some freaky stuff going on you guys have to deal with. That's why we had our Major Crimes team call you two in; you handled that Thomson and Thomson mess," the crime scene investigator said.

"I don't see how they're related," Detective Matthews responded. His partner agreed.

"We need to find out what's on that floor; it could be anything," Detective Matthews continued.

The two detectives returned to the parlor office and joined their supervisor and Father Yancy.

"Too bad there's no audio, we may have to get help from the FBI to run facial pattern recognition on those two men. But either way, if we do find out who they were, they're crispy critters now on the floor. So, wouldn't this be case closed?" Detective Green asked.

"Think about it, someone else was in the room talking to the men before they died," Lieutenant Wilson said.

"The video clearly shows the two men involved with killing the Cardinal. What did you want us to do?" Detective Matthews asked.

"Oh, I don't know, maybe act like detectives. Canvas the neighborhood and see if there are any witnesses who may have noticed anything strange over the last couple of days. The two suspects could've cased the house, and someone may've seen something. They may've seen if anyone else out of the ordinary was in the area. You can try to find out who these two were, and why they did it."

17

Lieutenant Wilson placed heavy emphasis on the word why. "They were looking for something after the Cardinal died. Were they working for someone else who could've been involved? If you do get a hit on the facial recognition, maybe you can find some known accomplices."

"That's all, huh?"

"They do look like they were professionals," Detective Green commented. "We can try, but I don't think we'll come up with anything. This is a pretty upscale neighborhood. I don't think a lot of people would've been out and about."

"I'd never believed you two would sound like defeatists. You two can sometimes be bulldogs on cases, not letting things go," Lieutenant Wilson replied. "We have to start somewhere."

"Yeah, but in weird cases like this, we end up running into obscurity. Remember Thomson and Thomson? The Feds came in and said gas leak, but the condition of those bodies said otherwise. Then they tell us case closed, end of story."

"I'm not saying this is going to be easy. But this time, you have more definitive proof of something malicious based on the video. Two men don't come in and kill a high-ranking member of the Catholic Church for no reason," Lieutenant Wilson said. "There's gotta be a motive."

"I have a question for Father Yancy," Detective Matthews said, turning around with Father Yancy having eased behind the police detectives.

"What's that?" the father responded.

"Wouldn't the Cardinal of had some sort of security team or something other than the surveillance system?"

"He does, they're usually dismissed once he's inside and notifies them when he's armed the alarm and they can go. We're trying to get in touch with them now, but they aren't returning our calls from the Diocese offices."

Lieutenant Wilson's face flinched with anger. He calmed himself down replaying mental exercises he had learned in a recent anger control class. "How come you didn't tell us any of this before?"

Father Yancy fidgeted with his collar and cleared his throat. "It didn't come to mind until we started talking about it. I mean with the death of Cardinal Millhouse, I was kinda distracted by that."

Detectives Green and Matthews unhappy with the father in his late revelation of information, spent time questioning him regarding the composition and specifics of the security team.

\* \* \* \*

It was 11:45 in the evening. The crime scene investigation team had completed their initial on-scene investigation. The entrance of the semi-circle driveway leading to the front of Cardinal Millhouse's residence was clear of police and spectators, with everyone departing after the police secured the scene with "Do Not Cross – Police" yellow tape across the main entrance. Father Yancy, after driving away, drove around for several minutes then returned to the house. He'd earlier made a call for Bishop Grielle to come and visit him, and he was pulling into the driveway.

Bishop Grielle, the ecclesiastical leader for the Diocese of Los Angeles, was the senior individual with direct oversight on the previous investigation of the angelic visit at Thomson and Thomson by Father Hernandez, Sister Justine, and Michael Saunders.

"Hello, Your Excellency," Father Yancy greeted as they exited their cars. "Thank you for coming."

"Theo, what's so important to ask me to come out here at this late hour?" Bishop Grielle observed the police warning tape draped across the front door. "Should we even be here?"

"There's something of the utmost importance I need to show you."

"What could be so important that you couldn't tell me on the phone or waited until the morning?"

Father Yancy implored for Bishop Grielle to follow him. He did. Walking around to the rear, a motion detector light illuminated the yard startling the senior cleric. Once they arrived at the rear patio entrance, Father Yancy raised the yellow police tape barrier, unlocked and opened the French doors, darted over to the alarm annunciator panel, and typed in the disarm code.

"Dining room lights on," Father Yancy commanded followed by a soft automated woman's voice, "Dining room lights on."

A warm glow radiating from the chandelier filled the dining room with light.

"We shouldn't be in here," Bishop Grielle said through the open doorway, frozen in place not wanting to step into the house.

"Please, Your Excellency, what I need to show you is of extreme importance."

"I'm not moving until you tell me what it is you have to show me."

Father Yancy capitulated. "It's a video showing the death of the Cardinal."

"Wouldn't the police already have it? Did you make a copy?"

"The police do have the security camera recording system to make sure there was no tampering based on the strange occurrence with the deaths."

"Deaths?"

Father Yancy remembered Bishop Grielle was not aware of the two alleged bodies seared into the wood flooring of the parlor office. "Please do come in, Your Excellency, and let me close the door and blinds. I'll tell you everything."

Bishop Grielle was captivated and entered, closing the patio door behind himself.

"The recording shows two men who somehow got through the security system and waited for the Cardinal to return home. That was after 5:30 earlier this evening. The video shows they were talking, and then one of the men killing Cardinal Millhouse, looking like they injected him with something."

Father Yancy headed off towards the kitchen while continuing his chronicling of the earlier events. Captivated, Bishop Grielle trailed closed behind to make sure he heard every word.

Father Yancy continued. "After the two men searched the room looking for some information, they…"

Bishop Grielle interrupted. "What type of information were they looking for?"

"I know you're aware of Aurora, Your Excellency, it has something to do with that project."

"You know about Aurora?" Bishop Grielle asked.

"Yes, of course, I've been Cardinal Millhouse's personal aide for some time and knew a lot about the project."

"Do continue," Bishop Grielle said, feeling a tad spurned that a junior member of the clergy may have had

21

more knowledge provided by Cardinal Millhouse than he had up to this point.

"Anyway, the two intruders looked like they were talking to someone else in the room, and then ended up dead themselves."

Father Yancy and Bishop Grielle arrived to the kitchen and entered the walk-in pantry, with the father reaching up underneath the second from top shelf where it buttressed the wall. He manipulated an intricate hidden lock assembly, releasing a latch and swung the wall of spices, canned and dry goods outward exposing a safe room. Two security monitors installed on the wall opposite the entrance, each with quad split views, displayed interior scenes of the rooms and external panoramas of the residence grounds. A table height communications equipment cabinet with a smoked glass front door sat on the floor below the display screens, and contained electronic equipment blinking with a display as if fireworks of blinking green and yellow lights and LEDs. On top of the cabinet was a telephone next to a keyboard and LED computer monitor displaying scrolling text. A first aid kit, several packages of boxed water and dehydrated meal kits, flashlight, and two folded blankets occupied the lower shelves of an open-faced wire framed shelving unit in the corner.

"What is this room?" Bishop Grielle asked.

"The Cardinal recently had this hidden safe room installed in case anyone would enter onto the residence and try to harm him. He also started to provision it to be an earthquake storage room as well. A security company recently installed a new independent video and audio security system inconspicuously around the house, with the monitoring of the system landing in this room. Most of the cameras are tied in together by an encrypted wireless network. We were letting the system burn in and then planning to test the new duress controls connected to the security firm over the next couple of days. When I arrived to assist his Eminence for the evening and found him in his office, I checked the video from the older CCTV, and then this new system with standard, infrared, and wide-spectrum range cameras. Afterwards, I called the police, but only told them about the older system in the other room when they got here."

The sophistication, image quality, and detail of the enhanced security and video surveillance system astonished Bishop Grielle. Most Cardinals in the Dioceses across the country weren't too concerned regarding their personal security. Several reportedly used public transportation to commute to and from work. "I didn't know there were any threats against the Cardinal for him to have such an elaborate setup."

Father Yancy went to the keyboard and entered several commands launching the wall displays to go full screen displaying the office parlor with a time stamp for 5:45 pm. Two men preceded Cardinal Millhouse into the room by five minutes. Bishop Grielle witnessed and listened to the entire events of the men accosting Cardinal Millhouse, their rummaging through the office and stopping to talk to a mysterious individual in the room. An audible muffled trombone-like sound was the lone evidence of a purported third party during the conversation. After the portly man finished the statement "…we'll analyze the files," a white streak advanced up to the portly man, and then to his partner. Their heads twisted 180 degrees with the men collapsing to the floor. A sudden burst of amber and red flames erupted and consumed the two bodies. Less than three seconds later, the silhouettes of two adults as if laying down appeared burned and etched into the floor, with wafting smoke from the anomalies dissipating.

"Dear God!" Bishop Grielle blurted out. "Father, don't you think it wise we should present this video and audio evidence from this new system to the police?"

"Maybe in time we'll give it to them, but would they believe what was on it? I'm not sure if I believe it. We need to make sure the Church isn't implicated because of what was on the recording. If this got out, it could put more people at risk. We should hold on to it and contact Rome as soon as possible for guidance."

"I don't know if I agree…"

Father Yancy interrupted. "Your Eminence, look at this." He cued the video to the point before where the two mysterious men collapsed to the floor, and restarted the play back at $1/8^{th}$ speed. The high definition replay displayed two large bright and translucent hands encroaching upon the pockmarked-face man, grabbing him by his temples and twisting his head. An enigmatic white streak originating with the first man, terminated in front of the second. The two large hands repeated the same actions. Both men dropped in slow motion and landed on the floor simultaneously. The following frames replayed the same scene they had earlier witnessed. Father Yancy paused the video playback.

The safe room was quiet. Bishop Grielle's eyes widened, and his mouth gaped open. He was numb with disbelief. Father Yancy wondered if the bishop was going to say anything since it was visible that what he had witnessed overwhelmed him.

"Now do you see why I want to hold off on telling the police?" Father Yancy said. "Something supernatural happened. When the police saw a similar version to this on the old security system, most of them didn't want to believe it. They even called in the two detectives who investigated the Thomson and Thomson incident. So, it's not like we're holding anything back from them. If an angel, who is what I think it is we saw, is involved, then who more than the Church should investigate."

Bishop Grielle agreed with reluctance. Why would an angel leave digital evidence of its appearance and malevolent actions? Whether during the earlier funeral visitations over the years, or the strange appearances and announcements across the world, he was never aware of any successful photographs or digital recordings taken of the angels.

"Stop by my office first thing in the morning, Father, we'll need to discuss our next course of action," Bishop Grielle directed. "Nonetheless, before the end of the day tomorrow, after we talk, we'll be presenting this to the police."

"Yes, Your Excellency, but think about the fact that the two men did mention something about Aurora. That could open up questions about the Church's involvement in the project."

"Let me worry about that, we still need to do the right thing."

After Bishop Grielle departed the safe room, Father Yancy burned a copy of the video recording onto a blank DVD. Next, he typed several commands onto the keyboard of the console, initializing the security system, including deleting all the video recordings saved to the hard drive of the security system's DVR.

* * * *

As Bishop Grielle drove away, he contemplated Father Yancy's comment concerning the Aurora project. Any fiscal impropriety that may appear since he hadn't been involved with the Diocese's relationship with Everest Bio-Medical Group didn't bother the bishop. Yet, the knowing diversion of monies in the company for contracted vaccines and medicines supporting overseas church missions over to Aurora could present another blemish for his beloved Church to try to overcome with years of earlier blemishes.

## *Chapter 3 – Visitation at Dawles*

"**B**ull report to psychiatric wing 2A immediately, Bull report to psychiatric wing 2A immediately," blared from the public-address system throughout the entire Dawles Medical Center and Research Facility for the third time in the last five minutes. This last time there was a greater sense of urgency in the panicked voice.

Bull picked up his pace. The reason he assumed for the urgency was if a patient had become belligerent, with extra staff needed to subdue him or her. Bull was accustomed to the staff in his assigned wing paging him more often than many of the other technicians, not because of his bulk and muscular girth, but because he wasn't afraid to subdue the patients with extra force if necessary. It prevented the patient from further hurting themselves or other staff members. A couple of the attending doctors or staff therapists considered him too strong handed at times. One doctor believed his point proven, when close to a year ago, Bull's colleagues struggled to remove an out of control and aggressive patient from the dayroom back to his room. Bull had arrived to assist. As the staff and patient tussled down the hallway, the patient broke free from the orderlies and attempted to bowl down a nurse he saw as a threat who

27

was entering the wing. Bull tackled the patient, with both passing through the doorway and tumbling down the stairwell. The patient broke his neck and died. Most of the staff in the mental health wing came to Bull's defense. The hospital's inquiry board cleared him of using excessive force.

Bull arrived to the second-floor station desk for the wing – the patients appeared calm and manageable, those not in their rooms were tranquil and placated, occupying the dayroom. It was the duty doctor and nurse's aide themselves trembling and shaken, tending to a nurse he knew crying hysterically. Her typical warm and rosy complexion was now ashen.

"Thank God you're here, Bull," the senior nurse's aide, Wilma, said. "I was getting ready to have you paged again."

"What's going on?"

"You've been through something like this before."

"Something like what?"

"Maybe it's better if I show you." Wilma began to walk down towards the section of the wing containing the rooms for the male patients. "Something scared the crap out of the staff."

Once they arrived to where the hallway junction T'd, and turning left into a dark corridor, the robust aroma of cinnamon, flowers, and sweet rain water displaced the antiseptic smell of disinfectant, Lysol, and mildew. When Bull tried to turn the light switch on, flipping the switch off and on several times, none of the fluorescent ceiling lamps illuminated. An amber-whitish glow radiated from the small square shaped plexiglass window in the door for one of the rooms halfway down the hall. A nurse and orderly stood outside the doorway. The orderly was

Davies, a coworker Bull had worked with during most his tenure at Dawles.

"What's going on?" Bull asked.

"Bull, this is weird. Remember this room?"

"How am I supposed to remember something like that? You know we have different..." The diffused glow escaping through the door window intensified. The window oddity and pungent sweet smell reminded Bull of the previous occupant assigned to the room months ago, Doctor Cochrane.

Bull reached to open the door. Davies grabbed his co-worker's wrist to keep him from touching the doorknob.

"Just like last time," Davies said. "The door is locked and you'll get a shock that'll knock you on your ass."

Bull knew there was no way to secure the door, since none of the rooms had any type of lock installed. If a patient attempted to hurt themselves, they would be unable to prevent the staff from entering the rooms.

Bull wrapping his hand around the steel alloy doorknob was like clutching a cube of ice. The sharp sting of the cold metal sent a momentary pain radiating through his hand and up his arm, as if someone stabbed his hand with a knife. There was no sensation of an electric shock this time as Bull turned the knob without resistance. The door opened. Bull took a step inside beyond the jamb. The radiant light diffused. After taking two more steps, the door closed on its own behind him. A shimmering ethereal figure, with a sword emanating golden translucent flames held across its chest, stood in the center of the room. Bull trembled, controlling the urge to urinate on himself. He'd seen an angel at the funeral of Doctor McCall, but that one presented a feel-good story and came across as if it were a used car salesman. The one before him exuded a different aura, more authoritative. Bull wanted to back up out of the room, but fear planted his feet to the ground. His leg muscles shook like Jell-O, wanting to give out and not hold up his body weight. The awe and magnificence of the heavenly visitor overwhelmed him with the impulse to show reverence. Bull began to drop to one knee.

"Do not kneel before me, I am a simple servant of the Most High," the angel said.

Bull stood straight up. He didn't understand the context of the angel's statement but did understand the instruction of not to kneel.

"One hundred and one," the angel said in a harmonic tenor voice, its face etched with fury.

"I…don't…understand," Bull replied, his voice cracking from nerves and fear.

"This room is to remain empty."

"I still don't understand…"

The angel disappeared. The light from the fluorescent fixtures re-illuminated the room and hallway. The antiseptic aroma mixed with mildew and dust returned. Bull stepped back out into the hallway closing the door to the room

"What the hell was all that?" Davies asked, only able to hear Bull's side of the conversation. He had tried to follow Bull into the room, but an unexplained emotional burst of fear flooded his emotions keeping him from moving forward out of the hallway. Attempting to look in, he couldn't see through the veil of brilliant light flooding the doorway.

Emboldened with the lessening of his uncomfortable emotions, Davies attempted to enter the room. He turned the doorknob. It wouldn't rotate. "This is weird, the door is stuck again." No matter how hard he tried to turn and shake the knob, pound, or push on the door, it wouldn't open.

Bull regained his faculties and tried going back into the room but was now unable to turn the doorknob.

"We may need to call Facilities to get us in," Davies said.

"I don't think it'll do any good. The angel said the room is supposed to stay empty."

"That's silly. You know the hospital wants to use this room for an incoming patient." Davies reached and grabbed the doorknob now receiving a massive static electric shock. "Son of a…what the…"

"What happened?" Bull asked.

"I got shocked. What's going on?"

"I know someone who probably does."

\* \* \* \*

Father Hernandez, listless and dejected, his face blanketed with several days of beard growth, sat watching television. More than three weeks prior, Bishop Grielle informed him of the Church's intention to begin formal excommunication proceedings with immediate restrictions to oversee the administration of his parish, or officiate over any services. He hadn't decided what he would do as a new career due to the unplanned change from his life's ambition. The day before, he found a religious journal at the local library. Many former priests who voluntarily left the church went to work in the business world to become salesmen, management trainees, office managers, journalists, administrative supervisors, economists, or personnel directors depending on their degree and background in church administration. Some went into government service or became teachers.

There was the possibility of ministering in another denomination or non-denominational church. However, Father Hernandez still held an affinity for the Catholic Church and enjoyed serving in his former parish. Until recently, his extracurricular activity was angel hunting. His discussion with the enigmatic clone child impressed a considerable number of questions on the connection between the heavenly creatures and their recent ecclesiastical influence.

The father flipped through several local and national news channels, talk shows, game shows, and syndicated reruns. His smartphone rang, distracting him from his channel surfing, with the station landing on one broadcasting the local early evening news. The caller ID on his mobile phone displayed the call originated from an out of state area code he recognized, Las Cruces New Mexico. It took a few seconds for him to recall that the number was from the Dawles Medical and Research Center. Hesitant, he answered. Even though the volume was low on the television, Father Hernandez muted the audio

"This is Father, sorry, Jose Hernandez."

"Is this Father Hernandez?" the excited voice on the other end of the phone asked.

The voice sounded familiar, but the father couldn't picture a face. "Sorry, I'm no longer a priest. May I ask who I'm talking to?"

After a momentary pause, the voice continued. "Padre, this is Bull from Dawles."

"I almost didn't recognize the voice. How're you doing Bull? Is everything all right?"

"I'm doin' fine, it's just that it's getting weird here in the psych wing again. With you being a religious man, maybe you can help figure out what's going?" Bull replied. "No one here has any answers for us."

"I'm sorry, Bull, I'm not sure what you're talking about. And besides, I'm being excommunicated from the Church."

There was a pause before Bull responded. "I don't get it. What does that mean?"

"It means I'm getting kicked out of the Church."

There was another short pause before Bull responded again. "What do you mean kicked out? How are you gonna help us down here if you're kicked out of the church?"

"Bull, there's a Chaplain staff on board who should be able to help."

"You don't understand, Father, an angel showed up again here in the wing. The chaplain here is saying it's all in our imagination."

"I'm sorry, Bull, there's nothing I can do."

"Padre, it's got a lot of staff members scared down here. It won't let anybody in the room. It's the same one where that doctor from that medical company stayed."

"Medical company?" Father Hernandez asked.

"That one where the suit from Los Angeles came out and got him released, that doctor."

Father Hernandez rummaged through several names in his memory before coming to a possible candidate. "Doctor Cochrane?"

"Yeah, him. Whenever the staff assigned someone to the room, the patient said it was haunted or felt like someone was in there with them. Today there was an actual angel. I saw it myself."

A picture of Cardinal Millhouse emerged on the television screen. It caught Father Hernandez's attention.

The lower third displayed "Cardinal of Los Angeles Archdiocese, Taylor Millhouse found dead in his residence, assumed natural causes. Police are still investigating."

"Bull, I gotta let you go, but I promise I'll call you back, something's come up," Father Hernandez said as he moved the phone from his ear and disconnected the call. Turning up the volume on the television, Father Hernandez finished listening to the news report. He didn't know why anyone had not called to inform him of the Cardinal's passing. He called Justine.

## *Chapter 4 – Relocation*

"Welcome to your new residence," Cardinal Picoli, the Camerlengo for the Holy See, said with a slight Italian accent, greeting his two new arrivals entering the guest house, first bowing to the child, followed by him shaking Gary Applethorpe's hand. Gary's tall and thin frame was a direct contrast to Cardinal Picoli's stout and round body. The oversized black cassock he wore partly concealed his pot-belly. "Mr. Applethorpe, thank you for your flexibility with all the last-minute changes and plans since leaving the states. We're sorry for what you and the child had to endure in the cramped temporary residences after all that traveling. It's such a tragedy to hear about the loss of our dear Sister Ilsae. We had received many good reports of her works during the upbringing of our young protégé here."

"Yes, she was a big help with the administering of his training," Gary replied, at the same time impressed by the foyer's opulent décor. Light stained white oak wainscot lining the walls augmented large white marble floor slab tiles interspersed with small dark brown marble squares laid in a diamond pattern providing a dynamic appearance. White crown molding framed fleur-de-lis and Tudor Rose styled patterns stamped into the plastered ceiling. The design carried over into the adjacent parlor and living room, both filled with antique Baroque styled furniture.

"It's such an honor to finally meet you, young man. I'm sure I don't have to tell you how special you are?" Cardinal Picoli said. The Holy Father and Cardinal President of the Pontifical Commission allowed merely a select few in the Order to interact with Gary and the child until their relocation into the guest house. Also, rumors circulated that two miraculous events had occurred since the child's arrival. Ironically, the Holy Father's health worsened.

The child remained quiet. His ocean blue eyes stared into Cardinal Picoli's rain cloud gray eyes, captivated by the Cardinal's bushy and untrimmed gray haired unibrow weaved with scattered strands of black hair.

"Let us know if there's anything we can do to make your stay comfortable," Cardinal Picoli continued. The intensity of the child's gaze made him unsecure. "We in the Order are here to serve you."

"Where's my room?" The child inquired in a reserved, yet commanding youthful tenor voice. "I would like to attend to my spiritual schedule and then take a quick nap."

"Of course." Cardinal Picoli signaled for the valet waiting outside the doorway to direct the child to his room. Once the valet and the child withdrew from the foyer, Cardinal Picoli guided Gary to the adjacent parlor room.

"Has he always been so...so..." Cardinal Picoli had started to comment before Gary interrupted.

Gary agreed. "Say no more."

"He's not what I had expected. Yet his features are so striking."

"Trust me when I say the child is special," Gary said.

"Is he truly a child? The way he carries himself, and his appearance, it seems he's more of an older teenager than a child. Yet I'm to understand he's said to be twelve years old?"

"Almost thirteen, you must remember the uniqueness of his advent. Before Doctors Cochrane and Valdez turned against us, they established the foundation for some magnificent work," Gary said. "And then there's the extraordinary events concerning him, but that's about all that I can tell you. But before I forget, will I need to do anything to declare amnesty under the Holy See?" Gary asked.

Cardinal Picoli pursed his lips and stared at the ceiling for a quick moment appearing aloof before he responded. "Mr. Applethorpe, we're trying to assess the climate of the events since you departed Los Angeles. I know the Cardinal President in the Curia had been working between you and Cardinal Millhouse, but he directed that any potential extradition requests would be best sequestered at this time. Plus, your stay in Chicago and follow on travels to here were a little longer than we anticipated. The Order did such a wonderful job in keeping you hidden. We became worried something had happened until we received word of your travels through Africa and Spain after South America. By the way, we're still putting forward the pretense you're both down in Argentina. The governing bishop at the retreat doesn't know of your final destination here. He believes you're at one of the retreat houses deep in the countryside. For yours and the child's safety, no one is to know that you're here, including establishing any type of formal amnesty request for you."

"Are you kidding me?" Gary asked.

Cardinal Picoli didn't want to yet disclose Cardinal Millhouse's death to Gary, nor the supernatural situation that followed as reported by the Archdiocese in Los Angeles. Although Bishop Grielle had reported the incident through formal channels, Father Yancy had already shipped a copy of the DVD from Cardinal Millhouse's new security system.

"Gary, have faith and be patient. Just as you request of us here in the Order in the Vatican to be patient in understanding all there is regarding the child and his development these last thirteen years, please provide us the same courtesy," Cardinal Picoli commented as he started to head to the front door.

Gary quaked with anger becoming incensed, anticipating more information. He was accustomed to Cardinal Millhouse keeping him informed. "Your eminence, you can't leave me in the dark like this. What's going on?"

"We've assigned Cardinal Tullono, the Cardinal Vicar, to assist with your acclimation to the grounds of the holy city. Restrict your communications and continue to watch over our heavenly gift. You'll have the most experienced Gendarmerie watching over the two of you."

Cardinal Picoli knew any of the Gendarmerie assigned to the child would be on special assignment from the Swiss Guard, the elite guards for the Holy Father. He and the Holy Father were the lone clergy and staff aware of the special security arrangement, yet he didn't know the reason.

Cardinal Picoli's phone rang. Answering it, after a quick minute, he said, "We'll be right over."

"The Holy Father is anxious to see the child. Someone will be over in about an hour to escort him over after he's settled in. You have a good evening."

"I was hoping to meet the Holy Father as well," Gary said.

"I'm sorry, but that won't be possible anytime in the near future," Cardinal Picoli replied. He then departed leaving Gary fuming.

\* \* \* \*

The Holy Father's aged, slender body, though not thin and frail, shook from small uncontrollable tremors. The more violent shaking lessened after an injection his personal doctor administered several minutes earlier. His two aides supported him over to his prayer bench in the private oratory next to his bedroom quarters. They lowered him onto the kneeler of the prayer bench that sat in front of a small raised dais bearing a mahogany table with a small statue of the Madonna and child draped with a scarlet cloth. Several feet away, behind the table, suspended on the wall was a large wood crucifix with intricate carvings.

An angel as tall as the eight-foot ceiling appeared, its body and girth wider and stronger than any of that preceded it from what men had seen to date. It stood with four unfurled massive wings. It wore bright white linen garments and a purple sash draped from the upper right shoulder angled down to its lower left torso. A material having the semblance of tightly woven gold silk thread, appearing as if it were shimmering metal foil, veiled the countenance and physical features of the magnificent being's face and head. The garment reflected the subtle warm candlelight glow illuminating the room. The angel reached up and pulled it off. Uncovered was the head of an eagle melding into the muscular neck of a human-like body. Its eyes shone as if two amber jewels filled with liquid fire.

The Holy Father's trembling intensified, not out of fear receiving an angelic visitation, but to be encountering one with distinct inhuman features. The two aides dropped to their knees and executed the sign of the cross, taking their right hand to touch their forehead, to the middle of the breast, to the left shoulder, and the right shoulder.

"Fear not, I come on behalf of Aurora," the angel exclaimed. "How precious is the child? How precious is Aurora who imputed life unto the child? How blessed are those in the church who shelter over the child?"

The Holy Father's complexion became pale, not anticipating the unique facial features of the angelic creature. He had become accustomed to several angelic visitations by Aurora over the years, but the current creature was extraordinary.

"Do not be afraid. Do not lose heart," the angel continued. "Do not be discouraged by the setbacks of Los Angeles or Mexico. There will be those who will attempt to disrupt the established path. The child must be prepared, yet the time for his unveiling is not now, but will come soon."

The angel disappeared.

After everyone had calmed down from the excitement of the unforeseen visit, one aide observed the child escorted by two Gendarmeries, arrive and approach the oratory doorway.

"Your Holiness, the child is here," the aide whispered into the Holy Father's ear before he was to start his prayers.

The Holy Father stared with a furrowed forehead and his eyes flashed with annoyance at the aide, not happy with the interruption. The aide backed off. After finishing, the Holy Father turned and with a feeble hand gesture, signaled for the child to proceed over to a chair located next to the papal bed. He nodded at his two aides, who knew to provide help to stand and walk from the prayer bench back into his room.

The aides assisted the Holy Father into his bed, helping to prop him up and adjusting his pillows and sheets. "Leave us," he commanded, straining his weak voice. "I would like to become acquainted with our young miracle here."

# Chapter 5 – Elevation

Bishop Grielle was being a realist, Cardinal Trong, the Apostolic Nuncio, the position that represents the Vatican City for the United States as its ambassador and senior Cardinal, and based out in Washington D.C., was coming out to Los Angeles. He dismissed that the Nuncio could be coming out to appoint and promote him as the Archdiocese Cardinal. There was no way Cardinal Millhouse would have placed his name on the recommended list of eligible candidates to the Holy Father. The consideration consisted of three names submitted annually to the Holy See in case of a short notice retirement, or unfortunate death of the serving incumbent. Cardinal Millhouse didn't even esteem Bishop Grielle high enough for consideration as an Archbishop. The Cardinal continued to belay the promotion to the honorary position.

So why was Cardinal Trong coming out to Los Angeles? Continuing to read the communique, it stated Bishop Grielle was to work with the public affairs staff to coordinate news coverage, preparing the Chapel as the venue for a special event, and have his staff work with the security details. It made sense now – he was to be the Public Affairs liaison. Maybe the visit was to promote the bishop or monsignor for either the Diocese of San Bernardino or San Diego to Archbishop, as a preparatory step to take over as Cardinal, although not a formal requirement. With the Church still experiencing leadership shortages since the disappearances over eleven years prior, it would be difficult to transfer another Cardinal from another Archdiocese without having to backfill that vacancy. Maybe that was why there was no formal announcement as to who would replace Cardinal Millhouse?

The next day, Cardinal Trong arrived to the Diocese office building in downtown Los Angeles and met with Bishop Grielle in Cardinal Millhouse's former office. Bishop Grielle rendered his formal greeting. Cardinal Trong snubbed any form of a return salutation and proceeded straight to Cardinal Millhouse's office desk. Bishop Grielle trembled with anger. He found it hard to overlook the protocol indiscretion but constrained himself from making an outburst.

"Bishop Grielle, I'll be brief," Cardinal Trong said half-heartedly, as he sat at Cardinal Millhouse's office desk. "I came out for one reason, which you can imagine. With the unfortunate passing of Cardinal Millhouse, you're the one considered for his replacement."

Bishop Grielle found himself gasping for air before controlling his breathing and becoming lightheaded. "I find it a great honor to be on the Pope's short list for consideration as Cardinal for the Los Angeles Diocese," Bishop Grielle responded, holding back his enthusiasm. He would be hopscotching over the position of Archbishop, the tradition for the Los Angeles Diocese, if he was the one selected.

Cardinal Trong scooted his chair in closer to the desk leaning forward, resting his forearms on the desktop and interlocking his fingers. "Bishop Grielle, I don't think you understand what I'm saying, you're being selected for the position as Cardinal. The Holy Father has called a Holy Consistory for the College of Cardinals to elevate you and a couple others. Due to time constraints, you'll be elevated there in abstention. I'll be doing a sanctioned presentation here in Los Angeles. And so that you'll know, I understand that the reason for your consideration by elements within the Holy See is that they believed you should be Cardinal Millhouse's logical successor. They felt you would provide the greatest continuity for all that he had been working on. That's why the breech of formality and expediency for your appointment, you won't be going to Rome for the conferring of your position. The Holy Father is under the weather, and we want to move forward with the business of the Church."

Bishop Grielle sensed the tone of Cardinal Trong's voice expressed disapproval, rather than sounding congratulatory. Not to have the Holy Father confer his elevation in Rome was an indication of how the Vatican felt about the promotion. After the calling of a consistory, there could be a considerable amount of time from the candidate assembly until the announcement and publishing of the official elevation decree, followed by the ceremony. The impression was as if the Holy Father decided to stifle Bishop Grielle's honor of elevation amongst his peers with no respect to the position or person.

"Why not wait until the Holy Father is feeling better as well to move forward and select someone new and bring him up to speed on all that's going on in the Diocese?" Bishop Grielle asked.

Cardinal Trong detected Bishop Grielle's irritability by the timbre of his voice. "For some reason the powers that be find it imperative you're the one to succeed Taylor. You must know that you weren't on the list of submitted three as directed by the papal requirement."

"Evidently," Bishop Grielle snapped back.

Cardinal Trong's nose crumpled and the corner of his lips compressed, incensed by the ire in Bishop Grielle's response. "Consider it a blessing by God no matter how it occurs, and not to take this responsibility lightly," he said in a gruff and stern tone. "You were handpicked from within the Vatican."

"Nor do I intend to. I've always been faithful to the church, but what about the recent events of the angels making the announcement of a child?" Bishop Grielle replied.

"Most of the laity, and those outside the church, have no idea of their meaning. And the recent appearance of other angels has raised concerns. All the hierarchy has told me is that it is something to do with the impact of a special authority within the Church overseen by the Holy Father. Let me say that things at Vatican City are, dare I say, a bit uneasy."

Bishop Grielle's anger subsided hearing the worry in Cardinal Trong's comments, assuming his superior was referring to the Holy Father and the Holy See. "What's going on?"

"Many don't know this, but your predecessor was suspected to have been murdered."

Bishop Grielle's disbelief replaced his irritability. He didn't know how to respond with the news, particularly since he was aware of the situation concerning Cardinal Millhouse. Maybe Cardinal Trong was attempting to present a position of superiority. "Not to be disrespectful, but I'm fully aware of the circumstances surrounding Cardinal Millhouse. It was here in this Diocese that it occurred."

Cardinal Trong raised an eyebrow. "Yes, I suppose you are. Do the police have any idea who did it? Or were there any extenuating circumstances?"

Bishop Grielle hesitated before answering, unsure if Cardinal Trong asked the question as a test already aware of the two mysterious men and possible involvement of an angel. "No, from what I understand, they don't have any leads at this time. I wouldn't be surprised if it had to do with a special project he may have been overseeing."

Cardinal Trong didn't react to the partial withholding of information concerning Aurora or the child. "Taylor's death caught us all by surprise. And what I am about to tell you, you must not tell anyone else. With the ailing Holy Father, we were looking to make other arrangements in case the worse were to befall him. You should be prepared to attend the College of Cardinals if and when the word comes."

Bishop Grielle interrupted, astonished at the news concerning the Pontiff. "The Holy Father is dyin…"

"His health is failing, and please don't interrupt. We've been keeping this from press at this time. There are those who are pressuring him to resign. Anyway, all the while, I learned that there are some who were hoping he would be around for another seven or eight years to allow time for the…I've said enough."

Cardinal Trong paused before continuing. "If I could interject something else?"

"Of course."

"Back to your situation, although you weren't on the list of three potential candidates, I've had a couple of talks with Taylor concerning a unique venture he said he oversaw for Roman Curia, and I must say that he passed on to me the two of you hadn't seen eye-to-eye on a couple of issues. Yet he was a bit impressed by the tenacity you began to show since the incidents at Thomson and Thomson and Crestfield Funeral Home."

"That's Crestview," Bishop Grielle interrupted.

"Excuse me?"

"The funeral home is Crestview, not Crestfield."

Cardinal Trong eyes narrowed, his cold stare showed he didn't like Bishop Grielle corrected and interrupted him again. "Anyway, he considered you to be a bit of a weak leader, but he saw that you were beginning to show some backbone, although he didn't always agree with your decisions. The church now needs you to show backbone for her cause."

Bishop Grielle wasn't sure how to receive the last comments. "I've continually worked for the cause of the Church and ensuring I support the Bishop of Rome."

"Good, because from what I'm told with this venture of his, it may be required more than you realize. Events will transpire to test and determine those who are faithful to His Holiness and the Holy See."

"I don't understand."

Cardinal Trong took in a couple of deep breaths. "The situation in the Holy See has taken an unexpected turn. I don't know all the details and can't explain it at this time, but we need to remember our purpose on this earth. That's all I can say. Now you'll need to work and close out some of Taylor's open administrative actions."

The one that first came to mind was the excommunication administrative actions for Father Hernandez and Sister Justine. "I understand there may be some paperwork concerning the excommunication for two members in my Archdiocese."

"Excommunication, I wasn't made aware of any proceedings coming forth. Are you sure?" Cardinal Trong inquired.

"Yes, I was told the two are to be defrocked as soon as possible and separate their affiliation with the church," Bishop Grielle said. "I turned in the initial paperwork about a month ago."

"You do know how unorthodox that is? A formal inquiry and holy tribunal after submission of the request, and the appeals process must be followed before that could be accomplished after the paperwork is submitted."

"I'm aware," Bishop Grielle remarked. "But Cardinal Millhouse was adamant about this. It all stems from what the two who researched Thomson and Thomson had discovered and reported."

"Yes, he sent me a copy of the conclusions of your so-called research team. I will tell you that there are those who agree in part with their religious findings concerning what he called the Aurora during the review of the report by the Pontifical offices, but like I said earlier, I don't know much more than that. Not too much was described as to what Aurora was. Remember, we are still beholden to the Church and the Holy Father, anything about Aurora must remain confidential. Some sort of grand announcement was to be made, but that has been postponed due to the changes of the environment in Vatican City, considering the Holy Father's condition."

"Cardinal Millhouse mentioned he was going to request special circumstances to expedite the process from Vatican City," Bishop Grielle added concerning the excommunication.

"And bypass me? I would still need to sign off as Apostolic Nuncio for the United States. If you can't find any documentation for the formal proceedings, I say the issue is non-existent."

Bishop Grielle wanted to jump up and down, now filled with glee, but kept his composure. "I'll pass on to the two, news of your decision."

"No, it's your decision. If you are to be the new Cardinal, you will assume all the responsibilities. Recall that as soon as you're nominated, you have the rights as deemed necessary for your position until the consistory declares your name. Your elevation to the new position will be held four days hence."

"What, so quickly?" Bishop Grielle anticipated one or two months.

"Your name is to be read tomorrow in Rome. The Holy Father has already blessed your vestments. My staff has the new cassock and other new accruements for you to wear during the ceremony. You'll begin your fitting this afternoon. Your staff will need to continue the preparations for the event."

"Very well, and let me say despite the circumstances, I am honored," Bishop Grielle said.

"By the way, I was approached by Father Yancy, Taylor's aide-de-camp, and he would like to stay on and work with you. I believe it's a good idea. He knows the schedule, ins and out of what's going on, and can aid with your transition."

"I agree. That's a good idea."

"He'll also help in dealing with scheduling the lying-in state, formal service, and interment in the mausoleum here on the chapel grounds three days from today. I expect you to officiate," Cardinal Trong requested.

"Of course."

"Good, and many of the Cardinals and bishops across the country will be flying in over the next couple days to attend the funeral and your ceremony. The Protocol office at the Vatican is making the notifications today as we speak."

"The ceremony won't be held in Rome as per protoco…"

Cardinal Trong interrupted. "As I mentioned earlier, the Holy Father is not up to presiding over the ceremony, and with so many unique events going on around us, I'll be going to Rome to be conferred by the Holy Father, and returning as being able to preside over your elevation. I'll have some of my staff assist with the arrangements."

"That'll be wonderful. Our protocol office will appreciate the help."

"One more thing, due to the unique circumstances surrounding the death of his Eminence Millhouse, we'll need for you to be careful. Father Yancy informed me that the security detail for Millhouse was found to have been killed as well. That has us in the Church concerned."

\* \* \* \*

Bishop Grielle was pleased Father Hernandez accepted the invitation to visit him at his office early the next morning before his staff would come in and consume his time preparing for the informal elevation ceremony. Not wanting to show he was displaying any form of arrogance over his clergy, which Cardinal Millhouse had been accustomed to doing, Bishop Grielle ensured he arrived into his office at the chapel on time. Father Hernandez waited sitting in the leather chair in front of the desk.

"I'm glad you came out, Jose," Bishop Grielle said, as he displayed a broad smile exposing tea stained teeth, the bottom row shifting inward.

"So, you're advancing to Cardinal? Congratulations."

"Thank you and I have some good news to present to you."

"What's that?"

"It seems Cardinal Millhouse was a bit premature in admonishing you the way he did, and having you and Sister Justine cease from accomplishing your duties as clergy and servant for the church without going through the full formal process. As you know, it's a rare means of censure to excommunicate a member of the clergy and sister in the Lord. He didn't allow for an expiatory penalty designed to make penitence for the alleged wrongdoing against the church. He defrocked and expelled you as a vindictive means against the two of you for doing what you were asked, and not liking what you had learned and reported."

Father Hernandez smiled. "Are you saying what I think you're saying?"

"Father, I would like you and Sister Justine to attend the ceremony and sit in the front row as my special guests as a means to make up for the wrongs done to both of you."

Father Hernandez became lightheaded. "I'd be honored, but I can't answer for Sister Justine."

"I was hoping she would have been joining you here today."

"When I brought it up that you would like to see us, she sent her apologies as to being busy volunteering at the Women's Center. I better not mention what she said. It seems Michael Saunders may be rubbing off on her a bit."

"Well, if she is to return to her position in the church, ensure she makes full penitence. I may be a patient man, but I will not tolerate any type of insolence."

"I agree, but in her defense, she was slightly wounded during the incident back at Waterfall Industries. The last I talked to her she was only now getting over it."

"I'll let you work that out, but I hope to see all three of you the day after tomorrow at the ceremony."

"Three of us?"

"Yes, I'm sending an invite to Michael Saunders. It seems I need the expertise of the three of you in support of the Church, more so concerning the recent events occurring in the Diocese, but more on that later. I do have to return to my arrangements for the ceremony and Cardinal Millhouse's funeral services."

\* \* \* \*

Bishop Grielle presented the oath, following Cardinal Trong at the ascribed times. "I, Andrew Grielle, Cardinal of the Holy Roman Church, promise and swear to be faithful henceforth and forever, while I live, to Christ and his Gospel, with constant obedience to the Holy Roman Apostolic Church, to Blessed Peter in the person of the Supreme Pontiff, and of his canonically elected Successors, to maintain communion with the Catholic Church always, in word and deed, not to disclose to anyone what is confided to me in secret, nor to divulge what may bring harm or dishonor to the Holy Church, to carry out with great diligence and faithfulness those tasks to which I am called by my service to the Church, in accord with the norms of the law. So help me, Almighty God."

Dressed in his red and white vestments, Bishop Grielle knelt before Cardinal Trong, followed by the senior Cardinal sprinkling holy water. Cardinal Trong placed the four-cornered silk red biretta upon Bishop Grielle's head and gold, jewel-laden, ring upon his right hand, signifying the elevation.

"In the name of the Father, the Son, the Holy Spirit, and Blessed Mother, and on behalf of the power vested in me by the Holy Father in Rome, rise, Cardinal Grielle," Cardinal Trong commanded.

The audience in the chapel erupted in applause. Cardinal Grielle approached the podium looking out into the crowd. Father Hernandez and Sister Justine were sitting in their assigned seats amongst many of the other clergy leadership within the Diocese. The seat reserved for Michael Saunders remained empty. Father Hernandez wearing his collar demonstrated he made his decision to stay in the Church. Sister Justine wore a nice vibrant blue blouse and dress skirt. He wondered if she understood or accepted her reinstatement back into the Church.

The Cardinal delivered his speech, with the remainder of the ceremony completing on schedule. During the formal reception that followed, and after his short meeting with the Mayor of Los Angeles, members of the city council and other local dignitaries, Cardinal Grielle searched the Cathedral plaza for Father Hernandez and Sister Justine, finding them ready to leave after they had consumed a small plate of finger foods.

"I'm glad both of you could make it to the ceremony, but wasn't Mr. Saunders able to join you?"

"He sends you his warmest regards and wishes you the best of luck in your new position," Father Hernandez said.

"Really, am I supposed to believe that?" Cardinal Grielle replied, his question more rhetorical than inquisitive.

"That's what he would've said if he wasn't Michael Saunders," Father Hernandez said in a jesting tone.

"Father!" Sister Justine blurted out, realizing she made a scene with several bystanders peering in their direction. "That's no way to talk about Michael, especially since he's not here to defend himself."

"All right, take what I said, and imagine the opposite end of the polite scale."

"Father," Sister Justine exclaimed again.

Cardinal Grielle chuckled. "Don't worry, Sister, I don't take offense to it."

"I'm sure he's not serious," Sister Justine said.

"You know better than I, Sister, he's serious. That's what we appreciate about the father, he's shown himself to be straightforward. By the way, I would've hoped you would've come in your ceremonial wear. You look nice, but now that you're still associated with the church since your excommunication wasn't official, I would think…"

Sister Justine interrupted. "Your Eminence, do forgive me, but I'm still considering leaving the Church with all that's happened with the angels, and what we learned over the last several months. Looking at what the Church has been involved with, I don't know if I can agree…"

Cardinal Grielle now interrupted Sister Justine. "Look, I must attend to my peers and other guests, all being patient and wanting to vie for my time. I wanted to make sure I talked to you before they take over my time. Will both of you please stop by my office first thing tomorrow morning and allow me to explain? It's because of everything that's been happening that I would like for you to consider not leaving. And do see if Mr. Saunders would join you."

# Chapter 6 – New Employment

Cardinal Grielle's grin exploded as Father Yancy escorted Father Hernandez and Sister Justine into his office, followed by a wave of exhilaration to see Father Hernandez once again wearing his clerical collar. Sister Justine wore a simple dark blue skirt and light blue blouse and her short hair styled in a feathered haircut. The Cardinal had hoped she would be wearing a semblance of her religious accommodations as well, showing she had made up her mind to remain in the Church. Yet to see her, nonetheless, was a move in a positive direction.

"I'm glad you could make it," Cardinal Grielle said, stepping from behind his desk to greet his guests.

Father Hernandez bowed and kissed the Cardinal's ring. Sister Justine shook his hand.

"Father, I appreciate the gesture of respect, but here in this informal setting, you don't have to worry about accomplishing the baciamano."

"I don't mind, Your Eminence, with all that's happened, maybe that's why we're experiencing these troubling times with the Church moving away from tradition."

Justine turned and gave Father Hernandez a cautious stare, not anticipating his response. "Who are you and where is Father Hernandez?"

"And Sister, I see you're still wearing street clothing," Cardinal Grielle noted ignoring Justine's comment. "I would've hoped you had made up your mind with wanting to stay in the Church. No offense against Cardinal Millhouse, but with his passing, I would think you would see the manipulator of unfortunate events no longer involved with the affairs of the Church due to his tragic circumstances, would put you at ease."

Justine expelled two quick huffs as if a bull ready to attack but calmed herself. "Your Eminence, you were just as culpable as Cardinal Millhouse in coercing me to inform on my fellow sisters whom you two felt strayed from the path." She softened her tone, but ensured she inflected a sharpness to show she wasn't as forgiving as the Cardinal would have liked.

"And for that, I'm sorry. That was wrong, and I have confessed, and ask for your forgiveness," Cardinal Grielle replied. "Remember that we were all pawns of my predecessor's manipulations." The Cardinal would need to confess the fact that he lied in part to Justine. The apology was genuine, yet despite he hadn't agreed with all areas of Cardinal Millhouse's administration, he still maintained an allegiance to the church and considered her actions had helped to identify those sisters who he agreed strayed from following the Church's doctrinal position at the Women's Center she supported.

Cardinal Grielle's conciliatory words didn't help Sister Justine in considering a position. She took it as an insult there was no formal apology. Her viewpoint was that the church shouldn't be involved in the personal decisions of women, even though she herself may not agree with the implications of a woman's decision. The Diocese gave Justine a pass since she worked with homeless women. She provided counseling and spiritual support for those who experienced traumatic experiences on the streets, and tutoring services for young women who hadn't complete high school. Some became active members in their local parishes inspired by her magnanimous work.

The Cardinal continued. "Let me get straight to the point, with all that's happened, and the fact that you two spoke your mind with this angel situation, I feel I can trust you." The Cardinal paused to add emphasis to his follow-on comments. "I want the two of you to work as part of my staff here in the Archdiocese offices. Consider it an advancement of your positions. And I would like for you both to act as liaisons with the police to try and figure out what happened in the death of Cardinal Millhouse."

Flabbergasted, neither Father Hernandez nor Sister Justine could assemble any words to respond. Sister Justine was still contemplating Cardinal Grielle's apology and debating if it was genuine. Father Hernandez deemed it an honor the Cardinal considered him for a position at the Archdiocese. He had come to the peace of mind and resigned himself to remain at his parish for most, if not all his time as a priest. The promotion freezes after the mass disappearance across the world years ago struck many of the clergy's lower echelons the hardest.

"I see you both are a little surprised by the news. I know it is a big decision, but please get back with me in a couple of days after you think about it."

\* \* \* \*

Father Hernandez and Justine strolled onto the half vacant parking lot out to their cars after they departed the Diocese offices and cathedral. Many of the attendees for the earlier mass had already vacated the grounds. Neither the father nor Justine were able to find any words to say, both ruminating over Cardinal Grielle's proposition.

Father Hernandez broke the silence as they approached Justine's car. "I for one, Sister, may take up the Cardinal on his offer."

Sister Justine's jaw clenched and brows furrowed. "I don't know if I can."

"I understand there's some contention there…"

"Some," Sister Justine countered as she crossed her arms. "Hell, Father, when I look back on how I've been manipulated over the years, I still get upset. And what's worse, they took advantage of my naiveté at the time as well. Most times, when a sister wants to join an order, their background isn't that much an issue unless they were married, and have the marriage annulled instead of a divorce. There's an extended waiting time to ensure the sister is aware of the understanding with living a chaste life during that time, in preparation for what is to come. Damn it, they used me."

"Such language, remember, you're still a Sister in your order, and you must remember forgiveness. And part of forgiveness is to forget and move forward. I can't believe you're still struggling with this. The Cardinal is aware of his culpability. Remember the past is a guidepost, not a whipping post or hitching post to hang onto." Father Hernandez sneaked a peek down to Sister Justine's left hand and was relieved that she still wore her wedding ring. "Plus, don't forget that the ring you wear represents your commitment to the Church and

59

relationship to God, with looking to what good you can do for him, not what men may have done to you."

"And what about the Holy Father?" Sister Justine asked.

"I look to him as a symbolic representation of apostolic succession. He's still a man, just as Jesus was an archetype or model to how men should act."

"And what was that sucking up in there?"

"You know that despite what we found, and what I wrote wasn't against the Church as a whole. I still believe we need to be obedient if the Church is willing to make corrections. And I believe Cardinal Grielle is willing to make sure things move in the right direction."

"Don't forget that I accidently got shot in the arm as a result of the presumed direction of the Church."

At first, Father Hernandez didn't know how to respond, and didn't want to remind Justine that during the shooting incident at Waterfall, Michael had divulged he still held strong feelings for her while he administered first aid. The father then recalled her work at the Women's Center. "Think of all the young women you're helping even now. The fact that you still volunteer at the center despite all that's happened, and regardless Cardinal Millhouse had wanted us kicked out, show's you're still committed to the good works the Church provides."

Sister Justine relaxed her crossed arms, and then dropped them, easing her defensive posture. She began to fidget with her silver wedding band, worn to symbolize her marriage and faithfulness to the Church. It was a reminder she was a Bride of Christ.

Father Hernandez continued, his tone softening. "Please don't act hastily, think of all the good you've done, and all the good you could do, and why you came to the Church. Was it for Cardinal Millhouse and Grielle, or was it for God? Remember, we're not all without sin, we all have our failings."

Justine agreed. "You are such an idealist, aren't you, Father?"

"Because I try not to focus on men," Father Hernandez said, as he smiled. "We'll let you down every time."

He gave Sister Justine a gentle hug. She reciprocated with a placid embrace. He walked off to his car, not offended at her feigning a hug.

Sister Justine capitulated that maybe the father was correct, maybe she shouldn't act hastily. She had to consider her true reasons for becoming a nun, and it had nothing to do with either Cardinal Millhouse or Cardinal Grielle, it was a higher calling. If anything, she was hopeful that she helped prevent the manufacture of a deadly virus, and its release upon innocent people.

A bird chirping sound let Sister Justine know that she had received a text. Pulling her phone from her pocket, the notification center on the screen displayed a text from a private number with one character, "e." Since it originated from an unknown number, she ignored it.

# Chapter 7 – Staffing Dispute

Cardinal Grielle stood in the middle of his new office stroking his chin. The design style flaunted old fashioned and outdated, from the dark wood paneled walls to the older built-in shelving unit that held a collection of old, dusty biblical commentaries, devotionals and other related books interspersed with various religious accoutrements, including a large shiny brass crucifix and a brass candlestick on either side supporting a white candle. A small statue of the Madonna and child rested on one of the upper shelves. Cardinal Millhouse had displayed a crystal glass decanter with an engraved Chi-Rho symbol on the middle shelf. On the opposite side of the room was a half-height built-in shelf unit next to a built-in credenza with a computer workstation concealed by two wood doors. The carpet's red and black paisley pattern was unappealing. He would make remodeling one of his first priorities.

After a single knock on the office door, Father Yancy entered uninvited carrying a small bundle of tan and white sheets of paper, and what seemed to be a various assortment of note cards. Cardinal Grielle decided he would need to talk to his aide again about his annoying habit of entering his office unsolicited. Knocking first this time was a move in the right direction.

"Your Eminence, these require your review and signature," Father Yancy entreated as he laid the short stack of paperwork and documents atop of the desk.

"Can't some of those be sent over electronically?" Cardinal Grielle asked as he returned to his desk, sitting down in the king-size leather chair annoyed from signing copious amounts of policy letters, doctrinal statements, administrative documents, and legal forms over the last couple of days. "It's so much easier when I can sign them digitally."

"Only a couple, most of these though are letters of appreciation for the special guests and VIPs who attended your elevation ceremony, as well as thank you letters and notes for those who made significant gifts to the Church as well."

Cardinal Grielle started reviewing and signing the letters and note cards placed in front of him. Father Yancy stood erect and rigid behind him to his right with his hands cupped and fingers interlocked making the Cardinal begin to feel uneasy.

"Umm, was there anything else, Father? I can let you know when I'm finished," Cardinal Grielle said.

"I don't mind waiting, in case you have any questions. By the way, you look like you were thinking about something when I walked in," Father Yancy noted.

"That's very observant of you, I was thinking through some possible renovation ideas. I'm not a fan of this paneling or the overall décor of the office."

"Did you want me to contact the Facilities director and have her bring in a designer and decorator?"

Cardinal Grielle read the current thank you letter in front of him addressed to the Mayor of Los Angeles and signed before answering. "Not yet, I'm not sure which direction I want to go. I do know that I want to get rid of this dated midcentury modern style. Is there anything interesting on my schedule today? The meeting with the FBI earlier this morning mentally wore me out." Cardinal Grielle was thankful Cardinal Millhouse had kept him in the dark on most of the Aurora project. He could claim ignorance regarding the alleged misappropriations of monies within Everest Biomedical given by the Church for immunization and medical supplies to support medical missions to indigent nations and parishes. The financial records of monies transferred from the Vatican City donated to the church, and receipts of services from Everest were pristine and accurate. Although the FBI visit was lengthy, it was straightforward, and a good chance to eliminate the implication of the Church with any wrongdoing.

"Just a reminder about you being scheduled to preside over the mid-week mass today, after that you're to meet with the travel office to discuss your upcoming trip to San Francisco for a meeting of the North American Cardinals."

"If I recall, that's early next week? I may have some special undertakings for Father Delany and Father Hernandez while I'm gone."

"So, I understand that Father Hernandez is working with the police as a liaison for the church in the investigation with the death of Cardinal Millhouse?" Father Yancy asked.

Cardinal Grielle glanced up for a quick instant after he signed one of the pieces of correspondence. The way

Father Yancy had drawn out the word "so" raised his suspicions in the priest's intention. "Yes, why, is there something I should be concerned about?"

"Is that wise?"

Cardinal Grielle laid his silver-plated Cross pen on his desk blotter. His body tensed, then relaxed. "Father Yancy, do I need to remind you who's in charge here. It seems you may have forgotten that with the way you walk in here without being asked."

"My apologies, Your Eminence, it's just habit with the arrangement Cardinal Millhouse and I had."

"Yes, you told me that before."

"I was concerned with Father Hernandez and Sister Justine coming on staff, that's all," Father Yancy said, attempting to sound conciliatory.

"What does that have to do with any of this?" Cardinal Grielle asked. "If I want to bring Father Hernandez and Sister Justine on staff, I have the prerogative to do so."

"Your Eminence, it's not that I'm trying to be insolent, it's that they've put you through so much with their writings and controversial points of views in relation to the angel situation of late. I remember how much of a thorn they were for you and Cardinal Millhouse."

Cardinal Grielle rolled back in his chair and rotated to face Father Yancy, scratching his forehead for a quick moment in frustration. "Ever stopped to think that by having the two here on staff, I can keep a better eye on them, and keep them from being a nuisance?"

"That's a good idea. I didn't know that's what you had planned."

"I didn't know I had to explain my actions to you," Cardinal Grielle snapped back. "And don't think I've

forgotten about the video of Cardinal Millhouse's death."
Cardinal Grielle had forgotten. "We need to act upon it."

"About that…" Father Yancy said, followed by an
uneasy silence and hesitation. He continued. "I decided
you may have been right, and we should turn in the video
to the authorities. I went back to the residence since I had
to prepare it for you. Since the security system was new,
the settings weren't tweaked, with the length of recording
to be one day by default."

Cardinal Grielle scowled, making the aged creases in
his forehead more pronounced. "Are you saying what I
think you're saying?"

"The security video overwrote itself. We don't have
access to it anymore."

"How come I wasn't made aware of this? You should
have informed me as soon as you decided to work the
video and discovered the discrepancy."

"I did inform the police and they were supposed to
have met me there."

"That's not the point." Cardinal Grielle said, flustered
and frustrated. "You're an excellent aide, Father, but it's
getting harder for me to overlook your overreach. This
incident with the deleted video is a concern. And with
other recent incidents, I'm beginning to question our
working together. You're dismissed."

Cardinal Grielle began to deliberate on the possibility
of a new aide.

\* \* \* \*

"Do you know what I like about tea, Father
Hernandez?" Cardinal Grielle asked as he poured a cup of
tea joined by Father Hernandez in the staff dining area of
the Plaza Café of the Cathedral the next morning.

"What's that, Your Eminence?" Father Hernandez replied, bewildered by the Cardinal initiating a conversation over something as trivial as tea.

"I find it a much more tempered drink than coffee, smoother than coffee to be truthful. Maybe that's why Cardinal Millhouse enjoyed it as well."

"I'll drink either one, but I never developed a fond taste for either."

The two men began their stroll back to the office with Cardinal Grielle gingerly holding his Styrofoam cup of hot tea with lemon.

"Your Eminence, you know you have the Keurig brewing station in your office, or you can have someone bring that for you?" Father Hernandez said, breaking the lull in the conversation.

The piercing stare of Cardinal Grielle's pudgy face and green eyes signaled his dislike of the father's comment. "I'm aware of what I can have accomplished and what persons can do for me. I don't want to be like my predecessor and have you all wait on me hand and foot. I, too, am still a servant of God. I enjoy it when I can get a chance to step out and see the staff and parishioners. I would like to consider myself more accessible than the prior administration."

By Cardinal Grielle's tone, not only was it a jab at his predecessor's tenure, Father Hernandez sensed the Cardinal wanted to set himself apart from Cardinal Millhouse's management style.

"Father, there is something I'd like for you to do," Cardinal Grielle requested.

"Your Eminence?"

"I need for you to convince Sister Justine to remain in the fold," Cardinal Grielle said. "I haven't heard of any type of decision from her, and I'm afraid she may decide to leave. We can't afford to lose a hard-working Sister as Justine."

Father Hernandez smiled. "I'm already making that one of my priorities."

"Good."

"And I do believe her feelings for Mr. Saunders may be re-emerging."

"I didn't realize you'd noticed," Father Hernandez said.

"Considering the history of those two, is she still wearing her ring at least?"

Father Hernandez recalled the last time he and her were together in the parking lot. "Yes, she was the last time I saw her."

"That's good news for us."

The two men continued their stroll down the hallway back towards the administration wing of the Cathedral. Members of the staff would interrupt the Cardinal, approaching to ask simple administrative questions, congratulate him on his elevation, or discuss the specifics and details of future events and special masses he would need to officiate.

Father Hernandez's phone chime alerted him that he had received a text message. It stated "Ro." The originating number displayed "Private Number." He wondered why someone would send him "Ro," thinking maybe they were attempting to send Chi-Rho, sending only the last half. Even then, the sender misspelled it. He ignored the text.

Once the Cardinal and Father returned to the Cardinal's office, they were able to resume their conversation uninterrupted.

"Now that I'm working on your staff, there's one thing I would like to do. I'm not sure if you'd agree," Father Hernandez said.

Cardinal Grielle sat and leaned back in his high back leather chair. He motioned for Father Hernandez to take a seat in one of the chairs opposite his desk. "What is it?"

"One of the orderlies that I knew back at Dawles in Las Cruces New Mexico keeps calling mentioning an angel keeps appearing in a room back there."

"How come we haven't heard about this here in the Diocese?"

"Since the angel visitation seems confined to one of the lower security psych wings, they can control access to the room. And with the weird change of the angel appearances around the world, another one in another state didn't ruffle too many feathers to cause a major concern back here in California."

"So why would you need to go back there?"

"When the angel shows up, it repeats 101 over and over. Also, the room is the one where a Doctor Cochrane was assigned when he was admitted to the center."

Cardinal Grielle displayed a puzzled look on his round face. "What does those two pieces of information have to do with anything?"

"One hundred and one is the number of persons who died at Thomson and Thomson, and suspected to have died at a secret lab run by Everest in Mexico where they had worked on the Aurora virus. And Doctor Cochrane was believed to have been one of the doctors who worked at the lab."

Cardinal Grielle's eyes widened. "That is intriguing, but is it worth you going out there?"

"You have Cardinal Millhouse killed, and he was the primary liaison with Everest concerning Aurora, and Everest is the same company where an angel keeps showing up in a room of someone who was a key component of the project. I find that very interesting," Father Hernandez replied.

Cardinal Grielle contemplated for a couple of minutes and assumed the same before responding. "What you mentioned makes it more interesting in what I have to tell you. There's a reason I wanted Sister Justine to come onto the staff here, but not for what I'm about to tell you."

Father Hernandez was intrigued. "What is it, Your Eminence?"

"There was an enhanced video showing the death of Cardinal Millhouse. No one else is to know this, it's not public knowledge. We believe an angel is involved."

"What?"

Cardinal Grielle described what he witnessed on the video.

"That's unbelievable," Father Hernandez said, amazed by the revelation.

"I don't think the police are suited to handle this. If possible, see if Michael Saunders would be willing to assist. This may be up his lane."

"I'll try."

"Father, go with God's blessing."

Father Hernandez smiled, and rose up off the chair to leave wanting to skip out of the office ecstatic having permission to travel out to New Mexico.

"Oh, and Father," the Cardinal said.

"Yes, Your Eminence."

"Coach class."

Father Hernandez chuckled. "You know I like to take the train."

"I do, and don't tell anyone where and why you're going, especially not Father Yancy, I don't trust him."

"What about Sister Justine?"

"Of course, I hope she'll decide to go along with you."

# Chapter 8 – A New Threat

Xavier Durant, a young dark-skinned male, short afro dyed blond, the back of his hands tattooed with an image of an Aztec style sun, dressed in a custom-made pin striped suit, walked down a long dark hallway carrying a worn laptop case bearing scuff marks and a small tear. Each step echoed as the heel of his hard-soled, black Oxfords struck the concrete floor lacquered with peeling gray paint. The air in the corridor was damp, musty, and stale from the lack of any circulation. An uncovered incandescent lamp screwed into an exposed lamp socket every fifteen feet or so, hanging from the suspended framing of a drop ceiling with no ceiling tiles, connected to a draped brown power cord, provided illumination down the hallway. Xavier passed through an aged wood door covered in cracked varnish, into a large storage room with empty gray warehouse shelves towards the back half. In the middle of the room sat three individuals, each on a beige metal folding chair, behind a long, white plastic folding table. To Xavier's left was Nadia, a middle-aged woman, her skin showing signs of premature wrinkles, one would have the impression she would be older than the other men. She was the youngest of the three. She was his primary handler. The other two, Xavier never met. The male in the middle was bald, his ebony complexion glistening from his recent application of lotion to relieve his ashy and dry skin. To his left was a tall, thin, and light skin-tone Asian male. Atop the folding table was a star-shaped conference phone device connected by a wire to a small black box with an LCD display and numeric keypad containing keys printed with the letters A – F. Xavier recognized the device to be a wireless voice encryption unit.

"It's about time you got here, Xavier," Nadia said in an admonishing tone shrouded in a thick Russian accent. "Why did you call us together?"

"I have something of importance to show you," Xavier answered.

"Just so that you know, our directors and liaisons are listening in. They've been patient, and my two peers flew in for this and another project we're working on. To my left, his code name is Niru, and on the far left is Zho."

It wasn't abnormal for Xavier to have someone else listening in while he would provide a status update meeting or a debrief with his handlers, who were advisors or other intermediates working on behalf of the intelligence or secret service of nation states contracting his and his team's services. "It's about the two hired resources I sent to try and find out from the church liaison, and what happened to the monies invested to develop the proto-biological variant code-named Aurora."

"Say virus, we know you mean virus," Nadia said. "Millions of dollars have been lost."

"As well as personnel resources," Xavier said.

"Are you also talking about the two resources sent to take care of Cardinal Millhouse? Word is they were killed by some mysterious means," Niru said in a diffused African accent.

"We send agents to talk to several peoples at Everest under excuse they investigate as if working for SEC. Then I find out he was killed by unknown force," Zho said.

"That's why I'm here, I have something to show you regarding the death of Cardinal Millhouse and two of my colleagues on contract with me," Xavier said.

"Our source in police we have working investigation already tell us about odd reasons and security system video," Zho said.

"There was a new security system recently installed in the Cardinal's residence. Not many were aware of it. A priest kept this from the police. It had more enhanced features and captured something of interest on video. It also captured most of the conversation in the room at the time."

Xavier opened the laptop case and pulled out a large tablet device. Turning it on, and swiping through several applications, a video emerged on the screen. Xavier moved closer to the three sitting behind the table while flipping over holding the tablet to where they could view the display. He opened the video file with audio, displaying the playback of events leading up to and following Cardinal Millhouse's death. The audio sounded garbled from the point where the two men initiated a conversation with a mysterious unseen individual in the room. The two men looked as if talking to empty space. After half a minute, the death of the two assailants followed.

The three sat shell-shocked.

"Where did you get this?" Niru asked, his question close to being unintelligible due to the thickness of his accent from him not focusing on his word annunciation.

"From a Father Yancy, he was the aide to Cardinal Millhouse. He disclosed the video during a little persuasion discussion by one of my team members. I found it after he refused to give up anything about what happened to your investment in the virus, which I'm inclined to believe he knew very little about. He said the virus wasn't part of his primary responsibilities in working with Cardinal Millhouse. I used some pretty potent chemicals that yielded success in the past. All he did do was ramble on about how he would die rather than give up anything about some secret Society of the Holy Order of the Child."

"What is that?" Nadia asked.

"Well I've done some more digging. We believe we found out it may have something to do with what Gary Applethorpe and Everest siphoning off monies paid for in development of the virus. One of my associates was able to penetrate into the investigation team sent in to Everest, and was able to pass on what he found out talking to an Alder Dennison."

"And what did you find?" Nadia asked, her thick accent more pronounced.

"A clone child."

The room went quiet.

"A clone of who?" Nadia asked.

"We don't know, but the child is told to be around twelve, maybe thirteen years of age."

"How come we haven't heard of this before?"

"It seems while everyone was consumed with the development of the virus, Gary Applethorpe was good at keeping his other pet project close enough to his chest to protect what the Church and Everest were doing, but keeping the work in the open enough as not to raise suspicion. It was quite masterful actually. The Department of Defense had invested monies in the company to work on clones and rapid growth genetic 3-D fabrication of organs to stockpile and harvest body parts for soldiers, so in some ways their clone work blended in with their skunk work projects. That's how he was able to hide his side project, and why there wasn't that much of an uproar as to what happened in Eagle Rock. The contracted DOD research facility accomplished some of the same work as the child. That's why we think much of the investigation based on what's going on at Everest could be security theatre by the Feds."

"So, church backstab us?" Zho asked.

"The investigation at Eagle Rock is saying otherwise, some reports say there was unauthorized bio-medical viral research going on at the lab, but then something went wrong. The researchers, scientists, and technicians working on the project in a specialized sealed lab were killed. It's possible they were close to success and doing some finishing work as they reported," Xavier said. "All of that was covered up as not to expose the clone skunk works."

"They say same about Mexico at Aguascalientes," Zho, added. "That research lab over hundred persons die if we believe what they say. I bet clone child real prize. They used monies for child. Gary Applethorpe use labs to cover real purpose."

"So, what do you recommend we do?" Xavier asked.

"We strike at Everest and at Church," Zho exclaimed. "We got rid of Cardinal Millhouse – we take out figure head."

"What, take out the Pope?" Niru responded.

"No, clone," Zho said. "We strike heart of true project. It is possible virus way to fund true project. I bet original intentions not Jewish Sinai issue talked about in Council of Rome meetings. We take out Gary Applethorpe."

"Killing Gary Applethorpe is obvious, but how would killing the child provide retribution?" Nadia asked.

"It's said the child is venerated," Xavier answered. "One of the things Father Yancy did mention was that the child is alleged to be special to the Church and nations. He didn't say why."

"What so special about child?" Zho asked.

"It's said that angels worship him."

Nadia, Niru, and Zho's eyes narrowed. Each sat back in their chairs confused by the comment. Thoughts swirled in their heads while attempting to comprehend the "angels worship him" remark.

After a moment of hesitation, Nadia spoke up. "That's ridiculous. You're saying angels worship a child?"

"One of my case agents who managed to befriend a Stephen Williams and elicit information during a round of drinks, said the target mentioned he witnessed angels bowing to a child at the Cathedral in downtown Los Angeles," Xavier said. "I suspect it's the same child."

"This doesn't make any sense," Nadia said. "Angels bowing down to a child, it makes no sense. Are these the same angels helping some of our superiors?"

"I don't know, but Father Yancy was pretty adamant about all of this. According to the two men sent to handle Cardinal Millhouse, they said it was that same angel that told them how to enter his residence as the one who talked to our leaders. Recall that there was a short time when angels appeared and made one announcement, "The Child". That announcement energized many in the Church's secret order. They believed there's something special with him."

The room remained quiet for several moments.

"What's the status of Father Yancy?" Nadia asked.

"He stated it would be an honor to die for the sake of the child," Xavier answered.

"And?"

"We gave him that honor. We felt confident he didn't know anything else."

"So, where are Gary Applethorpe and child now?" Zho asked.

"I'm not sure, but Father Yancy implied they were in Chicago for a week, and then flew down to South America, we suspect Argentina. I haven't been able to find out for sure yet. Remember on the video Cardinal Millhouse mentioned two members of the church they used to investigate the alleged intervention of angels with the project," Xavier replied. "Their names are Father Hernandez and Sister Justine."

"You think they'll know?"

"Not directly. I researched the names and found out from Father Yancy that the new Cardinal still has plans to have them investigate angel sightings, and to try and find out why they're showing up. And if they were the ones as Cardinal Millhouse said, that interrupted the virus research in Eagle Rock. Maybe they'll lead me to Gary and the child if they found out more than they anticipated."

"Why does that name Father Hernandez sound familiar?" Nadia asked.

"He may be headed to Las Cruces, New Mexico," Xavier said.

A baritone voice interrupted from over the teleconference device. "Gary Applethorpe called for a cleaner from one of our intermediates to take care of a problem in Las Cruces. The target was a Father Hernandez, as well as a Doctor McCall who placed an inquiry with supporting data concerning Everest to the CDC, almost exposing our venture. Problem is the cleaner who went to Las Cruces was killed under mysterious circumstances after he eliminated the doctor. The father survived. I'll email more information to you and Nadia."

"Maybe there's some truth to the virus after all?" Niru commented.

"They tell us they were near success to having a product for us, and then out of nowhere, something happens, and no virus exists. Either way, Gary Applethorpe failed you. He still misappropriated millions of your resources according to some of the audit information my inside man found out," Xavier said.

"Yes, and if he applied all the monies he should, we now be discussing the implementation of plan to remove much Jewish nation and force their hand to embrace ecumenical religions of our nations. We could pacify them since they nothing more than infection on cultures and society," Zho said, his voice laced with contempt.

The three seated panelists leaned into each other and began to whisper amongst one another. They all remained calm during the discussion understanding the ramifications of millions of dollars lost over the years. The murmuring of their whispers ceased, with Nadia getting up out of her chair and retrieving a cell phone from the inside pocket of her blazer. She hit the disconnect button on the conference device sitting on the table after disabling the wireless voice tether to her cell phone.

"Did everyone hear all of that," Nadia queried into her mobile phone as she walked to the rear of the room. After several minutes, she disconnected the call, returned, and turned off the encryption device.

"So are we all in agreement, the nation states we represent all concur that Gary and the child are to die. Make every effort to find the two of them. We'll keep you posted with how to move forward in regard to the two clergy members."

Xavier secured his tablet device back into the laptop bag. He was thankful not having to explain that after Father Yancy had succumbed to the interrogation, the two interrogators had moved the body to a temporary location while attempting to dispose of it. Both claimed they needed to extricate the area to keep a passing work crew from discovering them. When asked why they didn't take the body, they thought they had stored the body in an inconspicuous manner. When they had gone back to complete their task, a stray hiker attracted by a bright light came along and found the body – he contacted the police.

Xavier's was upset that two of the most experienced team members acted like rookies. They knew how to remain calm and react in tense situations. They took care of the security detail protecting Cardinal Millhouse allowing the two older team members to enter the Cardinal's residence.

"I don't know why, but it feels like we're being played," Niru commented.

"Why do you say that, and by who?" Nadia asked.

"All the parties involved through Rome, the Church, angels..." Niru said.

"Did you say angels?" Nadia asked.

"Yes, angels," Niru said. "They influenced our leaders to invest in Everest and work with the Church in the search for the virus. We hoped it would take care of our middle east Sinai problem since we wouldn't normally work with Rome. Yet all the while they seem to be working against us. Let's be real, it was suspected that angels were involved down in Aguascalientes, then in Los Angeles at Thomson and Thomson, and possibly at Eagle Rock."

"Look what happen to the two resources who visit Cardinal Millhouse. Something strange," Zho added.

"An angel recommends for us to handle the problem," Xavier interjected, "even as much as to visit my colleagues before their visit, and then one seems to have killed the two of them afterwards. There's no other way you can explain what happened to them on the video that comes to mind."

"Ignore all of that for now and worry about the situation at hand, I believe you're overthinking it," Nadia said. "Remember, we were briefed that if our superiors were to head down this path, there would be those who would oppose the greater works. All of this wasn't part of the greater plan, we need to redress the losses of our superiors, and they decided what's to happen to Gary and the child. We have to continue to assume that there are angels continuing to help guide us with the covert political insights they've provided to some of our heads of state in maintaining order since the loss of the millions across the world."

"Nonetheless, I believe we should look at divesting…" Niru started before Nadia interrupted him.

"You may leave now, Xavier," Nadia said.

Niru continued after Xavier departed and considered well out of hearing distance. "As I was saying, we should divest from the front business and charities we used to funnel monies to the Church."

The other two agreed.

## *Chapter 9 – Persuasion Attempt*

Father Hernandez found the atmosphere of the Coffee Zone Coffee House and Cafe quaint, and not cookie cutter and sterile like many of the coffee house chains in the city. A row of dark stained wood-topped tables fashioned with legs made from piping and plumbing fixtures lined an ochre and red brick wall. Across the room on the other side of the sitting area were several couches with worn mismatched twill covered cushions, each with faded stains from earlier attempts at a deep cleaning. Placed in front of each one stood a short rectangular chestnut stained coffee table branded with coffee rings and littered with crumbs from long consumed pastries. A sea of small circular tables and white oak wood chairs filled the center of the coffee house.

Father Hernandez paid no attention to any of the patrons scattered across the room, except for Michael, who sat towards the rear of the sitting area, at the next to last table. The two men smiled and shook hands.

"I'm glad you decided to meet with me," Father Hernandez said as he sat in a dark wood-stained and cushioned chair opposite Michael. "How've you been?"

"Doin' good. Classes are going well, research is well. I'm going through the Book of Enoch again as part of my personal research. I find the interactions between the angels, Enoch, and man intriguing."

"It is, with what's happening these days, it makes you wonder if what happened in the book did occur," Michael replied. "I used to think a lot of it was more of an allegory."

"I remember reading that one years ago when I was interested in angels early in my career. I've sometimes wondered why the Church didn't add it as part of its official canon. The book is even cited in the Jude epistle."

"I kinda hinted upon that in my doctorate's dissertation, which by the way, I found out I have a date to go and defend it. If all goes well, tenure should follow shortly. As much as I hate to admit, some of what's been going on has helped in the process. I was able to make some changes in the final edits before sending it for review."

"Congratulations, I'll keep that in prayer for you," Father Hernandez said.

Michael picked up a beige ceramic cup resting on the table filled with a steaming dark liquid and took a sip.

"Is that coffee or tea?" Father Hernandez asked.

"Coffee. So, what is it you want, Padre?" Michael responded, knowing the father was circling around from arriving to his true intentions for meeting. "You said it was important, and I know you didn't want to talk about coffee."

"You're right," Father Hernandez replied, accustomed to Michael's episodic coarse attitude as demonstrated by the curt tone of his response. "It's just that something interesting has happened on the periphery of the Aurora situation,"

"Aurora? I thought that issue was closed, considering what happened at the Waterfall site and Everest."

"You'd think, but the news never did say what happened that evening back at the plant. We don't even know the true ramifications of what happened inside the lab."

"You mean like the bug still being around?" Michael asked.

"Exactly, I mean isn't it weird we haven't heard anything from Ashere?"

"And I'm thankful," Michael parried. The events on the grounds of Waterfall in Eagle Rock reawakened his fondness towards Justine. Although her gunshot wound was minor, he imagined his true emotions if she would have died. If reversed, would she feel the same.

Father Hernandez observed someone staring in their direction. Across the room, the familiar face of a young lady with brunette hair rolled into a bun, anger induced petite creased face, eyes lacquered with mascara, narrowed, and compressed lips, sat on one of the faded couches. She presented the two men with a stern gaze with her arms crossed in front of her chest, and ignored the cuddling gesture attempts of her thin, dark brown dreadlocked hair male companion.

Alicia's piercing stare made Father Hernandez uneasy. "Isn't that your ex-girlfriend over there with that guy?"

Michael took a sip from his coffee cup. "Don't pay her any attention, maybe she won't come over here. I think she's here to annoy me knowing this is my favorite coffee joint. I'm not going to give her the drama she's looking for." Michael took another sip of coffee.

"Without a doubt, I know I made the right decision with ending our relationship."

No sooner than when Michael finished his statement and placed his coffee mug on the tabletop, Alicia got up off the couch and walked over, weaving her way through the herd of small tables occupied with patrons.

"Great, you got her attention," Michael said as he rolled his eyes.

"Hello, Father, and where's your other friend, Michael?" Alicia asked in a snippety tone once she approached the two men. Her milky white porcelain skin flushed.

"What other friend?" Michael answered. He had an idea which friend Alicia was referring to but wanted her to state the name.

"You know which friend, your nun friend," Alicia countered.

"Nun friend, you know her name," Michael snapped back.

Father Hernandez wasn't sure of what to make of the dialogue between the two. The young man on the couch with Alicia stared at the three with a confused expression.

"Anyway, what do you care about her for?" Michael asked.

"I don't care about her since I'm with Vincent now. I don't know what I saw in you anyway."

"Well if you didn't care, why are you over here and not with your new boy toy annoying him?"

"Screw you," Alicia snapped back. "You were a pain in the ass to be with anyway and a crappy professor."

"And your crazy butt opinion matters to me how?" Michael said as he focused his attention back to Father Hernandez. "So where were we?"

Silence embraced the table. After a few seconds, Alicia spurted, "You're an asshole," and stormed back to the couch in a huff.

"Was that called for Mr. Saunders?" Father Hernandez said, in a disapproving tone. "That wasn't nice to say, and very disrespectful, regardless of the circumstances."

Michael ignored the father's rebuke.

"Should we at least leave?" Father Hernandez asked, feeling uncomfortable.

"You don't understand women, do you, boy toy?"

Both men became distracted watching Alicia's animated hand gestures as she stood in front of her companion. He sat dumfounded, confused as to what she expected of him. The ambient noise of customers' conversations and background music playing from the speaker system made it impossible to hear what resembled to be a scolding. A couple of customers at the tables next to Alicia and Victor watched and eavesdropped with curiosity. After a couple of minutes, she returned alone back over to Michael and Father Hernandez, her face flushed and cheeks candy apple red with anger. "You can go to hell," she snapped. "I don't know why I fell in love with you!" Alicia stomped off out of the coffee house with her companion getting up off the couch and following surprised she had left.

"Then again, neither do I," Michael said, after a short awkward pause after he and the father watched Alicia leave, with several of the neighboring coffee drinkers gawking at the interchange.

"Umm, so, where were we?" Michael continued.

"Mr. Saunders, I'm going to Las Cruces, and I was hoping you would join me."

"Why would I want to go back out to that place?"

"I'm going out to investigate an angel incident at Dawles."

"Does it call for you to head out there?"

"The angel is in the room that Doctor Cochrane was assigned to, and it said one thing of interest."

Michael eased back in his chair. "What's that?"

"One hundred and one, the same number of those..."

"I remember," Michael said, interrupting the father. "That's not coincidental at all considering recent events, but you're going back out there?"

"Yes."

Michael raised an eyebrow and hesitated before responding. "Let me get this straight, you're heading back out there where someone tried to kill you. Do you even know if the police found out anything about that man who tried to kill you?"

"No, but I was thinking about stopping by and talking to the detective who was investigating the case."

"You mean the one who came out here to L.A. from there? He was a real tool."

"He was, but ever since the incident at the Waterfall plant, it's been quiet, and now this happens out there."

A single chime rang from Michael's pants pocket. "Hold on," he said as he pulled out his smartphone. The notification bar displayed an incoming text from a private number. It stated the letter "m."

"Damn, that's weird," Michael continued.

"What's weird?"

"I keep getting the same text from a private number, and I can't seem to block it."

"A text, what does it say?"

"Just the letter m."

"Okay, that is weird. Same thing's been happening to me as well, except I keep getting "Ro" from an unknown number, and I can't seem to block it either. When I called the phone company, they say their records don't show a text being sent at the time shown on the phone."

"Same thing with me. I even tried changing phones and the same thing happened," Michael said as he put his smartphone back in his pocket. "Screw it. As we were saying."

"About you going back with me to Las Cruces."

"Yeah, your little angel crusade," Michael said. "I don't think so."

"I need your help. You're an intelligent man, understanding more than most in the arena of angels. And maybe we can figure out what happened with Cardinal Millhouse."

"Your platitudes aren't convincing me, boy toy. I can't accept a return to those who acted so repugnantly. Millhouse might be dead, but the man did try to have me fired from my job."

"And what man is without sin? Through our Father in heaven, we put up so much. A few men don't represent the whole. Look at what we have to put up with you."

Michael flashed a quick grin before it disappeared. "You suck at this convincing thing, boy toy…wait a minute…you said something about Cardinal Millhouse. How does going out to Las Cruces figure into Cardinal Millhouse's death?"

Father Hernandez leaned in across the veneer topped table. "It's believed that those who killed him were themselves killed by an angel right afterwards."

"You're saying angels were upset that slime bag was killed?"

89

"I don't know what I'm saying. The first thing that comes to mind is with what happened to me in the basement back at Dawles when that man tried to kill me, and something mysterious out of nowhere struck and killed him. Think about the premise we posited over the last several months during our writings. Who's to say what type of angels they are. Either way, why?"

"What about Justine?" Michael asked. "Is she going on this little excursion?"

Father Hernandez cleared his throat and gave Michael an intense stare. "I know that you still love Justine, and I know she's having re-emerging feelings for you. That's not what's important right now. Does it make a difference if she did or didn't go?"

Michael didn't know what to respond hearing the father being so direct. "I don't know."

"As of now, she's not. She's still debating if she's going to remain a nun or not. But my concern isn't Justine, it's you. Your knowledge and insight have been a valuable resource through everything we've experienced over the last year. Look, I know you didn't like Cardinal Millhouse, but there's more than him being murdered, and I think what's going on in Las Cruces may have something to do with it."

Michael contemplated that in his earlier experiences with Father Hernandez and Sister Justine, coincidences weren't mere coincidences. The millions of persons who remained on the earth, and all connected to one another as if a giant web, interacted with one another to different extents. If you tug on one strand, the entire web vibrates. Strange incidents tended to interact with other people and connected mysterious events. But Michael wanted to settle down and get back into his old routine of research and teaching, with the prospect of Justine being by his side.

"I do have a quick question, boy toy?" Michael asked.

"What's that?"

"The angels coming first and giving eulogies was pretty much innocuous, but things have gotten to be pretty serious, more so with what's happened back in Eagle Rock. Why do you think the game changed?"

Father Hernandez sat back in his chair and stared Michael down pondering the question for several minutes. "I don't know."

If Father Hernandez had given a reasonable response, Michael still made up his mind; he decided not to go chasing after angels and suspected viruses. "Boy toy, I'm not gonna go. Enjoy your trip."

"Please, you could be so much help with this. Are you sure?" Father Hernandez said, leaning in as he pleaded.

Michael smirked. "You are stubborn, aren't you? Padre, the answer is no."

Father Hernandez sighed as he got up out of his seat. "Well, when I return, I hope you will have made up your mind at least with helping us to try and find out about what happened with Cardinal Millhouse."

The father stepped back away from the table. "Oh, and give Alicia my regards." He presented Michael with an impish grin, winked, turned, and walked away.

Michael didn't know if he should be upset or impressed by the father's comment.

# Chapter 10 – Contention

Cardinal Tullono, Vicar General of His Holiness for Vatican City, sometimes called the Cardinal Vicar, was the one responsible to help with the spiritual administration for the Holy See Diocese. The Holy Father had assigned him to host and oversee the accommodations for Gary Applethorpe and the child. Tall and thin – almost emaciated, pale complexion, and large sunken green eyes brandished with black plastic rim glasses, the Cardinal stormed down the compacted gravel pathway that led from the private and secure guest house on the grounds of Vatican City.

As Cardinal Tullono rambled along the walkway through the manicured cut grass, large row hedges and an outcropping of evergreen and oak trees, en route to his office, he came upon Cardinal Picoli who was out taking an afternoon stroll near the Eagle Fountain. Its waters slowly cascaded onto five different levels, trickling into a small pond from down its artificially formed jagged rock façade made from the compacting of large and small natural stones mixed in with plaster. The gurgling waters flowing onto each level performed a soothing symphony relaxing Cardinal Picoli.

"Something seems to have you upset, Pieter," Cardinal Picoli noted.

Cardinal Tullono's pasty cheeks flushed. "It's that insolent, that…that…" he muttered with a scowl, unaffected by the tranquil influence of the fountain.

"The child again?" Cardinal Picoli asked, frustrated his peer was upset and complaining about the special guest having arrived to Vatican City. Tolerating Cardinal Tullono's attitude was made all the worse by the Holy Father installing the honorific title of Cardinal when he exceeded the maximum age of retirement. To elevate or bring back retired titles was a way of placating many of the senior clerics remaining after the worldwide disappearance, with many told they would need to remain in their current positions for an indefinite amount of time. Despite rumors of past indiscretions with one or more younger female lay members in his former Diocese, the Roman Curia in Vatican City relocated Cardinal Tullono from Northern Italy to backfill the critical vacancy, and elevated him from bishop.

"He goes off whenever he likes to wherever he likes without keeping me informed. He even dared to tell me he expects to be moved to his new quarters sooner than we had scheduled."

"As Camerlengo, the Bishop of Rome has selected me to run the city-state, and I say who stays where and how the facilities are managed, not that little self-righteous kid who believes he's smarter than everyone else," Cardinal Picoli responded, hoping his attempt to feign indignation fooled Cardinal Tullono. Cardinal Picoli had to admit there were times when the child would upset him.

"And I don't care about, or how he's a special guest we're to give reverence to. I don't know how you put up with his insolence." Cardinal Tullono said.

"It's because the Holy Father asks for me to put up with it. He is his guest and from what I understand, a prominent VIP."

"VIP or not, it doesn't give reason to disrespect any of us. Who does that child think he is? I don't care if he's some sort of important prince. How long is he supposed to be staying here anyway?"

"Two, maybe three months." The answer to the question was much longer, but the Camerlengo lied. The child's stay in the guest house was to be three or four weeks until the completion of the remodeling in his permanent residence within the guest section of the Mater Ecclesia Convent.

"That's two to three weeks too long if you ask me," Cardinal Tullono responded.

"We ourselves must remember humility. We heard that the angels across the world are announcing of a child. This could be him," Cardinal Picoli replied.

"Why is he so special? Am I supposed to be impressed some arrogant brat who some consider some sort of prophet is more of a pain in…"

Cardinal Picoli interrupted. "I wouldn't want you to sin, my brother. I'll go talk to him."

"Thank you. I may be the interim aide to the child and his guardian, but I'm considering going to ask for the removal from the duties for my peace of mind and spiritual centeredness. This child is arrogant and obstinate. When I recommended he should confess his…"

"You recommended reconciliation?" Cardinal Picoli asked.

"He's just as sinful as any man born," Cardinal Tullono responded. "And it is my job to maintain the centeredness of those in the Holy See."

"From what I understand, he is not like any man." Cardinal Picoli had to admit that since the arrival of the child onto the Vatican grounds, he wasn't aware of him partaking of confession.

"You can't be serious? Each person born is declared sinful, and confession a requirement and sacrament."

"Let me go talk to him and his guardian." Cardinal Picoli didn't want to provide any type of response and marched off to the guesthouse leaving Cardinal Tullono standing on the garden pathway irritated and dumbfounded.

*　*　*　*

A thin, adolescent teen boy wandered along the grounds of Vatican City in front of the Palace of the Governate, the pontifical governmental administration building for the Holy See. He had climbed the short flight of a cobbled stairway near the building where an expansive topiary with multi-colored hedges and bushes formed the shape of the papal coat of arms. He followed a small tour group that had recently passed and was circumnavigating around the building to the rear for a visit to the connected Chapel of Santa Maria Regina della Famiglia. As the tour group strolled towards the church, he wandered in the opposite direction along the asphalt pathway that transitioned into compacted gravel, towards the Ethiopian College building and Italian Gardens.

A young nun in the vestments of a veil and gray habit approached the teen seeming out of place walking alone along the walkway.

"Are you lost, young man?" the sister asked, believing him to have separated from a tour group. She became enamored with the brilliance of his phosphorous blue eyes saturated by the radiance of the sunlight as it beamed onto his face. She turned her head slightly to the right to hear his response. She had been deaf in her left ear since birth.

"No, and thank you, Sister Abigail."

"Do I know you?" she responded, paralyzed with intrigue wondering how the teen knew her name.

"No, and don't be sorrowful about the deafness in your left ear."

Sister Abigail's eyes widened. "How did you know about my...who are you?"

The teen smiled, displaying straight and alabaster white teeth as he stared into her brown eyes. He reached up and stroked the sister's left ear lobe. A loud popping sound resonated in her left ear.

Sister Abigail jumped back after she realized what had transpired, disarmed by the teen's countenance. Hearing the barely perceptible audible sounds of traffic on the other side of the Vatican walls, birds chirping, and the rustling of a light wind through the trees entering both ears disorientated her.

She rubbed her left ear. "I don't believe it...how did you do...who are you?"

"You mustn't tell anyone what I did until the proper time," the teen said, as he sauntered over to the Vatican Library.

The sister stood alone snapping her fingers by each ear unaware the teen had moved on. A minute later, two plain clothes gendarmeries on special assignment from the Swiss Guard, dressed in dark purple suits appearing black, white shirts, and thin dark purple ties, rushed over to her still standing on the pathway by the Italian Garden. She continued to be amazed at the restoration of her hearing still snapping her fingers.

"Where's the child you were with?" one of the guards firmly asked.

Sister Abigail hadn't acknowledged the two, unaware of their arrival. "I'm sorry, what?"

"The child who was here, where is he? We were dispatched over here when the security center observed him with you on the CCTV."

"I don't know," she responded walking away from the two guards, rushing back to the Mater Ecclesiae Convent to discuss what had transpired with her Mother Superior.

The Gendarmerie questioning Sister Abigail reached up and pressed the transceiver device in his left ear. "He's not here, were you able to track him and find out which direction he went?"

The guards' wireless earpieces received, "No, it looks like he disappeared when he moved from one camera zone to the next. Return to the command center."

\* \* \* \*

The guest house valet led Cardinal Picoli to the dining room adorned with floor to ceiling religious murals upon the wall. Gary sat at the red oak table consuming a light sandwich, small side of pasta salad mixed with sliced olives, and a glass of rose wine. With the arrival of the Camerlengo, Gary stopped eating and sat back in the ornate red velvet French Baroque style chair.

"Camerlengo, what brings you by…again?" Gary asked.

"Mr. Applethorpe, you have to see to it that your ward restrains himself from traversing unsupervised on the grounds. Of the nearly 435 permanent residents here in the city, he's upset a good portion of them. It's already hard enough to explain why we have a child in the guest residence. Many here are not members of the Society of the Holy...wait a minute..." The child not being in the room with the two adults caught the Cardinal's attention. During previous discussions, the child would interrupt and begin to petition his own case in defending whatever actions or mischief he was involved with. It upset the Cardinal that the child always won. "Where is he?"

Gary returned to eating his lunch. "He's out again. He wanted to go to the library, at least that's where he said he was going."

"What? How? The Gendarmerie is supposed to contact me when he leaves, or if they see him with the video security system unaccompanied on the grounds," Cardinal Picoli said angrily. "And the Holy Father was making special arrangements to accompany him to the library when he was up to moving around. That child needs to learn patience."

Although an irritant, the child impressed those whom he encountered. His mannerisms and intellectual prowess put him on par with most of the clergy, staff, and fellows he had met since arriving. The Society of the Holy Order of the Child considered the potential threat against him high. Cardinal Picoli assigned a security team from the Swiss Guard attached to the Vatican Gendarmerie. Yet the child petitioned, with success, to have it dismissed from time to time while he was out on the Vatican grounds. The child told those in the Holy Order within the inner circle of the Pontifical government and Holy See, that his true guards were higher and mightier than any men.

"Trust me, I know, he's very good at this," Gary said after swallowing a bite of his sandwich and scooping up a serving of pasta salad with his silver-plated fork.

Cardinal Picoli pulled out his mobile smartphone and speed dialed the security control center. "This is Cardinal Picoli. Tell me you know where the high value individual is?"

"We watched him leave the residence several minutes ago. One of the teams managed to track him, but before you called, it looks like he disappeared again. One second he was there, the next, he was gone. They're scanning through the displays now to see if we can pick him up."

*How does he do that?* Cardinal Picoli now understood how some of the Holy Order members on the Vatican staff believed the child possessed unique powers and abilities. "Send a team to search the grounds if you have to. Find him. I believe he may be heading to the library. And make sure he doesn't mix in with sightseers or leave the grounds again."

The Camerlengo terminated the phone call and focused his attention back towards Gary. "Mister Applethorpe, I believed there was an agreement that you're to watch him and help keep him under control. Plus, you've spent the most time with him and we assumed he would've formed some sort of bond with you."

"Are you kidding me? There's something supernatural about the child. If anything, he's formed a bond with the angels that surround and protect him."

"Those of us newly initiated into the Holy Order of the Child have heard of his supposed divine visitations,"

Cardinal Picoli said, "but it's hard to believe with his attitude and obstinance he could be considered so special and unique."

"Is it obstinance, or tremendous self-confidence?"

Cardinal Picoli moved in closer to the table pulling out a chair and sitting down next to Gary and placing his phone on the tabletop. "Mr. Applethorpe, what is so unique about this child? He seems smarter and intelligent, and in many ways, more poised than most children, most adults for that matter. Why does the Holy Father consider this child so special? After the Holy Father established the Holy Order, he told many of us that the child is greater than we could ever imagine. We weren't there during the first visitations to the Holy Father all those years ago, and we were excluded from further dialogues up until a short while ago, but you must have some insight?"

"You know that I can't tell you everything," Gary replied. "When the Holy Father initiated you, remember that there's a wonderful destiny for the child, that's all we're to be concerned about. There are those in the church who would try and stop the ascension of the child if they knew the full truth."

"Ascension? There's nothing more you can mention."

"You shouldn't have asked, and I shouldn't have answered. Many in the Holy See aren't aware of the importance or nature of the child." Gary went back to eating.

Cardinal Picoli stared at Gary for a couple of minutes hoping to garner more information. Gary ignored him.

The Cardinal's phone rang. He maintained his fierce gaze towards Gary.

"Are you going to get that?" Gary asked, after hearing the fourth melodic tone from the Cardinal's phone.

The Camerlengo glanced at his phone. The caller ID displayed the incoming call originated from the Vatican grounds security center.

"Did you find him?" the Cardinal asked, answering the phone, upset at the interruption of his attempted stare down of Gary.

"He's in the library," the voice on the other end stated.

"How did he get into the Vatican Palace?"

"We don't know how he got to the building without being seen on the security system, but he got there somehow. We even had the facial recognition system turned on."

"What part of the library is he in, with the research scholars, or in the tourist section?"

"No, he's in the other section."

"What do you mean other section?" Cardinal Picoli asked, with trepidation.

"The other section, he's in the secured area housing the sensitive manuscripts, archives and artifacts."

Although there had been an edict two decades prior that the Holy Father would make the archives available for limited public review and research, after the mass disappearance across the globe, and mysterious appearance of the angels, he reversed the edict. A flood of requests by scholars and researchers had overwhelmed the library offices, all trying to seek answers.

"The Secret Archives? How? Only a select few can enter. The system's been updated with a state-of-the-art genetic blood checker and individual PIN system

101

recorded for the Holy Father, myself, and most of the Curia. And he still has to personally get past the Prefect of the Archives."

"You don't think we know that?" the voice on the other end of the phone snapped.

"Keep an eye on him, I'll be right over." Cardinal Picoli ended the call and secured his phone in an inner pocket of his cassock.

"I would like to finish our discussion later, Mr. Applethorpe, if you have time."

"I'm not sure I can tell much more than what I already passed on to you."

"Well the child is causing quite a stir. He's undermining our intentions to keep your residence here covert."

"Don't worry, I'm hoping the breadcrumbs of disinformation we've planted will help throw anyone looking for us off track," Gary said starting back into his meal.

"Let's hope so," Cardinal Picoli said as he stood out of the chair and departed the quarters.

Two plain clothes gendarmeries, on special assignment from the Swiss Guard joined the Cardinal along the way to the Vatican Palace. They navigated through an influx of tourists and sightseers while passing through the public area of the grounds. Once the three men arrived at the secured outer entrance of the private library, the child walked out through the door displaying a confident stride with erect posture, and hands behind his back, fingers interlocked. Cardinal Picoli wondered if the child had experienced a growth spurt, with his height increasing another one or two inches since arriving.

"Why is a Swiss Guard gendarmerie detail here? It was understood that a team wouldn't always be assigned to me while I'm anywhere on the grounds," the child queried in near fluent Italian.

"Who decided that, and since when do you go breaking into the secret archives of His Holiness' library? What are we supposed to do?" Cardinal Picoli, answered in Italian. "How did you get in there?"

"I'll tell you, but you have to dismiss the security team."

"I can't do that."

"Dismiss the security detail," the child demanded in a forceful and commanding tone.

Hearing the authoritative voice of the child, Cardinal Picoli wanted to comply, but resisted. He wanted to instruct the security detail to go over, take hold of the child and haul him back to his residence. The directive from the ailing Holy Father was that no one was to handle the child in any physical manner.

"Let's try this again, the security detail stays," Cardinal Picoli directed.

The sensation of static electricity formed in the air causing tingling on the guards and Cardinal Picoli's skin and his arm hairs to stiffen. Queasiness assaulted his intestines. The scent of rain and dust mingled with pine filled the air. The light from the overhead ceiling fixtures and brass trimmed sconces along the walls flickered. Two handsome robed figures, one whose skin was like alabaster, the other his skin shone like bronze, both, their hair like wool, stood behind the child. The gaze of the two guards fixated on the appearance of the angelic apparitions. The bronzed complexioned manifestation pointed and gestured for the men to leave the corridor. They started to back away.

"Where are you two going?" Cardinal Picoli asked, overcoming a sense of dread. "Stand fast."

"Those two angels want us to leave. We're not wanting to disagree with them," the broader of the two guards said.

"Who wants you to leave?"

"The two angels...you don't see them?" the other guard asked.

"You're joking, right?" Cardinal Picoli responded, observing the child standing by himself.

Neither guard answered, both preoccupied by the broad, square-jawed faces of the two angels, eyes with irises and pupils black as coal staring with a fierce intensity. The guards took small steps backwards, remaining focused on the two ethereal creatures, until they turned the corner at the end of the hallway. The flickering of the lights ceased.

The child stood with his hands behind his back. He presented the Cardinal a sly smile. "Now that we're alone, I can tell you," he said. "The Holy Father was the one who gave it to me."

Cardinal Picoli snickered and rolled his eyes. "You expect me to believe the Holy Father gave you his PIN?"

"Yes."

"Only a few members of the Holy See and Curia have a unique PIN to enter, and they all know better than to reveal it. Still, you have to have the preprogrammed genetic code in your blood to..."

The child interrupted. "I know how it works. You as the Camerlengo also know the Holy Father's PIN." The child named off the Pope's birthdate, date of ascension to the position, and date of the first angelic visitation by Aurora.

Cardinal Picoli did not expect the child to state the exact digits he knew to be the Holy Father's PIN. "That's unbelievable, and how did you get past the genetic reader?"

The child smiled and didn't answer, strolling past the Cardinal who stood dumbfounded in the middle of the corridor. The Camerlengo regained his faculty catching up to the tall adolescent child walking by his side. "And what were you looking for?" he asked.

"That's none of your concern," the child answered.

Infuriated, Cardinal Picoli's neck veins throbbed as he expelled a large puff of air to keep from reacting angrily. "Has anyone told you how disrespectful you are?"

"How can I be disrespectful when I do what my father has directed me?"

"Your father? The Holy Father?"

"No, not the Holy Father."

"Then who?"

The child ignored answering the Camerlengo as they continued walking down the corridor where they reached and ascended a set of brown and white whirlpool patterned marble stairs. Once they reached the top of the main floor landing, the two Gendarme guards rejoined the child.

"I'm going to go and take a nap," the child said as he departed with his security detail.

Cardinal Picoli thought how this reminded him of the incident in the gospels where Jesus' parents believed he disobeyed them, but he responded he was obeying his true father.

# Chapter 11 – Return to Las Cruces

66"I hope you don't mind, but I'm not feeling well, and I thinks I mights throw up a cuple of times," a thin, aged man spouted off after sitting down onto the aisle seat next to Father Hernandez in the coach car of the Amtrak Texas Eagle train. "I seems to gets a bit of motion sickness whenever I takes the train."

*Why take the train?* flashed into Father Hernandez's mind as a question he wanted to ask of the man. "Sorry to hear that," is what came out.

"Yeps, I gets serious motion sicknass, hopes I don't throws up on you."

"Excuse me but I need to get by," Father Hernandez said, getting up out of his seat and stepping over the passenger who had boarded during the stop in Tucson.

Making his way down the center of the car swaying from the motion of the train gliding over the uneven tracks, Father Hernandez tripped over the leg of a young man in his early twenties, sleeping with his legs stretched out into the aisle. The man was unaffected by the father's unintentional jolt after bumping him in the ankle. At the end of the coach car, after the father pressed the release button, opening the sliding door leading into the lounge and café car, the train lurched upward causing him to stumble and bump into a petite young mother carrying her infant child heading in the direction opposite him. The bald infant wore a light pink head band embroidered with little flowers.

"Sorry about that," Father Hernandez said as he grabbed onto the candy cane painted hand-hold rail in the transverse between the cars.

The woman observed Father Hernandez's clerical collar. "No, I'm sorry, Father, I didn't see you there. I was trying to hold onto my little one," the mother responded, with a much huskier voice than Father Hernandez anticipated.

"She's cute, what's her name?" Father Hernandez asked.

"Flora."

"That's a pretty name."

"Thank you," the mother said, followed by her resuming the trek back to her seat.

Father Hernandez strolled into the lounge car. Most of the observation chairs installed facing the immense viewing windows were empty. All the lounge tables in the opposite half of the car, except for one, were unoccupied. Sitting down at the first open table, Father Hernandez stared out the oversized window. The sand, splotches of dried desert grasses, scattered sage and mesquite bush, and cactus of the arid landscape flowed by, interrupted by an infrequent solitaire ranch house, or abandoned and dilapidated barn or farmhouse. The truss of a bridge as they crossed over a dry river jostled Father Hernandez's attention from the view of the bronze and dusty backdrop of the arid New Mexico desert.

"You're a priest, I see," a voice said from the side of Father Hernandez, minutes later as the scenery changed to small swatches of homes, streets, and small buildings aside the Rio Grande River off in the distance.

A man with thinning hair, splotchy skin, and untucked, dingy white, button up, collared shirt, and faded blue jeans stood next to the table. Father Hernandez assumed the man asked observing his collar.

"Yes, I am," Father Hernandez responded.

The man sat across the table uninvited and smiled, revealing partly rotted teeth.

"You have to tell me what you think about all this angel stuff that's been goin' on all these years," the man commented.

"I'm not sure I know what you're talking about?"

"I mean here it is I thought that when we die, we become angels up in heaven. But when they started showing up at funerals, I wasn't sure what to think," the man said.

"Well, it doesn't quite work that way," Father Hernandez replied.

"So, angels aren't us then? I mean those who died before and are coming back."

"No, they're not," Father Hernandez responded in a frustrated tone.

"How do you know they aren't?"

"I've studied them quite a bit while at seminary and post seminary. I've done a considerable amount of research on the subject."

"You don't know what you're talking about. You don't have all the answers."

Father Hernandez forced himself from responding with an undignified and debasing outburst that he knew would reflect badly on his character and professionalism. "I realize I don't have all the answers, but I've studied on how to search for the answers instead of guessing and speculating."

"What could you possibly study that would talk about angels?" the man asked.

"Well, for beginners, the Bible," the Father responded in a sharp tone.

"Then how do you know the Bible is true? We weren't there when it was written. How do you know it wasn't made up by some men to create a religion as a way to control other men?"

"Because we have writings carried down over the years that've been inspired by God and proven true by archeol…"

"You have no idea what you're talking about," the man roared, interrupting Father Hernandez. "You think just because you're a priest you have all the answers."

"No, that's not what I'm sa…"

The man stood not waiting to hear the father's response, and stormed down the aisle in the direction of the diner and sleeper accommodations. Father Hernandez hoped he wouldn't run into him back in the coach section of the train. The emotional unease resulting from being self-conscious due to the man yelling and a few other passengers staring, didn't take long to subside.

Several minutes later, a black woman who looked to be in her early sixties was carrying a small cup of coffee covered with a lid and several napkins from the café. She sat at the table across the aisle from the father and gave him a quick smile exposing two missing front upper teeth. She removed the lid from the coffee cup – steam from the hot beverage wafted upward. Taking a napkin, she dipped it in the hot liquid and wiped the display of the smartphone she pulled from the pocket of her sweatpants, attempting to remove finger smudges from its glass surface.

"Miss, I don't know if that's a good idea to use coffee and a napkin like that on your phone. You might scratch and dull the display."

"Because you thinks you'z a priest, you can tells someone what's right and wrong?" the woman snapped back.

"My child, I was simply trying to help, that's all."

The woman grabbed her coffee and smartphone moving back a couple of tables. "Well, I don't needs yor help. And I ain't your child," the woman responded, followed by the ramblings of short fractured and incoherent rants, several lacquered with obscenities. Father Hernandez considered a couple of the mumblings blasphemous.

The bell chime on Father Hernandez's smartphone alerted him to a new text message. It showed "Ro." As with the previous times, the originating number displayed "Private Number." This was his third time since he awoke, he received the cryptic word. Now it was becoming annoying.

The announcement blared from the public-address speaker of the train car that they would arrive in El Paso in ten minutes. Father Hernandez was relieved, and hoped he wouldn't have to deal with any other discourteous passengers.

* * * *

As Father Hernandez stepped off the shuttle from the El Paso train station arriving at the designated Amtrak pickup and drop off location in Las Cruces, a familiar face floated amongst the several awaiting patrons. It was

Bull and he had a grin on his face painted with excitement to see the father.

"Padre, how's it going?" Bull said, as he shook Father Hernandez's hand with enthusiasm, clenching too hard.

"I'm doing well."

"How was your trip?" Bull asked, reaching for and picking up the father's carry-on luggage.

"I can truly say, different. What are you doing down here? I was going to get a taxi to the guest residence of the parish house where I'm staying."

"Don't worry about that, I can take you. Your email said what day you were arriving, so I decided to look up the time and come and get you."

Bull began heading to the parking lot with Father Hernandez joining him.

"Well, I wanted to get situated first," Father Hernandez stressed.

"But I want to get you down to Dawles and see if you can figure out what's going on as soon as possible."

"I don't think you understand, Bull. I was hoping to spend the rest of the day to complete my daily prayers and devotionals and go there tomorrow." The earlier passengers had irritated Father Hernandez. He was anxious to meditate and unwind.

"You can't come out today?" Bull pleaded, his grin distorting into a frown. "It's just that we were hoping you would come out as soon as possible to help."

"Don't worry, Bull, whatever's happening, I'll help you figure it out. I want to get settled in first."

\* \* \* \*

The next morning, Bull was waiting outside of the parish house on time at eight o'clock to pick up the father.

His excitement had returned and during the short drive to Dawles, he described the strange occurrences within the semi-private room. No one except for himself had been able to enter since the incident.

Upon arriving to the treatment center and parking, they proceeded straight to the nurses' admin station of the low security, low risk wing. As if an arriving celebrity, several of the waiting hospital staff members, orderlies, nurses, clerks, and a couple of doctors came up to greet the father as soon as he entered the ward. Some of the personnel he recalled from during his prior assignment at the hospital as the Catholic chaplain. Many assailed him with questions he didn't have the answers to – why did the angel pick that room, why is it keeping the room locked, how come it won't let anyone in, is there some sort of message it's trying to tell everyone? After a couple of rounds of nonstop questioning, staff members started to repeat themselves, or attempted to ask their question in a different manner hoping to elicit a response other than his repeating answer of "I don't know."

Bull led Father Hernandez down the hall to the room. A mini entourage followed. It was beginning to feel more like a circus than a pursuit to attempt and learn the reason for the alleged angel visit. The hallway lights were all illuminated, different than what Bull described from what had occurred during the earlier incidents. Father Hernandez wondered if an angel had shown up in the semi-private room, would it now show up with the glut of curious spectators flooding the corridor.

The door to the room looked normal. The crowd hushed as Father Hernandez reached to grab the doorknob. Bull warned him to expect some sort of unnatural electrical shock. The Father's hand wrapped around the cold metal of the knob and turned to release the latch. Gently pulling on the door, it cracked open. Father Hernandez paused for a few seconds. Nothing happened. He continued pulling to reveal a sparsely furnished room – a simple wood-framed bed, desk, chair, and a six-drawer dresser unit. He stepped in finding nothing strange or any signs that showed a paranormal event had occurred. The sweet aroma that would accompany a visitation was absent. The fading pungent smell of latex paint lingered in the air. Behind him, all Father Hernandez heard was the grumbling of the disappointed spectators not to have an angelic being waiting for him. Several of the staff members entered to confirm nothing of interest occupied the room. The hallway and room emptied after a couple of minutes, except for Bull.

"Well, Padre, this was a bust. I swear an angel was here. What do you think happened?" Bull asked.

"We can't think an angel will show up simply because we want one to show up," Father Hernandez replied. He worried if the trip would prove to be useless.

"Yeah, but no one could come into the room until now. Why would you be allowed?" Bull asked, strolling around the room to see if anything odd stood out.

"I don't have an answer for you, Bull, but it looks like everything is normal in here. Nothing new has happened since you called me?"

"Nope, only what I mentioned about the angel showing up. It was right after the room was repainted."

"The room was painted over?" Father Hernandez asked. "Why did they do that?"

"Sometimes Facilities will need to paint the room if the patient moves from being controllable to unstable, and starts to write crazy stuff on the wall, and we need to move them to the more secure wing. You don't want to know what they use sometimes. We have to clean and sterilize the walls, sometimes the entire room to be safe. It's amazing what some of the more unhinged patients can do in a short amount of time."

Father Hernandez didn't need to imagine the context of Bull's comment. Since most of his duties were associated with providing spiritual guidance for the staff and facilitating support groups, he had spent a small fraction of his time in the current wing during his earlier residency on staff. This was part of the daily protocol. "So, that's why you can still smell paint in here." He examined the walls to search if any earlier scrawls or penned ramblings were visible under the coats of paint.

"Wait a minute, was there anything odd Doctor Cochrane wrote on the walls when he was in here?" Father Hernandez inquired.

"Yeah, I think there was."

"You wouldn't happen to remember what he wrote would you?" Father Hernandez asked still surveying and massaging the surface of the wall.

Bull didn't answer. Father Hernandez turned to see him with raised eyebrows and a look of bewilderment. "Really, Father, did you just ask me that?"

"Wait a minute, when I talked to him before he was transferred out by Everest, I don't think it was in this room, was it? There wasn't anything on the walls."

"Nope, this was his primary room. We had moved him because of the weird stuff that happened with him the first time, and he'd written all over the place. He was moved to a temporary room once we got word he was going to be released."

"I wish we knew what he'd written on the walls. It'll be interesting to find out if there was something that would provide some light on all of this."

"You know what, Padre, check the hospital record archives. Most times pictures are taken in case the head shrinks want to review and analyze what was written for their upcoming sessions with the patient."

"That's a good idea, but I can't look in patient records."

"No, go to the archives, sometimes Facilities will keep a set as part of their maintenance records."

Father Hernandez darted out of the room wanting to waste no time to head down to the administrative section of the medical center and treatment center. He was halfway out of the building before he realized he forgot to ask Bull the exact location of the archives records office. A passing nurse was able to assist.

\* \* \* \*

For ten minutes, Father Hernandez contended with a records clerk refusing to provide him access to any of the photos or notes regarding Doctor Cochrane's room.

"That's great that you can remember your work access information and that you use to be on staff here, Father, but without a valid ID and current employment, we can't release that information to you," the records clerk emphasized. "Even then, a director or higher has to approve it."

"Look, I'm working on an investigation, and the details about one of the rooms for one of the low risk patients may provide some valuable information in helping to…"

The records clerk interrupted, not holding back his frustration at the insistence of Father Hernandez. "Father,

I don't care," he said in a loud voice, "but if you were the police working on an investigation, it could be a different story. The El Paso police come up all the time requesting information since that's where most of our patients reside or are transferred from," the records clerk finished, with the tone of his voice returning to a normal volume, realizing he was bringing attention of the other office workers to himself.

"I don't care about the El Paso police," Father Hernandez countered.

"Then the Las Cruces police office."

"And who would I know on either the El Paso or Las…" An idea came to Father Hernandez causing him to stop mid-sentence. He could attempt to contact the police detective who was investigating the murder of Doctor McCall, and the alleged attempt on his life in the basement of the older mental hospital building. Thing was that with the amount of time that had passed, Father Hernandez had forgotten the detective's name.

\* \* \* \*

The taxi conveying Father Hernandez pulled up to the single story, contemporary-modern designed, off-white sandstone covered police station. Past the front double doors made of smoked glass was an information desk occupied by a well-dressed, young Hispanic woman. Father Hernandez anticipated a desk sergeant, but recalled the sign on the front wall of the building that it also housed the Public Safety Administrative offices.

"May I help you?" she asked.

"I hate to admit this, but I'm looking for one of your police detectives, but I'm not sure which one."

"Well, what does he look like?" the receptionist asked.

"Father Hernandez, right? What are you doing out here, Father?" said a voice to Father Hernandez's right. Turning to look, Detective Henderson entered the lobby through a set of clear glass double doors that led into an office bullpen area humming with moderate activity.

"That would be him," Father Hernandez said to the receptionist. "I came to talk to you," he said as both men shook hands.

"We can head back to my desk," Detective Henderson replied.

"So, are you getting relocated back to Dawles?" Detective Henderson asked, as they sat at the detective's desk cluttered with file folders and papers.

"No, I came out to check the report of an angel sighting over at the hospital, but something else popped up."

"We heard some wild rumors about something going on with an angel over in one of the low security psych wings. What's all of it about anyway?"

"It may have had something to do with when I was assigned out here. I also came to follow up and see if you found out anything else about the man who killed Doctor McCall and tried to kill me?"

"Father, after all that weird stuff when I went out to L.A. with supposed angels and Gary Applethorpe disappearing, things went cold. Do you have something for me? And I don't mean that cockamamie story about Everest and the Church conspiring about some vaccine or something."

"Virus, actually."

"Whatever, unless you have something concrete, I can't be wasting my time," Detective Henderson said.

"I need your help with retrieving some information from the archives at Dawles."

Detective Henderson raised an eyebrow. "Why can't you do it? You use to work there."

"I'm not on staff now, and if I was, of course I wouldn't be here."

"What exactly are you looking for?" Detective Henderson asked, getting up and meandering over to a coffee pot and accoutrements that sat not too far away over against the wall, and pouring a cup of coffee.

While Father Hernandez didn't desire any coffee, he considered it a bit rude the detective didn't offer him a cup, but overlooked the minor transgression. "There was a patient admitted to Dawles who was an employee of Everest."

"I remember that. I approached Applethorpe about him when I was out there. What's so special about him now?"

"The patient's name was Doctor Cochrane, and he went through some sort of breakdown. I found out he may have written something on the walls, and the hospital's facilities department may have pictures of the room before they repainted that could help in my investigation."

"Your investigation?" Detective Henderson asked, sitting back down at his desk followed by him taking a sip of coffee from his mug.

"The Cardinal for the Los Angeles Archdiocese was killed by a couple of mysterious men."

"Who are you guys pissing off that they want to kill you?"

"We tried telling you when you came out to L.A., but you didn't want to believe us. What's going on out here may have something to do with it."

There was a long pause from Detective Henderson, with him giving Father Hernandez an intense gaze, attempting to size up the father's comments.

"We've pulled room records before for a couple of cases where what the patient wrote on the wall were used during an investigation for the police down in El Paso. But you know it can't be part of their medical records in any way," Detective Henderson said.

"I'm aware of that, but there may be facility records concerning the room you could have access to. I have a feeling that whatever you can help me with will help considerably."

There was another long pause from Detective Henderson. "I'll let you know what I decide sometime tomorrow."

\* \* \* \*

It was the early evening when Father Hernandez's host notified him that he had a guest in the living room of the parish house. Waiting was a man with a mahogany complexioned skin tone and mildly protruding pot-belly, dressed in a casual outfit and holding a 9x12" manila envelope. It was Detective Henderson

"Detective, what are you doing here?" Father Hernandez asked. "I was under the impression that you were going to decide to help or not in the morning."

"I was, but this case is intriguing, so I went to Dawles and managed to work some of my magic to have these printed from their digital archives. What I have here looks interesting. I imagined that you might want to see these pictures right away."

"You have the pictures of the walls?" There was a slight amount of excitement in the father's voice.

"I do, but before I turn them over to you, you promise to keep me in the loop on this?"

"I don't understand."

"When I was out in L.A., the FBI said I'd be lucky to get a chance at Gary after they build up a case against him, but if this'll help crack Doctor McCall's murder case, and the attempt on your life, I can pretty much tell them to go fu..." Detective Henderson caught himself. "I can tell them to go scre...I can tell them to go play with themse...ugh...you know what I mean." He opened the envelope pulling out several photographs and handing them over to the father.

Father Hernandez took the pictures showing images of a cinder block wall. Though not completely covered, sprawled over large sections were numerous words, numbers, and random chemical formula fragments.

"These were taken in Doctor Cochrane's old room?" Father Hernandez asked.

"Yeah, but they've had a couple of other occupants since then. Why are these pictures of what's on the wall so important?" Detective Henderson asked.

"I can't answer that one, detective," Father Hernandez replied, still flipping through the pictures. Perusing through one of the images, the number 101 written several times, along with the words, "bloodline" and "aurora" stood out. Towards the back of the room, midway down the wall to the baseboard, the words "aurora - child" accompanied a combination series of the letters A, C, G, and T, interspersed with a few of the letters X, Y, and K. On another picture, the word "enhancement" and "splice" was intermingled along with the previous scribblings and wrapped along the wall.

"So, do you have any idea what all that stuff means?" Detective Henderson asked, who was now standing next to Father Hernandez reviewing the pictures.

Father Hernandez was too concentrated on the pictures to be concerned with the fact Detective Henderson had invaded his personal space. "No idea. I wonder if my companions would know."

"And there's nothing in those pictures that could tell us why anyone would kill Dr. McCall, or try to have you killed."

"Like I said, detective, I have no idea."

## *Chapter 12 – Decision*

Michael observed someone standing on his small front porch as he was returning from his jog. As he got closer to his house, he recognized Justine. It reminded him of the time when she showed up with Father Hernandez after the reported alleged return of Abriel at the Thomson and Thomson incident.

"Justine, what are you doing here?" Michael asked, elated she was standing with him on his small porch. He hadn't expected to see her, wanting to leave her space as not to pressure her. At first, he tried to see why she seemed so different. Then it hit him, it was the light application of eyeliner, mascara, foundation, and blush that accentuated her blue eyes. Her wearing makeup was out of the ordinary. She also styled her short brunette hair with a small bang over the front of her petite face. He'd forgotten how beautiful she was.

Michael motioned for Justine to enter after he unlocked and opened the door into a small living room where the interior decorating was sparse and Spartan. She assumed that after Michael ended the relationship with Alicia, he erased her influence of vibrant throw pillows, colorful throw rugs, and wall pictures of northeastern snow sceneries.

"Wow, you didn't waste any time changing things back to plain, did you?" Justine noted.

"What brings you over here?" Michael asked, as he guided Justine into the kitchen. "I know it's not about my interior decorating style, or Alicia for that matter." Michael hoped her visit was Justine's attempt to make a segue way to build a path for the two of them to attempt and see if they could renew their relationship after an eleven-and-a-half, almost twelve-year separation. They were aware of their re-emerging emotions for one another, and he needed to keep his composure.

"I haven't seen you in a few days," Justine said. "And Cardinal Grielle missed you at his elevation ceremony."

Cardinal Grielle was a name Michael didn't want to hear. "Well, I didn't miss him," he responded in a sour tone. "I read in the news that Cardinal Millhouse may have been killed, and it wasn't natural causes like they first reported. I wouldn't be surprised if it was Grielle, which was the only way he was going to become Cardinal."

"Michael!"

"I'm not gonna lie, Millhouse, in my eyes, was a slime bag, and Grielle is a spineless snake. You already knew that though."

"But you have to feel something for Cardinal Millhouse's passing? You can't be that cold. And Cardinal Grielle was helpful when we were investigating the Aurora incidents."

Michael didn't want to agree with Justine that she was correct concerning the aide Cardinal Grielle had provided. But it was still hard to accept him. "I'm not gonna sit here and justify their actions. What did you want, Justine?" Michael asked, upset the tone of the conversation wasn't going as intended.

"Did you hear about Cardinal Grielle mentioning Father Hernandez and I weren't excommunicated from the church?"

"Yeah, when Father Hernandez called to let me know about the ceremony, he told me. And he reminded me of that fact when he tried to get me to go out to Las Cruces with him on his angel crusade a couple of days ago. But that doesn't mean anything about you leaving though," Michael noted, pulling a glass from the cabinet and filling it with water from the filtration system's miniature faucet spigot. "What is it you want, Justine?"

"Michael, I wanted to let you know that I'm deciding to stay in the church."

Michael's intestines turned as if he had been gut punched. "Wait…what…what about us?"

"There can be no us, not right now. With all that's happened, I have to reaffirm if this is what I want to do. I know we hinted at maybe we could start over again, but things have changed. I've been giving this quite a bit of reflection and prayer. You have to understand…"

"Understand?" Michael snapped. The light copper complexion of his bi-racial background saturated with a ruby color. "You expect me to say something like, if I did understand, I'd support your decision no matter what?"

"Well…yes."

"It doesn't work that way. The Church took you away from me once, and I'm supposed to sit by and let it take you away from me again."

"Michael, don't be this way. With the events at Everest, someone trying to kill Father Hernandez, and then the murder of Cardinal Millhouse, something is telling me this isn't over. I feel like I still have a higher purpose to serve. Cardinal Grielle and Father Hernandez have been helping me to see this."

"Grielle, I should've figured, he's still a snake and you want to go back to serve under him. And when I was getting ready to like boy toy, he goes and does this. I don't know why you're going back?"

"Cardinal Grielle promoted Father Hernandez to work on his personal staff and help oversee many of the parishes at the Diocese office in downtown L.A."

"Yay, good for him," Michael said.

"Michael, Cardinal Grielle offered me the opportunity to assist with overseeing the programs administration of all the sisters who serve at the Women's Centers in the Diocese. If I accept the position, I get to work as a coordinator with the Mother Superiors of the convents supporting the various health and education centers as the liaison for the Cardinal."

"Oh great, so now he's gonna make you his head snitch," Michael jabbed.

Justine's facial complexion inflamed. "Go to hell." She stormed out of the kitchen and proceeded towards the front door.

Michael, shocked, did not expect for Justine to react with uttering the harsh expletive. Since she didn't hold back and it was not normal for her to curse, he knew he crossed the line. Michael followed catching up with her outside on the front porch.

"Justine, wait," Michael pleaded.

She kept walking, stepping down off the porch.

He gently tugged on her shoulder as she started down the steps onto the sidewalk. "Justine, I'm sorry,"

Justine responded to the gesture and stopped.

125

"I feel as if I'm losing you again," Michael said. "Maybe that's why I'm upset."

Justine turned around to face Michael. She had made up her mind that she was going to return to the church, but looking into his eyes reignited the emotions she once experienced for him. "Michael, I have to be honest, I don't know if there was going to be an us. We've been down this road before when I first wanted to become a nun and began the process. I'm not a hundred percent positive that I'm going to return to the church, but I'm leaning in that direction. You have to be patient, and if you do care for me, you'd support me no matter what decision I may make."

Michael dropped his shoulders, bowed his head, and expelled a heavy breath feeling defeated. "You're not gonna make this easy, are you?" he asked, as he raised his head up and stared into her eyes glistening as if two sapphire blue gemstones.

"Don't get sappy. And if anything, you can at least help Father Hernandez investigate more about this Aurora situation and Cardinal Millhouse's death," Justine pleaded.

Michael stepped back. "Wow, you and boy toy are putting up a serious full court press, aren't you?"

"I know many think you're a pain in the butt...well...actually...you are...but I bet you're also concerned that the right thing is done, and just as intrigued as we are. We need your help in figuring out what's going on."

Michael grinned. "Listen to you with that potty mouth of yours, talking as if you're of the world. You sure you want to stay in the church?"

"You got me flustered and you know it's not that bad. I'm only human. Besides, I'll confess that later. But look what's happened, Cardinal Millhouse was killed with an angel somehow involved, and an angel showing up in Las Cruces around the same time. I had planned to go down with Father Hernandez to New Mexico, but some things popped up here in LA that I need to get started on to help a couple of the centers I'll be responsible for. You don't know how important I feel being able to help young teenage mothers and abuse survivors. With Cardinal Grielle, he's letting me take what's working at the Allison's Women's Center and bring it to the other centers in the Dioceses in Southern California. Think about the all the good myself and the sisters in my Order here and the other Dioceses could do."

Michael didn't know if he should be happy or upset. As much as he wanted to be excited for Justine, his emotions caused him to endure the selfish feelings that began to emerge wanting her to abandon the church, so they could be together. "Let's try this, I'll consider going if God were to call me on my phone and say go."

"Michael, be real."

"Okay, if one of his representative calls, how's that?"

Sister Justine smirked. Michael's smartphone chimed from his sweatpants pocket. Pulling it out, the display read "Father Boy Toy."

"You got to be kidding me," Michael commented.

"Who is it?" Justine asked.

"Father Hernandez."

Justine chuckled. "Be careful of what you ask for."

Michael snickered in response as he answered the phone in a callous tone. "What do you want, boy toy?"

"Wow, you sound happy to hear from me," Father Hernandez responded.

"Padre, I really don't have the time."

"I received a call from Cardinal Grielle."

"That concerns me how?" Michael snapped.

"He needs our help. The police approached him with something they want us to review regarding Cardinal Millhouse's death. And then I want to talk about what I found out here in Las Cruces. I should be back the day after next."

"And why do you think I'm gonna help?"

"What if I told you that there may be video proof of an angel. I also came up with some additional information about Doctor Cochrane. I was going to call Sister Justine to let her know and have her join us."

Michael didn't respond, tempted to first tell the father no, but leaned to deciding otherwise.

"Michael…Michael…are you there?" Father Hernandez asked, after a few moments not hearing a response.

"Sister Justine is here if you want to ask her."

"Umm, she is?" Father Hernandez replied, Michael not picking up on Father Hernandez's subtle concern as to Sister Justine being with him.

"I'll need to let you know," Michael said. He handed the phone to Sister Justine.

\* \* \* \*

The next morning after his semi-daily jog, Michael continued to mull over Father Hernandez's request to review the video and assist Cardinal Grielle. The father was being persistent. Not going to Las Cruces should have implied Michael wasn't interested in helping. And with Justine deciding on remaining in the Church, instead of her leaving, left a bit of distaste for the Diocese. He had flirted with the belief there would be an opportunity for the two to renew their relationship, but circumstances changed the outcome.

And Michael was still interested in angels. It all started when as a young teenager, his holy roller aunt would tell him stories of angel lore. One of the most intriguing was when his aunt and uncle were driving in Chicago. While at an intersection waiting at a red light in the Hyde Park district on the south side of the city, the light turned green and his uncle pressed on the accelerator. The vehicle lurched forward and then stopped after moving a couple of feet. The engine continued to rev, the transmission was in gear, yet the car didn't move. A dark blue car streaked in front of their vehicle and attempted to turn left having run through the red light for the cross traffic. The dark blue vehicle failed to brake, went wide, and crashed head on into a street lamp post on the corner. Michael's aunt and uncle's car was able to move forward again. They navigated to the opposite corner, pulling up to the curb parking next to a liquor store to see if they needed to render aide. They got out of their vehicle glancing back kitty corner across the intersection at the blue car, the front-end crumpled with a geyser of steam erupting from under the hood. A young man with glazed eyes and looking dazed got out, wobbled for a couple of steps, broke off running, and disappeared underneath a viaduct.

"God has his angels watching out for you two," a voice said from next to the wall of the liquor store.

Startled, Michael's aunt and uncle turned and found a transient camped out on the sidewalk who made the comment. "His angels was busy keepin' your car stills to

129

keeps you from getting hits. God mus' be watchin' out for you," the transient continued.

The piercing warble of approaching sirens broke his aunt and uncle's attention for a few seconds before their focus returned to the transient sitting by the wall. He was no longer there, nor anywhere in the vicinity.

Michael's aunt would tell him other stories like this one. He would ask, why did they have so many alleged encounters? Her response, "no one knows the purpose or ways of the Almighty, and why he sends his agents at the times when he does. It's important to remember that whether they're good or bad, there's still a greater purpose at work in the lives of men."

Michael called Father Hernandez after pondering his request from the day prior for a few more minutes. As soon as the father answered, Michael said, "I'm in, text me where and when." He ended the call and went to shower.

## *Chapter 13 – Meeting in Los Angeles*

After his train arrived into Los Angeles, Father Hernandez had first chose to walk from Union Station to the Archdiocese offices next to the Cathedral of Our Lady of the Angels, since the distance wasn't far, a little over a mile. After short consideration, taking a taxi would be less burdensome not having to carry his briefcase and a large roller bag in tow. He weaved through the river of commuters and long-haul passengers that flowed through the voluminous Great Hall of the station depot as if a raging torrent of bobbling heads. Apart from the occasional nudge or bump, a tall man with dark skin and a short afro dyed blond, jostled the father on his right shoulder as he passed. Father Hernandez thought nothing of it until another man jarred into him against the other shoulder seconds later distracting him from the first bump.

"Sorry, Father," the second man said, briskly walking away.

Father Hernandez accepted the fleeting apology, proceeded towards the main entrance, and then to the taxi stand where he flagged down the next available conveyance. After giving the driver the address of his destination, and knowing he'd arrive in a few minutes, he reached into his rear pocket to pull out his wallet. The pocket was empty. Thinking maybe he placed it in his other rear pocket, it was empty as well. Checking his briefcase yielded the same results, no wallet. He searched about his seat and the floor, still unsuccessful. He started to run through his mind the possible places he could have misplaced or dropped it. The train and train station came to mind.

"We'res here," the driver called out causing Father Hernandez to panic. He had no means to pay the taxi driver.

*Crap*, the father thought. "You know, this is going to sound funny, but I can't seem to find my wallet."

The taxi driver's face recoiled with anger. "A man of God tryin' to stiff me? This ain't no mercy trip," the driver said.

Father Hernandez's bronze skin blushed, embarrassed wearing his collar didn't help in this circumstance. "Look, let me call inside and have someone come out to pay you." Finding his phone was missing, the father started going into a frantic search reaching again into his pockets and rummaging through his briefcase, "I don't believe this, I swore it was in my pocket."

"Lemme guess, yours phone is missin' too."

Father Hernandez's stomach turned. Different options of how to pay the driver evaded him. He glanced out the window to see Sister Justine and Michael walking by on the sidewalk approaching the small set of steps that led to the front entrance of the cathedral offices.

"You gotta believe me, those two walking up to the building should be able to help me," Father Hernandez said, beginning to step out of the taxi.

"Where's you going?" The taxi driver bellowed, ready to jump out and hold the father back thinking he was trying to skip on the fare.

"Sister, Michael, I need your help," Father Hernandez yelled out.

After overcoming the surprise of who could be calling their names, Michael and Sister Justine recognized the father. He advertised a look of desperation with puppy dog eyes and a droopy frown.

"Are you all right, Father?" Sister Justine asked as she and Michael approached the taxi.

"I need your help. I can't seem to find my wallet, and I need to pay the driver."

Michael grinned. "In a bit of trouble, are you?"

Sister Justine glared at Michael, and then focused her attention back to the father. "How much do you need?"

"$9.10," the taxi driver blurted out.

Sister Justine pulled out ten dollars from her purse and paid the taxi driver as Michael helped Father Hernandez pull out his roller bag and briefcase. No sooner than the father and his luggage was out of the taxi, it sped away.

"That's a bit embarrassing, isn't it, Father?" Sister Justine asked.

"I know I had my wallet and phone a short bit ago. I called you two to meet me here at the Archdiocese when we left the Ontario station before coming into L.A. And I know I had everything when I got off the train."

"You lost your phone too, boy toy?" Michael asked.

"Yeah, I don't understand it. I talked to Cardinal Grielle as well as I got off the train. By the way, he's going to be waiting for us. Let's go up so I can throw my stuff in the office. And I need to see if someone from the

133

staff can call the lost and found at Union Station for me in case anyone turned in my wallet and phone."

* * * *

When Father Hernandez, Sister Justine, and Michael entered Cardinal Grielle's office, they recognized the two men sitting in front of the Cardinal's desk who wore machine stitched, poorly fitting, polyester blend business casual suits and scuffed up Rockport styled Oxford shoes.

"Of course, you three remember Detectives Green and Matthews from the Thomson and Thomson incident," Cardinal Grielle said.

"Not to answer for my team, but it's been some time, I do," Father Hernandez said.

Two Archdiocese staff members brought in three additional chairs, placing them next to the chairs occupied by the detectives.

"Detective Green, still into your puzzles?" Michael asked.

"That would be Detective Matthews," Detective Green fired back.

"I knew it was one of you two."

"What are you two doing here?" Father Hernandez asked, going over to shake the hands of the detectives, followed by Sister Justine doing the same. The father and Sister Justine sat in one of the empty chairs. Michael went over to the credenza leaning against the top, avoiding the remaining empty chair, not wanting to be near Cardinal Grielle.

"We're the ones assigned to the Cardinal Millhouse case," Detective Green started, with a troubled look on his face, "and we think we ran into some roadblocks. Since you worked with us in the past, maybe you can help us now. This time, we know something…bizarre happened."

134

"You can join us over here, Mr. Saunders," Cardinal Grielle requested, Michael interpreting it to be a couched command.

"I'm good," Michael fired back, a bit crossly.

Michael and Cardinal Grielle engaged in a staring contest.

"So how can we help you, detectives?" Father Hernandez interjected wanting to avoid a potential uncomfortable confrontation sensing Michael's suppressed hostility.

Cardinal Grielle grabbed a remote on his desktop and pointed it to a seventy-two inch, large display mounted on the wall opposite the desk. "Watch this."

Michael inched over from the side of the room towards the group to get a better view of the screen. A video of Cardinal Millhouse's death and follow up incidents played on the oversized unit. Cardinal Grielle paused the playback after the blacked-out segment disappeared. The video image of the room displayed the shapes of two figures burned into the wood floor.

"Did I see what happened, happen?" Michael asked.

"Did those poor men somehow end up on the floor?" Sister Justine asked.

"Poor men?" Cardinal Grielle exclaimed. "They killed Cardinal Millhouse."

"We tested the results of the materials on the floor," Detective Green said. "The first set of results from the soot we collected we considered inconclusive, so we had the sample tested again. The lab stated the chemical analysis of the ash is nearly identical to what remains after as if a body is cremated, including wood ash and the chemical elements for wood stain and veneer considering the finished wood floor."

"Cremated?" Michael asked.

"And what appears to be the remnants of a USB and slagged metal we think were keys," Detective Matthews replied.

"Do you know how hot that has got to be, for something like what we saw to happen?" Michael commented.

"We can't explain anything that you witnessed. And I can't believe that I'm gonna ask you this, but you saw the weird streak, is it possible...an angel was involved?" Detective Green asked.

"Why do you think an angel was involved?" Michael countered.

"You guys are the religious experts and saw what happened. We want to rule them out, but not discount anything. It looked like the two men were talking to someone who wasn't there before they dropped to the ground," Detective Green replied. "Do you think something superna…"

"Doesn't mean someone else wasn't in the room," Michael said, interrupting the detective. "The video could've been doctored. We have to be realistic here."

"Watch, we added a copy of the original video with playback at a slower frame rate. And our digital forensics team verified what you saw was untouched."

Cardinal Grielle pressed the play key on the remote. The video they had viewed replayed at a slower frame rate. Pronounced ethereal hands, briefly visible, showed the twisting of the victim's heads before the blacked-out segment.

"Okay, that was trippy," Michael remarked.

"Was there a sweet or flowery smell in the room, detectives?" Sister Justine asked.

"Nothing like when we were investigating the funeral home incidents," Detective Green answered. "Just weird smells and bodies."

Michael glanced over to Father Hernandez who had remained quiet during the conversation and displayed a pensive facial expression. "Uhm, boy toy, how come you're not saying anything?"

"I already knew about the video."

Sister Justine's jaw dropped open.

Michael rolled his eyes. "And you didn't tell us?"

"You didn't want to get involved before now, so I don't think there was a problem."

"So, the big question I have," Detective Green interjected after Father Hernandez's reply believing the discussion was drifting off topic. "Why would someone want to kill the Cardinal?"

No one responded.

"You three are going to tell me there's no reason you can think of that those two men would want to kill Cardinal Millhouse?" Detective Green asked of the group. "All this weird stuff going on, and you have no idea why someone would murder a high-level clergy member?"

"We don't even know who the men are," Father Hernandez interjected.

"Facial recognition was able to come up with something on one of the men. He was retired military with an intelligence background, and with some investigating, so was the other," Detective Matthews said.

"You're telling us that there's the possibility of a state sponsored attack behind Cardinal Millhouse's death?" Cardinal Grielle asked.

137

"I don't know what we're saying," Detective Green commented. "All of this is strange. And you saw the video, this is an assassination, not a simple murder."

"Assassination?" Cardinal Grielle queried of the two detectives. "Wouldn't the FBI be involved?"

"Not necessarily, but we're trying to stay ahead of the Feds on this just in case," Detective Green said.

"We kinda suspect that Everest Biomedical was involved through all of this somehow," Father Hernandez commented.

"Everest International?" Detective Matthews asked.

"Yes, you might not believe us," Father Hernandez answered. "But we think Everest was somehow associated with the Thomson and Thomson and Crestview funeral homes incidents. Prominent members from Everest were killed at both."

"And we think an angel was to blame," Sister Justine added.

"Wait, what you're telling us is that the FBI saying Thomson and Thomson was a gas leak isn't the case?" There was skepticism in Detective Green's voice.

"I'm not quite saying that," Father Hernandez said. "Maybe they don't have any way to explain what happened because it wasn't natural. You remember what happened to all the bodies when they got to the morgue."

"Then why make something up?" Detective Matthews said.

Father Hernandez, Sister Justine, and Michael ping-ponged glances back and forth between each other, wondering if and what they should respond. When one of the three would throw a quick glimpse over to Cardinal Grielle, he made sure neither one of the detectives was looking in his direction. With minute movements, he shook his head back and forth signaling not to disclose any additional information.

"By chance, did you receive any information from my office?" Cardinal Grielle asked breaking the awkward lull in the conversation and round robin of glances.

"What type of information? We haven't received anything," Detective Matthews replied.

"My aide, Father Yancy, was tasked to research and provide any information concerning Cardinal Millhouse and get it over to you. Maybe he didn't find anything."

"So, is there anything you can give us to help figure out who may have been involved with the Cardinal's death?" Detective Green asked.

"No, but since you have all worked together before, I had intended for Father Hernandez here to be our liaison on this investigation, and for us to provide anything that may help to solve this."

"That'll be fine, and if you come up with anything substantive and concrete, and not conspiracy theories or magical angel tales, you need to give us a call."

Frustrated, the detectives departed Cardinal Grielle's office.

"What was all that about Father Yancy? Should we be aware of something else?" Father Hernandez asked.

Cardinal Grielle leaned back in his chair. "There is. I'm a bit concerned because Father Yancy hasn't shown up to work or in his dormitory apartment for the last couple of days. We submitted a missing person report with the police."

Michael made his way from standing near the front of Cardinal Grielle's desk and sat in the empty chair next to Sister Justine. "And you didn't want to mention any of this to those two yahoos?"

"What is it Father Yancy was supposed to tell them?" Sister Justine asked.

Cardinal Grielle described the new panic room at the residence, along with the contents of the recorded video on the newly installed security system. All three were not only intrigued, but worried by Cardinal Grielle's exposition to learn that Cardinal Millhouse had referenced two of their names, and his knowledge with the intentional misappropriation of funds by the church for use towards the Aurora project.

"We should be thankful that after the Cardinal named the sister and myself, the two men aren't around anymore according to the video," Father Hernandez said.

"Let's pray it is a blessing. That's why I didn't mention about Cardinal Millhouse being the Church's point man with Everest as one of the primary suppliers for some of our medical missionary work down in Mexico. It could cause the police to investigate further. Thank goodness we hadn't found any paperwork stating as such."

"Listen to us, a blessing that two men are dead?" Sister Justine said.

"Two men who murdered a Cardinal. Who knows what would've happened if they came to talk to us," Father Hernandez said.

"We should show a little mercy," she responded.

"How did things go in Las Cruces?" Cardinal Grielle asked, wanting to divert the conversation.

Father Hernandez jumped out of his chair. "I'll be right back." He darted out the room and returned after several minutes carrying a large manila envelope, handing it to Cardinal Grielle.

"What's this?"

"It's a good thing we didn't mention anything about these pictures and Aurora to the two police detectives," Cardinal Grielle said, while reviewing the pictures. "It would invite more questions on their part. We need a way to clear the church."

"Yeah, I don't think that's happening," Michael inserted. "Thanks to Cardinal Millhouse, the church is knee deep in this mess."

"Michael's right," Father Hernandez added. "We have to work and make sure none of this gets out to embarrass the church, and mitigate the damage right now."

"Don't we sound like the politician," Michael commented.

"You don't understand, Michael, I still have a duty to God and the Church, not to find filler material to fill a book for you to make tenure," Father Hernandez replied.

"Enough, you two, zip it," Cardinal Grielle commanded. "I need you to work together and try to figure out all of this. What you have here may be a big piece," he added waving the pictures. After viewing the final hard copy of the image, he passed the set to Sister Justine, who then passed them to Michael.

"Do any of you have an idea of what those writings might mean?" Cardinal Grielle asked.

"Maybe something to do with the virus or the child. That's my guess," Father Hernandez said.

"You have two unknown men kill Cardinal Millhouse, an unknown man tried to kill Father Hernandez when he was assigned back in Las Cruces, and maybe the same man killing a doctor who was helping us investigate the virus. This is getting pretty serious," Sister Justine added.

141

"With an ex-intelligence person involved, what does that mean?" Father Hernandez asked.

"Considering the potential genocidal impact of Aurora, and then the clone kid, is there anything special about him?" Michael asked.

"Remember what Stephen told us about the angels he saw and how they acted around him, what makes him so unique?" Sister Justine asked of the group.

"And it was an angel who may have guided my return to Las Cruces, even though I didn't see one. You know who may be able to answer a lot of these questions?" Father Hernandez inquired.

Cardinal Grielle, Sister Justine and Michael waited patiently for the father to answer his own question. He assumed one of the other three had deduced the same.

"Well, boy toy?" Michael commented.

"Gary Applethorpe. We find him, we should be able to clear up a lot of this mess, and with it, the church," Father Hernandez responded.

"Or implicate it further," Sister Justine suggested.

"You three need to be careful, and I need to alert the Holy See," Cardinal Grielle commented. "I promised I'd keep them informed. I don't know about the pictures though. We should keep that amongst ourselves for now."

"On my way back here to the office, I found out I need to officiate a mass in about an hour, so we may need to get back together to discuss where we go from here," Father Hernandez said.

* * * *

Xavier inspected every inset and pocket of Father Hernandez's wallet that he pick-pocketed after bumping into him while in Union Station. Apart from a couple of credit cards, several worn business cards, an AAA auto club card, a few receipts for food and beverages, and thirty-one dollars in denominations of fives and ones, nothing was of interest. He snapped front and back pictures of the credit cards to have an analysis team initiate a search for all the purchases made over the last several months.

His partner, Sanger, had stolen the father's cell phone.

"How's the phone cloning coming along?" Xavier asked of his partner who was in the middle of a high-speed data transfer from Father Hernandez's cell phone to copy the contacts, phone numbers, texts, and other data into a blank phone device.

"Almost there," Sanger responded.

Seconds later, the miniature LCD panel displayed "Transfer Complete."

"It's done," Sanger said as he disconnected the cable from the phone devices.

Xavier completed returning all the items back into Father's Hernandez's wallet. "And you loaded the listening override software as well."

"Yep, I worked with the boys to upgrade the transfer software so that it'll upload and download at the same time. We'll be able to hear everything going on whatever room he's in. Hope he keeps his phone charged because the software can be buggy and drain the battery prematurely."

"We'll have to risk it. You know the plan. Send the phone and wallet as if a good Samaritan found it. I'll see you back at the office in one hour," Xavier directed. "And hurry up, if he's already realized he's missing his phone, we don't want him turning on his locate my phone feature while we still have possession of it."

"Yeah, yeah, got it," Sanger said grabbing the wallet and phone, and getting out of Xavier's black Audi detailed with dark smoke tinted side and rear windows.

* * * *

Father Hernandez shook the hand of the last parishioner leaving after the end of the mid-week afternoon mass. Returning into the chapel, Claudia, one of the Archdiocese administrative staff members, approached before he was going to enter the changing room to remove his robe and ceremonial vestments.

"Father, I have some good news for you, someone turned in your phone and wallet at the Union Station lost and found. You can pick it up anytime."

Father Hernandez smiled as he removed the stole. "Could you do me a big favor, Claudia? I have a budget meeting with the Cardinal's staff, and then I'm working with the scheduling team on the assignment for the masses next month. Could you see if someone can go over for me?"

"Of course."

## *Chapter 14 – A Body Found*

When Detectives Matthews and Green walked into the exam room of the morgue, Doctor McKay, the lead Medical Examiner for Los Angeles County Coroner's office, was finishing eating a banana as he stood over a body covered in a dingy white sheet on the exam table.

"Should you be eating that in here?" Detective Green asked.

"Hey, I've been working for the last five and a half hours straight, and I was getting hungry. Besides, I know when and where to break the rules."

"As long as it doesn't break our case," Detective Matthews said.

Doctor McKay went over to the knee operated sink next to the automatic door entrance to the locker room and offices and discarded the banana peel into a black plastic lined trash container. He washed his hands and put on a set of latex gloves and returned to the two detectives.

"What do we got, doc?" Detective Green asked.

Dr. McKay pulled back the sheet uncovering a naked, dark-skinned male with curly hair. "I finished the autopsy on this body that was found."

"People find dead bodies all the time, what's so special about this one?" Detective Green asked, scanning the corpse.

"He looks familiar," Detective Matthews noted observing the lifeless male lying on the examination table, staring hard at the bloated decomposing face. "Crap, I know we saw him before."

"The guys from Homicide wanted this passed onto you two. Someone found him in the Angeles Forests, and once we ID'd the body, he was flagged as a missing person from a report submitted a few days ago. Entomology is running through their analysis to see if they can determine the estimated day and time of death."

"So, it's sounding like he went for a hike, and got lost or something."

"There's evidence he was murdered, or maybe someone attacked him," Dr. McKay said. "His face is somewhat disfigured, and not from exposure after death. That didn't help in the facial recognition."

"What's the probable cause of death?" Detective Green asked, moving in closer to examine the naked body on table from head to toe. Multiple blackish splotches painted the face distinct from the already dark and decomposing skin. Splotches also covered the abdomen area. Detective Green was familiar with the marks based on similar cases. "This is bruising we're looking at, isn't it? It looks like someone had been beating up on him?"

"Yep, there was extensive ante-mortem bruising on the body, along with ligature marks, possibly zip ties, around the wrist. There was duct tape residue around his mouth. And we're running tox screens," Dr. McKay said, picking up the corpse's arm and pointing to the wrist, followed by his pointing to the mouth area while

146

describing the abrasions, lacerations, bruising, and oddities on the body.

"Whoa, you're saying it's a possible body dump after he was held and beat up?" Detective Matthews asked. "Because that's what it sounds like."

"That's not my job to figure out, but yours. Crime Scene has all the pictures of where they found him and the surrounding crime scene. There's no physical evidence from the scene that matches up with what happened to the body or that could've led to his death."

"And I imagine he was clothed as well," Detective Green said.

"Yep, the crime scene folks are examining his clothing for trace. We also pulled for trace from his body. I left him here on the slab until you got here."

"What type of clothing was he wearing? And do you have the workup of what you found so far?" Detective Green asked.

Dr. McKay meandered over to a desk near the entrance of the door, picking up a tablet device and bringing it back to the detective. "Here you go."

Flipping through the virtual electronic sheets of paper that comprised the preliminary coroner's report, Detective Green read information matching what the doctor already presented. The clothing report and the missing person's report caught his interest. "Wait, is this right?"

"What's that," his partner asked.

"It says he was wearing a priest's collar and shirt, and Cardinal Grielle's office was the one who initiated a missing person's report. This is Father Yancy, the one who assisted at the scene of Cardinal Millhouse's death."

"Now you see why you got this one," Doctor McKay said.

"Let me guess," Detective Matthews said. "We're going back to the Archdiocese offices?"

"Not yet," Detective Green answered. "Doc, expedite the results from toxicology. I want have a full picture of what's going on here before we head over."

"That'll be a week."

"That long? What if I give you something specific to look for, can I have it by tomorrow?"

"You're joking, right?"

"Nope, I got a hunch, the tox report from Cardinal Millhouse had a specific substance we know he was injected with. I don't care what it is yet, but can you see if it can be found in our church friend here on the slab."

Dr. McKay groaned. "Yeah, you're gonna owe me. Earliest is tomorrow afternoon, evening at the latest."

"Thanks, doc." Detective Green turned towards his partner. "In the meantime, let's go check out his residence."

## *Chapter 15 – A Rebellious Guest*

As soon as Gary stepped out of the confessional, an olive complexioned, stocky man shorter than himself, dressed in a black cassock, stood a couple of feet away from him. He stared with his rain cloud gray eyes distorted by the thick lensed glasses he wore. It was Cardinal Picoli. Gary didn't recognize him right way, startled with the shock of someone standing right outside the door of the confessional.

"Camerlengo, what are you doing here?"

"Where's the child now?" the Camerlengo asked.

"Should we talk out here in the open?"

Cardinal Picoli knocked on the confessional booth door for the priest's chamber, and politely asked the father presiding over confessions to leave for a few minutes.

Cardinal Picoli waited to hear the side entrance door close after the father departed before continuing. "We have the place to ourselves."

Gary surveyed inside the cathedral as they waited for the father to leave. The Vatican staff members scattered amongst the pews within the nave who had been engaged in silent prayers earlier, were no longer about. Cardinal Picoli dismissed the administering priest and nun preparing for the next mass and reception for a later tour group. The remaining individuals in the sanctuary were the two-plain clothed Gendarmerie who stood behind the Cardinal. Two more stood by the entrance into the cathedral.

"So, where is your charge?" Cardinal Picoli asked. His stern voice conveyed his current temperament.

"Where do you think if he's not at the guest house? I told him I was coming over for reconciliation, but he said he had no need at this time. He could be in one of the cathedrals praying, but I bet he's in the library again."

It was still upsetting to the Camerlengo as to how the child had been able to move about the grounds unobserved. More upsetting was his ability to clandestinely proceed to the private library and archives of the Holy See. The security specialists in the control center viewing the monitors, claimed that while watching him move about the grounds while surrounded by his guard escort, the display would freeze or blank out. Several seconds later after the video resumed, the child mysteriously showed up on another screen monitoring a different section of the city. The guard escort from the first video displayed they became unnerved and initiated a search of the immediate area. A frantic call from one of the guards to the control center hollered, "The prince is code five. Again, the prince is code five."

Cardinal Picoli guided Gary over to one of the nearby wood-stained pews and prompted for him to sit down.

"Mr. Applethorpe, there's something we learned concerning Cardinal Millhouse's death I think you should be aware of."

Gary raised an eyebrow. "What's that?"

"We have reason to believe that two men were involved in his death, and they may've been representatives for one or more national entities, namely our sponsors. It's suspected that an angel dispatched both?"

"He was...what happ...the news didn't...and when you say dispatched, you mean?"

"The two men were killed," Cardinal Picoli said. "And Cardinal Millhouse was murdered."

Gary collected his thoughts, continuing to comprehend and process the news.

Cardinal Picoli continued. "We're calling it what it is, an assassination. We've been able to keep the media from calling it as such. More so because of the spiritual implications, and that it appears it has to do with Aurora. The local Archdiocese assigned three persons in Los Angeles to investigate the spiritual implications of his death."

"What three?" Gary asked, with unease.

"A Father Hernandez, Sister Justine, and Michael Saunders. They're looking into potential religious implications of the Cardinal's death and the involvement of angels."

Incensed, Gary's skin tone flushed. He managed to maintain a calm demeanor. "Why would they be involved? You don't know how much trouble they've caused."

"According to Cardinal Grielle, they've already found some additional information in Las Cruces that could be of concern. I've requested for him to email whatever he's found right away, and to keep us abreast of anything new."

151

It was hard for Gary to hear the new title of Cardinal for Grielle. During several private conversations with Cardinal Millhouse, the Cardinal would never condone the elevation of any type for Bishop Grielle, who had proven himself to be neither an effective administrative or spiritual leader.

"Do we know why he was assassinated?" Gary asked.

"We know for sure they're upset about the failure of the virus."

Gary didn't hold back his anger this time and interrupted the Cardinal. "The virus wasn't a failure," he snapped. "If it wasn't for the interference by those three, we would've been running tests and field trials right now."

"Calm down, that's behind us, and we have to look to the future. We're speculating they could be coming after you and the child."

"What? Why would those three be after us?"

Cardinal Picoli continued. "I don't mean the three church representatives sponsored by Cardinal Grielle. I should let you know that envoys for the nations working with us on the first phase of Aurora are upset to learn of the child," Cardinal Picoli stated.

"They know of the child? How much do they know?"

"I pray not enough," Cardinal Picoli replied. "We may have had you come here to the Vatican prematurely and need to move the child to a safe house. We can't put him in jeopardy."

"They wouldn't be that bold as to try something here in the Vatican, would they?"

"You don't know how upset they are," Cardinal Picoli said, his gray and black hair unibrow scrunched. The timbre in his voice conveyed severe distress. "When I

152

learned that a common antagonist of the Sinai plague had helped to sponsor our venture, those of the Islamic faith tend to be very unforgiving."

"We anticipated fallout, but not to this level where they're this upset. We knew we'd be successful, and you know what, we were."

"Despite that, there are those here in the Curia who are upset as well. We became elated with the efforts of your scientists to help make the doctrine of Replacement Theology a reality. And then there is Cardinal Tullono. He and some others are extremely upset at the effect of the child. Not being members of the society, they don't know of his uniqueness, and they act as if they don't care much about him."

"So, I take it L.A. is no longer the conduit for the project. With what happened at the plant, the chances of anyone giving us resources to continue the viral research…"

"Don't say another word, it looks like we'll have to not consider that portion of Aurora anymore, and find some way to placate our sponsors before things get way out of hand." Cardinal Picoli wished the Holy Church and Roman Curia hadn't formed a clandestine allegiance with Russia and Islamic nations, even if angelic influences prodded the collaboration of resources. The Muslim religion left a severe distaste with Cardinal Picoli. When he was much younger, a Muslim group called the Aseleka, killed his step-brother, also a priest and assigned to a church in central Africa.

Gary leaned back on the pew. "Do you think they'll be that forgiving? Look at what happened to Cardinal Millhouse." Gary had used the resources of those who killed Cardinal Millhouse to eliminate individuals who

153

had risked the project, looking back to Jeffery Brassfield, Doctor McCall, and the attempt on Father Hernandez. He wondered if the same resource pool was involved with Cardinal Millhouse's death.

"We can't risk presenting the child, now is not the time," Cardinal Picoli said. "We're hoping to have time for him to grow up so we can establish a legitimate background with him attending college and seminary, and then…"

"Wait a minute," Gary interrupted. "I imagined his path was to be one more secular so that he could become the acceptable political face of the Church. That's what I imagined he's being prepared for."

"Those in the hierarchy of the Society, and those within the church who are aware of the project, now propose a different course for our little prodigy," the Cardinal replied. He didn't want to mention he himself had learned that the new plan was the original plan all along. Also, many in the Holy See were becoming enamored with the child.

As Cardinal Picoli fidgeted with his hands, he pulled a small square of microfiber cloth from the inner pocket of his cassock and took his glasses off. The nervous tapping of his right foot as he began to clean his lenses made Gary doubt if the senior cleric had communicated the entire truth.

Gary followed his intuition. "What is it you're not telling me, Your Eminence?"

"You may not know of the weak and failing condition of the Holy Father, but the child managed to make it to his quarters and converse with him a couple of times."

154

"I assumed he'd been going to the library all these times," Gary responded.

"So, you're just as surprised as we are when we found this out. There's a rumor that the child is the originator for one of the doctrinal decrees to be issued by the Holy Father. And if the decree itself does go out, I can see it causing quite the disruption."

"What are you saying?" Gary asked, amazed if it was true hearing that the child had an influence over the Holy Father. "A child influencing the Holy Father, can you imagine what that would do to the authority and prestige of the Church Universal if word of that was to get out?"

"You've noticed how rebellious the child has been since he's arrived, it's becoming quite the scandal. The Holy Father is cognizant of all that's going on, of that I'm convinced. Yet with the deteriorating condition of His Holiness, there are those calling for his resignation."

"Can they do that?"

"Yes, based on the code of canon law in 1917 that made it judicious to do so by the regulations established by Pope Paul VI in 1975 and reintroduced by John Paul II in 1996. The quorum of highest Cardinals in the Holy See may see it wise to do so, one who would include Cardinal Tullono, who we imagine is antagonistic to the Order of the Child. We tried to indoctrinate him by having him manage the oversight of the young man to divert any of that from happening. All this would give Tullono an excuse to press for the Holy Fa…"

Gary interrupted. "I already know that didn't go well at all." He stood and walked out from between the pew, and began wandering back and forth in the aisle. The child became more than he anticipated. They engineered high intelligence into his genetic make-up, but Gary never

155

anticipated this level of maturity and charismatic impact for the child at this age. Add to it over the last few weeks, the child grew in stature and poise. He appeared more to be fifteen or sixteen than a month past turning thirteen.

"So the child has been visiting the Holy Father?" Gary asked.

"A personal medical attendant to Holy Father revealed to me that he saw the two communing on more than one occasion. You're the one person who seems to have any influence over him. You have to get him under control."

Gary chuckled. "Influence over him? If that was the case, we wouldn't be having this conversation."

\* \* \* \*

Gary returned to the guest house to find the lack of a security detail posted outside the main entrance, indicating the child was somewhere about on the grounds of the city. The guest house valet greeted Gary when he strode into the residence.

"Where did our little prince go?" he asked, in a stern tone.

"He didn't say, he said he needed to continue his spiritual schedule."

The front door swung open, followed by the child walking in sandwiched by his two body guards. The activity surprised Gary and the valet.

"Where've you been?" Gary questioned. The Gendarmerie guards cast a disapproving look over his harsh tone. Gary didn't care, and both knew to keep quiet.

"Over to the library," the child answered.

"Again? Why do you keep going over there?" Gary asked, wondering if this was true based on what Cardinal Picoli had divulged.

"I can't learn what I need to know by reading books of the world," the child said, continuing straight down the main hallway. Gary followed. The security detail went back outside under the portico and posted on each side of the front door.

"And what is it you need to know?" Gary asked.

"That's not important right now."

"Well, a situation has come up, we may have to leave to a safe house," Gary said.

The child stopped and turned to look at Gary, his expression stone-faced and emotionless. "What situation might that be?" he asked.

"That's none of your concern."

"I know more than you realize. My father and brethren will protect me. We'll be fine if we stay here."

The statement of his Father and brethren puzzled Gary. "Why do I think when you say your Father, you're not talking about the Holy Father?"

"Mr. Applethorpe, you forget that I know that I am a clone of the Holy Father, and also that he isn't my full biological father."

"I know that, then who are you talking about?"

The child smiled. "I know about the miraculous event of the angel Aurora breathing the breath of life into my body upon my birth, and the other circumstances surrounding my inception. Other than that, we don't have to worry about leaving, no matter who comes or what may happen. And that's all I'll say for now."

The child continued to his room, leaving Gary standing alone and frustrated in the hallway. No one was supposed to have told the child that piece of information. Who was the leak? Would the Holy Father have told him, or Cardinal Picoli, if he knew?

# Chapter 16 – Room Examination

Claudia walked up to Father Hernandez and Michael in the artwork adorned corridor of the Archdiocese offices carrying a wallet and phone. "Father, here's your wallet and phone picked up from the lost and found. I was going to give it to you yesterday, but my little boy got sick, and I had to take the day off. It was locked up. I'm so sorry. I meant to have one of the other staff members bring it to you, but I got distracted."

"Claudia, don't worry about it," Father Hernandez said, hearing sniffling as if she wanted to cry. She tended to be one of the more hyper-emotional members of the administrative staff. "I didn't even miss them because I knew they were in good hands. Besides, I've been so pre-occupied with everything, and I don't want to mention the larger than normal tour groups through the grand Cathedral lately. So many people are hoping there's gonna be some sort of angel event. Anyway, I was busy with the weekly evening mass last night and went straight home and rested."

Claudia handed the found items to the father.

"Thank you," he said.

"I'm so sorry again," Claudia said as she expelled a breath of relief that Father Hernandez wasn't upset or going to unleash a verbal rebuke.

"Don't worry about it," Father Hernandez said as Claudia turned to return to her cubicle in the office area. He had heard rumors the working conditions in the administrative offices were tense under the previous tenure of Cardinal Millhouse.

Examining his wallet, it contained his driver's license, credit cards, auto club card, medical insurance card, several business cards, rosary card, miscellaneous receipts, and thirty-one dollars, the exact amount prior to losing it. Nothing seemed missing.

"Surprisingly, all my cards and money seem to be in here. There are still good people in the world," Father Hernandez said as he smiled. "Whoever turned it in at the lost and found didn't take anything. I did cancel my credit cards though to be safe."

"What about your phone?" Michael asked.

"I don't know if anyone has tried to get into it to see who it belongs to. I set up the security to wipe after too many unsuccessful tries."

Powering up the phone, the battery power level indicated 7%. Swiping his thumb over the fingerprint reader displayed the normal home screen. Navigating through several of the icons gave Father Hernandez the confidence his phone was in the proper working condition. Reviewing his missed texts, most were inconsequential, including three with the word "Ro." He had already viewed them on his workstation. He deleted them.

"Anyway, you got me down here this morning wanting to go take a look at something. Where are you planning on taking me?" Michael asked.

"I'll explain along the way," Father Hernandez said, patting his pants pockets. "First I need to go back to my desk. I need to pick up something. And I should leave my phone to charge it. I won't need it anyhow."

Father Hernandez went back to his office and as soon as he stepped through the door, his phone chimed alerting him to a new text message that displayed "Ro." He discounted it and placed his phone on the desktop. The father connected it to the charging cable and grabbed a set of keys signed out from the facilities office earlier in the morning.

\* \* \* \*

The seasonal morning blanket of a misty marine layer over the city of Los Angeles had begun to dissipate. Father Hernandez and Michael drove up to an Adobe colored duplex housing unit at the end of a block with similar homes, minutes away by car near the downtown Cathedral. Michael learned it was the rectory apartment complex where Father Yancy had resided.

"Do all of these units belong to the church?" Michael asked as they exited the car.

"No, we rent a few of them for some of the single or younger church clergy members who either work or are interning at the Cathedral."

"Justine should've come with us," Michael commented as the two men approached one of the duplex units, the varnish on the front door yellow and cracked from age. He believed that Justine would have been insightful during their pending examination of Father Yancy's residence. And he wanted to see her again.

"I don't think it's right she should be here while we do this," Father Hernandez said as he rang the doorbell. For the father, it would be improper for Sister Justine to assist in this circumstance. "Females are solely allowed in community rooms or offices with separate outside entrances for the pastoral rectories, but not in the residences proper. Of course, there's the exception for cleaning staff."

"Wow, you're still in the dark ages, aren't you?"

"Tradition is one of the strongest foundations of the church," Father Hernandez replied, again ringing the doorbell, followed by him pounding on the door.

There was still no response, and after waiting a couple of minutes, Father Hernandez reached into his pants pocket and pulled out a set of keys, each with a small attached label. Flipping through each key, he came across one labeled Carson/Yancy, inserted it into the keyhole and turned unlocking the deadbolt securing the door.

"You have a key to his apartment?" Michael asked with unease.

"Of course, the church has a spare to all the residences, in case of emergencies. Most times it's if someone becomes incapacitated, or heaven forbid, pass in the night, and we don't hear from him in a day or two. We tend to think the worst. A priest is dispatched in case we need to administer last rites."

Father Hernandez swung open the front door. "The church doesn't want to publicly admit it, but there've been priests in the Holy See who've committed suicide over the years. Regardless, I thought his dorm mate Father Carson, would be home."

161

"Yeah, you mentioned that as we were driving over here," Michael said. "Maybe he's out shopping or something."

Father Hernandez and Michael stepped into a color coordinated living room with ultra-modern abstract patterned black and maroon couch with chrome trim and matching side chairs. A light color stained coffee table with an inlay smoked glass top sat in front of the couch. Two smaller matching end tables, each with a lamp made of ceramic base fire kilned with a dark maroon paint and cream-colored lamp shade guarded each side. A whiff of Lysol and detergent circulated through the apartment home as the men passed through to a small hallway on the right leading to a bathroom and two bedroom doors. The one closet to the front of the residence displayed a name placard "Fr. Carson," the other "Fr. Yancy."

"Hello, this is Father Hernandez," Father Hernandez announced as they moved through the apartment, not wanting to surprise Father Carson in case he was either napping or indisposed.

"And Michael Saunders," Michael added.

Father Hernandez grabbed the doorknob to the door for Father Yancy's room and paused before turning to open.

"What are you waiting for?" Michael asked. "It's not like you're gonna find him in the room. If you did, that'll be one hell of a magic trick."

Father Hernandez's facial expression soured. He didn't appreciate the comment as he opened the door, but Michael was correct.

The uncluttered room could have passed a military inspection. The bed appeared undisturbed made with taut sheets, hospital corners, and the top cover folded back over the blanket. Next to the bed atop the nightstand was a lamp with a beige pleated shade and black ceramic base decorated with the Chi-Rho symbol in gold paint. A worn Bible, a small devotional book, and a small bottle of Polo cologne rested on the semi-barren top of the dark wood dresser.

"You sure someone lived here?" Michael commented. "It looks like a museum in here."

"It does, doesn't it," Father Hernandez replied.

Michael examined the closet. Father Yancy's pressed religious garments hung evenly spaced on the right side of the hangar rod. An assortment of jeans, casual pants, a few earth tone colored polo shirts, and a couple of dress shirts, hung spaced in the same meticulous manner as his clerical outfits on the left side. Black Oxfords, brown Hush Puppies and a pair of gym shoes lay well-ordered on the closet floor.

Father Hernandez sifted through the dresser unit. In each drawer, the clothes whether underwear, socks, gym clothing, or light winter wear sweater tops, were each folded square and placed in perfect order.

Michael moved over to the bed. "Let's see what's under here," He said as he lifted the mattress from the box spring.

"Why're you looking under there? I doubt you'll find anything."

Michael dropped the mattress down finding but the top of the box spring and disheveling the tucked in sheets. "Hey, you never know, and maybe the father was into some stuff you don't know about."

"That's not a nice thing to say about Father Yancy, show some respect. And you don't have to make a mess of everything while we're looking."

163

"It's not like he's going to…"

A deep male voice bellowed from the entrance of the room interrupting Michael. "Who are you two and what are you doing in here?"

Father Hernandez and Michael turned to see a young, skinny and acne faced priest wearing brass colored wire-oval framed glasses, standing in the doorway. Father Hernandez recognized him right away as Father Carson. Father Carson expressed relief as soon as he recognized Father Hernandez.

"Father, you startled me," Father Carson said. "I was concerned when I walked into the apartment and heard you two and saw you in here."

"Our apologies," Father Hernandez responded. "We came to see if we could find anything of interest concerning the disappearance and death of Father Yancy."

"Well, the police already came through and took what they deemed to be of interest yesterday evening."

Both Father Hernandez and Michael didn't expect to hear the police had already examined the room considering its impeccable condition.

"Like what?" Father Hernandez asked.

"His laptop, tablet, I don't know, some other stuff. I know that it's upsetting hearing what's happened to him."

"Father Yancy was a bit of a neat freak, wasn't he?" Michael asked.

"Yeah, he was, but not overt with his OCD, just here in his room. He was observant as well and would notice if something seemed out of place. It's a good thing he's not here to see what you two did to his room. Even the police weren't this disruptive."

Father Hernandez flashed Michael a look of irritation.

"What? It's not that bad," Michael countered.

"Did he mention if anything specific seemed outta place, Father?" Father Hernandez asked.

"A couple of times he believed things seemed like they had moved whenever he was gone for a while. But he imagined maybe he was being paranoid," Father Carson said as he began to remake Father Yancy's bed.

"Why?" Michael asked.

"He could've sworn he was being followed. I don't know why, but considering what happened to him, maybe he was right," Father Carson said in a somber voice.

"He didn't say by who, or anything?"

Father Carson finished tucking in the bed cover. "No, but he did notice when he would drive from the store or one of his parish duties, a couple of times there was a black car down the block with dark tinted windows that looked a little out of place for this neighborhood. I think he said it was a newer Audi."

"So, I take it the police impounded Father Yancy's assigned vehicle."

Father Carson moved to the half-opened dresser drawers rearranging the articles of clothing in proper order. "No, we share, I mean shared, a vehicle. I've had it for a while. I'd been out in the Inland Empire during the last week interning in one of the San Bernardino Diocese parishes when they suspect for him to have gone missing. I was staying in the guest room of the rectory out there to keep from commuting. After they questioned me, and verified the onboard nav system, they decided not to take it. They had their forensics team do a full on-site examination."

Father Carson moved back over with Father Hernandez and Michael.

"They didn't have the church turn it over?" Father Hernandez asked.

"No."

Michael stepped over to the dresser and shifted the devotional book about an inch to the right, and the Bible an inch to the left. Father Carson went over and moved the items back to their original position.

"Did they find anything?" Father Hernandez asked.

"Nothing that the police would be interested in."

Father Hernandez sensed a subtext to Father Carson's comment.

Michael overlooked the remark, curious as to Father Carson's actions in tidying up the room. "I bet you and Father Yancy were compatible roommates?" he asked.

"Why do you say that?" Father Carson answered.

"I'm curious as to why you're straightening up? I'm not trying to be cruel, but Father Yancy isn't coming back."

Father Carson gave Michael a curt glance and went back to rearranging Father Yancy's clothing and accruements. "His family is flying in to collect his remains and personal effects, and I want the room to be as it should be, a representation of him."

"Weird," Michael said, attempting to whisper, but it was loud enough for Father Hernandez and Father Carson to hear. They ignored him, although Father Hernandez did agree.

"You said the police didn't find anything they would be interested in; is there something we'd be interested in?" Father Hernandez asked.

Father Carson froze, paralyzed by Father Hernandez's comment. He went back to finish repositioning Father Yancy's clothing, and then over to straighten up the closet. "I'm not sure what you're talking about father."

Both Father Hernandez and Michael caught Father Carson's momentary restlessness.

"Don't jerk us around Father Carson," Michael snapped. "You know you want to tell us something."

Father Hernandez gave Michael a disapproving look, but was glad he was direct in pointing out the same thing he had been thinking after Father Carson's odd response to his prior question.

Father Carson sat on the edge of the bed and fidgeted with his fingers. "I'm new to being a priest, and felt I would never have to experience something like this...Father Yancy was scared about something...he wasn't sure who to trust after Cardinal Millhouse was killed."

Father Hernandez and Michael moved in closer.

"Go on," Father Hernandez requested. "You can trust us. We want to find out the truth of what happened to the Cardinal and Father Yancy."

Father Carson hesitated before he responded. "They may have been looking for this." He reached into his pocket and pulled out a thick silver pen with blue trim. "Father Yancy wanted me to pass it on if someone from the church came looking for something."

"A pen," Michael quipped. "What's so special about a pen?"

Father Carson separated the pen towards the middle of the shaft. Instead of a pen refill insert was a miniature USB type C male connector, implying a concealed data storage device. He handed the faux pen to Father Hernandez.

"Why didn't you pass this on to us sooner?" Father Hernandez questioned, with a slight irritation in his voice.

"Father Yancy wanted me to be careful who I gave it to, and to consider that I should be careful of you, Sister Justine, and Cardinal Grielle."

"So why are you giving it to us now," Michael asked.

"I kinda followed Cardinal Grielle more as my mentor. He had me set up a private VPN and disposable e-mail address that could be untraced to use to send some provocative writings to a friend of his who had in roads to a couple of religious journals. I thought they were intriguing."

Father Hernandez became ecstatic to meet someone who had helped with getting some of his unauthorized writings published, and appreciated the content.

"You helped with that?" said the father as he smiled, and his voice filled with glee.

"Like I said, I considered the writings intriguing. I liked reading the challenges to orthodoxy, and I was more than willing to help the Cardinal."

"What do you think was one of the most interesting topics?" Father Hernandez asked, interested in Father Carson's viewpoint.

After a moment of hesitation, Father Carson responded. "The casting of good versus bad angels, it was interesting to see how many people accept them and anything they say without questioning. Yet to say that malevolent ones could use the devices of good to deceive and perpetuate false doctrines with the misapplication of religious practices irked the hierarchy in the Diocese."

Father Hernandez's smile exploded on his face. "I bet it did. I'm aware of the hypothesis. Was there anything else?"

Michael glanced at Father Hernandez with a smirk and wide eyed, confused as to the motive for letting Father Carson continue, but kept quiet.

Father Carson continued. "I never considered the fact that even though we consider angels supernatural, they have to be real in some way since they manifest themselves in our physical world. Some of them even appeared as humans. The angel that Jacob wrestled...come on...you can't wrestle an ethereal being. Even the angels today, no one's gone up and touched one. But persons felt the effects like what happened a couple of years ago at Thomson and Thomson. I was still in seminary at the time, but a lot of stories came out about what happened."

"You know that Mr. Saunders here and myself investigated that."

"Was he the second person who helped you with the writings?"

The question from the young priest caught Father Hernandez off guard.

"Busted," Michael commented.

"He was. When did you find out?" the father asked.

"I figured it out a minute ago."

"Cardinal Grielle didn't tell you?"

"No, he made sure I didn't know in case Cardinal Millhouse found out I was helping. I wouldn't be able to expose anything if he questioned me. There were a couple of times we believed he'd discovered the names of the authors. But we deduced Cardinal Millhouse was pretending to know more than he did. Bishop Grielle...I mean Cardinal...I mean Bishop... anyway, Cardinal Grielle wanted to call his bluff, but ended up playing it safe and backed off."

Michael saw the conversation had lost its focus. "Back to the USB, do you know what's on it?" he asked.

"I don't. I didn't want to take the chance of finding something I shouldn't have. Besides, he said it was encrypted."

"We need to get back to the office, see what's on this and talk to Justine," Father Hernandez said. "And Father Carson, I'm going to ask something important of you that you may not agree with."

"What's that?"

"Don't tell his Eminence about this, at least not yet. We need to see if we can crack into it, and determine if there's anything of importance."

Father Carson launched himself off the edge of the bed and clenched the disguised USB device. "What. Why would you want me not to tell the Cardinal?"

Father Hernandez reached out and wrapped Father Carson's small hands within his larger hands and pressed firmly to keep him from pulling back, without seeming too assertive. "I beg of you, I plead of you, please give us this one mercy. We want to make sure it's of importance first, and foremost, not put Cardinal Grielle in any danger if there is anything on the USB." Father Hernandez turned to Michael maintaining his grip over Father Carson's hands. "Michael, please back me up on this."

Michael, mesmerized by the interplay between the two clergy members and Father Hernandez's passion, was now annoyed that the father drew him into the interaction.

"Padre, I'm simply along for the ride. I want to learn more about these angel events that've been occurring and help you with what happened with Millhouse, but I'll only go so..." Michael paused a few seconds after Father

Hernandez flashed him a slight frown and sad puppy eyes. "And as for Father Hernandez, you can trust him."

Father Carson released his grip on the USB device.

# Chapter 17 – A Warning

This was the first time anyone could recall an angel visitation in quite some time. Stephen Williams was in attendance of the mid-week morning mass after having decided to attend church regularly, influenced by earlier supernatural incidents. Although confronted with what was in some ways a repeat performance to the Thomson and Thomson visitation, this time there wasn't the urgency to get up and rush out to leave.

Parishioners, however, worried something harmful or evil would occur. No one could force open any of the closed sanctuary doors. Cell phones no longer functioned. Cascading memories of impending fatality flooded their imaginations. Many recalled the news reports of similar circumstances at the earlier incident where everyone inside had died, except for one man, Stephen.

Stephen sat in the second-row pew enthralled by the mysterious being. The angel's appearance although beautiful, displayed a stern and forceful countenance. It held a broadsword across its chest as the blade shimmered with a bluish aura. For five minutes, the majestic creature stood motionless. The air was still. A floral scent and spicy fragrance similar to fresh ground cloves overwhelmed the congregation's sense of smell. The hairs on Stephen's arms stood as if a static charge filled the room. The remainder of the small congregation in the chapel was at unease, most trembling with a sense of fear and anxiety. Those who hadn't urinated on themselves came close to doing so.

Stephen, earlier besieged with the ability to observe and commune with angels, and not witnessing one for weeks, hoped they wouldn't plague him with any further appearances. He was the one person brave enough to consider conversing with the angelic visitor. Trembling, his heart racing and palms sweaty, he stood. Father Wilkerson, who presided over the mass, and the congregation all gawked at him. Most were concerned he would offend or upset the ethereal being.

Stephen gathered the courage to speak. "Do you have a message for us?"

Father Wilkerson worried if it was smart to ask such a question, or any question.

The angel fixed its gazed towards Stephen. It said, "Behold, in the day that comes, beware the child." The angel's voice carried the words in a bassoon-like tone. The parishioners in the chapel unable to distinguish any intelligible words assumed its voice blared like a trumpet blast.

"I don't understand, behold, in the day that comes, beware the child?" Stephen murmured in response, not sure he heard or comprehended the angel's statement.

"Yes." The angel disappeared.

Father Wilkerson and the congregation expelled a sigh of relief. They were still alive. The few in Stephen's vicinity rushed over and assaulted him with a barrage of questions, curious as to the conversation that had transpired. Others dropped to their knees and began praying or reciting the rosary.

Before Stephen could reply to the flurry of inquiries, Father Wilkerson interrupted. "Ladies and gentlemen, we are in God's house. May we please continue with the holy mass in doing his work and paying homage to him and the Blessed Mother? We must not become occupied with what's happened," he said, bellowing from the altar.

Stephen was relieved for the interruption. He wouldn't have to deal with the congregation right away.

Father Wilkerson himself was interested in what had occurred and wanted to talk to Stephen. He rushed through the remainder of the order of service to where the portions cited in Latin sounded unfamiliar and as if he spoke in a mysterious tongue.

"I would like to speak to Stephen Williams alone privately as we depart this morning," he said after closing out the mass and presenting the benediction prayer.

The moans and grunts from the congregation indicated their disappointment and disapproval not being able to talk to Stephen right away. Stephen would have forgone talking to anyone about the visit, but if he didn't discuss the event with Father Wilkerson right away, the father would request for him to come back later. Stephen did want to talk with him concerning the Blessed Mother. And since Stephen was endeavoring to become active in the church, certain practices and doctrines began to trouble him based upon what he had read in the Bible, and what his parents had begun to discuss with him and his sister before they disappeared with the countless millions.

\* \* \* \*

Father Hernandez found himself busy with the intensity of activity in the administrative offices and

Archdiocese chapel. Today, the schedule had him performing the morning and noon mass due to the presiding priest calling in sick. The father focused on fine tuning his homily as he worked on his computer workstation. A pop-up notification alerted him he had received a text on his phone that he had set to silent. He was about to ignore it until later, believing it was another message containing the letters "Ro" which he had been receiving on an infrequent basis, yet enough to be annoying. Instead, the header information specified the message originated from Stephen Williams. The father opened it. *An angel showed up at your old church and said behold, in the day to come, beware the child. Don't know what it means, but I believe you might be interested.*

Father Hernandez pondered the message by a solitaire angel, wondering if other angels had presented similar messages. Researching the Internet and the church's angel tracking database for similar reported visitations yielded no results. Another question came to mind, why present the warning to Stephen, not even a lay person in the church, and not to himself, Sister Justine, or even Michael?

## Chapter 18 – Following the Trail

Xavier dedicated a considerable amount of time managing his team's efforts to track down Gary Applethorpe. They discovered that after his stay at the convent in Chicago, he traveled to South America. Nadia authorized Xavier to send an agent down to investigate the Roman Catholic sanctuary in the country. Apart from the pedophiles, sex addicts, and abusers, and other clergy residents there for repentance, spiritual renewal, and rehabilitation, Gary and what came to be known as the special package, were there for several days before traveling to a remote sanctuary retreat in the country. Xavier suspected that to be a false trail, as the agent found a plane chartered by the facility traveled to Pretoria, South Africa. From there, another charter plane establishing a false flight plan departed to an unknown destination. This was where the trail went cold. Xavier was impressed on how clandestine, yet discoverable, the travel arrangements made by the Church had been.

Could they have traveled to Rome? When Xavier attempted to bring up this possibility to Nadia, she dismissed it. It would be careless for the Vatican to have Gary head to Rome. That would be too obvious a place for anyone looking for him. Nadia directed Xavier to disregard Rome or Vatican City and pursue any potential leads stemming from Los Angeles or Argentina. Her analysts had noted that the flight from Chicago to South America may have been genuine, what followed had a high probability of being a ruse. They brought to Nadia's attention that over a year ago, Gary and Cardinal Millhouse reported that after the second catastrophic event in Mexico, it came close to destroying the Aurora virus. They oversaw the transport of a surviving sample to a facility in Canada. They stopped in New Mexico to pick up a key research doctor. Gary then chartered a plane that he used as a diversion to mislead three individuals who had the potential to expose and shutdown the project. The three were Father Hernandez, Sister Justine, and Michael Saunders.

Xavier considered sending one member from his team to Rome to investigate. However, since various entities contracted he and his team, he didn't want to upset his employers. If he was successful in finding his mark while disobeying his orders, the possibility existed they would terminate their working agreement, not reimburse him for expenses, or disavow, by means of termination, his entire team if something went wrong. The two members killed in Cardinal Millhouse's residence, and the blunder with Father Yancy's body, stressed the current working relationship, even if external circumstances did cause both incidents. Xavier needed to explicitly follow Nadia's instructions and the others she represented.

# *Chapter 19 – Adoration*

"It's said he's progressing well on his Latin lessons, and he's now reading historical books on military tactics, politics and the like. He's even completed reading the Art of War by Sun Tzu," Father Roberts, a staff aide to Cardinal Picoli, said as he and Cardinal Picoli traversed the primary pathway through the English Garden situated towards the rear of Vatican City. "And let me tell you about his debate sessions with some of the scholars here doing research for their thesis or treatises."

"Why, what's happened?"

"They're amazed not simply at his grasp of facts and knowledge of history but that he's able to apply what he's learned in practical ways. Simply put, he's taken some of them to task. One researcher had to scrap his work on a thesis he'd been working on after talking to the child."

Cardinal Picoli stopped. "I'm supposed to believe that? I know the child is extraordinary and advanced in his intellect, but is he as special as you say he is?"

Father Roberts didn't notice Cardinal Picoli had stopped walking. "The priests who are here for their sabbatical, rejuvenation, and doctrinal development and training are taken to task. He's teaching them things they didn't know or comprehended and providing insight on some difficult doctrines."

"How was he able to interact with the priests? Wait a minute, do you mean some of the advanced training for the priests located outside the wall of the See? He's not supposed to leave for fear of his safety." Cardinal Picoli's complexion reddened with anger. "And no one's informed me," he said in a loud outburst that distracted two clergy members taking a stroll nearby in the garden.

"Your Eminence, it was only a couple of times, and I just found out myself." Father Roberts's voice cracked as he responded to the Cardinal. He was under the impression that Cardinal Picoli was aware the Holy Father had approved the off-site excursions by the child. He decided not to tell the Cardinal concerning one of the child's trips to visit several of the historical sites in the city.

Cardinal Picoli continued. "He's supposed to be sequestered from the staff and clergy here in the Holy See as best as possible. Does anyone even know what the word sequester means?"

"You can't sequester the brilliance the child exhibits. He is so charismatic and persuasive, that he's talked his security detail into letting him experience what the priests go through."

"So many are beginning to admire, if not adore him. And if it's true with the rumors of what's happened with him and the Holy Father when he arrived…"

"What rumors have you heard?"

"That he's demonstrated several wonders such as communing with angels. Also, days ago, there was a sister who was deaf in one ear…"

"What do you mean was deaf in one ear?" Cardinal Picoli asked.

"Sister Abigail claims that while meeting the child, he somehow knew of her affliction, rubbed her left ear, and she could hear again. An audiologist confirmed her hearing is perfect in both ears."

"Do tell," Cardinal Picoli replied, raising one eyebrow in disbelief.

"During his physical, he possessed more strength for someone his age. Your Eminence, many in the Order, and those who are supporting him, understood him to be a blessing unto the Church, but he is greater than anything any of us anticipated. They're beginning to establish an adoration and veneration for the child."

"If they are, and to honor the Church, they are to keep their mouths shut. It is not his time to be made known unto the world."

"When Sister Abigail reported what had happened to her Mother Superior, who is a member of the Holy Order, instructed her not to mention it to anyone."

"Good."

Cardinal Picoli began to see more into the intelligent and gifted child than he first considered. He believed those in the Holy See would merely groom him to become the future Bishop of Rome once he was to finish seminary. The child surpassed everyone's expectations, both intellectually and spiritually.

With the unwanted attention, there was a possibility those looking for him could become aware of his residence in the city. "Make sure the word gets out that anyone who meets with the child is to maintain the strictest confidence, otherwise they would deal with a censure from the Holy Father and myself. Is that understood?"

"But shouldn't we…"

"Nothing else needs to be said. It is not yet the child's time to be revealed to the world."

Cardinal Picoli may have been frustrated with the actions of the child, but he couldn't help admitting to himself a growing sense of elation and awe when in his presence. Yet it didn't take away that the child's openness could jeopardize his and Gary's safety.

## *Chapter 20 – Open Files*

"**W**ell, Padre, we're here, what do you got to show us?" Michael asked as he and Sister Justine walked into Father Hernandez's office.

"Yes, what's so important, Father," Sister Justine queried, her interest piqued by his enthusiasm in urging for her and Michael to rush over to his office.

"Come on over behind my desk, I want to show you something," Father Hernandez said.

A sly grin blossomed on Michael's face. "You dirty boy toy," he said, with Sister Justine not finding Michael's comment funny.

Father Hernandez didn't comprehend the wisecrack too fixated typing and navigating the mouse on his desktop computer. Michael and Sister Justine went and stood over each shoulder of the father, looking down onto his workstation display.

"So, what are we looking at?" Michael asked.

Father Hernandez sat back in his chair to make sure he addressed both at the same time, to allow for plenty of room to ensure his screen was visible. "When I inserted Father Yancy's USB device, a warning screen popped up stating the disk is encrypted. It's the same notification used for all the removable storage devices used here in the

Archdiocese. So, I took a wild guess and called our IT department to see if they could help. I mentioned this USB device was assigned to Father Yancy, and with a little convincing, they said it shouldn't be a problem." Father Hernandez navigated through the interface of the computer's operating system to the disk's file system.

"You guys encrypt your files?" Michael asked sitting on the edge of the father's desk.

"Of course, especially those on USB drives and laptops, the Church has to protect the files as a part of HIPAA. We have to maintain confidentiality of our journaled official counseling and discussion sessions with parishioners since we have some priests who are state licensed therapists. Some of the clergy are involved with local support groups needing to maintain personal and counseling records. So, if one of the devices get lost or stolen, then the information would be near impossible for someone to read."

"Hmm, didn't know that," Michael responded.

Sister Justine asked, "So how was the IT department able to help?"

"Since the encryption key is associated with a user's login account, if the user forgets their password, you wouldn't be able to access the information on the device. All the removable storage devices have a master unlock key in a database to override."

"And they gave you the key?" Michael asked.

"It took a little convincing, but I mentioned I was working on investigating the father's death. They told me how to connect to it with my login and attempt a high-level access since I told them I was working for Cardinal Grielle. Then they gave me this encryption recovery key to try," Father Hernandez said pointing to a sheet of paper printed with a long string of characters composed of upper and lower-case letters, numbers, and several special characters. He rolled his chair back to his desk and began working on his computer again.

Michael and Sister Justine repositioned themselves again to view Father Hernandez's monitor as he worked. He typed in the forty-eight-character recovery key. Hitting the enter key, the screen displayed "Incorrect key entered. 1 of 3 Attempts."

"Damn," Father Hernandez blurted out.

Michael chuckled. "Yep, you're human."

"Father, is Michael rubbing off on you?" Sister Justine asked.

"Let me try this again," Father Hernandez said. He re-input the recovery key realizing where he made the mistake, using a numeric one instead of the lowercase letter L in one of the positions. Once he finished typing in the last character, the file directory listing for the contents of the USB key displayed on the screen.

"I'll be darn, you're in," Michael said, amazed they were able to open the encrypted disk.

Father Hernandez navigated through the directory and files in the file explorer window to see if any looked relevant. Most of the file names appeared inconsequential until he came to one that caught his attention labeled "SHOC." When he attempted to open it, a dialog box displayed on the screen prompting for entering a decryption key. Although the input box looked shorter than the current forty-eight-character string given to him by the IT department, he tried to type it in. After fifteen characters, no other letters, numbers, or symbols could fit. He selected the "Enter Secure Password" selection button with the mouse. An incorrect passphrase message appeared. After two more attempts, the file remained closed. He tried to input the last fifteen characters of the passkey printed on the paper, still with no success.

"He double encrypted the file," Michael commented. "This is getting interesting. What the heck was he trying to hide?"

Father Hernandez tried opening several other files with no success. Continuing his search in another unencrypted directory, he recognized an offline email database and configured his email program to connect to the file.

"How do you know how to do that?" Michael asked.

"It's not that hard, I had to work through a couple of issues with my email before. The IT staff here trained us in case we needed to work at different desks and store our email offline on portable storage devices or personal laptops."

He finished configuring the application and opened the email program. An index tree on the left side of the email folders window displayed "Mail – Yancy, Ian"

Father Hernandez clicked on the folder. Reading the subject headers for the emails, he spotted a message addressed from a Cardinal Picoli at a Vatican email address.

"Here we go," Father Hernandez said as he moved the mouse pointer over to the email header list. "Here's one from a Cardinal Picoli at the Vatican."

"Who's Cardinal Picoli?" Michael asked.

"He's the Camerlengo in the Holy See," Father Hernandez answered.

"Wait, you have a low-ranking priest emailing one of the most prestigious and important positions in the Church?" Sister Justine queried.

Father Hernandez and Michael stared at each other astonished by the Sister's observation.

After a minute of their disorientation, Michael grew impatient. "Umm, the email, you two, what does it say?"

Father Hernandez clicked and opened the email.

*Thank you for your help in assisting Cardinal Millhouse in making travel arrangements with Mother Superior Lucinda in regards to the precious cargo and escort to the convent home of Society members in Chicago. The arrangements to their final destination are being worked out and will be ready in several days. A representative from the Vatican secretary of state will meet up with the two once they arrive to the center down in South America. We're working with the appropriate offices to expedite the necessary paperwork for travel of Doctor Kaughman once friendly allies establish a safe haven.*

"Wait a minute, Mother Superior Lucinda, Chicago," Sister Justine cried out in a shrill, interrupting her companion's reading of the file. "I can't believe Cardinal Millhouse." Her flushed complexion and heavy breathing signaled she was attempting to control her emotions and keep from going into an angry tirade.

"What's wrong, Justine," Michael asked, sensitive to the change in her emotional state. The last he recalled her being this upset was back at his house when she informed him of her intentions to remain a nun, and years ago when they had dated. Nor had she shown being worked up like this over the last year and a half during their current investigation into the angel incidents.

186

"Mother Superior Lucinda was in charge of the convent where they sent me after separating us a year ago," Sister Justine remarked, the tone of her voice laced with suppressed rage. Cognizant of her location, and with Father Hernandez's office door open, she didn't want anyone to hear if she had lost control and began yelling. She walked over to the office entrance and closed the door, leaving it cracked open. "I bet it was to keep watch over me looking back at how I was treated there. I suspected she was a member of that Society, like Sister Ilsae. This proves it, now I know why she was such…such a…"

Michael expelled an expletive in a joking tone.

"Michael!" Father Hernandez and Sister Justine said in unison, snapping at Michael.

"That's totally uncalled for," Father Hernandez continued.

"Hey, she's the one all upset and angry. I was trying to help fill in the void on how you feel."

"I was going to say such a pain. I was too upset to finish my sentence," Justine retorted, stepping back over to the father's desk rejoining her companions.

"Calm down, Sister. What happened in Chicago is in the past, it'll be all right," Father Hernandez said in what he hoped was a calming tone. "Although I would've hoped after all this time we spent together, Michael would've learned to watch his mouth more."

"Point taken, my apologies," Michael responded. Father Hernandez and Sister Justine both grinned sensing he was genuine with his apology.

"And what is it about you guys in the church and your alternative secretive societies – The Illuminati, Opus Dei, and now this one," Michael questioned, attempting to further diffuse Justine's anger, and deflect their annoyance at him for his expletive.

"For some, it allows a greater sense of fraternity and brotherhood within the church for those who espouse similar doctrines," Father Hernandez responded.

"You came up with that answer pretty quick, boy toy. So, what order are you a part of?"

"I'm not, I'm simply a diocesan priest. I decided to research a bit more on them when Sister Justine had mentioned the Holy Order of the Child to see if I could come up with some information about them," Father Hernandez said.

Sister Justine had now calmed down. "And don't forget, Michael, I'm a member of a teaching order of nuns," she said, while taking a closer look at Father Hernandez's display monitor. "Does this mean that Cardinal Picoli and Father Yancy were members of the Holy Order of the Child?"

"And who else high up in the Holy See could be involved?" Father Hernandez commented.

"Okay…anything else on the USB?" Michael asked. "This is getting interesting."

Father Hernandez attempted to access the remaining files and subdirectories on the USB drive, with two opening and having no significance to their investigation. He was able to open many of the other files in the other directories, closing those realizing most consisted of transcribed notes, meeting records, and related counselling forms. "Unless we can get into the other files, what we found so far is pretty much useless."

"I don't know about that, but if I had to make a guess, it looks like Gary and the child traveled through

Chicago. We need to try and find out if they did go down to South America," Michael said.

"I can try calling a dear friend of mine at the convent to see if she can find out anything about visitors staying at the guest house, and any suspicious travel activities," Sister Justine said.

"Maybe finding them, somehow that could help us figure out why Cardinal Millhouse was killed and who killed him," Father Hernandez added.

"Could his death have something to do with the child?" Sister Justine asked of her two partners.

"That reminds me," Father Hernandez said. "When I logged on this morning, I received a text via an instant message on my workstation from Stephen Williams. There was another visitation, and this time it was at the church I had formerly pastored. The angel said – Behold, in the day to come, beware the child."

"What the…In the day to come...beware the child? What the heck does that mean?" Michael asked with hesitancy. "It can't be about the same one we talked to, the clone kid from Everest…could it?"

"What do we have, a Cardinal and priest killed, and possible members in the Order of the Child," Father Hernandez said, pushing back on his rolling chair away from his desk a few inches.

"You know, we haven't discussed one other important thing either since the Cardinal's murder," Sister Justine said.

"What's that?" Michael asked, with Father Hernandez answering the same thing in unison.

"The virus," she answered. "Do you think they're still working on it?"

Neither one of her companions had an answer.

"I think there's more going on that we're not aware of. We need to do whatever we can to try and figure out what that is," Father Hernandez said with intensity. "We need to make this our number one priority."

"What's this we need to make it a priority? You're sounding a little obsessive about this, Padre," Michael said. "I have other priorities in my life."

Sister Justine remained quiet, but agreed with Michael. Father Hernandez demonstrated he had become preoccupied with the investigation. A couple of her new acquaintances since becoming a member on staff at the Diocese offices noted he'd been late for meetings, and came close to missing a mass he was to officiate. He'd become consumed with some alleged pictures and had spent excessive time from his duties doing research in the library.

"Think about the seriousness of this, two of the church's clergy were killed, and the possibility of a deadly virus," Father Hernandez stressed.

"And that's why you have the police," Michael retorted.

"Will you two settle down, I swear, it's getting tiresome," Sister Justine said.

Father Hernandez and Michael hadn't expected Sister Justine's chastisement, but recognized she was correct.

"I know I may be getting a little aggressive with finding out what's going on, maybe I'm frustrated not knowing what we might be missing," Father Hernandez said.

"There's one person who could help provide insight for us," Michael said moving over to one of the lounge chairs in the office and plopping down. "Ashere."

"The problem is we can't get in touch with her," Father Hernandez said. "She shows up when we least expected her."

"She is our Deus ex Machina," Michael replied.

"I call it God's providence," Father Hernandez said.

"Could Stephen help us? He still seems to have the ability to see angels, or be where they're likely to show up," Sister Justine recommended. "Maybe he knows how to get in touch with her."

Michael and Father Hernandez glanced at each other wondering why they hadn't come up with that idea.

"You should give him a call to see if we can head over there this evening," Michael said springing up from the lounge chair.

"That's not a bad idea," Sister Justine added.

After a quick knock on the office door, Detective Green and Detective Matthews entered the office not waiting for an invitation by the father.

"We need to talk, Father," Detective Green said.

"You could've waited," Father Hernandez snapped back. "It's kinda rude for you to barge into my office like this."

"You guys want to tell me why Cardinal Millhouse and Father Yancy had trace amounts of a chemical substance in their bodies that our tech researchers have no idea what it is."

"What the sam hell are you talking about?" Michael asked in response, puzzled by Detective Green's revelation. Father Hernandez and Sister Justine, also curious, were oblivious to Michael's expletive.

"We had our Toxicology lab run exhaustive tests on the work up for Cardinal Millhouse seeing that he was injected with something during the video. For grins and giggles we had the same run up done for Father Yancy, and guess what, the same chemical compound showed up. It's pretty advanced stuff. It looked like it caused the Cardinal to have a heart attack. Thank goodness we knew what to look for. It metabolizes in the body differently and wouldn't show up on the normal tox scan."

"What do you want us to say?" Father Hernandez asked, perturbed that the detectives expected he or his companions would have knowledge regarding the chemical. "We're just as much in the dark as you."

"What could they have been involved with that they would be murdered?" Detective Green asked.

"Would you believe that's what we're trying to find out as well," Father Hernandez said.

"Did the two somehow work together? Father Yancy found Cardinal Millhouse's body and assisted us the night his body was discovered."

"Father Yancy was Cardinal Millhouse's aide. He would assist with managing the residence, security, cleaning, and maintenance staff."

Detective Matthews advanced over to Father Hernandez's desk. "Come on, Father, you can help us out," he asked in a soothing and mellow tone. "You have to know something."

"Your counterparts at the FBI and police investigating what happened at Everest and Waterfall Incorporated could help. Cardinal Millhouse was the primary coordinator between the Church and the company for vaccines and other services. Father Yancy was his aide. One of the persons we came across, Gary Applethorpe, a guy in charge there, seems to be involved with some indiscretions. We keep going in circles, with us coming back to him."

"And why him?" Detective Matthews asked picking up and examining one of the baubles on Father Hernandez's desk.

"He was the main person Cardinal Millhouse would liaison with at the high level in the company."

"Wait, I think I remember hearing that name on the news, he disappeared the evening of the Waterfall event, a nun and rumor was a bunch of lab people had died, but it came out it wasn't as bad as everyone reported, thinking it was caused by some sort of virus or something."

"We were there that evening," Father Hernandez said.

"Wait. What?" Detective Green interrupted. "What were you doing there?"

"Like I said, we were trying to see if it was Gary Applethorpe who attempted to try and have me killed when I was assigned out in Las Cruces, New Mexico."

"Someone tried to kill you?" Detective Matthews asked. "And you think it was this Gary Applethorpe?"

"Yes, we were investigating Everest and their connection with what happened at Thomson and Thomson and Crestview and the Church."

"So, what does our earlier working together have to do with all of this?" Detective Matthews continued.

"Some of the people killed at the two locations were research doctors for Everest and Waterfall, a subsidiary of Everest."

"And how are they associated with the church?" Detective Matthews asked.

"They were working on the projects sponsored by the church," Father Hernandez said.

"If I recall, that came up before, but we didn't think anything of it at the time. What type of projects?" Detective Green asked.

"Maybe because some of the stuff they were supposed to be working on for the Church, wasn't quite what is was, and the Cardinal found out."

"And let me guess, Gary Applethorpe was the company representative working with the church?" Detective Matthews asked.

"Yes," Father Hernandez answered.

"Now we're talking, thanks. Maybe he hired those two men to silence Cardinal Millhouse and Father Yancy when they learned the truth," Detective Green said.

"We'll be keeping in touch," Detective Matthews added. "I know there's going to be more that we'll want to talk about."

Both detectives hurried out of the office intent on putting out a bulletin for Gary Applethorpe. They came up with a motive and suspect. Father Hernandez was thankful they both jumped to a conclusion on the information given.

"That was brilliant, Padre," Michael commented. "You told them the truth without telling the truth. I'm impressed. You use to be straight and narrow, but now you're becoming more like us stretching the truth."

"It seems to me you lied, Father," Sister Justine said.

"I didn't tell them the whole truth," Father Hernandez responded. "I didn't want to implicate the church, because Cardinal Millhouse did know about the monies being shifted. But the detectives wouldn't believe me if we said that angels were involved with instigating as we suspect, Everest and the Church having malicious plans with a deadly virus, all the while another group of angels are trying to prevent Everest and the Church from doing the same. And we saw what happened with Cardinal Millhouse, angels are involved. They wouldn't believe something supernatural happened. Hopefully what I told them will keep them busy for a while."

Michael plopped back down in the office chair he had occupied. "With what you had explained to the detectives, and what we talked about, there's quite a bit to digest."

Sister Justine became a bit disheartened agreeing with Michael's earlier comment that Father Hernandez was becoming more morally ambiguous. "I don't know if I agree with all of this."

"I promise, Sister, once we learn more, we'll inform the police. But we want to make sure that nothing implicates innocent laity, clergy, or the Church. We need clarity, and maybe if we could learn more about the involvement of angels could help."

"We do need clarity," Sister Justine noted, franticly twisting the ring on her finger. "I think maybe we need to visit Stephen Williams."

# Chapter 21 – Stephen

Michael broke the long silence in the car as he, Father Hernandez, and Sister Justine drove to Stephen Williams's house. "The more I think about where we're going, the more I think this may be a waste of time." He stated, with force from the front passenger seat of Father Hernandez's Ford Taurus, making sure he stressed his point of view to the father and Sister Justine.

"What choice do we have? No other major leads are presenting themselves," Father Hernandez replied in response. "Stephen was the one who gave us the message about the angel visit and its warning. And of course, it would've happened at my old church that I don't serve at full time anymore. That's a bit ominous."

Father Hernandez gazed into the rearview mirror. Once he adjusted his view to remove the glare of the setting sun low on the horizon now beginning to impair his vision, a black car traveling three to four car lengths back, matched each turn and lane change he made move for move during the last five minutes.

Sister Justine interjected into the conversation. "Well, I'm hoping Stephen could somehow lead us to Ashere, and since she used to work for Everest, maybe she could provide some insight again."

"So, what about the two men who killed Cardinal Millhouse?" Michael asked. "And Father Yancy? Whoever killed him, could they be connected like the police think?"

"You mean with them finding out from the FBI that one of them may have been some sort of ex-intelligence agent? That would be disconcerting," Sister Justine said. "What have we gotten involved with? And how is Gary Applethorpe involved in all of this. Does it mean more than the church being involved with the virus?"

"What if he does know something about the deaths, would he even talk to us. Besides, we don't even know where he is. And with Cardinal Millhouse dead, I bet either one could've answered a lot of questions about the virus and the child."

"Hey, you two ever get the feeling that you're being followed," Father Hernandez asked in a worrisome voice.

"Great, now you're becoming paranoid, boy toy?" Michael responded.

"No, I'd swear there's a black car that's been following us for the last ten minutes or so. It's weird, that's all."

Michael and Sister Justine turned to look over their shoulder to peruse the traffic behind them to see a black Audi several car lengths back.

"So, it's a black car in traffic," Michael commented.

"What kinda car did Father Carson say Father Yancy noticed before he ended up missing?" Father Hernandez asked.

"What are you talking about?" Sister Justine asked.

"An Audi," Michael answered in response to the father's inquiry.

"We never did fill you in on that, did we, Sister." Father Hernandez said.

"No, you didn't. Are you becoming like Cardinal Millhouse and Grielle now?" Sister Justine said coldly.

"Ouch," Michael said, "that's gotta sting."

"A simple oversight on my part, my apologies Sister. We'll fill you in when we get to Stephen's house. Back to the car, what is it they say, if you make three rights, you're being followed?"

"Does that mean anything since there're means of technology to track people?" Michael paused for a few seconds before continuing. "I don't think you have to worry anyway. It looks like they're turning."

Sister Justine looked back over her shoulder. Father Hernandez glanced into the rearview mirror. The black car turned at the intersection they had traversed.

"Well, that was pretty much empty excitement," Michael said.

Several minutes later, they arrived at Stephen's residence and walked up to the house. The front door swung open with Stephen broadcasting a large grin as Father Hernandez reached out to ring the doorbell.

"I can't get rid of you three, can I?" Stephen playfully jibed. He stepped outside and hugged Father Hernandez, then Sister Justine.

Michael flinched when Stephen approached. "Whoa, I didn't know we'd become so close."

"I'm glad to see you guys," Stephen said pulling Michael in and embracing him.

Michael nudged Stephen back. "Dude, I prefer we didn't."

"Whatever. Come on in." Stephen stepped back into his house.

"You two go in, we'll be in in a sec," Sister Justine said. "I have something I need to talk to Michael about."

Father Hernandez gazed at his companions with furrowed eyes as he followed Stephen in through the front door, bumping into the jamb not watching where he was walking.

"Michael, I don't know what it is, but throughout this entire investigation, you've been rude and irritable too many times to count," she whispered in a sharp tone. "You're not the same man I knew all those years ago. I don't care what's going on in your life now, that's no reason for you to be acting like this. Stop it." Sister Justine stormed through the front door into the house making sure to take a couple of deep breaths to calm down.

Michael, at first surprised by Sister Justine's unexpected chastisement, overcame the shock of her outburst. He did realize she was right. He held onto the past too long, and it influenced the way he acted around others over the years. She finally called him out. He followed her into the house.

"You're right, Justine. I'm sorry." Michael then focused his attention towards Stephen. "And angel boy, I'm sorry. I didn't mean to be so abrupt outside. I'm still not hugging you though, but it's good to see you again."

Father Hernandez's jaw dropped momentarily. Sister Justine smiled.

"Not a problem," Stephen replied as he sat in his lounge chair. "I'm just glad we have this chance to talk."

"We're glad you agreed to meet with us this evening," Father Hernandez said.

The living room wasn't as sparse as the three had remembered. Several pictures and large photographs adorned the walls. On one wall opposite the couch was a large screen television with the image of a game show, the audio muted.

"Please go ahead and take a seat," Stephen offered, gesturing towards the couch with his hand.

"Excuse me, but before we get started, could I use your restroom?" Father Hernandez asked.

"Of course." Stephen directed the father to the small bathroom. As he closed the door after entering, his smartphone rang. The unique ringtone identified the caller as Cardinal Grielle. Reaching in to pull out his device, it snagged and caught on the lip of his pants pocket. Overcompensating using too much force, it tumbled in the direction of the toilet. Fumbling to keep the phone from falling in proved unsuccessful. He inadvertently propelled it to the side followed by the device slamming face-downward onto the tile floor landing with a loud crackling sound. Father Hernandez winced – his shoulders recoiled as he clenched his teeth. Picking up his smartphone, the fractured glass revealed a visible, but dimly lit screen displaying an incoming call notification. The phone rang startling the father. Again, he dropped it, this time into the toilet.

"Darn it!" Father Hernandez was thankful the bowl contained nothing but water. He extricated his phone with care, dried it off with copious amounts of toilet paper and placed it on the counter. He washed his hands and lower forearms several times. After relieving himself and washing his hands again, he returned to the living room. Stephen, Michael, and Sister Justine stared at him quizzically.

"What happened in there, Padre?" Michael asked, giving the father an impish grin. "You missed?"

Stephen chuckled. He then realized the ramifications of having to clean up if Michael was correct. Sister Justine rolled her eyes to Michael's comment, but also curious as to the father's outburst while in the bathroom, hoping the reason wasn't as crude.

"I dropped my phone on the floor and then in the toilet in there, look," Father Hernandez said reaching out to show the phone to his companions.

"I'm not touching that," Michael retorted.

"I don't want you to grab it, just look at the face. I doubt it's functional. I'll have to get a new one."

The phone's glass face bore an extensive spider web of cracks.

"Anyway, the reason we wanted to talk to you, Stephen, was due to the angel visit you witnessed at the church," Father Hernandez continued as he sat on the remaining lounge chair in the living room.

"Like I said when you called after you got my text, behold, blah, blah, blah, beware the child was the only thing the angel said. But you wanted to come over anyway. I don't know what else to tell you."

Father Hernandez leaned in towards Stephen. "Some tragic events have occurred over the last several weeks since you were involved with all that happened at your company. We lost the overseer of the Los Angeles Archdiocese, Cardinal Millhouse, and a young Father Yancy. I'm going to be honest with you, we think there was foul play and angels involved with what the Church and your company was working on."

"Well, that makes sense," Stephen said.

"What do you mean?" Michael asked.

"The FBI talked to me a little bit about some post R&D production in Gary's division over at the Waterfall facility. One agent said he was involved with the investigation way back during the Thomson and Thomson affair. He asked a lot about the books, but as he continued, they seemed more interested in finding out if certain projects had leaked out. I think some were from the CDC and Department of Defense, and I was getting worried."

"Department of Defense? Was a lot of what was found out somehow associated with the military?" Father Hernandez questioned.

"We were responsible for general accounting, and our R&D section was known to work on proof of concept projects to try and secure full contracts from the government, so they were considered confidential within the company. But I got the impression that other labs in the company, like over at Waterfall, is where it sounds like live production was going on."

"Could explain why possible intelligence agents may be involved," Sister Justine said.

"Yeah, but whose?" Michael added.

"What about Ashere, do you remember anything that could help us find her?" Father Hernandez asked leaning forward.

"Whenever Abriel showed up, she wouldn't be that far behind," Stephen said.

"So, she didn't show up when you saw Abriel and he gave you the message at the church?" Father Hernandez asked.

Stephen tilted his head to the side confused by the father's question. "Who said that angel was Abriel?"

"I assumed…"

"Father, I've dealt with Abriel quite a bit, and without a doubt, this was a different angel."

"It didn't give its name?"

"Nope."

"Then could the warning about the child be the one we met?" Michael asked, directing his question to Father Hernandez.

"Right now, that would be my guess."

* * * *

"Something happened," Sanger said, manipulating the software on his portable tablet.

"What do you mean something happened? Why, what do you got?" Xavier asked looking over at his partner sitting in the passenger seat of the car with a convertible portable tablet in his lap. Sanger was gnawing at the fingernails of his left hand.

"The father's phone stopped beaconing. I'm not getting anything," Sanger responded. "No voice, no GPS, nothing."

"Don't tell me that, we had to pull back when we were listening and they caught us tailing them. I didn't know I had gotten so rusty."

"Or maybe over confident taking him for granted thinking a priest wouldn't expect to be followed," Sanger said, in a cold manner while frantically typing attempting to troubleshoot the cause for the lack of data from the malware on Father Hernandez's phone.

"You're not helping," Xavier snapped back.

"Without knowing what happened, it may be a while before I can set up a data stream of info. What type of timeline are we looking at, and should I have the brothers snatch of one of the three?"

"No, there're too many dead bodies in our wake, and with the screw up of Father Yancy's body being found, one of these three going missing would raise a lot of

203

suspicion with an active police investigation. And somehow, they found out something of our associates' backgrounds. We should pull back and regroup. It sounds like the police suspect there's a connection. It doesn't help either that these three are as much in the dark about Gary's location. And they mentioned someone called Ashere. We may need to follow up on that lead. I think I may have seen it reviewing the case history. I need to get with Nadia to provide us the full case file for review."

"I can do a name data analysis cross-reference search and see if something comes up once we get access to the system," Sanger said, enthused he'd be able to use some of his data research hacks.

"We still got the tracker on his vehicle? It's still hot isn't it?"

After a pause and a couple of touchpad maneuvers and keystrokes, Sanger responded. "Yeah, it's broadcasting. So maybe it's something with the phone."

"You know what, we should go old school. Have the brothers tail the priest and the nun, put Red on Father Hernandez and Ben on Sister Justine. For the father, it should be easier since we tagged his car. He seems to be the lead on all of this." Xavier paused for a minute. "Could something have happened to his phone, or could he have turned it off for some reason?"

"The load is designed to keep working in the background even if the phone is off, unless the battery died. The software is taking advantage of the carrier's signaling still operating to provide location services as long as there's power. Something must've caused it to stop phoning home."

"So, what was the last thing you managed to capture?"

"Let's see, he was receiving a phone call…from a …Cardinal Grielle."

"I would've loved to have captured that conversation."

"Wanna know something else weird?" Sanger asked.

"What's that," Xavier responded, as he shifted the car into drive and pulled out from the half-empty parking lot where they had taken temporary refuge.

"I've been doing a quick scan on a couple of his texts, and he's been getting several strange ones, some with the word Ro."

"Ro? What the hell is Ro?"

"How do I know, just the letters capital R and little o, maybe it's some sort of code."

"We may have to look that up to find out what it means, along with the name Ashere. Do we know who sent those texts?" Xavier asked.

"This is weird, no matter what I do to find out the number or system of origin, nothing comes up. It's as if there's a ghost in the machine sending those texts. Each time I've hacked into the phone system before on previous assignments, I've been able to find out what I've needed."

Occupied with attempting to find the "Ro" texts' originator, Sanger missed the text from Stephen to Father Hernandez – "An angel showed up at your old church, and it said behold, in the day to come, beware the child. Don't know what it means, but I believe you'd be interested."

# Chapter 22 – Rebuke

A couple of hours after Father Hernandez arrived at his desk and settled in the next morning, he pulled out the pictures taken of Doctor Cochrane's room, scattering them atop his desk. After analyzing one for a few minutes, he would shift it to the side and replace it with another to attempt and try to decode the strange formulas, characters and writings written on the walls in the photographs.

It was after twenty minutes of studying the pictures and becoming frustrated not making any headway as to interpreting anything helpful, and deciding to work on a homily, Claudia from the administrative staff walked into the office carrying a mobile phone like the one he had damaged the day prior. He had dropped it off at the staff bullpen as soon as he arrived to the Cathedral offices so they could work on getting a replacement. He was puzzled as to why she would already be bringing it back.

"Here's a new phone for you. I ported your old number over to this one," Claudia said handing Father Hernandez his new device.

He was ecstatic to be receiving one that was the exact same model as his damaged cell phone. It meant not trying to learn any new features or buttons. "That was quick. I can't thank you enough for taking care of this for me."

"That's what I get paid for," she responded with a beaming grin. "We have a couple of spares around in case something like this happens. I called first thing and had the billing and number assignment changed. All your contacts should be on there since they were backed up to the SIM and the information was able to be recovered from your broken phone. Your emails and messages look like they downloaded from the servers as well. You'll have to restore most of your apps."

"Praise the Holy Mother, that's awesome. You're a miracle worker." Father Hernandez navigated to the contacts app and scrolled through a fragment of the list, satisfied they all were on the phone. Curious, he opened his text messaging application. Of all the new texts received, included were two new ones from an unknown number. They contained the letters "Ro."

"Are you kidding me?" he blurted out, startling Claudia.

"What's the matter, did I do something wrong?" she asked, believing she configured something on the phone incorrectly.

"No, no, it's nothing you did. I've been receiving some strange texts, and no matter what I try to do, I can't seem to stop them, that's all. I was hoping now with a new phone, maybe they would've stopped."

"Was that what you had Bernie from IT try to figure out?" Claudia asked.

"Yeah, it was."

"It frustrated him like you wouldn't believe. The phone company didn't show him any love."

"Well, tell him thank you for trying."

A soft knock on the door jamb of his office entrance interrupted Claudia and Father Hernandez. It was Father Carson who was spending his day interning at the Archdiocese offices. "Excuse me, Father, Cardinal Grielle would like to see you as soon as possible."

"Did he say what it was about, Father?" Father Hernandez asked.

"No, but if I didn't know better, he looked like he might have been a little upset about something."

Claudia began to ease out of the office. "I'll pass on your message to Bernie."

"Thank you, Claudia, if I have any problems, I'll stop by your desk."

Father Hernandez collected the photographs, placing them back in the manila envelope and securing them in his desk before going down to meet with Cardinal Grielle.

\* \* \* \*

After Father Hernandez entered Cardinal Grielle's office, he sidestepped several boxes of carpet tiles and two crew members working in the middle of the room laying down new flooring.

"Father Hernandez, please take a seat," the Cardinal requested as he gestured for the father to sit down in one of the office chairs opposite his desk. "I have something of importance to discuss with you. And gentlemen, could you please excuse us for a few minutes, and close the door on the way out," he asked of the two laborers.

They laid down their tools and departed.

"Father, you know that I'm to keep the Holy See informed as to the progression of Cardinal Millhouse's investigation? And with the death of a young priest, they're interested in that as well," Cardinal Grielle noted.

"Yes, and unfortunately, we're not making much progress. We don't seem to have many leads. We went to talk to Stephen Williams, but that didn't turn up anything helpful. We had hoped that he would've had more to tell us about his angel experience that happened at my old church."

"I see. So, Father, is there anything else you'd like to tell me, or if you found anything else of interest up to this point?" Cardinal Grielle asked.

Father Hernandez picked up by the Cardinal's tone that he already knew the answer before asking the question. "What is it you want to know, Your Eminence?"

"I can't believe you would betray me the way you did."

"I'm sorry, but I don't understand."

"Don't play coy, how come you didn't mention the USB device Father Carson gave you from Father Yancy? You should've told me that's why the IT department needed my approval to authorize the release of a decryption key. They made it sound as if it was for someone else on staff."

Father Hernandez wasn't going to worry how the Cardinal acquired the information. He would need to be more careful in the future. "It may have been nothing. With most of the files on it related to Church administration, I wasn't sure it would've been any use," Father Hernandez said.

"This is no time to be cautious, Father," Cardinal Grielle stated, not holding back he was irritated. "And it's no time to keep any pertinent information from myself either. If I'm willing to provide you with any resources and information necessary, you should provide me with the same courtesy. I can't see why you would want to keep me in the dark."

This was the most dedicated to demonstrating sound leadership Father Hernandez had experienced all the years of working with Cardinal Grielle. "I didn't want to put you in danger if what was on the device was one of the reasons for the demise of Cardinal Millhouse or Father Yancy. Add to it Cardinal Millhouse's missing security detail, we should assume the worse, that's why I'm being cautious."

Cardinal Grielle's demeanor changed from restrained anger to mild discontent. "That may sound well intentioned, but you need to keep me informed regardless of the circumstances." Cardinal Grielle leaned forward from his desk. "I can't believe you would do something like that."

"Believe me when I say…"

"Father, stop, what did you learn? And don't hold anything back."

It wasn't hard for Father Hernandez to know that no matter how much Cardinal Grielle attempted to remain calm and seem unaffected, the fury in his eyes showed he was incensed. The father replied after a short pause of Cardinal Grielle waiting for an answer. "We didn't find much of anything to be truthful. We did learn that Gary Applethorpe and the child traveled through Chicago to some unknown destination."

"Where do you think they may have headed?"

"The message inferred they may have travelled to South America. Sister Justine contacted an acquaintance at the convent she was assigned to when you and Cardinal Millhouse exiled her from Los Angeles, who did some looking around and found out a couple of special guests travelled through there."

"Exile, that's a strong way of putting it," Cardinal Grielle said, adjusting himself in his chair showing he didn't appreciate the comment, yet his posture and mood relaxed. "Are you sure South America?"

Father Hernandez didn't miss Cardinal Grielle's inquisitive tone. "Yes, Your Eminence. Why? What is it?"

Cardinal Grielle drummed his fingertips on his desktop, debating if he should respond. After a minute, he did. "South America is where the Church has a safe haven retreat for sabbaticals, and a spiritual treatment center. When there are abuse issues or other indiscretions from clergy members known to be a problem and whose actions could blemish the Church, the offending member is sent there for rehabilitation before they're exposed, if they haven't been already."

"Maybe we should go down there."

Cardinal Grielle responded with a disapproving look. "That's not going to happen. We don't know for sure if that's going to help. And if you did, what could you do?"

There was an uncomfortable silence between the two men. Cardinal Grielle was frustrated trying hard not to respond in the same way in a similar situation during the discourse as his predecessor. To hear that Sister Justine had someone gather information in what he imagined to be an unethical manner made him uneasy. The Church considered records of travel to the treatment center confidential.

"And how did Sister Justine's friend come about the information on Gary going down to South America?"

Father Hernandez wasn't sure why Cardinal Grielle had asked the question. "To be honest, I don't know."

"Is there anything else, since we're being open," Cardinal Grielle asked.

"Yes, we believe that Father Yancy was a member of the Society of the Holy Order of the Child."

Cardinal Grielle raised an eyebrow. "What, another secret society in my beloved church? Do you know much about them?"

"No, I don't."

"I see. I knew there was a reason why I didn't trust him. I wonder if that's part of it. He seemed overly interested in the activities of my office in relation to this investigation, or you working with your companions. Was there anything on there as to who may be members of the society? I'm not sure who to trust, here, in DC, or at the Vatican."

"Sister Justine suspected the Reverend Mother at her former convent in Chicago to be a member based on some earlier notes she had received when she was assigned out there. Apart from that, after we got into the drive, someone, maybe Father Yancy, encrypted most anything doing with the Society. We were able to open and view official church administration records," Father Hernandez said.

"Encrypted, but I thought you had opened up the files on the USB?"

"We believe most of the files associated with our investigation were in another encrypted directory needing a different password to open. We did manage to read a couple of interesting email messages. Maybe he didn't have time to encrypt them, or he got distracted and forgot about them."

"If he took the time to encrypt the other files, would he forget a couple of them?" Cardinal Grielle asked.

"Unless he considered them unimportant," Father Hernandez replied.

"And you mentioned about the angel visitation at your old church?"

"Yes, the 'beware the child' message. Sister Justine, Michael and myself tried to determine what the message could mean. Our best guess is maybe something to do with the child we met at Everest. Then we have a set of other angels making a simple pronouncement of 'The Child.'"

"Not beware the child?" Cardinal Grielle asked.

"No, two distinct messages. I'm not sure if these two different sets of angels with the different messages are working in sync with one another," Father Hernandez replied.

"You have a lone angel making one pronouncement, and quite a few others making a different announcement. Who do you trust?"

"In the scriptures, how many times do you see a lone prophet speaking against the many, the many who were wrong?" Father Hernandez asked.

Cardinal Grielle fidgeted with his fingers. "We're talking angels here, not men and prophets of God. You've mentioned that in some of your earlier dissertations Cardinal Millhouse rejected your initial findings outright. Am I mistaken, but does it seem that what's happening now is centered on the child?"

"Possibly," Father Hernandez replied.

"I need a cup of tea to focus my thinking," Cardinal Grielle commented in response, bewildered by the discussion.

He rose up out of his chair and began to stroll over to a new coffee and tea bar with a mini-sink, tea kettle, coffee machine, coffee cups and condiments, and various flavors of herbal teas, built in as part of the new credenza extending along the entire side of the room. Not watching his step, the taxing discussion muddled the Cardinal's mind with him contemplating if Father Hernandez had been candid. The Cardinal's foot jammed the corner edge of a stack of carpet tile boxes left in place by the carpet installers he had asked to leave. The Cardinal stumbled and lost his balance, falling forward with his hands stretched out attempting to break his fall.

By the time Father Hernandez jumped out of the office chair to help, Cardinal Grielle was already lying on the floor. "Oh my God, are you all right, Your Eminence?"

"I'm okay," Cardinal Grielle replied. His response crackled from the surprise of the fall.

Pushing himself up, he stood with the assistance of Father Hernandez. A sharp pain radiated from his left wrist. "Ow, ow, ow," he whimpered, grabbing the joint, now tender to the touch, turning blue, and showing signs of mild swelling.

"That doesn't look good," Father Hernandez said. "We should get you to Urgent Care at Mercy Memorial."

\* \* \* \*

Lieutenant Wilson found Detectives Green and Matthews in the Canteen break room after searching for them throughout the precinct headquarters. Detective Green finished paying for a cup of coffee and cheese Danish, while Detective Matthews contemplated which puzzle game to play on his smart phone, deciding on advanced word scrabble.

"The info finally came back on the known accomplices for those two men involved with the Millhouse investigation and we need to talk."

Detective Green's complexion flushed as he became irritated. Months after being able to tolerate Lieutenant Wilson, and not looking at him as a young political opportunist, Detective Green wondered how his commander ended up with the information from the FBI. The case was his and his partner's.

"Why in the hell do you have that?" Detective Green asked. "That's our case."

"Calm down, the FBI called me. The facial recognition flagged their local offices, and they were debating about releasing the search results to us."

"What do you mean?" Detective Matthews asked.

"I don't want to talk about any of that here. We need to go somewhere to talk about this, but I want to get a cup of coffee first." Lieutenant Wilson went and prepared himself a café latte from the automated cappuccino machine. After paying the cashier, he led the two detectives upstairs into an empty office near the top of the stairwell.

"As I was saying earlier, a couple of agents are coming over later to talk about the case," Lieutenant Wilson said, walking up to a dusty and empty desk, placing his coffee drink on the desktop, and turning around and lifting himself up to sit on the top with his legs dangling from the front.

"What's all this about?" Detective Green asked.

"They want to find out if what you learned centered around the Church and Cardinal Millhouse could have anything to do with some sort of domestic espionage activities. They're talking about helping out and collaborating with the case."

"They're gonna take away our case," Detective Green snapped. "That's what they're gonna end up doing."

"That's not what I said. They're coming over to talk about it."

"Call it what you will," Detective Matthews said. "They'll end up wanting us to back off. We've been down this road before during the Thomson and Thomson investigation."

"You don't know that," Lieutenant Wilson responded. "I contacted our guys working with the Feds on the incident in Eagle Rock at Everest's Waterfall. They think they may've found some discrepancies during their investigation at the Everest headquarters. I wouldn't be surprised after they talk to you, they head over to the Church and talk to them. It may lead to some insight in to why those two men killed Cardinal Millhouse."

"What type of discrepancies?" Detective Matthews asked.

"The amount of monies the church provided for vaccines versus what was spent."

"What? The Church did something wrong in giving money to Everest?" Detective Matthews asked.

"That's not what I'm saying," Lieutenant Wilson said. "The Church contracted with Everest for a bunch of medicines and vaccines to support their sponsored missionary clinics. They want to know if the Church knew about the possible reallocation of monies is what I was told. If they did, that could show some sort of collusion or conspiracy. The issue is, what was the real use of the monies?"

"Wouldn't the church have to receive some sort of gain as a result of the collusion, if there were any?" Detective Green asked. "Or what if someone in Everest was responsible, afraid that Cardinal Millhouse discovered some of the monies had been misallocated and siphoned off."

"That could lead to motive," Detective Matthews said.

The lieutenant moved in closer to the two detectives. "Gary Applethorpe is told to be a person of interest. It's suspected he left the country and he was involved with cheating some foreign companies as well."

Detectives Matthews and Green glanced towards one another as if their next thoughts had mirrored one another, and darted out of the empty office to their desk so they could log in and pull up the detailed profile information, including known accomplices for the alleged two men involved with Cardinal Millhouse's death.

Detective Green typed in the password for his workstation and accessed the LAPDOnline web portal's Background Queries portlet. The status message notification bar noted, "1 Active Query Completed." Clicking the link opened the pictures of three men showing each of their names and a query ID number. Selecting the ID number, a new window opened showing the background of the men, each having several aliases listed. The information for each man displayed, each having retired from the military or intelligence related agency five to seven years prior. The onscreen report output had the data fields masked for each of their employment backgrounds from the current date back to their military retirement dates, including much of their military history. The detectives could not make any inference as to their work history, citizenship, or specific nationality. The personal background information for each was scarce displaying their names, if it were their real names, ages, and physical attributes. The database record also displayed redacted place of birth and known address data fields. The detectives couldn't develop a complete profile for any of the subjects after they finished scanning through the four files.

"Who the hell are these guys?" Detective Matthews commented. "They might as well not have sent this crap."

"You know what we need to do?" Detective Green asked of his partner, sending each of the background reports to the printer.

"What's that?"

"Go talk to Father Hernandez and Cardinal Grielle before the Feds do. There's gotta be more to this. Why is there what looks like spooks involved in all of this?"

Detective Matthews pursed his lips. "How much you wanna bet the Feds are already aware of these guys?"

# Chapter 23 – Mercy Memorial

Detectives Green and Matthews tracked down and caught up to Father Hernandez and Cardinal Grielle at Mercy Memorial as the two walked out of the entrance for the Urgent Care Outpatient center. A temporary wrist splint covered the Cardinal's left wrist.

"Detectives, you made it sound like it was important that we meet," Father Hernandez said. "Couldn't this have waited?"

"No, we have our reasons in wanting to talk to you as soon as we could," Detective Green said. "What type of involvement was there between Cardinal Millhouse and Gary Applethorpe?" he asked.

Cardinal Grielle didn't feel comfortable talking about the investigation in the open with the periodic interruption of someone walking by going in, or exiting the Urgent Care clinic. He maneuvered away from the walkway over to an empty sitting area with a solitary, green painted, metal bench. He tried not to focus attention on his arm secured in a sling and radiating slight pain. "We talked about this before, I would call it professional. He would come over to the Archdiocese offices from time to time from what I understood."

"Do you know if the Church found out if Everest has been honest with all of your procured services or materials that they provided for your clinics and sites?" Detective Green asked.

"Of course. From what I can tell, and with the records and information I've gone through since taking over, everything seems to be on the up and up. I understand that when Cardinal Millhouse was alive, the FBI came over to review the financial records for the monies the Church paid to Everest. There was nothing illicit with any of the contracts or transactions. What's all this questioning about, detective? What are you trying to imply?"

Detective Matthews pursed one side of his lips. "There were some discrepancies with the monies benefactors gave to the Church, and other sources of revenue provided to Everest that didn't quite find their way to where they needed to go in the company. From what we understand, the auditors and investigators nearly missed it because of some capital expenditure and expense accounting codes mumble jumble."

"This sounds like it's going to be a bit time consuming. You mind if we go back to our offices to finish this discussion?" Cardinal Grielle asked.

"Hopefully the FBI isn't there," Detective Green noted.

Cardinal Grielle stopped walking and gave both detectives a bewildered look. "FBI, why would the FBI be there?" He was under the impression the FBI were through with interrogating him and his office staff.

"I know I shouldn't tell you this, but the FBI may be taking over this investigation, and we want to find out if there's anything we should know if we have to relinquish this over to the feds." Detective Green sensed the disapproving stare of his colleague, but ignored it.

Cardinal Grielle knew of the Church's clandestine sponsorship on the inception of the clone child when Cardinal Millhouse and Gary Applethorpe had revealed his existence. Reviewing the files and records of his predecessor, none disclosed anything of the project. It seemed Cardinal Millhouse was good at leaving no paper trail, and no reason to bring it up. "Then I guess we'll have to tell them the same thing that we told you. I couldn't find anyone or paperwork pointing to any wrongdoing in Everest on our part."

"Are you sure?" Detective Green asked, attempting to show unity with his partner.

"I'm pretty darn sure. If the FBI wants to come over and look at our files, they're more than welcome," Cardinal Grielle said, confident he found none that could implicate the church when he was able to get access to Cardinal Millhouse's files and email on the Church's network. "Like I said though, can we finish this up at my office?"

As the four men started to stroll back to their vehicles, Detective Matthews sensed someone tapping him on his right shoulder. He turned around to see no one was there. Yet something strange caught his attention. Several rows over and up in the parking lot, a young man, pale skin tone, sitting in a dark gray Audi and wearing wire-rimmed glasses, lowered what had the semblance of a camera with a long-range zoom lens out of view once the detective observed him. The man then turned away.

"Did he take a picture of us?" Detective Matthews asked, in a soft tone. From the distance, the man's face and red hair color was familiar. He couldn't remember where he had seen him before.

"What? I didn't catch what you said," Detective Green replied.

The man in the gray Audi raised the driver side window and began to pull out of the parking stall.

"Over there in that gray car pulling out, it looked like he was spying on…" Detective Matthews recalled where he saw the man before. "Son of a b… I think that man is one of the possible associates of those two men involved with Cardinal Millhouse's death." He began walking over to the gray Audi that was now beginning to move.

Assuming the detective was heading in his direction, the driver pressed down on the gas pedal. The finely tuned engine revved, accelerating the vehicle down the parking lot lane.

"Hey you, stop!" Detective Matthews shouted, breaking out into a run, weaving through parked cars. Detective Green followed. The driver peered over to determine the proximity and location of the encroaching detectives. Having diverted his attention, he clipped the rear of a SUV backing out of a parking stall propelling fragments of the car's headlight lens and the SUV's rear taillight into the air, mingled with the splintering sound of crunching metal, plastic, and fiberglass. The Audi continued to speed between the rows of parked cars and sped onto the street. He missed a pickup truck and Honda sedan, both braking to an immediate stop avoiding a collision. Detective Green diverted to the SUV to check on the condition of the driver and possible passengers. Detective Matthew's attempt to keep pace with the Audi to at least garner a glance at the vehicle's license plate was futile, unable to make a straight approach due to the angled layout of the parking stalls. In one row, where the front bumpers of two cars kissed one another, caused the detective to slow down and jump over the obstacle. By the time he got to the street, his quarry had already traveled a city block. Detective Matthews pulled out his phone and called dispatch giving the direction of the suspect vehicle before walking back to rejoin his partner.

"Were you able to get a license plate?" Detective Green asked of his partner engaged with interrogating the driver of the SUV to determine if she were able to get a look at the license plate of the offending vehicle.

"No, he managed to drive through traffic like nothing I've seen before. I've called it in though. Air ships are inbound looking for someone driving erratically in a gray Audi."

"I'll go ahead and let the Cardinal know we'll catch up with him later. We'll be here awhile," Detective Green said as a hospital security patrol vehicle pulled up.

\* \* \* \*

When Detectives Green and Matthews entered Cardinal Grielle's office, Michael and Sister Justine had arrived at the request of Father Hernandez. The Cardinal gestured for the two policemen to take a seat in the chairs opposite his desk.

"Heard you guys had quite the morning," Michael remarked. "How's it going, puzzle man?"

"Puzzle man?" Cardinal Grielle asked.

"He's good with puzzles, that's how we figured out we needed to return to Aguascalientes," Michael answered.

"Cardinal, do all three of them need to be here?" Detective Green asked sitting down in one of the chairs.

223

"They are three of my most trusted associates in working this investigation from the church's perspective."

Detective Green leaned forward placing his hands on the front of the Cardinal's desk. "At this point, this is a police homicide investigation, not a religious quest."

"I think that's where you're wrong," Cardinal Grielle replied. "This is also a supernatural investigation based on the video evidence we all witnessed in this office. And I get to say who and who doesn't work this. You know that there's something else going on here. For all intents and purposes, the two men who killed my predecessor are known quantities. I believe there may be a spiritual impact to the church with the possible involvement of angels. That's not a police issue."

Cardinal Grielle and Detective Green locked eyes.

Father Hernandez was again impressed with the growing tenacity of his spiritual leader. Cardinal Grielle demonstrated increased confidence and determination each passing day.

"Any luck with finding that stranger who may have been watching us, and involved with that hit and run at the parking lot at Mercy Memorial?" Father Hernandez asked to break up the staring contest.

"No, we were hoping the hospital security cameras would have caught the license plate, but no luck," Detective Matthews replied, thinking the friction between his partner and the Cardinal was futile.

Michael, holding his cell phone in his hand, sensed it vibrate from receiving either a voice mail or text message. The notification bar on the display showed one text message from an unknown number containing the letter m. At the same time, Father Hernandez experienced the sensation of his cell phone vibrating in his pocket. His phone display showed he received a text composed of the letters "Ro" from an unknown number. He ignored it and placed the phone back in his pocket. A single bird-like chirp sound filled the office. Sister Justine pulled out her phone to see that she received a text message – the letter e. A few seconds later, the mystery texts replayed two more times on all three phones before all three decided to ignore the texts and attempt to reengage the conversation. Father Hernandez, Michael, and Sister Justine distracted and annoyed Cardinal Grielle and the two police detectives with the three interacting with their phones.

"Excuse me, you three," Cardinal Grielle remarked, "but is there any reason you continue to check your messages? It's a bit of a distraction."

Father Hernandez responded first. "Sorry, Your Eminence, but I keep getting these weird text messages. Someone keeps sending me the letters Ro."

"Same for me," Sister Justine said, frustrated. "Except I keep getting the letter "e" from an unknown number. Nothing else."

"Okay, this went up on the weird meter," Michael added. "I'm receiving the letter m."

"The three of you are receiving the letters "Ro", "e" and "m" in random text messages?" Detective Matthews asked.

"Yeah, why?" Father Hernandez asked.

"You know that those letters make up the word Rome?" Detective Matthews noted. His observation caught everyone off guard. "Those are the same letters for the word more, but being the Roman Catholic Church, I would think Rome has more relevance to you," he continued.

"I'll be damn, puzzle boy did it again," Michael remarked.

Detective Matthews' furled eyebrows and clenched jaw exposed he was annoyed by Michael's comment.

"So is it important somehow to the four of you," Detective Green inquired of the church team. "What does it mean?"

Cardinal Grielle ruminated through a couple of ideas, but decided it best not to disclose them. "Detectives, I wish we could say, but we're as much at a lost as you are."

"You sure, it has to mean something," Detective Green said.

"Maybe we'll figure it out somewhere down the line, but back to our original discussion," Cardinal Grielle said.

"Yeah, we've noticed there seems to be some guys who's background we're not able to pull much on. Why would someone like that be involved with all of this?"

"What're you talking about?" the Cardinal asked.

"The men involved with Father Yancy's death may have been spooks," Detective Matthews said. "Why would that be?"

"We know that Everest was working on classified projects for the DoD," Father Hernandez said.

"And why would the Church be involved?"

"Maybe he learned something in working with Gary Applethorpe, and they killed him for it."

"Like what? We've been down this road before. There's gotta be more if you're still being followed."

"We don't know, maybe because it's classified," Father Hernandez said. "Maybe they think we know more than we actually do."

The detectives spent another thirty-five minutes with the interrogation before receiving a phone call requesting their return to the precinct station. After their departure, Cardinal Grielle dismissed his team and drafted an updated message for Cardinal Picoli. He refrained from mentioning the mysterious texts, and minimized the incident in the parking lot.

## *Chapter 24 – Confirmation Sacrament*

Twelve members of the Vatican clergy from the Roman Curia and members of the Society of the Holy Order of the Child, and the child sat in the front row of pews of the neo-Baroque styled Santa Maria Regina della Famiglia chapel, which was adjacent to the Pontifical Government building. Several senior clergy members of the Society, including Sister Abigail and her Mother Superior were in attendance. The Holy Father directed Cardinal Picoli not to invite Gary Applethorpe, even though he was a qualified deacon to participate in the procession. Also, the Pontiff's office told Holy See administrative clergy and staff throughout Vatican City that the Holy Father would officiate over a special private mass of intercession for a high-level dignitary. Cardinal Tullono, misled by Cardinal Picoli, coordinated a ruse car convoy to pretend a VIP had arrived onto the grounds, and deployed gendarmerie and the Swiss Guard posted outside each entrance of the chapel.

Pride filled the young priest selected to preside over the special evening mass and perform the confirmation of a VIP child with the Holy Father in attendance. The priest, vested in a blessed stole and chasuble, followed two candle holder servers and an assigned deacon carrying the Book of Gospels down the main aisle. None of the attendees were concerned that the procession did not contain an acolyte carrying a processional cross.

The weakened Holy Father ensured he would attend, though he needed support as he sat in the pew. The Camerlengo, or any of the other attending Cardinals or bishops were more qualified to administer the rite. The child informed them that they should sit in the pews to witness a significant event. They were all also aware of a confirmation accomplished back in Los Angeles officiated by the late Cardinal Millhouse. A divine announcement voiced that the evening's ceremony was to perfect the preceding event months prior.

The candle-holder servers lit the ceremonial candles. The priest reached the pulpit and altar that rested upon the raised dais of the sanctuary, when the domed vaulted ceiling above glistened as if the plaster, stone, and concrete had become translucent. A veiled, muscular angel, donning four wings manifested itself and hovered several feet in the air before gliding down with its feet touching upon the floor towards the rear of the sanctuary behind the communion table. The angel removed its veil to expose the head of a human-bird like face. Two members of the congregation recognized the angel, witnessing the same one in the Holy Father's private oratory. The new arrival's facial features startled the others in attendance. The awestruck, yet angst filled officiating priest stepped back away from the raised dais. Several of the spectators knelt onto the kneeling board performing the Rosary, others began reciting rote prayers. The congregation, except for the child, became enthralled when two additional angels materialized, one behind on the right, the other behind on the left. The first angel gestured with his hands for the child to approach. The child rose from the pew, stepped into the aisle, and up to the raised dais. He dropped to one knee and bowed his head.

The first angel approached, passing through the ornate cherry wood communion table as if it didn't exist, and laid its broad hands with six fingers each upon top of the child's head. The child exuded the same ethereal shimmer as that of the angels.

"As I lay my hands upon thy prince, you are bequeathed and sealed with the gift of the spirit that has conferred life upon you. How precious thou art, do you confirm your gift?" the angel with four wings asked, its voice resonating as if it were a trumpet.

"I do," the child answered.

"Do you confirm the path established by your father?"

"I do," the child said.

"Do you confirm the purpose conferred by Father?"

"I do, understand, and accomplish without hesitation what is expected of the father," the child said.

The two angels in the rear sang a short melodic choral duet during the confirmation.

The first angel stepped back three paces as the child stood, the radiant aura subsided. All three angels dropped to one knee and bowed. "This is our pledge, we are bound to serve."

"Go in peace," the child remarked.

The first angel stood, soberly staring at the small congregation with its eyes glistening as if amber jewels filled with liquid fire. "What man and the divine have joined, do not disrupt the blessed path of the child." the angels disappeared.

The child turned to face the captivated onlookers. "I would like to return to my residence."

"We haven't started with the official confirmation ceremony," the presiding priest whispered, still shaken with amazement from the angelic visit.

The child gave the priest a wry smile. "Haven't you witnessed the amazing events here? We're done." He strolled out of the chapel followed by his security detail.

*   *   *   *

A rush of excitement raced through the housing quarters, offices and workplaces in the Vatican. Witnesses on the grounds at the time of the visitation observed a strange ethereal violet aura appearing over the chapel at the same time as the alleged special mass. Many of the preceding angel and funeral eulogy visitations reported the accompaniment of a similar type of glowing aura, but never with the distinctive purplish palette.

The Holy Father made an urgent plea for those in the Vatican City not to discuss or release information concerning the visitation to anyone outside of the Holy See. Word still leaked out, although not the specifics of what happened. The Holy See leadership was thankful no major news agencies pursued the story or ignored it outright due to the recent resurgence of visitations across the world over the last forty-eight hours. Individuals were more interested in what was happening in their cities or communities than Rome. Now, eulogies weren't the primary focus of exposition by the manifestations, they made pronouncements like "All hail, the time of his glory is to come."

Clergy and staff members of Vatican City not in attendance during the special mass approached Cardinal Tullono the following morning asking a barrage of questions concerning the suspected visitation. They assumed he would have answers for their inquiries with him being the assigned spiritual leader assisting the Holy Father in the Diocese of the Holy See. They expressed interest as to the rumored prominent unique features of the angelic creature. Some were concerned if it was an ominous sign, or the visit to the church by something other than benevolent manifestations. Cardinal Tullono himself not witnessing the visitation, wasn't able to answer any of their questions. He rushed over to Cardinal Picoli's office to discuss the recent visit.

Also, after learning of an alleged secretive society centered on a child, Cardinal Tullono wanted to inquire if he was a senior member as rumored. Adding to the urgency to talk to his peer, a sister assisting the administrative staff for the Vicar of the Holy See, handed him a requisition form for coordination governing the commissioning of a non-descript artwork project initiated by the child.

Cardinal Picoli greeted his visitor into his office. "Welcome Pieter, what brings you by?"

"I'm sure you know why I'm here, Silvio," Cardinal Tullono said, walking up to Cardinal Picoli's cherry wood desk, carrying the requisition form.

"Let me guess, the visitation we had last night?" Cardinal Picoli asked as he gestured for Cardinal Tullono to take a seat in the chair opposite his desk.

Cardinal Tullono remained standing. "Yes, here it is I'm supposed to be the spiritual leader for the Holy See, and I seem to be in the dark on quite a bit with what's going on in the Santa Maria Chap..."

Cardinal Picoli interrupted, "Pieter, calm down. My team has been making sure to schedule use of the chapels through your office."

"That's not what I meant. From what I understand since that mysterious visit by the suspected angel Aurora over ten years ago, things have been upside down in the See. I've been appointed here over the last two and a half years, and everything's been calming down to being orderly. Since the arrival of that child, things have become chaotic. And there's all these rumors being bantered about that there was a mysterious angel visit yesterday evening."

Cardinal Picoli sat back in his chair and crossed his arms, but then relaxed and moved forward resting his forearms on his desktop. "Yes, you should know, we did have an angel visit last night, three angels to be exact."

Cardinal Tullono's eyes enlarged exposing the fullness of his green irises through his glasses. "Three? What is it that they want?" he asked.

"The lead angel was the same one that heralded the preparation of the child to the Holy Father after his arrival here to the Holy See."

Cardinal Tullono considered now would be a good time to attempt and probe for more information regarding the recently discovered secret society. "I don't know why, but I'm troubled by a lot of this. Doesn't it seem strange that some of what's going on is out of the ordinary? And is the Holy Father agreeable with everything around here. Are we sure there are those around here who aren't operating under their own autonomy and outside of canon law and Biblical principles?"

Cardinal Picoli took longer than expected before responding. "What are you driving at, my friend?"

233

"You, I, and the Vicar of the Holy See are to work together for the purpose of administering the church, so we all should be knowledgeable with what goes on around here," Cardinal Tullono replied. "Yet it seems that there's quite a bit of administrative workings having the appearance of operating in a clandestine manner."

"We've told you many times before, divine guidance directs a lot of what we do. Our intention is not to undermine you or the Church. If anything, we're strengthening its foundation, leading the church into the future."

"And you don't see anything wrong with what's going on? You know you can rally more to your side if you were open instead of working in the shadows," Cardinal Tullono said.

Cardinal Picoli reflected on Cardinal Tullono's remark, sensing the comment was a veiled attempt to solicit some information.

"We should be working together, one in union for the church," Cardinal Tullono continued as he sat in the chair opposite Cardinal Picoli's desk, crossing his legs under his cassock, and watching his peer Cardinal Picoli get up out of his chair and now pace his office back and forth.

"Before you came over, I was reviewing several older email communiques concerning angels, and I looked back at the report from Cardinal Grielle in Los Angeles. There was a report of an angel at one of the parish chapels presenting a unique and conflicting message, behold, in the day to come, beware the child," Cardinal Picoli said. "The question is, what was he driving at when he sent this? And with what his so-called investigators are telling him, they're not painting a positive picture."

"What are they saying?" Cardinal Tullono asked.

"Let me jump back for you. The three gave a conclusion, albeit a little weak, as to the nature and state of the angels involved with Thomson and Thomson, versus the ones involved with the messages that had been presented across the globe at multiple funerals, casting the two in different and opposing lights."

"That is interesting. Is there any chance of me being able to review some of what they stated for my own edification later?"

"His Holiness saw it fit to limit for view what came out of the Southern California Diocese," Cardinal Picoli said.

Cardinal Tullono wanted to question more about the report, being he was annoyed his peer didn't want to provide more information. He decided to let Cardinal Picoli continue the discussion to infer his true motives.

Cardinal Picoli continued. "You may not be aware, but several regional religious journals in the United States had published some heretical writings, which we believe originated from one of the investigators under the administration of Cardinal Millhouse."

"Cardinal Millhouse? Wasn't he the one murdered back in Los Angeles?" Cardinal Tullono asked.

"Yes. The writings implied the likelihood that the Church was under the influence by spiritual entities at enmity with the true nature of the Church. The first angel that appeared years ago when all of this started said that we should expect much of the resistance occurring these days. To be truthful, I don't know if all of this was foretold."

"First angel?" Cardinal Tullono noted, pushing his black rim glasses that had been shifting down his nose, back up. "What do you mean by first angel? How long has these visits been going on?"

"The first Papal visit by an angel occurred I think twelve, maybe thirteen years ago now, at least a year or two before the mass disappearance. The church was working on a special project with various patrons and national entities, when a divine influence inspired and generated a unique future blessing for the world. Right away there was a major setback for a portion of the project that occurred over in Mexico."

"And what was that unique blessing?"

"The child himself, of course, but I can't tell you too much more."

Cardinal Tullono raised an eyebrow and adjusted his body weight in the chair that was now uncomfortable. "That's quite a bit to take in," he said. "You and some of the others here in the Holy See saw it fitting to say little about our special friend during our weekly administration meetings and assemblies. We knew of some sort of divine revelations and the child, but nothing compared to what's been going on around here. Now add this recent incident with several supposed angels, there was bound to be some sort of opposition. It would be asinine not to anticipate an adversary concerning the child."

"That's an odd way of putting that. What are you trying to say?" Cardinal Picoli asked.

"Last I recall, the Holy Mother already provided the blessed child whom we revere."

There was a reason Cardinal Picoli didn't immerse Cardinal Tullono into the full plan regarding the child, their doctrinal viewpoints differed. "You don't like the child, do you, Pieter?" Cardinal Picoli asked, his pacing stopped. He now stood by the side of his desk staring down at Cardinal Tullono.

"If we're going to be truthful, no, I don't. I think many around here are beginning to give undo reverence to him," Cardinal Tullono replied. "I look back when he and his guardian arrived, and how that child believed he owned the place."

"Yes, he is a child, but I tell you this, he's a special and unique child."

"Did you know that the child managed to convince some of the staff in the Holy See to commission a couple of pieces of art work?" Cardinal Tullono inquired as he slid the requisition form over to Cardinal Picoli atop his desk. "I was told the child claimed it was sanctioned by the Holy Father. I found out a short while ago myself."

"I wasn't aware of that," Cardinal Picoli responded, becoming a bit angered hearing of the unexpected news, not being informed by the Holy Father or the staff providing aid to the child.

Cardinal Picoli examined the form as Cardinal Tullono continued speaking. "This request doesn't say what type of artwork either. Regardless, we have special committees for that, one that I sit upon to ensure the artwork represents the proper spiritual tone of the church. I'm not going to blindly sign this form."

Cardinal Picoli sat in his desk chair. "I understand, but these are special circumstances. We have to overlook these trivial indiscretions."

Cardinal Tullono became flustered, aggravated by the complicity of Cardinal Picoli. "Special circumstances. Inconsequential indiscretions. Silvio, is there a piece of art being commissioned?"

The angel's comment stating not to disrupt the path of the child came to Cardinal Picoli's mind. "I can find out if it's true, and if that's what the Holy Father has agreed to, we'll act and see to it that it's completed."

Cardinal Tullono rocketed out of his chair, his nostrils flared. "You're kidding me, right? I can't believe we're going to commit to this…atrocity. This goes against all protocol. His Holiness wouldn't approve this request if he wasn't as incapacitated as he is, would he?" Cardinal Tullono took a deep breath before continuing. "I'll come out and say it. Are there those who are taking advantage of him due to his failing condition?"

"Calm down, Pieter. The Holy Father is more aware of what's going on than you give him credit for. As the Camerlengo, I can assure you, he is in full control. The divine activities are a sign that God is working in the Church."

"Even if you say that, I don't agree with the situation with the child either, or should I say abomination," Cardinal Tullono said.

The way Cardinal Picoli's gray eyes narrowed reminded Cardinal Tullono of an asp ready to strike as he stood, leaned forward and planted his hands on the desk. His light bronzed skin tone flushed. "Pieter, I'll say this, and then this discussion is over, no matter what you may think, the child is considered a miracle. To oppose him, one may question your loyalty to the Church. Now leave, I have other duties to attend to."

Cardinal Tullono submitted to his colleague's request, knowing he would go and attempt to contact Cardinal Grielle in Los Angeles to probe where he stood on the situation. He hoped that he might be of like mind, and know the author of the alleged heretical writings.

Those writings, might help him understand the secretive sect within the Vatican.

## Chapter 25 – Reemergence

Michael found himself doing something he hadn't done over the last several years. After waking up, he would go online to review the daily news after his morning jog. He had avoided the news whenever possible, not wanting to read about the trivial and meaningless things people were doing in their lives. Reports of angels showing up at numerous locales across the country flooded the news headlines and articles over the last couple of days. Once again, they no longer focused on presenting eulogies at random funerals. They would appear at churches and other religious edifices and make a quick announcement, most containing the same like, "The dawn of a new age is approaching, the dawn of a new spiritual understanding and joining of beliefs, be prepared for the glory to soon come upon you."

Another twist was that nations across the world now began to report distinct and unique manifestations of spiritual and alleged heavenly creatures. In Japan, most appearances asserted they represented the indeterminate number of deities associated with Shintoism. Called Kami, they claimed the earlier funeral eulogies reinforced the way of the one who was deceased, and remembered as joining the ancient ancestors of family clans. To demonstrate that after their death, the eulogy would report if the departed were able to embody the values and virtues of Kami in life. Shinto tradition stated that there are "eight million million" Kami in Japan.

Under Hinduism, similar correlations occurred with the ancient religion. The manifestations had reported the coming universal brotherhood of all religions, and one, an ascended one, who is to come and reconcile the beliefs systems across the world.

Two hours drifted by. A soft knock at the front door distracted him from his informal research. Answering the door, it was Alicia, with her thin and petite lips pursed and face distorted with anger. She wore less makeup than their last encounter in the coffee house.

"What are you doing here?" Michael asked, scrunching his eyes.

"I came to pick up some of my stuff," she answered, storming past him into the house.

He followed her leaving the front door open. "Um, excuse me, but I think you already got all your stuff when you moved out."

"I would've known if I got everything," Alicia snapped back, stomping off towards the back bedroom going and rummaging through the closet, followed with digging through the dresser drawers and nightstand shuffling folded shirts, underwear, and socks askew.

"See I told you, you don't have anything here," Michael said, irritated she had ransacked the room. If he had come across something of hers that didn't seem important, such as a small makeup kit, or something else inconsequential she wouldn't miss, he threw it out to avoid having to contact her, knowing it wasn't worth the trouble. Michael found little items of hers in obscure places throughout the house. He doubted some were misplaced and wondered if Alicia was marking her territory.

Alicia looking as if she were going to begin a second round of searching shriveled Michael's patience. "Are you done yet?"

"I want to make sure your old girlfriend doesn't use any of my stuff," Alicia replied, perusing the room making sure she didn't miss any place to search. She moved to the bathroom and began looking through the medicine cabinet and vanity drawers.

"First, ewww, and second…wait a minute, what old girlfriend?"

Alicia ignored Michael with her now foraging through the towel and linen closet.

"Wait a minute, did you come here to see if Justine was here?"

"Nooo."

Michael could tell she was lying by the change of tone in her squeaky voice. "Why are you really here?"

Alicia stopped rifling through the bathroom. "You're not back with Justine?"

"For goodness sake, no, she's still a nun." Michael didn't want to tell Alicia that Justine had earlier considered leaving the church.

"I know that, but I heard you both…never mind. If you're not getting back with her, why did you break us up?"

"Oh, I don't know, maybe because of how you're acting now. I don't need crazy in my life."

Alicia's light amber brown eyes flashed with fury. "Screw you," she screamed, her shrill voice broadcasted several octaves higher than its normal pitch. She wanted to storm out of the house, yet her feet remained in place. She didn't know why she stayed.

Michael regretted verbalizing the disrespectful remark. Maybe having Alicia back around wouldn't be that bad. The house had been quiet without anyone else around. "Look Alicia, I'm sorry. Maybe we..." His phone rang.

Reaching into his pocket and pulling it out, the caller ID displayed "Father Boy Toy." "Hello, Padre," he responded, answering the call.

"Michael, are you busy?"

"Not really, hold on." Michael turned to Alicia who was staring at him crossly. "Can we finish our discussion later? I need to take this call." He was thankful for the interruption.

"No, there's nothing else to discuss. You and me, we're done," she snapped as she huffed out of the bathroom. Seconds later, the front door slammed.

Michael was appreciative of her leaving, and happy he hadn't made the mistake of asking her to consider getting back together. "Sorry, Padre, what did you want?"

"Have you been keeping track of all the angel visits that seem to have been occurring recently?" Father Hernandez asked.

"Strange that you mention it, I have been. I was doing some reading about them, more so about the ones in Japan this morning."

"Have you noticed that the number of these recent visitations seems two or three times as many as before?"

Michael paused before responding. He hadn't considered the quantity, only the change in their preferred locales and the messages they conveyed. "I'll admit things have been getting strange around their appearances.

Their overall actions seem so different now, evolving and changing. I'm not sure what their intentions are, not that I knew before."

"So, you noticed it too. The world seems so distracted by these manifestations that they're forgetting what could be the true source of these angels or their purpose? Or are the people even listening to what they're saying or not saying. As messengers of God, they've been inclined to…"

Michael interrupted. "Now you're starting to steer this into a going religious discussion. What is it you want, Padre?"

"Would you be up for investigating some of these visits and starting a formal case study? I wanna talk to the witnesses to see if we can find some sort of pattern and collect background information like where, when, who was there, and anything else that may be relevant. I can't explain it, but so much of this seems connected. Maybe this'll lead to the strange occurrence associated with Cardinal Millhouse's death. And I've heard rumors of strange visits in Vatican City."

"Let me see if I heard you correctly, you want to start going around talking to complete strangers about the strange things that they saw?"

"I do. Cardinal Trong recalled Cardinal Grielle to D.C. with all the other Cardinals in the country for an emergency meeting. I've off-loaded some of my duties to accomplish the formal masses to the junior priests here, so I have some extra time. I was also thinking of asking Sister Justine to join us."

"Sorry, Padre, but I have to focus on my classes. I've already spent too much time with you and Justine. But I wouldn't mind getting together when you gather some of your information. I'd be interested to see what you found out."

"Please reconsider, Michael. I think…"

"Sorry, Father." Michael disconnected the call. *Today is going to be one of those days, Next thing you know, he'd want me to go with him to some place crazy like Rome.*

Michael chuckled at the thought, and prepared for his late afternoon lecture and class.

# Chapter 26 – Communiqué

Cardinal Picoli entered the small office in the guest house, where Gary sat viewing the display of his laptop computer.

"It's interesting that you requested me," Cardinal Picoli said. "I was coming by to show you something. But first, what do you have?"

"A couple of things, I heard something about an angel visit the night prior?" Gary asked.

Just as with the other clergy and staff members who had been asking, Cardinal Picoli answered the question with a pre-fabricated response to conceal the actual agenda of what had occurred. He was confident no one had informed Gary the visitation was preplanned. And due to Gary's background and prominence, the Cardinal included a bit more information in his response. "You heard correctly, there was an angel visit. It turned out to be for the exultation and confirmation of the child. We should be so blessed."

"What happened? I would've liked to have been there," Gary commented.

"It was a surprise to us all. We were performing a special mass for a VIP when the angel showed up and requested for the child. The angel then laid hands and blessed him."

"It reminds me of the visit with the child in Los Angeles. We couldn't witness any angels then, but we sensed a great power and presence there with us."

"These were very much visible. Was that what you wanted to talk to me about?" Cardinal Picoli asked.

"No, but what if we can redeem ourselves with being successful completing the viral components of the Aurora project?" Cabin fever had set in for Gary. He searched for ways to placate those who were searching for him and the child. If successful, he could work with his contacts in the DOD and CDC, such as Doctor Ingram, to terminate their formal investigation into the Waterfall incident. He was upset they hadn't come to his aid already, or provided some form of official immunity since the company was successful with new advances in its research and development into clone technology for the Department of Defense, thanks to the work with the development of the child.

Cardinal Picoli wanted to groan in frustration, but maintained his composure. "Mr. Applethorpe, that portion of Aurora is over. The damage is done. We need to move forward and focus on the child whom Cardinal Millhouse and Father Yancy died helping to protect and advance."

"I've been catching up on some emails, and going over some old ones from Doctor Kaughman. He had assumed most if not all of the key notes concerning the virus project had been destroyed, but he found some obscure ones from some of the original research team members, and their possible launching pad leading to their later successes."

"We mustn't focus on the past."

"Synthetic DNA," Gary said, with enthusiasm.

"What?"

"Synthetic DNA, it explains a lot the way Doctor Kaughman described it according to his email."

"I don't understand," Cardinal Picoli responded, somewhat fascinated. "What're you talking about?"

"From what the virus geeks stated in their notes, the problem is virology genetics. DNA is wanting to revert to its preprogrammed structure. By replacing portions of a virus' DNA strain with synthetic DNA, you can better manage and control any programmatic mutations. Likewise, they reported to have found advanced uses in other areas of Aurora. I'm guessing that's in relation to their success with the child."

Gary's explanation didn't help to clarify the issue for the Cardinal. "That sounds way too technical for me, and as promising as it may sound, that portion of Aurora is indefinitely suspended. The Church isn't going to invest any more into it, and our benefactor nations aren't either – they've made that quite clear. It's over, and our main focus is the security of Aurora's Child."

"Is that how we're referring to Jude?" Gary retorted.

"That's not the point, and you need to limit, if not eliminate your communication with the outside world. You know that you're a definite person of interest to the Los Angeles police according to Cardinal Grielle's report, albeit it's quite lean on other information as to what's going on. Given the loss of Cardinal Millhouse and Father Yancy, and the fact we believe unknown entities are following some of our clergy in Los Angeles, they're intensifying the search for you and Jude. It's a miracle of God they haven't found that you two are here."

Gary sat back in his chair as he massaged his forehead, attempting to hide he was concerned. "The sponsor nations are still looking that hard?"

"Yes, and there may be more to upset them. Diplomatic back channels from those involved with the Rome Council II meetings conveyed that the church betrayed them in some way. And, did you read the new edict put out by the Holy Father?" Cardinal Picoli asked passing a couple of sheets of paper to Gary across the desk.

"No. What edict?" Gary asked as he began to read the papers handed to him.

*At the time of receiving this message, it is to notify you that the Church leadership, through the Apostolic Nuncio-Secretary of State for the Holy See in Vatican City, has presented an official letter of announcement to the nations of the world. The Holy See will publish a modified and condensed version of the letter concurrently on the Vatican social media sites. It is to inform the world governments that The Holy Father is grooming one who will be a compassionate, wise, and spiritual representative for the Church Universal in moving forward to embrace the ecumenical religious and bridge the political desires for many of the nations across the world. Through him, a wonderful opportunity for universal peace is before us. Add to this the past announcement by the appearance of angels several months ago making the pronouncement of "The Child" across the world, we believe one is being prepared to guide the way in peace.*

*We will reject the advent of increased hostility between the religions that has existed in the past and over the last eleven years since the mass disappearance of millions across the earth. As such, we must be willing to pursue peace for the advancement of all mankind and all religion. We should work together to secure a bright future for our brethren, of all whom we are all members of the human race, and fend off any future spiritual threats against the potential of universal brotherhood.*

*One objective to meet this goal is that the Holy Church will begin a diligent pursuit to normalize relations with Israel, and dissuade any adverse...*

Gary didn't want to read any further. "Is the Holy Father serious? How did he come up with this? This goes against everything we had been working towards. Are you going to send this out?"

"It was sent out yesterday morning to our Nuncios and Secretaries of State across the Holy See in different countries to alert their local Dioceses," Cardinal Picoli responded. "The official release went out late this morning making it public."

"What? Parts of this is years ahead of where anyone imagined we should be in relation to the formal revelation and ascension of the child. It wasn't supposed to happen until he turned at least twenty-one..."

"We think this treatise was drafted with the child's influence. Then he somehow convinced the PR staff and Church Doctrinal team to distribute this out to the field."

Gary sat back in his chair. "What?"

"Jude somehow convinced the..."

"I heard what you said," Gary interrupted. "I was being rhetorical. The child can't be doing this unilaterally?"

"Of course not," the Cardinal responded. His voice softened. "We know the child isn't acting unilaterally."

Cardinal Picoli's voice tone bothered Gary. "What is it you're not telling me, Your Eminence?"

"A divine revelation inspired His Holiness and Jude to act."

"A divine inspiration? What are you saying? What happened during that visitation you're not telling me?"

When the Holy Father first indoctrinated Cardinal Picoli into the Holy Order of the Society of the Child, and told him that Jude was special, he had expected someone more of a prodigy, humbler, and more obedient. He now became in awe witnessing an increase in supernatural incidents centered on the adolescent and his ability to perform miracles. Cardinal Picoli believed a new age was upon the Church.

"I've told you all that I know. We should consider ourselves blessed to be witnessing what is before us firsthand." Cardinal Picolo stood and departed the quarters.

\* \* \* \*

Xavier read the encrypted memorandum from Nadia, his primary handler, along with an attached communique from the Vatican offices. When she drafted her accompanying text message, she didn't bother to edit out the numerous misspelled or missed words in the sentences. Her Russian dialect had influenced the message's English grammatical and semantic accuracy. Add the livid tone of the composition, it conveyed she was upset. The embassy in Moscow had received an official communique that the Church will work harder to establish warmer relations with the nation of Israel. It also stated there will be the coming of one who will help to

251

bridge the ecumenical divides that exist between the world religions, governments, and people. All the sponsors of the Aurora virus believed that Vatican City betrayed them, and were convinced that the clone child was their end goal all along. The virus project as the intended primary objective, no matter how well intentioned, was subterfuge. Many of the partner nations are beginning to disavow the supernatural guidance their leaders had received, believing their influence as diversionary in collusion with the Church.

Xavier's main objective was to continue the search to find Gary and the child. Then it hit him, the formal message sent by the Church may have inferred the possible location of the two. Where it stated "The Holy Father is grooming…," where was the most logical place? Vatican-City – Rome. Where else would the Holy Father groom one to become prominent in world affairs? Xavier was confident he could now reallocate the resources following and tracking the local persons of interest to verify the Vatican theory. If validated, he could report back to Nadia for her not to dismiss Rome out of hand. Xavier would need to contact his colleague Ben, the primary associate responsible with following Sister Justine, to prepare his special gear for possible use against two high value targets in Rome.

* * * *

Father Hernandez, Sister Justine, and Michael received a group text message from Cardinal Grielle containing a link to a web page and the comment "First Document." They each clicked on the hyperlink opening the Apostolic Constitutions page on the Vatican's website. Reading the list of articles and announcements, the most recent posting at the top of the list titled "The

Imminent Religious Ascension of a Special Representative for the Holy See," matched the candidate story noted in the text.

Once they each read the article, the gravity of the declaration was yet still to be absorbed. The body narrative hinted of a unique member of the laity embodying a special blessing to the church, and would help to yield an understanding to the recent proliferation of angelic manifestations. Unsure if they should call one another to discuss the document, another text followed minutes later. It requested for each to report to Cardinal Grielle's office at the Archdiocese to debate future options when he returned the day after next from having attended an emergency conclave convened for all the Cardinals in the country by Cardinal Trong, the Apostolic Nuncio of the United States.

# Chapter 27 – Women's Health Center

Working in the Julie Allison Women's Alternative Education and Health Center energized Sister Justine when she was not assisting Father Hernandez and Michael. Over the last several days, she spent less time working at the Archdiocese offices, finding it more rewarding helping the young ladies at the center.

She had read and digested Cardinal Grielle's text after completing a guidance session with a young woman interested in starting the high school evening completion program for dropouts. Sister Justine departed the empty counseling room and stepped into the waiting room to receive her next counselee. The pungent scent of two distinct floral perfumes worn by two of the recent arrivals competed with one another annihilating her sense of smell. One of the overpowering aromas was familiar. It belonged to Megan, the next appointment. She was a nineteen-year-old high school dropout due to an earlier pregnancy, and was close to finishing the evening adult program.

Megan, considered full figured, was tall, broad shouldered, and tomboyish most of her life. When Sister Justine once met her boyfriend Jason, she considered him to have several attributes making him more effeminate than Megan. It was unique on how they complemented one another in their relationship. Once becoming a mother, Megan sought to become more feminine, to the extreme opposite of her normal self. She wore excessive amounts of perfume, over applied her makeup, let her hair grow out, and wore bright floral or paisley blouses and skirts that didn't always match. Since Megan didn't have any close female friends, the center was going to assign a sister and peer-mentor to work with her on how to groom oneself with humility.

Sister Justine greeted Megan with a warm embrace. She sensed something was bothering her.

"What's wrong?" Sister Justine asked, as they strolled from the waiting room down the hallway to an unoccupied counseling room.

"There was this creep staring at me when I walked in."

Sister Justine stopped. "Did he look familiar? Should we call the police?" She dismissed the stranger being associated with Jason, since he'd been supportive of Megan working to get her diploma. Knowing of her history, it surprised Sister Justine and Jason that she had decided to drop out of high school after becoming pregnant and having the baby.

"I didn't recognize him, but you know how sometimes someone seems creepy. This guy did, with his sunglasses and all. He's probably harmless."

Sister Justine understood that not only husbands, boyfriends, ex-boyfriends would be antagonistic to the purpose of the clinic, but sometimes estranged family members. If they didn't show up themselves to intimidate the women, they would use a proxy. For Megan, it was her father who was hostile to her coming to the center.

During her counseling sessions, she communicated he believed himself to be a failure as a parent. He'd yell at her because she had asked for help.

Many men didn't understand the full extent of the education center in providing training for undereducated women who may have been involved in abusive relationships or made flawed life decisions. Sometimes the Sisters would counsel women on reproductive preventative options. This was one of the policies that offended the Church. It made no difference to the hierarchy that most all the nuns and volunteers recommended abstinence and adoption over birth control or abortion. It didn't mean one or more of the Sisters condoned the practice. They still recognized their duty to God. Sister Justine never made the recommendation, but didn't judge if one of the young ladies decided on the procedure. During her relationship with Michael before becoming a nun, they believed that she may have been pregnant. Justine could have faced the same decisions as the women she had been counseling. She stressed for prayer before they made a final decision.

"What did he look like?" Sister Justine asked.

"I don't know, old, like somewhere around thirty-five years old, I guess, tall, skinny, greasy hair, and wearing sunglasses."

Sister Justine wanted to chuckle regarding Megan's concept of old, but kept her composure. "You never noticed him before?"

"No, I don't remember seeing him when I came to class last night after work."

"I'll see if security could maybe make an extra round outside to make sure. Wait for me in the room, and then we can talk."

Sister Justine went back out to talk to Cynthia, the receptionist.

"Cynthia, could you please have the security company make sure they make themselves known? Megan mentioned a stranger making her feel uncomfortable."

"He's back?" Cynthia said with an excited tone. "A couple of the young women have been complaining about him. He's been out across the street the last week or so. He'll show up, and then a day or two, he won't show up at all."

"Well, I wasn't here yesterday," Sister Justine said. "Did anyone mention if he was out there then?"

"No, but that doesn't mean he wasn't out there." Cynthia glanced up, pursing the left side of her mouth, and closing her left eye, looking intense on attempting to recall some information. "You know what's weird, it's when you're here that anyone seems to notice him outside. He never seems to stay long though."

"What does he look like? Did he do or say anything to any of the women?"

"All he does is seem to watch the front of the center...maybe it's you that he's following," Cynthia said followed by a slight uncomfortable chuckle, attempting to lighten the mood.

Sister Justine overlooked the comment, wondering why she herself hadn't noticed the man before. The parking lot for the center was to the side of the facility, and no one seemed strange or out of the ordinary when she would drive to the building, park and enter. Who was he, and was he watching her and not the women coming and going into the center? Going over to the large picture window to look outside showed a busy thoroughfare with

257

a couple of empty parked cars across the street. She went and resumed her counseling session with Megan.

* * * *

A young woman swung the door open into the counseling room occupied by Sister Justine and Megan, and rushed in without knocking. "Something strange is happening at that old abandoned church around the corner."

"Lily, please knock before entering like that," Sister Justine said, irritated and not paying attention to Lily's comment.

"Sister, something weird is happening at that old run-down church around the corner. We're all heading over to see what's going on."

"What do you mean weird?" Sister Justine asked.

"Someone thinks they saw angels."

Sister Justine and Megan's eyes popped wide open. They jumped up out of their chairs, following Lily.

A small flock of women and men from the center streamed down the sidewalk of the side street and joined a modest crowd that had already formed in front of a small deserted neighborhood church halfway down the block. Peeling and faded white paint as if dying skin flaked off the rotted, insect infested wood siding. Weather aged unpainted plywood sheets covered the windows and front entrance. The condition of the building mirrored other boarded up houses on the block. It was a reminder that after the disappearance of millions, there were streets where most of the residents went missing – their clothing, jewelry, eyeglasses, dental fillings, artificial body parts, or other personal effects remained. Many parts of cities across the world had resembled a ghost town. This street was one of them. Sister Justine wasn't sure where everyone in the crowd had come from.

The sound of trumpets or trombones playing in a low register emanated from the abandoned and dilapidated structure.

"What's going on?" Megan asked one of the strangers in the crowd.

"Som'thin weird's is goin' on ins ther," an older black man in the crowd replied.

"What?" Sister Justine followed up.

"Them noises you hear been goin on. Someones walked up to theres and supposed it sounded like two peoples fightins when he gots close. He gots to the doorway and peeked in through the crack in the wood, but ain't see anything cept darkness at first, then swore he saw two angels."

"How long has it been going on?"

"Bout's ten minutes," the man answered

"A couple of kids claimed they heard voices arguing and fighting in there, no one else could hear anything like that," a woman in the crowd added. "All we hear is muffled sounds of something going on."

A police patrol car with two officers pulled up with the crowd parting like a zipper opening to make room on the street. The church structure trembled and rattled as if experiencing a violent earthquake. The ground outside the old building, and all the other occupied and abandoned homes in the neighborhood remained motionless.

With the crowd gawking at the run-down church, someone caught Sister Justine's attention. A dark complexion man having Mediterranean features with slicked back hair, wearing black rimmed sunglasses, and standing taller than most of the crowd, had focused his gaze watching her every move. Sister Justine's skin cringed as if assaulted with thousands of miniature pins as she sensed his piercing eyes staring at her through the dark tinted eyewear. He didn't attempt to be discreet and displayed no interest with the ongoing phenomena occurring inside the old church.

The two police officers inched their way up to the front entrance. A sense of dread overwhelmed both men. They gripped their holstered Taser handles as a precaution. The sound of trumpet blasts wailed inside as if from two different locales and two different volumes. A portion of the roof towards the rear exploded outwards along with an abrupt and concussive boom. The flash of a bright translucent aura spewed out like a volcano for several seconds before dissipating. The large sheet of plywood covering the front door propelled outward and struck the nearest officer sending him falling backwards onto the front portico of the church. Visible for an instant, a radiant and brilliant robed figure darted out of the entrance, followed by another. Both jumped becoming orbs of radiant bluish-white light, and ascended before vanishing. Most everyone second guessed what they had witnessed, discounting it as too surreal. The entire crowd continued gazing upwards attempting to track the mysterious objects. A thunderous rumbling and loud popping sound reverberated in the clear skies.

A female's petite and bronze complexioned hand with unpolished and dirty fingernails firmly grasped Sister Justine's wrist. A pungent musky body odor scent assaulted her nose. The owner of the small hand revealed a middle-aged Latina having dark brown eyes with a prominent mole over the right eyebrow, and dark hair mingled with silver streaks towards the front. It was

Ashere. Her face conveyed for Sister Justine not to resist and follow her.

A large trumpet blast blared from inside and high above the church continuing to distract the mysterious man. The one policeman who had fallen and was picking himself up with the aid of his partner, jumped back as he stood. The two officers approached the open doorway, peered inside the vacant structure illuminated from the fresh void in the rear, and found the building unoccupied. The activity inside and out had ceased.

The man who had been watching Sister Justine turned away from peering into the sky and focused his attention back onto the crowd. He scanned for her. She was no longer among the bystanders. Down the street he observed two women running and getting ready to turn the corner; one resembled Sister Justine from the rear. He sprinted after her, upset she already had a large lead. The other question, who was the other woman?

\* \* \* \*

Sister Justine had taken lead, with Ashere following her down the street, around the corner, and down to the middle of the block into the Women's Center that was vacant, except for one pregnant teenager sitting on a couch in the waiting room wondering where everybody had disappeared. Sister Justine glanced out the large window to see the man approaching the front of the building. She closed the blinds and peeked from an angle hoping he wouldn't see her. He reached into his pocket and pulled out his phone. After a brief conversation, he returned the phone to his pocket and darted across the street through traffic into his car and drove off.

The teenager was relieved to see Sister Justine enter the waiting room, although puzzled by her odd actions and the unkempt woman accompanying her. She didn't know the sister personally, but recalled her working in the center during previous visits.

"Whoa, Sister, I was getting worried," the teenager said, as she rose up from the couch. "I wasn't sure if you guys were opened today, or if my appointment got canceled or something and no one told me. I saw all the cars in the parking lot and the door was open, I kinda got confused."

"I'm so sorry, what was your name?" Sister Justine asked, still panting to catch her breath. She hadn't realized that the entire office staff and clients had all left, leaving the center unoccupied.

"Liza," the teenager replied.

"Liza, everyone had stepped out for a minute, but they should be back in a bit. Would you mind waiting here?"

"Sure." Liza lounged back down onto the couch and started perusing a celebrity lifestyle magazine on the coffee table.

Justine guided Ashere to her counseling room.

"What happened back there?" Sister Justine asked as she gave Ashere a warm hug, who was still breathing heavily. She ignored Ashere's musky and mildew body odor, and pulled up a rollaway office chair for her guest. "What's going on?"

Ashere sat and rolled up next to the counseling table, catching her breath before she responded. "I was hiding out in that old church the last couple of days trying to somehow come and visit you, but you were being watched. I was afraid whoever it was may also be interested in me. Gary and others aren't very happy with me right now."

"To be truthful, Ashere, we don't know who may be following us, or why. We don't think it's Mr. Applethorpe. We heard he may have left the country. Father Hernandez believed someone may have been following us as well when we went to go talk to Stephen Williams."

"Do you have a glass of water by chance?" Ashere asked.

"I'm so sorry. I should've offered you something to drink. Do you need anything else, and not to be offensive, but maybe you'd like to take a shower? We have the facilities here. Sometimes the women who come here are under duress and we provide a temporary place of sanctuary until we can set them up in a fully equipped shelter. I can provide you with some clean clothing."

"I'm fine, darling, simply a glass of water."

"Of course."

Sister Justine went out to the kitchenette to prepare the glass, hearing several of the staff members and clients returning from around the corner. She returned to the counseling room and handed Ashere a dark blue plastic tumbler filled with ice and water.

Ashere gulped the contents without stopping to take in air. "Thank you, that was much needed."

Megan walked into the counseling room startling both women. "Uhm, hello, Sister, I thought we were gonna finish with the education plan for my final semester," she said, scrunching her face as she noticed Ashere's slovenly appearance and caught a whiff of the air. "And maybe you could explain a little bit about what we just saw."

"I'm so sorry, Megan, but this is a very important friend, and an emergency has popped up," Sister Justine said. "Could you please reschedule with Cynthia, and I promise I'll make it up to you."

After flashing a quick facial expression of disdain towards Ashere, Megan turned to Sister Justine and presented a forced smiled. "Sure, that's not a problem." She politely left the room.

"So, where were we?" Sister Justine asked.

"I was hiding out in the church, and I've been trying to get in touch with you here at the center, but I noticed someone was following you. And I don't know if you're aware, but there's been quite a bit of angel activity lately."

"Was that what was going on a few minutes ago?"

"How do I say this...my guardian was busy. I was going to try to get in touch with you, but unexpected entities had other intentions. It turns out that what happened at the old church was a fortunate distraction. It gave reason for you to come over and when I saw you, I had the perfect opportunity to get your attention."

"Your guardian?" Sister Justine said, confused by Ashere's phrase. "Your guardian angel?"

"I guess that's what you call him...or her...heck, I don't know, but I'm thankful for the help. Where're your two friends?"

"You mean Michael and Father Hernandez?"

"Yes."

"I should call and have them come down."

"Will we be safe in here?" Ashere asked.

"We should be – I saw him drive away. But if whoever is following us does come back, he wouldn't be bold enough to come in here, would he?" Sister Justine asked. "Wouldn't your guardian protect us?"

"It doesn't quite work that way, darling."

264

\* \* \* \*

The pictures taken of Doctor Cochrane's room lay atop Father Hernandez's desk, a ritual he would do every free moment while at his desk when not working Archdiocese administration issues for Cardinal Grielle, or administering mass in one of the cathedral chapels. After viewing one for a few minutes, he moved it to the side and picked up another one to attempt and try to make sense of the image. Some of the writings in the photographs weren't hard to figure out, "101," "child – aurora," "bloodline"…this made sense, but how did the information correlate with the unfamiliar mathematical or scientific formulas, or was it a mad man's scribblings? The father tried cross referencing information in the pictures with verses in the Bible concerning angels, genealogies, and other categorical topics. He was unsuccessful.

One person that came to mind who could help decipher the images was Ashere. There was no way of getting in touch with her. She would show up on her own schedule.

Frustrated, Father Hernandez engaged in a quick mental prayer, *Holy Father, please provide insight into what I have before me so that we may continue to pursue and find the truth, if it is your will.* Moments later, Father Hernandez's cell phone rang. The caller ID displayed Sister Justine.

"Hello, Sister," the father said, answering the phone.

"Can you come down to the Women's Center right away?" Sister Justine asked.

Father Hernandez sensed the excitement in her voice. "What is it? Everything all right?"

"Ashere is here."

Father Hernandez couldn't find the words to say.

"Father, are you there?"

"Sorry, yes, I am. I'll be right down. We need to call Michael and let him know."

"I already called him, he's on his way. Please hurry." Sister Justine ended the call.

*She called Michael first.* Father Hernandez wondered if Sister Justine's emotions did lay in her return to the church. Immediately, he chastised himself for his unwarranted thoughts. It shouldn't make a difference who she called first. Despite the time that had transpired working together during the investigations, she was still more comfortable with Michael having known him longer.

The father grabbed his wallet and car keys. As soon as he stepped out of his office, he returned to his desk and retrieved the pictures.

# *Chapter 28 – Discussion with a Lost Friend*

When Father Hernandez entered the counseling room at the Women's Health Center and saw Ashere, a smile burst onto this face. He hurried over giving her a powerful hug. Michael followed next and extended his arms to give her an embrace, but pulled back when he caught the aroma of dirt, odorous sweat, and a hint of mildew. "I'm not trying to be mean, but when was the last time you had a shower?"

"I'm sorry I don't meet your standards of personal hygiene, Mr. Saunders, but I've been trying to keep a low profile."

"I'm only saying," Michael commented, still inching back away from her.

"Michael, be nice and give her a hug," Sister Justine demanded.

Michael moved in and held his breath as he gave Ashere a firm hug.

"What're you doing here?" Father Hernandez asked, wanting to move the conversation forward.

Ashere sat at the head of the small, aged faded wood stained meeting table. "I had a feeling you were looking for me, but I know how dangerous everything still is since what happened at the Waterfall site in Eagle Rock, and

Cardinal Millhouse. I was talking with Sister Justine before the two of you arrived that the angel activity has increased, and despite what many may think, it's not all good. A lot of what's going on is an attempt to lead men astray regarding their presence and the child. I had to try and talk to you regardless of the risks. I've been looking for the right time."

"We are so lost. We don't know where to go from this point on," Father Hernandez said as he sat in a chair at the aged wood table across from Sister Justine. "And there's so much we need to ask you."

Michael pulled a chair from the wall and sat next to Justine. "Wait a minute, roll back, you said there's a lot going on leading men astray? What do you mean by that?"

"You and the father are the religious ones who have the extensive background in angels. You should have a pretty good idea of what I'm talking about."

"We've been speculating, but there's been nothing to say one way or another which angels we should consider on one side or the other." Father Hernandez noted. "So many people seem enamored by their appearance without questioning, we're not sure we can put together an accurate picture of which side of the aisle each angel stands upon."

"And how does all of this play together?" Michael asked.

Father Hernandez leaned in resting his forearms on the table top. "Do you know what we found in Doctor Cochrane's room?"

Ashere smirked at the question. "Of course not."

"101 was written all over the wall, we think we know what that points back to, but we found the word bloodline drawn on the wall. What does it mean?"

"He would've been the one who could explain exactly what that would mean. But I do know that Everest spent a great deal of the monies on geneticists outside of the virus project, and it was crucial to their end goal. Rumor was that they'd been part of the research going on for centuries in the Church, tracing back the detailed lineage of the Holy Father and cataloging the information to the Vatican Library."

"Whoa, whoa, whoa, what do you mean for centuries?" Michael asked. He shifted in his chair, turning his torso in the direction of Ashere.

Father Hernandez and Sister Justine leaned in, intrigued.

"When the company brought myself and many of the other researchers into the project, they told us a secret many in the Vatican weren't told. For us, it was crucial to ensure our awareness on the significance of the genetic research for those outside of the virology portion. Whenever the College of Cardinals would meet to select a new Pope, they now confer and collect information on one's family history. They then correlate it to the information in the Vatican Library's genealogy database. The prerogative is that the Cardinal selected will be the one in line closet with the approved bloodline."

"So how come we didn't know about this before and why are we learning about it now?" Father Hernandez asked.

Ashere reached over to Father Hernandez, placing her hand on his cheek. She caressed it with smooth, gentle strokes. "It's because now is the time for you to learn this," she said in a soft voice and then sat back in her seat.

"You mentioned something about the child's lineage, since he was a clone, wouldn't he have the same genetic make-up as that of the donor?" Father Hernandez asked.

"For his acceptance as the face of the continued apostolic succession, yet future leader for man and church, they searched his lineage attempting to go back close to 2,100 years. They recorded what they found in the private archives at the Vatican."

"So, they went back 2,100 years for what? What happened bac..." Father Hernandez had started. His, Michael's, and Sister Justine's eyes widened and jaws gaped open. They all came to the same revelation.

"Jesus would've had a multitude of descendants from his mother's side. Mary had multiple children, and each one of them having married, would have multiple children. That's why the Church down plays such flights of fancy," Father Hernandez said.

"Yes, but there are many who fall into the fallacy of thinking that there's something unique about his lineage. That's why they venerate the Virgin Mother. They consider anyone in direct lineage blessed," Ashere said.

Father Hernandez sat back in his chair. "But in many ways, we're all of the same lineage as Adam, then Noah by extension for that matter taking the flood into consideration."

"But why a clone child? The Holy Father could've been the vessel for whatever they were attempting?" Michael asked.

Ashere turned towards Michael. "They looked to create someone so special, so unique, and so perfect, that the world would be amazed, someone's humanity who wouldn't have the same failings and negative traits we associate with our frail, fallen condition."

"Then what about the rest of what Doctor Cochrane wrote on the wall?" Father Hernandez asked. "Could this be it?"

"Why, what else did he write?"

Father Hernandez handed Ashere the 9x12 manila envelope. She opened it and pulled out the set of pictures with writing on the walls in Doctor Cochrane's room at Dawles. As she perused the images, she came upon one with the writing of the words Aurora and combination of the letters A, C, G, K, T, X, and Y in various combinations. Her bronze skin tone lost its vibrancy. Lightheaded and dizzy, Ashere gently pushed the pictures away. "This can't be? Did they actually do it?"

"You don't look too good," Sister Justine said. "What is it?"

"The child, the clone child, yet not any clone child."

"Uhm, you said he was the one considered unique earlier with the angel Aurora breathing the breath of life into him," Michael said. "Wouldn't that already make him more unique than any clone child?"

"No, I think there's more to it now." Ashere's voice became tense and fractured with fear. "I assumed it was the wild ideas some of the genetic researchers were working on."

"Working on what?" Sister Justine asked, moving in closer and massaging Ashere on the back of her shoulder to comfort her, sensing her agitation.

Ashere pointed at one of the pictures displaying a pattern of letters. "Where you see the patterns of A, C, G, and T written in triplets called codons. That's representative of human RNA and DNA. The additional

271

K, X, and Y mixed in are variable representation forming unique triplets considered to be …it's impossible…isn't it?"

Michael moved in to get a closer look. "For us laymen, what are you driving at?"

Ashere bit her lip as she looked up at Michael with fear in her tear-soaked dark brown eyes.

Father Hernandez's and Sister Justine's fascination with wanting to hear the answer caused both to miss the expletive in his question.

Ashere hesitated responding. The three waited with patience. Ashere continued after several moments. "In short hand, it's saying there're foreign DNA building blocks in this genome."

"Foreign DNA?" Father Hernandez asked. "What do you mean foreign, like a race of someone other than the Holy Father's?"

Ashere attempted to calm herself overwhelmed by the seriousness on the implications of the picture. She tried to present a composed demeanor, aware of Father Hernandez's, Sister Justine's and Michael's ignorance. "No, it's something more than that. When I say foreign, I mean not human."

All three exchanged quick wide-eyed glances with one another, not anticipating that answer.

"Not human, what do you mean by not human?" Michael asked, with Father Hernandez asking a similar question, and both leaning in at the same time.

"What I mean is an angel."

Again, emotionally knocked off balance, they didn't expect the answer she furnished.

Michael got the courage to ask the question his two partners were hesitant to ask. "Angel DNA? Are you serious? How do you mix the DNA of an angel and a man?" Sister Justine asked.

"The process started many years ago. I don't know if you heard about the news story years ago when geneticists were able to produce florescence in a pig with genes from a bio-luminesce jellyfish. There was also a genetically engineered goat where a spider web could be extracted from its milk."

"What the..." Michael said, smirking and sitting back in his chair. "You're kidding, right?"

"No, I'm not kidding. I was a research grad student at the time when I first learned about one of the many processes in doing something like this. Geneticists spliced, or let's say added, the silk-spinning gene of the golden orb-weaving spider into a goat's embryonic DNA, in this case with the genes responsible for producing milk. After the goat's birth and when it reached maturity, it produced milk that could be strained leaving web-like fibers used to weave an extremely strong fabric."

Father Hernandez rested his elbows on the table top, placed his face down in the palms of his hands and stroked his forehead. "I don't think we understand."

"I know you may not understand much of this, but it explains a lot. The goat-spider experiments worked well because the geneticists spliced an infinitesimal fragment of DNA. This was like when I studied about pig DNA spliced with the DNA of jellyfish, and the fusion caused pigs that did glow. However, the more foreign DNA you try to add in the original host, the bigger the problem with DNA wanting to revert and correct back to its original format. I heard the researcher's beginning attempts at the lab resulted in more than a handful of stillborn, primarily because the natural processes couldn't hold. But they must've found some way to create an arrester protein or blocker for the human DNA preventing reversion back to its original form. And why…" there was a long pause.

Father Hernandez and Sister Justine wanted her to continue when she felt ready, not wanting to rush her.

Michael was a bit impatient. "And why what?" he asked.

"And why the angel Aurora was able to impart the breath of life to the clone child, whose DNA was imbedded with angel DNA. We heard any other time Aurora tried to impute its breath of life, it didn't work until that one time."

"How can an angel have DNA?" Sister Justine asked.

"Because an angel is nothing more than a created being like us," Father Hernandez answered. "They're considered both natural and supernatural. Most everyone always thinks of them as only non-corporeal."

"And if you could impute a portion of its DNA during the cloning process…" Ashere started to say, pausing to allow time to see if anyone of the three would fill in the gap.

"You have a human who takes on angelic attributes," Father Hernandez added. "Angels are capable of taking on physical characteristics. Supernatural still has natural components. Look at the times when the mention of angels occurs in the Bible, and how they sometimes physically interacted with men and women. It's theorized they can sometimes appear as humans, and would have greater abilities than we can imagine, doing things that would seem supernatural to us. I'm thinking of the Book of Genesis and the two angels who appeared as men in Sodom."

"You have an angel helping Saint Peter escape," Sister Justine said.

"Then there's all the visits over this last dozen of years," Michael said.

Father Hernandez voiced another premise that came to mind. "You know they're believed to have mated with humans."

"As in Genesis 6," Michael added, standing up and beginning to pace back and forth in the room. "The B'nai ha Elohim."

"B'nai ha Elohim?" Sister Justine asked.

Michael stopped and stood behind the chair he had sat in, grabbing the top back rail. "That's Hebrew for the Sons of God. The term is said to be one representing manifestations for fallen angels in the Bible. It's used in both the books of Genesis and Job. Within Genesis, the fallen ones are implied to have come down and mated with women according to some scholars."

"Wait a minute, Jesus mentions in the Bible that the angels aren't able to procreate." Sister Justine said.

"Right, in the New Testament, Jesus said the angels don't marry or are given into marriage, thus consummate a marriage-like relationship via, well you know." Michael said. He wanted to be respectful to his two companions. "But if what Ashere says is true, it doesn't mean they could still impute their DNA during the cloning process."

"I see you still remember quite a bit from seminary," Father Hernandez said. "Many think that's a misinterpretation."

"I refer to parts of what we're discussing in one of my classes. I cover angels in the various religious cultures of the world. In Genesis, many accept the angel viewpoint because in the book of Job, the same term is used, and there it's definitive of angels inferring to the fallen ones."

"Some theologians consider the term means the godly line of Seth in Genesis, or the sons of nobility," Father Hernandez replied. "It was in the fourth century St. Augustine who posited this modern prevalent view."

"You're right, yet ancient rabbinical sources, as well as the Septuagint translators, refer to fallen angels and call out the exact same term is used in the exact same context according to the Hebrew texts," Michael said.

Ashere smiled. "I have to agree with Michael on the historical viewpoint. I know that you can take the DNA of a higher creature and integrate it into a lower creation, not the other way around. With us frail humans, our DNA is corrupted, we use a mere small percentage with a big portion considered to be junk where we still don't know its purpose. Imagine if we could turn on or repair our entirety of DNA material. We could be as angels are in many ways, or near like them anyway, super-intelligent, with the potential to possess abilities we couldn't begin to comprehend. One inspirational divine visit told Church leaders that we would break the bond between divine and natural – a child conceived of both."

Michael sat down in his chair again, curious with a specific point on their discussion. "So, how do you get DNA from an angel if the theological inference is that angels don't procreate anymore? Do they have blood, or maybe some have semen, I mean how does that work anyhow?"

"Michael!" Sister Justine blasted.

"Hey, I'm keeping it real," he countered. "We should remember that we're dealing with some natural processes when we talk about procreation. We can't be too prudish

276

about that. It's a natural and biological process that God implemented since the creation."

Ashere interjected into the conversation as she wiped away tears that began to form in her eyes. "We learned of something from my research years ago and it looks like they were able to apply it, my guess is again with divine inspiration."

"We've been coming across that term divine inspiration, what are you talking about?" Sister Justine asked.

"Angels, but more importantly, synthetic DNA. Quite a few years ago, geneticists developed it and found you could accomplish gene splicing and gene editing to help overcome DNA replication and repair issues. It turned out to be helpful with my work on viruses. But the advances we found must've helped with overcoming the limits of major incompatibilities between species. They must've used it to bridge the gap. The pictures you have here show a small fraction of what was accomplished, but enough to show they succeeded."

"This sounds too unreal," Michael said.

Ashere continued. "So, taking what you've learned, imagine if they blended a small portion of an angel's DNA with that of a human. He or she could be taller, stronger, smarter than you can ever imagine. I don't know if we could comprehend the abilities he would have."

"I bet he would come off as being God like. Imagine how men would accept him if he demonstrated supernatural abilities? They could see him as some sort of Messiah figure," Father Hernandez said with despondency.

"Could he have two hearts?" Michael asked. "Remember, we learned about the two hearts."

"Yes, and imagine if he were to sustain an injury that would be fatal to most men. With him, his ability to survive would seem superhuman, almost miraculous." Ashere's complexion waned as she placed her elbows on the table top and her forehead into the palms of her hands. "So, it wasn't simply the breath of life Aurora imputed, but part of its genetic make-up to make him more human than human."

Ashere began to tear up again. "Justin, I can't believe we did this, I assumed you were going to stop."

"Justin? Who's Justin?" Father Hernandez asked of Ashere in a soft and compassionate manner, seeing her distraught.

Ashere raised her head; her eyes glistened from holding back crying. "Doctor Cochrane. We began to have second thoughts and question what we were doing. He had decided to take a short leave of absence before the first event incident in Aguascalientes. They must've convinced him to return to the project and he helped them move forward before becoming conflicted again much later in the project."

The room was silent.

"So, what do we do?" Sister Justine asked, after several minutes.

"Do you all know how crazy all of this sounds?" Michael asked. "A human with angel DNA."

Father Hernandez now stood and paced the room. "We know more of the child, but could this be the secret why someone had Cardinal Millhouse and Father Yancy killed? If an angel was involved in killing those two men, is it the same at Thomson and Thomson and…"

"What about the two men who killed Cardinal Millhouse?" Ashere inquired. "An angel was involved with the killing of the Cardinal? I heard about his death, but I'm not aware of any details. And who is Father Yancy?"

Sister Justine discussed the early portions of the video captured in the Cardinal's residence.

"After the two men killed the Cardinal and started searching through his home office, we saw what we think may have been an angel that killed the two men who killed the Cardinal. It doesn't make sense though," Father Hernandez said. "The persons involved with what was happening at Everest and Waterfall, angels became involved with taking out those who had devised some bad stuff. Why would an angel act out against the two men when it looks like they would be doing them a favor?" he asked. In some ways he considered his question rhetorical, and didn't expect an answer.

"Maybe they killed the Cardinal for other reasons," Michael surmised.

"What other reasons would there be to kill him?" Sister Justine asked.

"Remember the church wasn't the direct sponsor of what was being developed at Gary's company," Father Hernandez replied. "What was told to us of what was heard on the video pointed to those upset at the work lost at the labs."

"That's correct, Father," Ashere said. "Quite a few nations invested considerable resources into the work down in Aguascalientes, mainly for the virus. I'm not sure if they knew how much of their investment Everest divested over to the child research. Our directors in the company overseeing the project told us to keep isolated records for the research and follow on implementation for reporting purposes. We shared a lot of that research with

279

the Waterfall site in Eagle Rock outside of Los Angeles. We were briefed on the dangerous implications of doing so."

"So, if one or more nations were involved with Cardinal Millhouse's death and an angel killed the two men in retribution, or whatever reason for killing the man sponsoring such proposed evil, are there angels heavily vested in the Aurora projects?" Michael asked.

"Yes, that's been the case all along," Ashere said. "Foremost the angel called Aurora."

"I have a question," Sister Justine wondered. "What started all of this? I mean, you say maybe an angel, but why is the church so vested in the virus and the chi…"

"The virus is no longer the issue," Ashere injected, interrupting Sister Justine. "The events that occurred at Waterfall after your visit helped more than you realize to destroy the virus."

Father Hernandez, Michael, and Sister Justine didn't know what to say. All three had assumed the virus might still be of a concern, believing its research and development moved to another location.

The focus of the discussion troubled Sister Justine. "What would motivate the church for getting involved in all of this?"

Father Hernandez believed he had answer. "When Michael and I were involved with our writings in defense of our findings from after the eulogy of angels months ago, I came across some of Cardinal Millhouse's treatises. He was a staunch advocate of Replacement Theology, dismissive of key verses in Romans 11. I even recall that he agreed the nation of Israel and her people were a hindrance to the Holy Church. This goes with extreme elements in the Russian Orthodox Church and other belief

280

systems. They feel that the Jewish belief system is more a stigma in the efforts by the United Nations to establish an ecumenical system to bring about a brotherhood of peace. For the Holy Church, Cardinal Millhouse held fast that through the Lord, and with the establishment of the new Covenant, the Church Universal was destined to receive the promises made to the nation of Israel, with God removing them from his grace. I believe that's why he was seen as the Church's vassal to lead the Aurora project."

"Some of what the father said was part of our secret mission statement in the company. Many of the scientists felt they were doing a godly work," Ashere said, with melancholy in her voice.

"Well now that we know that, why the child is unique, and considering the circumstances around Cardinal Millhouse, where do we go from here?" Michael asked.

"Gary Applethorpe has to be aware of all this, and why the angel involvement," Sister Justine said. "Wouldn't he?"

"It would help if we knew where he was," Father Hernandez said. "We need to expose all of this."

"You're both crazy, expose what?" Michael remarked. "How much you wanna bet Gary Applethorpe wouldn't even talk to us."

"I can't help you there," Ashere said, as she stood and acted as if preparing to leave. "I already feel guilty for all that I've done. Besides, your calling is different than mine. God gives to each man his own destiny, and each decision made is a brick laid upon that path." Ashere paused before continuing. "I need to go, but I need to sneak out of here. The man following you may be outside, and I want to make sure he isn't aware of who I am, just in case he is working for Gary Applethorpe. We know he's not shy about having someone killed."

"We can have our security check to make sure he's not around," Sister Justine said. "Even though he drove off, we want to make sure he didn't return."

"What are you two talking about?" Michael asked. "Someone's following you?"

"I learned this place may have been watched," Sister Justine said. "Ashere and something that occurred around the corner kinda confirmed it."

Sister Justine continued to describe the earlier incident at the small abandoned and run-down church.

"So maybe there was someone following us earlier when we visited Stephen Williams," Father Hernandez said.

Michael agreed. He glanced at Sister Justine who was staring with an unfocused gaze, her eyes glazed over and fidgeting with twisting the silver band on her ring finger. He leaned back in his chair and swung his legs on the table top. "I know you, Justine – something serious is on your mind."

"It's nothing. I'm trying to digest everything," she responded, not wanting to acknowledge Michael was correct. The revelations for what the church had sponsored, and potential of its future direction, disturbed her.

The same was true for Father Hernandez, but he was more successful with hiding his concerns.

## *Chapter 29 – Dispatch*

Cardinal Grielle entered his office, his left wrist still bandaged and arm resting in a sling, found Father Hernandez, Michael, and Sister Justine waiting patiently. The three had arrived responding to his earlier text requesting their presence to discuss the Holy See's recent communique and press release. "Thank you for coming," he said.

Father Hernandez and Sister Justine rose and stood from two new brown leather chairs in front of the Cardinal's desk. Michael rested leaning next to the new coffee and tea bar built in as part of the new credenza extending along the entire side of the room. Cardinal Grielle ignored Michael's breach of etiquette.

"How was the trip, Your Eminence?" Father Hernandez asked.

Cardinal Grielle yawned. "My apologies." He had considered postponing the meeting and coming in later to adjust from the jet lag of returning from the east coast the prior evening. "It was interesting. The recent activity of the Holy See has caused quite a bit of consternation for several of the Archdioceses around the country," Cardinal Grielle replied as he strolled over to his desk chair and sat. "I can only imagine what's going on across the entire

Holy See. Add to it the emergence of new angels and their messages, no one is sure what all this means. Did all of you get a chance to read the information that I texted?"

Father Hernandez answered for the three. "We did."

"That's the reason Cardinal Trong recalled all the U.S. Cardinals to D.C., it was to let us know of the Vatican's pronouncement face to face before hearing it in the news or from other secondary sources. It was to ensure that the Nuncios develop national strategies for working with the press, and passing on to the Dioceses answers to questions bound to come in from the parishes. There're going to be future statements and communiques coming out of the Holy Church with the potential to cause quite a bit of disruption. While I was back there talking to my counterparts, a couple, like myself, are worried by the spiritual direction in the Holy See."

"I hope my companions agree," Father Hernandez said. "Strategies for what? I'm not sure we understand what you're talking about."

"You three came across something that could have a pivotal impact on the church." Cardinal Grielle leaned forward resting his forearms and interlocking his fingers atop his desk. He grimaced from the pain in his wrist for a brief instant before he continued. "Father, I believe it may be a good idea for the three of you to go to Rome and meet with a Cardinal Tullono."

"Who's he?" Father Hernandez asked.

"The Vicar General of His Holiness for Vatican City."

"It's been a while since I had to know the workings of the Vatican, what's the Vicar General?" Michael asked.

"He's a member of the Roman Curia and the highest official entrusted with the ecclesiastical spiritual governance and facilities administration for the Holy See proper of Vatican City. Since the property within the city-state has few true residents, his offices are also responsible for visitors to the Vatican, overseeing on-site masses, along with managing the use of the smaller chapels for weddings, baptisms, and confirmations by church parishioners."

"Do you trust him?" Father Hernandez asked.

"He mentioned he and the Camerlengo, Cardinal Picoli, have been at odds concerning a point of doctrine regarding the future of the church. I got the feeling Cardinal Tullono was attempting to feel me out since the two had discussed the unfortunate events surrounding Cardinal Millhouse and Father Yancy."

"Your Eminence, that may be true, but do you trust him," Father Hernandez asked again. He came off as stern and demanding, close to irritating Cardinal Grielle.

"We have no choice. You read the memorandum published by the See, who is the one the Holy Father is grooming? The fact that the angels made the pronouncement of a child, is it the one associated with Gary Applethorpe. Are all these circumstances connected? Plus, you still have a charge to determine why someone would kill Cardinal Millhouse, if angels could be involved with the death of the two men who killed him, and who was involved with the death of Father Yancy. I'd also like for you to take the pictures and show them to Cardinal Tullono. Maybe he could provide insight."

The three remained quiet not sure how to respond.

Cardinal Grielle continued. "Tell me you don't think this is all connected?"

"Why don't you go, Your Eminence?" Sister Justine asked.

"Me going to Rome without being summoned would be too obvious to those in that damnable Society. The next official scheduled gathering for all Cardinals is a couple of months out. But if you go for other ecclesiastical purposes, maybe you won't show up on anyone's radar."

"Not that I'm one to turn down a free trip to Rome, but I don't trust him," Michael grumbled. "This doesn't sound right."

"Michael could be right," Sister Justine said. "Why don't you send an email?"

"I read a small fraction of mine, less these days. Besides, I may be paranoid, but I don't trust that our correspondences are secure from eyes within the Vatican. I'm convinced the IT department is well versed in facilitating the scanning of our emails. Remember when Father Hernandez and I collaborated and distributed his writings to the journal, we used security measures to ensure their secrecy. We had to go as far as using private commercial email accounts. Since I've taken charge of the Archdiocese, I learned Cardinal Millhouse was aware of more than I realized. And you three mustn't forget there's the strange occurrence with your text messages that you received from unknown sources. What word did the police detective think the letters compose?"

"Rome," Sister Justine replied.

Father Hernandez wasn't confident with Cardinal Grielle's plan. "We can't walk into Vatican City and start looking around and asking if anyone knows of a clone child."

Cardinal Grielle interrupted. "You and Sister Justine are going for your official religious sabbatical to spiritually refresh your relationship with the Church. Mr. Saunders will be going under the guise as one you're attempting to convince and bring back his return to the fold. You can say that you're his spiritual mentor, and all these issues with the angels have reawakened his interest to perhaps finish seminary. You're helping him to research the topic of angelology and church history."

"So, you want us to lie?" Michael asked. "If I remember correctly, isn't there a commandment about that?"

"We're stretching the truth on your part, Mr. Saunders," Cardinal Grielle replied.

"You're good at that, aren't you," Michael said.

Cardinal Grielle's neck veins throbbed. "Mr. Saunders, I may be patient, but I will not continue to tolerate your insolence. There are things more important than any of us in the room that threatens the sanctity of the Holy Church."

"All Michael is saying," Father Hernandez interrupted, "is he wants to make sure we don't end up in pursuing the fallacy that the ends justify the means."

Cardinal Grielle and Michael engaged in a stare down across the room.

"I implore both of you, please, we all want the same thing," Father Hernandez said.

Cardinal Grielle and Michael backed down.

Cardinal Grielle continued. "As I was saying, Father, you'll be staying at the priest dormitories outside the back of Vatican City. Mr. Saunders, you'll be staying at the church run apartments down the street from the father.

Sister, the travel coordinator was able to schedule for you to stay at the convent on the grounds of the Vatican."

"What's Cardinal Tullono going to do that he could help?" Father Hernandez asked.

"He's concerned with the direction of the church and noted there's quite a bit of strange angel activity going on. That's where you three could help in sorting through that. Maybe someone from the outside could get a better view than someone on the inside. There're rumors swirling about that someone may have undue influence over the Holy Father. That's the biggest concern. Maybe you can see if that appears to be the case."

Sister Justine sat forward in her chair. Interested, Michael stood from leaning up against the credenza and moved over to join the group.

"Influenced by who?" Father Hernandez asked. "Angels?"

"He wouldn't say," Cardinal Grielle responded.

"Yep, I'm sure of it, as the big bubbly-bug-eyed guy in that old Star Wars movie said – it's a trap," Michael said, attempting to deepen and alter his voice to mimic that of the movie character. "It'd be crazy to think we'll have access to the Pope."

Cardinal Grielle, Father Hernandez, and Sister Justine glared at Michael with disapproval, even though they agreed with the point of his statement.

"Look," Michael continued, "all I'm trying to say is that they may be trying to get us there to find out what information you have and if you turned it all over to them. They could try to force us to squelch it, that's all."

"I believe this is the best course of action," Cardinal Grielle responded. "And there's something else I need to tell you on what convinced me to consider you going on this excursion. One of my counterparts approached me during a sidebar believing me to be a member of the Holy Order of the Child. He presumed I had the same level of knowledge into Aurora as Cardinal Millhouse since I was elevated so quickly and outside of the normal protocol."

All three leaned in a little closer to Cardinal Grielle as he continued. "He mentioned something that came out of left field, about how we should be ecstatic that the Council of Pisa II tenets could soon be fulfilled, despite the outcome from the Council of Rome having been disrupted on three different occasions."

"I've heard years ago about a Council in Rome, though nothing was presented to us in the field," Father Hernandez said. "And what's the Council of Pisa II?" He asked, not hearing of an official Vatican Council during the last several years, apart from a well-known one called the Council of Rome prior to the mass disappearance on the earth.

"I don't know. I was fortunate Cardinal Millhouse divulged a small bit concerning the Rome Council before his demise. I tried to bluff my counterpart to continue, and at first it was working since I knew pieces about what happened twice down in Mexico and here in Los Angeles. But the Pisa part, I had no idea, and he caught on and separated from me. I did find out what happened was a reported secret tertiary council that occurred during the Rome Council at the same time. When I had a free chance, I did some quick research and found that in 1409, the Church had convened an unsanctioned Council in Pisa. It was an attempt to end the schism in the west at that time by removing Benedict XIII who was in Avignon and Gregory XII who was in Rome. Instead they ended up electing a third papal claimant, Alexander V. I think the second council meeting in Pisa was unsanctioned with ramifications on the future leadership of the Church."

The sense of intrigue motivated Sister Justine to lean in and speak in a soft voice. "Do you know who attended the council?"

"Or when it occurred?" Father Hernandez asked, in a subdued voice.

Michael found himself drawn into the discussion. "Yeah, who did attend?"

"That's an original question, Michael," Sister Justine said, giving Michael a sly grin.

"Ha, ha," Michael replied. "It was a good question."

"Do you know what was discussed?" Father Hernandez asked.

"I don't have an answer for any of your questions, that's why I need you three to go and find out."

"How are we supposed to do that?" Michael asked.

"By Church tradition, the location of a Council archives maintains a copy of working documents, along with the doctrinal statements derived during the gathering, so you'll need to first go to the Cathedral of Pisa. The original treatise and notes are more than likely in the Vatican Library, which would be hard to gain access and review. Cardinal Tullono mentioned that access has become extremely restrictive. Maybe we'll get lucky and they recorded at least the broad strokes of their meetings; afterwards, head down to Rome to continue your research."

"We can't just walk in and ask to see the derived treatises for a Council of Pisa II," Father Hernandez said.

"Cardinal Tullono is working to give you access to the archives on the Cathedral grounds for the Diocese of Pisa by means of his position. He anticipates it could be easier than we imagine. You'll head there first as if you're researching for your special project. It'll be a history of the early Church during the Renaissance in Italy, and the influence it had on today's Pontifical Succession. Using the guise to research the first Pisa Council will help legitimize your visit. Make your arrangements to fly into Milan and then head over to Pisa. From there, you can take the train down to Rome. Plan on leaving here three or four days earlier than your scheduled date to arrive at the residences in Rome to give yourself time," Cardinal Grielle said.

"Wow, you pretty much got most of this figured out, don't you?" Michael asked.

"I'm serious, Mr. Saunders," Cardinal Grielle replied.

"And so am I," Michael snapped back.

"With God's blessing, I'm sure everything'll be all right." Cardinal Grielle said.

"I'll think about it," Michael said.

"Please do, I'm sure you'll be a big help for your two companions when they go over."

Father Hernandez cleared his throat. "All this time you make it sound like we're going."

"A bit ago, you sounded like you were. I didn't want to formally direct you and Sister Justine to go, but imagined you'd want to of your own accord and continue the research and investigation. Regardless, it's a done deal. I expect no less than you two to be on a plane as soon as possible." The Cardinal's voice was stern and firm.

Father Hernandez didn't expect Cardinal Grielle to demonstrate his growing tenacity towards himself. The father glanced over to Sister Justine. The Cardinal's comment shocked her, demonstrated by her wide eyes and raised brows.

Cardinal Grielle continued. "Now if you excuse me, I do have other duties to attend to. Father, please stay behind for a moment? I have something important to discuss with you."

"Of course." Father Hernandez turned to Michael and Sister Justine. "I'll meet you back in my office."

Michael and Sister Justine, puzzled, considered the father would let them know if the private discussion would be relevant.

"Father, can I trust you?" Cardinal Grielle asked, after Michael and Sister Justine had shut the door as they walked out the office.

"Of course."

"Father, can I trust you?" Cardinal Grielle asked again, his green eyes focused on the father with a deft intensity.

Father Hernandez pondered why the Cardinal repeated the question. "You know you can. Why are you asking me again?"

"Because I need to know that you'll present everything to me without holding anything back. Remember that we're doing this for the sake of the Church and God."

"I'm aware of that, unless you commissioned Sister Justine to spy on us again."

Cardinal Grielle's visible facial capillaries on his cheeks and spider-webbed on and around his nose, engorged turning his round face ruby in color. "Father, remember your place. You've been around Mister Saunders too long."

"No disrespect intended, but you know there's no need in asking me such a question."

Cardinal Grielle stared hard at Father Hernandez and took a couple of deep breaths before continuing. "So, what can you tell me about this strange woman you, Sister Justine, and Mr. Saunders had a discussion with down at the Allison Women's Center."

"What woman are you talking about?" The conversation with Ashere came to Father Hernandez's mind. "You mean Dr. Vasquez?"

"I don't know her name, only that somehow she's involved with what's going on."

"She used to be a doctor working on the Aurora project at Everest." Father Hernandez presented Cardinal Grielle with the narrative of her background and support she had provided to his investigation team, withholding the full extent of the discussion in the Women's Center knowing he was aware of the photographs.

"She's the one helping us figure out what's going on with the pictures helping to tie all of this together."

"I do remember you bringing her up with what happened at the Waterfall company when Cardinal Millhouse was alive. So, she's one of your primary sources?" Cardinal Grielle asked.

"Yes."

"Well, I'm glad you're letting me know all of this."

"Don't think we're trying to hold anything back. It skipped my mind about what happened with you being gone back east, and then getting back with all that's going on around here."

"Thank you, you're dismissed."

Cardinal Grielle was taking a risk sending the three researchers to Italy. Although the Camerlengo requested any updates on the investigation concerning Cardinal Millhouse, Father Yancy, or events around Aurora, he had condensed the reports. If Cardinal Picoli were to find out, the Holy Father would recommend some form of censure against Cardinal Grielle.

* * * *

Father Hernandez returned to his office to find Michael and Sister Justine staring at him.

"Well, Padre, what did the Cardinal want to talk to you about?" Michael asked.

"He asked if he could trust me."

"Ouch, that's a blow."

"Why would he ask me that?" Father Hernandez seemed hurt.

After a short moment of silence, it was Sister Justine who answered. "Maybe not telling Cardinal Grielle about the USB from Father Carson upset him."

"I was talking in general. It wasn't about the USB. We'd already cleared the air about that. He felt that I was trying to keep information from him because I forgot to mention our discussion with Ashere," Father Hernandez said.

"Why are you so concerned anyway?" Michael asked. "You didn't know if you could trust him. Think about what he's done in the past."

"I'm concerned because I'm trying to find out what happened for the sake of the Church and what I believe," Father Hernandez said. "I can't keep faulting his Eminence when he's seeking the same as I am for the sake of the Church. Don't forget how helpful he was in our little side writing projects. We're upset at what we see happening."

"How can I when you keep reminding us?" Sister Justine said in a subtle snarky tone, surprising Michael and Father Hernandez.

"Where did that come from?" Michael asked.

"I'm sorry, Michael, I was thinking about something else." Sister Justine wondered how the Cardinal learned of Ashere's visit to the Women's Center. Did he have an informant in the center? Was he becoming more like his predecessor? Maybe Michael was accurate with him becoming more duplicitous. She didn't want to make any unwarranted assumptions and dismissed the idea.

"I agree with his Eminence," Father Hernandez said. "We should go to Pisa and Rome as soon as possible. I'll make the arrangements."

"Hold on, boy toy, I didn't agree to that," Michael stated, beginning to contemplate the impact of the discussions. "You don't think I have classes to worry about?"

"We should go, Michael," Sister Justine said. Despite her apprehensions with Cardinal Grielle, the trip could be helpful.

"What," Michael responded.

Sister Justine continued. "I may not be as well versed on angels as you and Father Hernandez, but I do know we have a purpose greater than ourselves in searching for the truth. Think about what Ashere told us, and what we've found out up to this point."

Michael wasn't sure on how to respond. His companions' eyes conveyed the same appearance of supplication. Justine's round eyes glistened as if tearing up and displayed genuine sympathy.

Michael conceded. "Fine, I've never been to Rome anyway."

\* \* \* \*

"I'm positive, we know that Gary Applethorpe going down and staying in South America was a ruse," Xavier noted on the phone call to his handler Nadia.

"I understand that," Nadia replied. "You said that he wasn't found to be anywhere in the country."

"No, he wasn't. It does seem they tried to put up the pretense he was in one of the retreats deep in the countryside. They put up a good front since it was what they described to be a restricted access monastery. They wouldn't allow any outsiders, nor for the longest time could we find out who was staying on the grounds. We tried subverting a couple of individuals, but didn't succeed on that front. We did manage to infiltrate the site a couple of times but couldn't get a full recon of the entire grounds or any relevant information up until a couple of days ago."

Xavier didn't want to mention they wasted an inordinate amount of time chasing a shadow, not with only the South America lead, but also a couple of other inconsequential leads. He continued. "The team suspects that someone with Gary Applethorpe's description stayed there about a month with a teenage boy. My counterpart reported that they allegedly slipped out and traveled to South Africa, followed by a couple of other locations. One agent even checked to make sure they didn't double back to the States. Each leg of their trip was under the guise of diplomatic representatives on a Vatican flight with a special diplomatic package of high value. Each passenger manifest contained different names and nationalities. We suspect they ended up in Rome."

Nadia remained quiet.

"I need to go to Rome," Xavier said. "I want to pass on to you that the tracking on Father Hernandez's credit card, and information Sanger pulled from a contact he made in the Los Angeles Diocese travel office shows he's making arrangements for travel to Italy, Pisa and Rome to be exact. We know they have an interest in wanting to find him."

Nadia acquiesced and disconnected the call.

Finding out Father Hernandez, Sister Justine, and Michael Saunders arranged for travel to Italy, confirmed Xavier's suspicions about Rome or Vatican City as the next possible step in finding his two targets. He planned to increase surveillance of the three again after considering they may have been inconsequential.

Would he run into some of the same issues as his colleagues? Since learning more of the history for the Aurora project from various sources during this assignment, Xavier became unsettled with what some of his team members called paranormal road blocks. The nations that had backed the virus project did so under the supernatural influence of an angel called Aurora. Yet a suspected angel was to have killed the team that terminated Cardinal Millhouse. Supernatural circumstances of alleged angels reportedly interfered with the disposal of Father Yancy's body. When one of Xavier's team members was about to approach and interrogate Sister Justine, a supernatural event occurred at an abandoned church distracting him. It allowed her time to temporarily elude him before his recall, believing she couldn't provide much information. Xavier also learned of the earlier death of another contract agent sent to Las Cruces to kill Father Hernandez and a Doctor McCall. The medical examiner's report noted traumatic impact by an object causing severe internal organ damage. The coroner equated the force focused on his abdomen to being hit by a fast-moving automobile. On the torso, they found bruising that developed postmortem leaving what looked like the imprint from the blunt side of a large sword.

After a day of preparing his and his partner's travel arrangements, coordinating local contacts, and studying of the Vatican grounds, Xavier became elated when Nadia relayed from counterparts in Rome, they had developed two human intelligence assets within the City. One was a priest, the other a former high-ranking bishop, now a Cardinal. The two were involved in past major acts of indiscretion, and currently blackmailed to provide intermittent information on visiting heads of State, heads of government, governmental ministers, ambassadors, or other dignitaries.

The compromised Cardinal when questioned by the local operative in Rome, if he knew of any high-profile guests, more specifically Gary Applethorpe, responded he was unaware of anyone. The Cardinal noted guests visiting Vatican City would stay in designated lodging quarters off the grounds of the Holy City if they stayed longer than overnight. Senior clergy, including the Holy Father, the Swiss Guard, and key laity staff members resided in the city-state.

Xavier finalized a time to meet with the local Rome operative for assistance facilitating access onto the Vatican grounds.

# *Chapter 30 – Cattedrale di Pisa*

Weary from the intrigue back in Los Angeles, the transatlantic journey for Father Hernandez, Sister Justine, and Michael was uneventful. Thankfully, this was also the case for the trip from the airport to the hotel. Suffering jet lag and displaced by a nine-hour time difference, along with the anxiety of the trip and what they could find, emotionally weighed down the three. They checked into their rooms, settled in, and later spent time together enjoying a modest dinner. As they ate, apart from a few trivial comments regarding the city and atmosphere of the café, their conversation was non-existent.

The next day, after a simple breakfast of pastries and coffee, they strolled over to the Cathedral offices in the Palazzo dell'Opera to meet Bishop D'Arcy at nine o'clock. He was the representative Cardinal Grielle and Cardinal Tullono had coordinated with to assist with their research to find any information on the secret meeting called the Council of Pisa II.

As they traversed the Piazza dei Miracoli and approached the historical Romanesque styled Cathedral of Pisa resting on beautiful alabaster white marble pavement on their left, the Leaning Tower of Pisa loomed closer on their right. Tourists had already started to amble about the plaza to view the historical structures.

"So that's the famous Leaning Tower, huh?" Michael remarked, fascinated by the marble covered limestone structure designed with layers of intricate columns and arches. He'd seen pictures, but to witness the attraction in person was moving.

"We're here to research, Mr. Saunders," Father Hernandez replied, "not sightsee."

"I'm aware of that, Padre. I'm making a comment about the building, that's all," Michael said, grumbling. "Ease up, you can't tell me you're not impressed with the tower and chapel?"

Father Hernandez regretted that he had responded in a chastising tone. Michael was right, the structures were beautiful. "My apologies, I'm a little tense about our meeting, and I'm not sure what to expect from Bishop D'Arcy. I'm trying to stay focused, that's all."

Michael sympathized. "Not a problem, Padre."

Sister Justine smiled that the two reconciled and didn't go into one of their squabbles.

The three approached a row of two and three-story brown brick buildings enclosing the north side of the plaza. They searched for the entrance specified in their instructions, and entered after finding the correct door. A nun wearing conventional vestments and conversing with a young, skinny security guard advanced to greet them speaking Italian. Father Hernandez understood a few of the words with his knowledge of Spanish helping to interpret and understand her remarks. He'd forgotten most of his Italian. He recognized "excuse me," "wrong entrance," "no visitors," "front," and "father."

"I'm sorry, we don't speak Italian," Father Hernandez said in Italian, one of the few phrases he, Sister Justine, and Michael had memorized. "We speak English. We're here to see Bishop D'Arcy."

The nun's eyes widened hearing Bishop D'Arcy's name. She gestured for the three to stand fast, turned and departed down a narrow corridor consisting of a low gothic vaulted ceiling with faded paint and dim lights. The guard remained, staring at the three with a fierce intensity. The nun returned a couple of minutes later with a tall, young olive complexioned priest, his hair slicked back.

"You three here to see Bishop D'Arcy?" the priest asked, with a heavy Italian accent.

"Yes, we are," Father Hernandez responded.

After the priest verified their identities viewing their driver's licenses and passports, he guided the three to where the bishop would be waiting. As they passed through the open chambers of the Chapter Archives that preserved and exhibited various papal and imperial diplomas and documents, some of the placards dated many of the displayed articles back to ninth and tenth centuries. There was a framed eleventh century Exsultet Easter Hymn sheet music faded from the age, a collection of fourteenth century miniature books, autographs of historical Italian artists, and other various historical documents in display cases. Father Hernandez found himself stopping every several feet to view one of the many artifacts.

"Hey, Padre," Michael said in a soft voice after multiple stops, "we're here to research, not sightsee, remember."

301

Father Hernandez smiled. "Point taken. I can't get over the history here."

They continued into the Chapter meeting room lined with wainscot topped with a molded chair rail. Gold-tinted wallpaper with vertical stripes and a maroon flower-patterned felt fabric covered the upper half of the wall. Portrait oil paintings of former bishops and Cardinals responsible for the archives and art collection hung around the room. A late middle-aged clergyman, mildly creased skin, dressed in a black cassock and large gold pectoral cross, stood waiting next to a long cherry wood conference table in the center of the room. Something unique concerning the bishop's eyes caught their attention. Most noticeable, his right eye danced around in a natural manner while the left eye remained stationary and lifeless, even though it glinted from the room light. They deduced it was a glass prosthetic, almost indistinguishable from his right eye. The color and details of the iris and pupil was a near match to his natural eye.

"Good morning, welcome to Pisa," the bishop said with a thick Italian accent.

Father Hernandez and Sister Justine rendered their formal greeting.

Michael shook the bishop's hand still fascinated by the artificial eye. "Not to be rude, Your Excellency, but I noticed your eye; it looks fake. Is it? What happened?"

Bishop D'Arcy arched his eyebrows not expecting the question and presented Michael a small smile. "No one normally direct like that, they pretend not to notice. It is because of eye surgery, afterwards, it get how you say, badly infected and needed be removed."

"That sucks. Sorry to hear that."

Father Hernandez and Sister Justine agreed, although forward, Michael by his standards was delicate and polite. They had anticipated an inappropriate comment to follow. One didn't come.

Bishop D'Arcy continued. "Cardinal Tullono request me to meet you and discuss your visit, and help if we can."

Father Hernandez and Sister Justine still staring at Michael surprised by his behavior, made the bishop believe neither one was listening, but preoccupied with something else.

"Father? Sister? Everything all right?" Bishop D'Arcy asked.

"I'm sorry," Father Hernandez responded, "you were saying."

"We meet normally at my admin offices in Archbishop's Square, but here in archives building seems like it be better location for your research from what was asked."

"Thank you, that's very considerate," Father Hernandez replied.

"I have staff assist in doing early search for you, but Cardinal Tullono recommends we not get too involved. What is he worried?"

Father Hernandez, Sister Justine, and Michael flashed quick glances toward each other, all three wondering if one of the other two would give a reply.

"I don't think this is in my wheelhouse," Michael said after a tense minute with no one responding. "You got a better handle on this, Padre."

Father Hernandez wasn't sure if he wanted to comment, but decided Michael was right, decorum called for him to answer the bishop. "We're looking for

303

information concerning the Council of Pisa II, believing it may lead to information that may have led someone to kill Cardinal Millhouse and Father Yancy back in Los Angeles."

"I hear of Cardinal in Los Angeles passing, but wasn't aware of priest. You think there is something that Church involved that could cause their...what do you say...demise?"

"Your Excellency, how long have you been assigned here?"

"Much my twenty-year career with sometimes assignment across the country, but Church history my passion, being assigned here is wonderful blessing."

"Were you aware of any sort of high-level Holy Council meeting during your time here?" Father Hernandez asked.

Bishop D'Arcy chuckled. "My son, meetings held here all the time by staff of the Holy See as off-site location. They do so not interrupted if they hold on grounds of Vatican City or in Roma. You need be more specific."

Father Hernandez detailed the estimated timeline, with Bishop D'Arcy attempting to recall events around the suspected timeframe.

"If around when you mention, I not here when there was supposed official gathering. I remember because it odd my governing Cardinal ask me questions on beliefs and where I stand on different religious, social, and political stuff about week before. I think nothing of it. My Diocese later ask I support Diocese in another region for two weeks. I learn of meeting while I gone. When I return, I hear rumor that Camerlengo represented Holy Father. He and few of the Roman Curia, and high-level laity meet here for private meeting. They discuss church doctrine and ecclesiastical ambition during my absence. They claim they discuss and make formal a future direction of church, but I not remember anything official published. I forget all about it, I didn't think it be considered a doctrinal convention as Cardinal Tullono noted."

"Please understand we're not sure what we're looking for. We're following a wild hunch for any possible information or recorded administrative documents that could provide some insight or background on many of the angelic incidents," Father Hernandez said. "We think they may have named the private meeting the Council of Pisa II."

"You think they record the meeting contents if it secret, no?" Bishop D'Arcy asked. "To call it Council, that is important. That makes it official church doctrine."

"If that's the case, doesn't the Church have some sort of rule calling for administrative documentation or records for special meetings like that?" Sister Justine asked.

"Especially if it's being referred to a Council, even if not a sanctioned one," Father Hernandez noted. "Throughout the Church's history, that's how we know of alleged past secret councils brought to light. If the results of the hidden conclave transpire, then the claim can be made that it was sanctioned and endorsed by God."

"This have to do with announcement released few days ago?" Bishop D'Arcy asked.

There was a silence before anyone responded.

"Yes, we think so," Father Hernandez said.

"Secret Councils, controversial announcements from Holy See, you say there is reason for concern. I know when I talk with Cardinal Tullono, he upset too by announcement, as I am," Bishop D'Arcy said as he began walking the room. "You not think what you look be found on Vatican Library online archives?"

"Nothing we would have access to. I tried before we left, as did Cardinal Tullono according to Cardinal Grielle. We realize coming here is like looking for a needle in a haystack, but we have to try. By the grace of God, maybe we'll find something."

"Very well, I leave you be, I return to administrative duties. Ask Sister Lucia for whatever you need. I believe you lucky what we find so far. Most meeting records and documents in Italian. We find these copies in English and French recorded for attendees from America, France, Mexico, and Canada. These records here in English journaled in archives. Good luck."

* * * *

After a couple of hours of examining pages of documents, journals, and other records, nothing conveyed anything to indicate or point to a high-level Council meeting.

"You know that the organizers were probably intelligent enough not to leave any evidence or records in the local archives," Michael commented.

"We shouldn't let that stop us from trying," Father Hernandez replied. "They would still have to maintain Church protocol."

Bishop D'Arcy entered with Sister Lucia who was carrying a small stack of papers and a couple of black leather-bound journals.

"What's this, Your Excellency," Father Hernandez asked, standing up, followed by Sister Justine, to greet the bishop.

"In today's computer age, and disruptions since mass disappearances, paperwork still important. After you explain more of what you looking for, I have Sister Lucia do more detailed search for time around the meetings and pull archives for special events, ceremonies, meetings."

"Thank you, these could be helpful," Father Hernandez said.

Sister Lucia placed the items on the table and then left with Bishop D'Arcy to return to their normal duties.

"Great, more hay for the haystack," Michael said.

"You have to stay positive, Michael," Sister Justine said. "It doesn't seem to be that much."

"I agree with Michael, even with this, it seems like we're getting nowhere, doesn't it?" Father Hernandez added while flipping through the pages in one of the journal books he picked up.

"Wait a minute, I think I found something," Sister Justine said, after passing through a couple of pages from several of the sheets she had grabbed. "It looks like this could be relevant."

Father Hernandez and Michael rose from their chairs and joined her, looking over her shoulder. On each sheet, along with the text, was the word Draft in the header and footer on each page.

*As noted in the background of the recent discussions and meetings in Rome, two types of antisemitism differ over time from a direct method to an indirect method. With the direct method when we look at history, the Nazis achieved unparalleled depth with shocking speed. Long term, this was encumbered by the traditional hindrances of logistical execution. As the effectiveness of their program increased, backend throughput capacity was overwhelmed.*

Father Hernandez interrupted. "Wait a minute, this begins with the Council of Rome, why would this be here since Cardinal Grielle noted the inference of a Council of Pisa II?"

"Good question, Padre," Michael answered. "Let's keep reading."

*The Kremlin's more calculated maneuvers, by contrast, have spanned far greater geographical breadth, and over a longer period...The former Romanian Securitate official Ion Lacera documents how the KGB spotted Muslims' anti-Israel animus as an excellent opportunity. The Kremlin viewed Muslims as malleable due to their ancient animosities — a spectacular Orientalizing, which the most ardent of our self-appointed anti-Orientalists today studiously ignore.*

*The Secret Police chief and later Secretary General Yuri Leonopov undertook a program of spreading anti-Semitic propaganda throughout Muslim populations. Suddenly, this produced new Protocols minted in Arabic (elements and terms translated verbatim into the 1988 Hamas Charter), and later displayed for practical intake as far away as the main airport in Malaysia. In Leonopov's view: "We needed to nurture the Nazi-style hatred for the Jews throughout the Islamic world, and to turn this weapon of the emotions into a terrorist bloodbath against Israel." This course of action will dictate time and patience.*

*The establishment of another attack vector is then necessary to further strike at the one nation that other nations properly consider a blight in the Middle East. A biological tool is one potential, and potent, course of action to assist with inoculating and purifying the land. With today's advances in genetic engineering, designer genes with the ability to target and exploit the smallest of attributes of a target group is possible in ways never imagined. Thus, now we can approach the Sinai thorn on multiple fronts – social, economic (explained in Comrade Kroshomev's writings), military, political, and the now new to the arsenal, biological. The purpose of meeting in Rome was to focus on the latter front.*

*The Holy Roman Church, and other Protestant worldly religious members of the World Council of Churches in opposition to the unlawful occupiers of the Holy Land, were inspired by the most beautiful and holy of divine visitor to move forward on this front. The same divine inspirations, we're learning as unpredicted visitations that cannot explain, have allegedly influenced the leaders of several national entities. The Church of Rome is to take lead in coordinating and managing the development of a future biological agent capable of supplementing the other course of actions taken by like-minded nations. The Church will help to obfuscate the true work under the guise of medical clinics, missions, and services. To facilitate moving forward, it is with all intensity that the Holy See coordinates the resources from the represented nations, and those in proxy, at that council. They have promised extensive financial resources to assist with the execution of these plans.*

> *Private organizations and companies will need to recruit like-minded laity members and organizations to assist with bridging the religious-secular gap that exists in accomplishing the research, development, and implementation for the solution.*
>
> *Moving from the secular from the above mentioned, another divine calling has resulted in moving forward with the special conclave here in Pisa, the Holy See with the aid of laity dedicated to the inception of the miraculous true gift provided by Aurora. The recommendation is that those nations and governments assisting with the Sinai-Southwest Asia-Middle East project must not be told or involved. The divine inspiration has revealed whether they're successful or not, with known disruptions and attempts to halt the forward progress, their resources towards development of the biological agent will be a bounty to heaven's Holy Church here on earth, not only in the endowments to be bestowed, but that the fruits of the research will yield a wonderful gift of one divine and natural, a Holy...*

The text stopped at the end of the page. The three frantically searched through the remainder of the newly delivered documents to find one or more pages with the continuation of the exposition. None of the other documents in their possession provided any additional insight.

The pages they did review incensed Michael, but they had a greater effect on Father Hernandez and Sister Justine, whose stomachs experienced the sensation of a gut-punch. By their estimation, the information chronicled the genesis of the virus project leading to its development.

All three believed responsibility had rested with a localized rogue group within the Church. To see active high-level involvement in the upper echelons of the Holy See, in alliance with multiple external entities, was disturbing and appalling. The other question, who or what was the suspected divine angelic inspiration? It would have been more acceptable if they read that the malevolent supernatural forces did have a greater influence than anticipated.

"I can't believe we found something like this," Father Hernandez said as he began to arrange the paperwork into neat stacks. "There's gotta be more that we may've missed."

"Maybe, what we found was a fluke and misfiled or overlooked and was supposed to be destroyed or transferred to the Vatican Library," Sister Justine said assisting with the restacking of the documents.

"I dunno," Michael said, drawn off to the side of the room taking an interest in the pictures on the wall, "we already knew a lot of this. It doesn't tie into what happened back in Los Angeles though. We're going in circles."

"Possibly," Father Hernandez replied. "The religious impact from what we found is unfathomable. There were other nations involved and remember what we saw and heard on the video; they were upset about the virus project. And don't forget that Cardinal Grielle mentioned someone had approached him and said how ecstatic they were to be witness to the fulfillment of all this. How can that be if the virus is no longer a concern?"

"If they know that, they have to mean the child," Sister Justine said.

"He's not directly mentioned," Michael countered.

Sister Justine continued, pointing to and reading the text on the page. "Recall the last sentence of the page we read stating 'the fruits of the research will yield a wonderful gift of one divine and natural. She focused her attention back towards her companions. "It's inferred the research could help yield the child. It's like what Ashere told us, we may not have all the information here since it looks like there could be more. Yet this could point to a possible beginning for all of this."

"We should get this to Cardinal Grielle, and down to Cardinal Tullono," Father Hernandez said. "He has to be told what we found, to see what the Church had planned, and to know this is what they were supporting. I can't help but to see how all of this is but an affront to God in some way. And the influence stems from Aurora."

"This is serious. Can we trust the bishop with any of this?" Sister Justine asked.

"We have to, he's the one working with Cardinal Grielle and sponsoring us coming here," Father Hernandez said.

"Weren't we also getting those weird texts as well, and then that communique that the Church sent out? Like Justine said, even though nothing here directly mentions anything about the kid. I think that's telling," Michael said jumping back into the conversation.

"The way this reads, the primary focus of the Council was the virus. The child may've been a silent side project for the church. They must've wanted to limit what was documented, maybe that's why there's not much here."

"Or there's more than they want to disclose. Maybe Tullono does know something about the child," Michael interjected.

"We need to get down to Rome. We also need to show him the pictures from Las Cruces," Father Hernandez commented.

"Shouldn't we brief Bishop D'Arcy on everything?" Sister Justine asked of her companions.

"I don't know, but protocol would call for it. He's been very helpful," Father Hernandez replied.

"Let's hope he's not a member of the Holy Order of the Child, or whatever it is they call themselves," Michael snickered. "If he is, and he alerts the ones down in Rome that we're coming, you can bet we won't get anywhere."

"Don't worry, Father, Sister, Mr. Saunders," Bishop D'Arcy said. "I'm not member of that society."

Father Hernandez, Sister Justine, and Michael turned to see the bishop standing in the main doorway leading into the corridor and holding a black journal book.

"I admit, I been here couple of minutes listening. My apologies not letting you know. I come back because I read some of what we gave you, supposed it was important, but waited to after you read. Cardinal Tullono placed great deal of trust in me because we do not agree with ungodly Order of the Child. And listen to you three, you don't either."

"Sorry, Your Excellency," Father Hernandez said, "no disrespect was intended."

"None taken." Bishop D'Arcy stepped over to the conference table handing Father Hernandez the journal. "My staff continuing to collect documents for your review, they find this. It looks like it be of interest, many of pages dated around same time as the supposed council meeting."

Michael and Sister Justine huddled around Father Hernandez to view the pages in the journal. Apart from the date atop many of the sheets, the hand writing on each was in Italian. Interspersed with the writing various doodles, drawings, and indistinguishable side notes in the margins.

Michael and Sister Justine couldn't interpret the sheets. Before either one could make a comment, Father Hernandez spoke. "Your Eminence, it's been years since I've used Italian, I can barely make anything out."

"These appear working notes that got overlooked somehow," Bishop D'Arcy responded. "They get mixed in with other archived documents. The pages read coming of blessing, a child believed in eyes of some pre-told a miracle. A company in America help bring forward this blessing, a blessing not shown on these pages. It confirms Council held here was secret and different from one in Rome."

"I bet these were supposed to be destroyed, or at least taken down to Rome. How did they get overlooked?" Michael asked.

"I not worry how they got overlooked," Bishop D'Arcy said. "We should be thankful they are found."

Sister Justine rummaged through the pages of the journal intrigued by the dates. "Just looking at the dates of the meetings, this confirms the Church held other meetings after the non-church entities had left."

"I'll need to send a quick brief to Cardinal Grielle back in L.A. tonight before we head out tomorrow," Father Hernandez said. "I think a lot of this is important."

"You not hear?"

"Hear what?" Father Hernandez asked.

"Yesterday, College of Cardinals called together and immediate report to Holy See for special Holy Conclave."

"What? There's going to be a vote for a new Pope?" Sister Justine asked.

"No, not call for Papal conclave, all Cardinals, those over age of consideration attend to. They not meet in Sistine Chapel, but nave of St. Peters Basilica. My Diocese Cardinal already go to Rome. Gossip is Holy Father in deteriorating health, but receive supernatural sign upon Holy See. Holy Father make public announcement in Saint Peter's square after conclave."

"This means that Cardinal Grielle should be in attendance," Father Hernandez said. "How much you want to bet he's already on his way to Rome?"

"This'll be interesting," Michael quipped. A quick glance over to Sister Justine revealed an unfocused downhearted gaze, as if lost in a vortex of disassociated thoughts attempting to absorb the recently discovered information. "You all right, Justine?"

Sister Justine's brooding dissolved as she shrugged her shoulders. "I'm fine."

"You sure?"

She returned a dispirited stare and attempted to recover with a small smile. "Yes, I'm fine. Let's just get out here."

\* \* \* \*

When Sister Justine returned to her guest room in the convent, she debated whether to go out to dinner with Father Hernandez and Michael or eat with the religious order hosting her stay while in the city. If she stayed, she'd be isolated. Most didn't understand English, and her limited Spanish didn't help bridge any communication gaps the same way Father Hernandez was able to engage in rudimentary conversations. The time alone would allow her to ponder the abundance of information discovered

315

over the last couple of weeks, discovering that a small faction guided the future leadership of the Church to sponsor a plan accommodating the genocide of a race many considered a nuisance. She recalled reading through the paperwork that the Holy Father sanctioned the projects. Sister Justine deduced that not only the Society of the Holy Order of the Child, but many sympathizers in the Church leadership could be involved. Thinking she had absolved the past indiscretions with Cardinal Millhouse and Grielle, the recent activities reawakened her disdain of their earlier behavior. Yet she needed to maintain a heart of forgiveness, but with the Church still moving in a reprehensible direction, could Father Hernandez, Cardinal Grielle, Cardinal Tullono, or even Michael, help turn that around?

# Chapter 31 – Travel to Rome

Minutes before sunrise, Father Hernandez, Sister Justine, and Michael boarded a high-speed Trenitalia train destined for Rome. Michael sat opposite Father Hernandez and Sister Justine in the aisle seat at a business class table near the end of the car. The train's momentum, and the window scenery of the station transitioning into a view of the early dawn city scape passing by, indicated the train had begun its two-and-a-half-hour journey south. Sister Justine found interest in a novel she had bought while on the trip. Father Hernandez began to consume his time scouring through the pictures retrieved from Las Cruces, and reviewing photocopies of the paperwork discovered in Pisa, having made digital copies of all the documents and images on a USB drive. He replayed the conversation with Ashere in his mind as he examined two pictures he held. What was so unique about the genetic makeup of the child if mixed with angelic DNA?

After ten minutes of reading a couple of thesis arguments on his tablet submitted by his students, Michael became bored and turned off his device. "Why are you still going over that stuff, Father?" he asked, noticing Father Hernandez sifting through the hard copies of pictures and documents relating to Doctor Cochrane's room. "Before we left Los Angeles, on the plane, dinner last night, you should give it a rest. Ashere kinda explained a lot of that stuff."

"Do you know that you called me Father and not boy toy?" Father Hernandez replied.

"Maybe because you're not as annoying as you used to be," Michael said, displaying a slight smile.

"Why, Michael, I think that's one of the nicest things you ever said to me."

"Hey, I was simply asking a question about the papers and pictures. I didn't know you were going to turn it into a love fest."

"I don't know what it is, but I think there's something here that we're missing. I went over all of this in my room last night after we had dinner, and nothing is jumping out at me."

"No, we're not obsessed, are we?" Michael said.

"I have to agree with Michael," Sister Justine said, "you've been absorbed by those pictures and documents."

"I'm hoping these help lead to the true spiritual source of what's going on in the church, and what's so special about the child."

"What's going on in the Church?" Michael chuckled sardonically. "I can tell you what's going on in the Church – you had men like Cardinal Millhouse, Father Yancy, and others in that Order of the Child driving a subversive agenda. Besides, Ashere pretty much told us about the child."

"You see, Michael," Sister Justine said, "that's where I think you and the father and I differ. We believe the Church is good, it's men who pollute it. Remember we're all not without sin, even though some men sin more than others. We put our faith in God, not men, regardless of their position or status."

Father Hernandez smiled. "Well said, Sister."

Michael knew Justine, it sounded as if she didn't agree with her own statement. He decided not to pursue the contradiction in case he misinterpreted her subtle inference. "Well, you're still spending a lot time with those pictures," he said as he rested his head on the headrest and closed his eyes.

Father Hernandez decided to take a break from viewing the images. "You know these trains are much nicer than the ones I rode years ago coming here to Italy," he said laying the paperwork he had held in his hands onto the table surface. "They were the archaic square boxy style trains you used to see in the old movies. The second-class cars had the hallway on the one side, little rooms with opposing wood benches, and glass looking out into the corridor. They didn't even have air conditioning. You had a window you would roll down."

"Geesh, how long ago was that?" Michael asked, his eyes still closed. "From what I read earlier, these streamlined trains have been in service for two or three decades."

"Probably about thirty-five years ago, about a year or so before they took the last of them out of operation. I had just become a priest and was here for my first sabbatical for indoctrination and ordination into the ministry."

This was the first time Michael thought about Father Hernandez's age. His vigor and passion during their investigation, as well as his lack of gray hair, gave Michael the impression he was closer to his age of thirty-six or south of forty.

"Just how old are you, Padre?" Michael asked, opening his eyes. As Michael did, he glanced down the aisle several rows back to see a thin, dark-skinned male, blond afro, direct his eyes away from looking at him to viewing a tablet device.

"I'll be fifty-seven in a couple of months. Why, you thinking of getting me a present?" Father Hernandez quipped.

Sister Justine chuckled.

Michael focused his attention back toward his companions and smiled. "That's pretty funny." Glancing back down the aisle, the man was still engaged in viewing his tablet. "I'm gonna try and take a nap." Michael closed his eyes again.

Twenty minutes passed. Michael awoke not anticipating the change of motion with the intense lean of the car as the rhythmic movement of the high-speed train negotiated a turn. The man down the aisle was once again looking in their direction. His eyes locked with Michael's. The man returned to staring at his tablet. Michael narrowed his eyes and stared at him for a couple of minutes. He shifted in his seat, closed his eyes, and reopened them seconds later. The man remained engaged in viewing his tablet. Michael readjusted himself in his seat again, closing his eyes for a moment longer than his preceding attempt before reopening them. The man's position and activity remained unchanged, apart from a quick glance in Michael's direction before returning to viewing his tablet.

The way Michael fidgeted about in his chair, Sister Justine sensed something was bothering him. "What's wrong, Michael?"

"What makes you think something is wrong?"

"The way you keep moving around in your seat. Is something on your mind?"

Michael peeked down the aisle before answering in a soft tone. "There's a man sitting a few rows back. He keeps looking away each time I look at him."

Sister Justine began to twist her head to peer around the glass panel separating the seating sections to look behind and down the aisle.

"Don't turn around," Michael said in an anxious tone.

"Why? You think we're being followed?" Sister Justine asked.

"I don't know what I'm saying, it's weird, that's all."

"Maybe he thinks you're not your typical obnoxious American tourist, well, American tourist anyway," Father Hernandez said, followed with a wry smile.

Michael rolled his head in the headrest to face Father Hernandez, who had returned to scanning through the pictures and documents on the table top. "You're on a roll today, aren't you, Padre? I'm impressed, but something seems off."

The train slowed down. The public-address speakers blared an announcement in Italian, followed by an announcement in English, "Florence, now arriving, Florence. If this is your station, please gather your belongings. This is Florence."

Michael stared down the aisle to witness the dark-skinned man with blonde afro grab a camouflaged patterned backpack resting in the seat next to him, stand, shoulder it on his back and walk down the aisle in his direction. Michael caught the glimpse of an Aztec style sun tattoo on the back of the man's hand, as he glanced away not wanting to look like he suspected someone may have watched him and his companions. None of the three noticed the man scan the papers and pictures on the table top as he strolled by to the train car door.

The train stopped. The man exited onto the platform after the doors opened.

*   *   *   *

In Rome, Father Hernandez, Sister Justine, and Michael weaved through the throng of passengers in the busy Termini station out to the street to search for a shuttle or taxi service. It was Sister Justine who spotted a white Ford mini monovolume passenger van several car lengths away from the station entrance towards the end of the loading zone. Standing on the sidewalk next to the vehicle was a middle-aged man holding a placard displaying Hernandez – Gates – Saunders.

"Is that for us?" Father Hernandez asked as they approached the man.

"You names the ones on the sign?" the man responded with a heavy Italian accent.

"I'm sorry, yes, I'm Father Hernandez, this is Sister Justine and Michael Saunders," Father Hernandez said.

"Excellent, Cardinal arranged this for you."

The three assumed Cardinal Tullono made the shuttle arrangements since they conveyed their schedule to him and Bishop D'Arcy.

"Get in, I load your luggage," the man continued. Along with the suitcases, he reached for the father's attaché as the father went to enter the van.

"Thank you, but I'd like to keep this with me," Father Hernandez said, holding onto the case's handle with a firm grip.

"You be more comfortable with it back here," the man said.

Father Hernandez released the attaché succumbing to the driver's determination and sincerity displayed in his eyes. The driver loaded the remaining baggage into the rear of the vehicle as they situated themselves inside the van.

"Where do you go?" the driver asked after he entered the vehicle. "Residences, Vatican, off site Vatican offices?"

Father Hernandez stated the address.

The driver placed a call on his smartphone. "I have the three from train station headed to dormitory residences located on Viale Vaticano," he said using the vehicle's hands-free audio system connected by the Bluetooth of his mobile device.

A voice responded blaring in the interior of the van from the vehicle speakers. "After you drop off passengers, Cardinal Dimitz needs pick up from meeting at Piazza di San Giovanni offices."

The driver acknowledged. En route to their destination, he flooded his passengers with a torrent of questions. "This first time in Rome?", "How long you here for?", "What part of America you from?", "What do you think of city?", "Will you have time to tour city?", "Do you need to know good restaurants?" Before anyone could finish answering a question, he continued onto the next, frustrating each one of the three.

Just under ten minutes, the van pulled up arriving to the dorm residences half a block from the rear administrative and clergy entrance of Vatican City.

"Sorry I rush, I need hurry and do another run, I unload your luggage," the driver said as he braked, put the vehicle in park, and jumped out leaving it running.

"Wow, he can talk, not one of us could get a word in edgewise," Michael said.

"Michael, ssshhh," Sister Justine said as the rear panel door of the mini-van opened. "Be nice."

Father Hernandez, Sister Justine, and Michael got out and stepped to the rear of the van finding the driver closing the rear door after unloading the luggage, placing the final roller suitcase in formation on the sidewalk.

"Have excellent day," the driver said as he dashed back into the van and sped away.

"You're right though, Michael, that was one heck of an experience," Father Hernandez said. He reached for his roller suitcase but didn't find his attaché. "Hey, my briefcase, it's not here."

The father circled the other pieces of luggage to make sure he didn't overlook it.

"You mean it's still in the van?" Sister Justine said.

"Hey wait," Michael hollered as he began running down the narrow street and waving his arms, stopping after several seconds realizing the fast-moving van was too far away as it rounded a bend in the roadway.

\* \* \* \*

Father Hernandez, Sister Justine, and Michael spent the remaining morning hours talking to personnel in the Vatican City's transportation services attempting to track down the vehicle and driver who inadvertently drove off with the father's attaché. They became worried after contacting Cardinal Tullono's office for help when his staff reported they weren't aware of any of the white minivans owned by the Vatican City used as a shuttle service to the train terminal or airport. Protocol called for use of commercial livery companies or taxis. When asked to recall if the license plate began with the letters SCV or

324

CV just in case Cardinal Grielle or Cardinal Tullono did coordinate special arrangements with the transportation office, Sister Justine remembered the plate on the van displayed Roma followed by a series of letters and numbers. The transportation staff instructed the three to contact the Rome police and file a theft report. Vehicles assigned to the city-state would not have Rome or Italian plates.

# Chapter 32 – Infiltration Planning

W hen Xavier arrived at his hotel room in Rome, he reviewed the paperwork and pictures his Rome counterpart had stolen from Father Hernandez. He didn't anticipate the plan to retrieve the father's briefcase would work so well with such short notice. He scanned and forwarded digital copies of the documents and images to Nadia. Then he destroyed the physical copies after she verified receipt of the electronic transfer.

Xavier had deliberated on ways to enter the grounds of the Vatican to recon and see if Gary was on site. One of his objectives would become more difficult. Learning the Holy Father summoned every Cardinal worldwide posed complications for himself and members of his team's ability to penetrate the Vatican City with the anticipated increased security.

* * * *

Late in the afternoon, Xavier arrived at the Caffè Tazza D'oro down the street from the Piazza della Rotonda as instructed when he received a response to the information he transmitted to his handler. He hadn't expected to hear anything back so soon. As Xavier strolled up to the entrance, a pale broad-shouldered, middle-aged man, cratered face, wearing wire rim glasses, balding with a comb over, approached holding his arms out as if to give him a hug. The man with the cover name Angelo matched the description of the local operative he was to meet. They embraced and greeted one another as if long lost friends.

Angelo whispered the pre-arranged phrase into Xavier's ear. "I understand a babysitter vacancy may open up soon."

Xavier responded. "Sometimes the wrong person is hired."

Angelo backed up and smiled. "My friend, look at you, you're looking well."

"Thank you, so do you."

"I almost didn't recognize you. You changed your hair color, I see," Angelo said. "Our mutual friend told me it was blond."

"Yes, I was getting tired of it."

"Good, I was going to recommend you do so, so you didn't stand out amongst the other press members."

They ordered an espresso shot from the café, drank, and left to meander down a narrow gray brick lined pedestrian thoroughfare. Angelo guided Xavier to an area with few tourists and shops.

"Thank you for assisting in acquiring the information from the priest," Xavier said. "When I passed by him on the train, I sneaked a quick look. It looked interesting. I hope it was helpful."

"Very much so," Angelo replied. "With what the church team has learned about what happened at the meetings in Rome those years ago, it's disturbing on how the divine influences led so many of our leaders astray. We heard rumors of a meeting in Pisa at the same time. And thank goodness the notes and papers didn't identify any prominent names or countries from what we reviewed. The information helped to show the church did willingly deceive the benefactors. A scientist and an analyst who reviewed the images and documents retrieved and forwarded have proven that point. We want to reemphasize that no matter how you do it, clean up the fruit of their efforts and remove the company caretaker. Do it as soon as possible. The Church has been sending out bold and inflammatory statements our bosses don't appreciate and could undermine the ground work for some future plans."

"I understand, and does Nadia send her wishes?" Xavier wanted to ensure his handler concurred with the final actions.

"Nadia won't be able to assist anymore, she's been reassigned. Her not moving forward to investigate Rome as a potential location to find our friend based on your earlier recommendation seems to have hurt our cause. Because of the delays, we could have moved sooner, but now with all the Cardinals in town, and the information about our common interest coming out, security is going to be a bit of an obstacle, but not impossible."

"Will we be able to use one of the Vatican assets you groomed for me and my team's access?"

Angelo scratched his ear. "We're still working on that and any credentials you may need. I'm waiting to hear word, but he's determined to assist us not wanting to have certain pieces of his background exposed in the media. Be patient, if successful, the contact will coordinate with me and validate your access. Then, if the opportunity arises, you can do your research and final interview with the babysitter. With the short amount of time we have, we have intermediates working on your backstory. You and your team's background, and being contract make it a little harder. Also, with this event they're planning, it's turning out to be both good and bad for us."

"How's that?"

"They've invited quite a bit of press to cover whatever it is they're planning to reveal."

"You should be able to use some of my team's earlier credentials."

"That's what we're updating and building on to fill in holes since you last used them. We also estimate it'll be harder to move around with the extra security and personnel on site, but it's doable. Regardless, get the job done at the first opportune time."

"Why not wait?"

"We want to take away the Church's momentum, especially since our employers feel betrayed. If you're effective, expect a bonus."

"Would your aide on the inside be able to help direct us to our mutual friends?" Xavier asked. If the subverted clergy member was able to assist with providing access onto the grounds, he could know the location and whereabouts of Gary and the child.

"The friends on the inside have all been insistent that they're not aware of any special guests, although the strange supernatural events identify something is going on."

Angelo stopped and turned to Xavier. "We should do dinner next time," he said, as he gave Xavier a cordial embrace. "I'll send you information about where and when after I hear back about the reservations I made."

"Yes, we should," Xavier replied, knowing the context was that the two will not be meeting again face to face.

\* \* \* \*

Cardinal Tullono hadn't expected the email so soon after a phone call from the man he knew over the years who worked for a small press bureau as Angelo. The official email package would be a request for two members from the American bureau of the new wire service. They would collect information for a news documentary.

The Cardinal forwarded the email to the Vatican City Public Affairs email address, and walked down to the office to follow up. The Public Affairs administrative assistant had opened the email and attachments. The first document with the letterhead logo and business information for one of the lesser known news wire services was an official press credentials request for two of their staffers. The other attachments consisted of the resumes and personal background information for a reporter and photographer/videographer assigned to the American news wire's European office.

"You should've gotten this to us sooner, Your Eminence. We're not sure if we have time to do a full background check with our security services and Interpol. We're rushing to finish the badges and identification for the different press events as it stands now. We learned the Camerlengo added a last-minute reception event at the Santa Maria Regina Chapel that we need to clear."

"I understand," Cardinal Tullono said. "But I received this a few minutes ago, the news bureau wasn't sure they would be able to send someone, but managed to have a team free up at the last minute. They called me up and asked if I could help this one through. I'd be so thankful if you could do this for me. The Bureau Chief is a good friend. We kind of worked together when I was assigned in the Ecclesiastical Province of Milan in Northern Italy."

The administrative assistant groaned.

Cardinal Tullono worried that if he couldn't get credentials for the reporter and photographer allowing for their attendance to the event, his blackmailer may consider it a slight, regardless that he had been able to provide information when requested in the past. Cardinal Tullono didn't want Angelo to expose his affair with a church staff member during his earlier years right after he became a Bishop while in Northern Italy. The result of his affair was an older teen now in high school, and years of monies for her and the child's support.

The administrative assistant sighed. "We'll see what we can do, but I can't promise anything. Maybe we can try and get them to attend the new smaller event since they're not assigned to one of the major TV carriers or newspapers."

"Thank you."

# Chapter 33 – Meeting with Cardinal Tullono

The following morning, Father Hernandez, Sister Justine, and Michael didn't anticipate the throng of tourists and worshipers visiting the Vatican City. Many travelled there to visit one of the most revered historical religious sites on the planet, and as a personal spiritual pilgrimage. They looked to the Catholic Church as providing guidance and insight to the supernatural angel events occurring across the globe over the last twelve years. The recent enigmatic angel events also spurred an increased interest in different religions across the world.

After the three presented their credentials, and validated the purpose for their visit after checking in through security, they waited for an escort to Cardinal Tullono's office located in the Pontifical Governate building. A couple of hours passed before someone was able to assist, with the administrative offices active in managing the arrival and lodging for all the Cardinals, the last ones from outside the Holy See having recently arrived on site.

* * * *

Cardinal Tullono received a memorandum on the finishing of the art pieces initiated by the Holy Father and child. Learning of their recent completion, he suspected that Cardinal Picoli had already commissioned them prior to the official submission request to his office staff for review. He continued to read and discovered that the Public Affairs office scheduled a press event for their showing the next day.

Cardinal Tullono slammed his hand on the desktop. "Damn them."

He jumped out of his chair and rushed out of the office down to the Chapel of Santa Maria Regina della Famiglia to view the artwork. When he arrived, two four-foot-tall paintings on large easels were resting behind a marble table that sat in the middle of the dais. They stood in front of the existing wall mural with the image of the Madonna enthroned with Child between two saints.

On an oversized easel to the right rested an oil painting displaying a throng of angels bowing to the image of the tall child within an obscure and abstract background. Cardinal Tullono's stomach turned at what he considered a sacrilegious and blasphemous piece of art, ignoring the second painting, and not aware of a new statue erected over in the left transept opposite the side entrance leading to the atrium hallway into the connected Pontifical Governate building.

Not wanting to remain in the chapel, he returned to his office finding Father Hernandez, Michael, and Sister Justine waiting in the reception area.

"You three are?" The Cardinal asked, in an overt gruff tone still perturbed by the artwork.

"Your Eminence," one of the administrative nuns said, "these three are here to see you arriving from Pisa after visiting Bishop D'Arcy."

Cardinal Tullono's aged and thin face displayed a broad smile. "You're the ones from Los Angeles?"

"Yes," Father Hernandez said, standing to greet the Cardinal, followed by Sister Justine and Michael, all three who shook the Cardinal's hand.

"Sorry for the delay in meeting with you. It's gotten to be busy around here the last couple of days finding out the Holy Father recalled every Cardinal in the See and scheduled some sort of historical event at the last minute. I went to go take care of some business concerning a special project in one of the chapels."

"You don't have to apologize, Your Eminence, we're very appreciative of your time to meet with us," Father Hernandez responded.

Cardinal Tullono invited his three guests into his office and offered for them to take a seat at a small meeting table off to the side of the large room. "My staff informed me about what happened yesterday with your briefcase and the mysterious vehicle. Were you able to recover it?"

"No," Father Hernandez responded. "I filled out a police report. I'm lucky that my passport and other identification were in my money belt. I doubt whoever took my attaché would understand what was inside anyhow. Yet I can't believe it was done by accident with someone going through that much trouble to steal what may or may not be insignificant."

"So, you think this was planned?" the Cardinal asked.

"They had a sign with our names and tricked us into their vehicle," Sister Justine said. "We had planned on taking a taxi over here, but assumed some other arrangements had been made. And with what happened to Cardinal Millhouse, Father Yancy, and someone following us back in the states, we never imagined something like this would happen over here."

"So, catch me up as best you can and why you would think that someone would want to steal your briefcase?"

Father Hernandez removed a thick silver pen with blue trim from his pants pocket and separated it into two halves to expose the thicker one containing a USB connector. Michael and Sister Justine gawked at each other upon recognizing the concealed storage device. They had anticipated the father to bring a backup set of documents and pictures in his luggage, or some sort of electronic USB device, but not the same one owned by Father Yancy. Father Hernandez avoided making eye contact with his two companions.

"Your Eminence, could someone on your staff assist me with printing some of the information on this USB key?" Father Hernandez asked.

"Of course," Cardinal Tullono replied. He escorted Father Hernandez out of the office.

The Cardinal and Father Hernandez returned a couple of minutes later. The three spent short of twenty minutes illuminating the Cardinal on the broad details of their earlier exploits, first going back to the Thomson and Thomson investigation, as well as the timeline of events leading up to their visit to Rome. Michael and Sister Justine included the events back to their first investigation in Aguascalientes and El Refugio, Mexico. They then emphasized the earlier incidents regarding Stephen Williams, since it had a major impact on their overall progress. They steered away from the core of the major religious or scientific sections, unable to determine how to best broach the subject on Ashere's most recent revelations.

During their chronicling of events, all three pondered if they could fully trust Cardinal Tullono. By the widening of his eyes and mouth gaping open at times, his reactions appeared genuine. He was either a good actor, or not entirely briefed by Cardinal Grielle, ignorant on many of the investigation details.

Likewise, during their exposition, Cardinal Tullono surveyed and scrutinized each one's body language, facial expression, and voice to help quantify the veracity of their extraordinary report. "That's quite an account of what you three have been through," he said, overwhelmed by the surreal account of the three Church investigators. "Nevertheless, some of what you've mentioned regarding angels in all of this sound too unbelievable for me to accept."

Although alleged strange angelic incidents occurred on the grounds of the city, Cardinal Tullono hadn't experienced any firsthand. It was easier for him to comprehend the fiscal and biological components of their chronicles.

The Cardinal sat back in his chair interlocking his long thin fingers on his chest. "What you're saying is that all the while the church received monies from various nations across the world for vaccines, medicines and other medical services to support medical missionaries, they paid Everest as the primary contractor, who then siphoned some of those monies to work on the virus, as well as added monies from the Department of Defense for the United States to work on clones. Why didn't they pay Everest directly and bypass the church?"

"A couple of nations did," Father Hernandez answered. "But for others, financial laws and auditing requirements meant a more stringent oversight by their governments is our guess. By going through the Church and Vatican City, it looks innocuous since the monies could be seen as donations, and the donations given to Everest as legitimate services for vaccines, medical supplics and the like to support the Church's missionary services."

"Basically, the monies were misused for other than their intended purposes," Michael added.

Cardinal Tullono leaned in and began tapping his fingers on the table top. "You know that the amounts I'm imagining to carry out such a venture, the group responsible for financial decisions is the Cardinal President of the Pontifical Commission for Vatican City State, which is the executive body as part of the Roman Curia. And you're saying some of the monies went to develop a deadly virus, and some used to develop a clone child?" the Cardinal inquired. "Both sponsored by the Church?"

"Yes," Father Hernandez replied. "We discovered paperwork showing the Councils in Rome and Pisa had planned a lot of this from the beginning with what appears to be an angelic influence. Who in the Church knew what at what level, we don't know."

"Enough," Cardinal Tullono said, finding it difficult to absorb the information, and not sure if he wanted to accept its veracity. He took off his glasses with his pale and gaunt hands, placed them on the table top, and rubbed his eyes in frustration. "You know what my next question is?" he asked. "The child is a clone of who?"

Neither one of the three wanted to respond, still unsure if they should trust him, despite having divulged a full exposition of their exploits up to the present. They were relieved when a staff member walked in carrying a small set of papers and the USB device concealed as a pen.

"Here are the documents and pictures you requested, Father," the staff member said.

"Good, let's take a closer look at them," Cardinal Tullono entreated, putting his eyeglasses back on.

Father Hernandez received the document and picture printouts, laying them on the table top, orientating them for the Cardinal to view.

"So, what do we have here?" the Cardinal asked.

Father Hernandez, Sister Justine, and Michael circled around him. The Cardinal picked up the pictures first, absorbed, but confused by the images. "What's going on here with all of this?"

"These are from the room of the doctor we mentioned who was in New Mexico. He scrawled information about the genetic makeup of the child, and it was validated by our primary source," Father Hernandez replied.

"You never did tell me who the child is a clone of," Cardinal Tullono said.

Father Hernandez, Michael and Sister Justine made passing glances amongst each other. If one of them did give the Cardinal a direct answer, they would betray an earlier agreement between each other not to reveal the alleged full scope of the child's genetic makeup.

Cardinal Tullono's face tensed, his neck veins began to throb. "I insist that you tell me. I was under the impression from Cardinal Grielle that you would be open with what you've learned. Why do I have the feeling you're holding something major back?"

Father Hernandez relented. "The Holy Father."

Cardinal Tullono was now lightheaded. He began to sway in his chair. "The...Holy...Father? Why would...what...the Holy Father?"

"Yes, the Holy Father," Sister Justine said.

"Why the Holy Father?" Cardinal Tullono asked. His question was both rhetorical and inquisitive. He mentally juggled different scenarios on how to disclose that Gary and the child resided on the city-state grounds. The Cardinal swore to the Holy Father not to mention the two guests' presence to anyone outside of the Camerlengo or approved staff members. He even withheld the information from Angelo knowing of the risks. Yet now, the implication was that elements within the Roman Curia were already aware of the revelations.

"There's more," Father Hernandez said.

"What do you mean there's more? Isn't that enough?" The Cardinal asked, still ill at ease.

"You sure you wanna tell him?" Michael queried of Father Hernandez.

Father Hernandez returned a sharp stare, signaling to Michael he was confident in wanting to divulge the information concerning the child's genetic makeup.

Cardinal Tullono, intrigued by the two men's interactions, took his glasses off again to rub his eyes. "What more is there? How can something be as disturbing as finding out that the Holy Father has a clone running around?"

Father Hernandez shifted the papers on the conference table top around, moving them in front of the Cardinal, refocusing on a couple of pictures. "Our source who's a specialist in the area of genetics told us the pictures show strong evidence the child may have angel DNA mixed with his own DNA."

"Angel...DNA?" the Cardinal asked, skepticism was discernible by the tone of his voice. "You mean like human DNA...like human genetic DNA? You've got to be joking? They're spiritual beings, there's no way you can have something like what you're talking about to happen."

"Angels are considered spiritual and at the same time physical," Michael interjected. "One example is what transpired in Genesis 6, and in the Book of Enoch. Then there are the multiple unique physical manifestations for the angel of the Lord when you look at his interaction with Abraham, Joshua, and Sampson's father, Manoah. Then you have the human like angel representations early in the book of Ezekiel."

Father Hernandez wanted to smile, again impressed with Michael's ability to recall biblical and apocryphal historical information.

"Enough, and how is it you, a layman has come to know so much about this?" Cardinal Tullono asked.

Michael presumed Cardinal Grielle would have mentioned his background, but decided to not let that distract him. "I studied them quite extensively while I was in Seminary to become a priest. I'm also a professor at a college where I research and teach religious studies, and I still have an interest in angels."

Sister Justine ignored the interaction between the three men, concentrating on the documents fascinated by something that caught her attention that seemed out of the ordinary. "Look at the date on a couple of the council of Pisa notes document in the header section, a year before the global mass disappearance."

"What about it?" Michael asked.

"The divine inspirations, we thought the appearance of Abriel before the missing of the millions to be an isolated event, and then the angel appearances giving their eulogies followed afterwards. It seems the influence of angels instigating all of this goes back further than we realized, months before Aguascalientes," Sister Justine said.

"Remember, in retrospect, the influence of angels goes back to the dawn of man, Sister," Cardinal Tullono said in a diluted condescending tone.

The three turned to the Cardinal, each one of their eyes went round and foreheads creased, their facial expressions entreating him to expound on his comment. Sister Justine wanted to snap at the Cardinal for his marginalizing her comments, but kept her composure. Father Hernandez and Michael sensed an underlying motive was for him to demonstrate his intelligence on the subject.

Cardinal Tullono continued. "Many believe what's going on with the angels is the dawn of something new or unique. But an angel instigated the fall of man, the fallen morning star who instigated the plunge of men into sin. And since we're talking about angels, what else can you tell me about the angel aspect of what's going on?" Cardinal Tullono asked. His tone was stern as he gave the three a piercing gaze.

"All of this deals with what we're investigating under the project unique with the name of Aurora," Father Hernandez said.

"Aurora?" Cardinal Tullono asked. "You've mentioned the name during your explanation of what's going on. What about the meaning of that word? Does that name have anything to do in context of what we're discussing here?"

Father Hernandez responded. "It's reasoned the name originated from the first influence of an angel, one called Aurora."

"Oh my God," Sister Justine said in a worried tone.

"What is it?" Father Hernandez asked.

"Do you know what the name Aurora implies? Michael, think about when we did some of our earlier research."

Michael responded. "Well, some associate it with the Aurora Borealis."

"I believe it means the…what if Aurora is not merely the angel's name, but more its essence – the dawn."

"And the Cardinal did mention the morning star, which appears in the dawn," Father Hernandez said, the cadence of his voice trailing at the end of the statement.

"So is the spawn of Aurora whom the angels bowed to?" Sister Justine asked.

Cardinal Tullono trembled with disgust. "Bow to…you're saying angels bowed to the child?" He asked in an infuriating tone wrapped with incredulity, now pausing to take in a couple of deep breaths. The painting in the chapel came to mind. He had believed it to be symbolic, not representative of a real-world occurrence. "Why didn't you mention this before?" The Cardinal continued, in a gruff tone.

The three couldn't determine if the Cardinal's tone was one of disbelief or derision.

"We're telling you what we learned and what was told to us," Michael said, attempting to defend Sister Justine from what he perceived to be an aggressive response by Cardinal Tullono. "We didn't know if that would be important, or how all of it would fit in."

The Cardinal's face reddened. "How does all of this fit in? What you're telling me is that angels bowed to that bastardization of a child living here on these holy grounds."

Father Hernandez, Sister Justine, and Michael's eyes widened. An uncomfortable silence followed. Cardinal Tullono realized he made a mistake making the comment without thinking first.

"The child…is… here?" Father Hernandez asked his voice cracking. Michael and Sister Justine remained silent, still stunned by the revelation.

Cardinal Tullono acted. "As far as you three know, I mentioned no such thing. I am under the strictest confidence of the Holy Father, and the Camerlengo, as to the child being here. We will mention it no further, and neither shall you."

"You can't…" Father Hernandez had started to comment before the Cardinal interrupted him.

"Father, no more about this will be said." The Cardinal's tone was forceful and resolute.

Michael became incensed. "You can't bring something like that up and…"

"Mr. Saunders," Cardinal Tullono said, holding back from yelling at Michael. "I've given you all consideration because of your two companions, please don't make this uncomfortable. Be respectful of your place."

Michael against his nature, acquiesced in deference to Father Hernandez and Sister Justine.

An idea came to Cardinal Tullono. If he couldn't openly talk to his three guests about the child, he could direct them to visit and examine the recent artwork commissioned by the Holy Father. "You three should go take a personal walking tour and look at some of the history and art in the Chapel of Santa Maria Regina della Famiglia. It's on the backside of the Governate offices here."

"Artwork?" Michael questioned. "Really? If you want to blow us off, you don't have to send us on a useless field trip to go gawk at some artwork."

"I believe you might be interested in taking a look at some of the artwork on display," Cardinal Tullono stressed.

Father Hernandez jumped in. "I don't see how this would be of a benefit to our discussion."

"I have other duties to take care, go view the artwork. Like I said, the chapel rests behind this building. But I'm afraid you won't be able to go through the hallway and side entrance linked to the transept. For security purposes, we temporarily blocked off that area in preparation for a press event, special presentation, and sensitive meetings in a couple of the offices scheduled to convene down there tomorrow. You'll need to go out and around to the main entrance to enter. Afterwards, we'll get together again later to discuss what you viewed and where we'll go from there."

"But..." Father Hernandez started before Cardinal Tullono interrupted him.

"Listen to what I'm telling you. Please go," Cardinal Tullono stressed in a softened tone, as he stood and guided his visitors out of his office. "I believe it may help to provide some answers and add context to what we're discussing here."

The Cardinal was anxious to attempt to see if he could corroborate any of the information with a peer on the Roman Curia.

\* \* \* \*

After leaving Cardinal Tullono's office, Father Hernandez, Michael and Sister Justine conceded to view the artwork. Approaching the outside main chapel entrance, a Gendarme dressed in a black suit, white shirt and black tie, stood arguing in Italian with a young couple. The guard, planted in front of the ornate designed double doors, shifted in front of the man and woman each time they tried to step around him to approach the entrance. Both knew not to rush and enter without his permission – to do so would invite banned access for use of the church, and possibly access to the city-state. With the similarity of several words and phrases in Spanish, Father Hernandez's best interpretation was that the disagreement centered on the couple's wedding scheduled to commence in three days. After the couple's fourth attempt of trying to circumnavigate around the gendarme, he bellowed the word "partire" and pointed away. The couple stormed off around to the front of the administrative building.

Father Hernandez advertised a large smile hoping to psychologically disarm the gendarme.

The gendarme raised his hand signaling for the three to stop and expelled a command in Italian.

"I'm sorry, we don't speak Italian," Father Hernandez replied, still displaying a forced smile.

"No one allowed in today or tomorrow Father because of special event," the gendarme said. "I sorry if they by accident double-schedule yours."

"No, no, we're not here with that couple, we're here on behalf of Cardinal Tullono, we would like to go in," Father Hernandez said.

"I sorry, because you say Cardinal Tullono's name means he not sent you."

Michael chuckled.

"What's so funny?" Sister Justine asked.

"No matter where you go, name dropping doesn't always work."

"Let's go back and talk to his Eminence," Father Hernandez said, pursing his lips, annoyed the guard prevented he and his companions from entering the chapel.

After an hour of tracking down Cardinal Tullono, who had departed his office to tend to other affairs, he validated approval for Father Hernandez, Sister Justine, and Michael to enter the Cathedral, but not until the following morning just after nine o'clock before a special ceremony and press event. A private dedication service and mass was underway, and wouldn't finish until the end of the day.

# Chapter 34 – A Quick Rendezvous

It was the early evening. An hour earlier, Sister Justine had requested a private audience with Cardinal Grielle to discuss a heavy concern on her mind. Entering the small meeting chamber, he was already sitting at an oak table in the center of the Renaissance period art filled room.

"You're here, Your Eminence," she said, not anticipating for the Cardinal to be in the room, with herself arriving ten minutes early to pray and meditate.

"Yes, your message sounded urgent." Cardinal Grielle wondered if Sister Justine had some disturbing news concerning the Women's Center back in Los Angeles.

After bending down to give Cardinal Grielle a warm, firm embrace, she pulled out an adjacent chair at the table and sat facing him.

"Well, you caught me at a good time. I wasn't planning to do much this evening before retiring. I'm still suffering from jet lag, plus it's getting a little tiresome listening to my peers with their incessant speculating on the purpose of the Papal audience tomorrow. So why are you being so mysterious wanting to meet in secret like this, and that you don't want me to mention it to your two colleagues."

*I can do this.* Sister Justine closed her soft blue eyes, expelled a deep breath, and focused on Cardinal Grielle's eyes. "Your Eminence." Justine took another deep breath. "I'm letting you know of my decision to leave the Church. It's final."

Cardinal Grielle sat back in his chair. His eyes enlarged as if softballs and glistened from repressed tears. He took in a gulp of air. "Wha...wha...what do you mean leave the Church, you had decided to stay. You've been so influential and blessed with what you've provided at the centers."

"I keep going back and forth on my decision, and I've come to the conclusion I can't do this anymore, not through the Church anyway."

"Do what anymore? You're no longer under service to inform on your Sisters, which was wrong of us to ask." Cardinal Grielle sensed his stomach become queasy as a wave of guilt flowed through his body knowing his words were counterfeit to his earlier stance on the situation, but he didn't want that to distract him.

"It's more than me having to deal with previously informing on my sisters, but tell me you're not going to support what's going on, or that you're at least concerned?" Sister Justine asked. "I was already upset about the Church's sponsoring what was happening down in Mexico and Los Angeles with the virus. But to continue to find out more about the child, and how what I assumed were marginalized factions attempting to lead the Church, and appear close to doing so, I don't know if I agree with that. Talking with Cardinal Tullono earlier

348

today opened my eyes onto how much of the Curia must be involved. It's what helped to finalize my decision."

"Sister, remember who the true spiritual head of the church is, God our Father in heaven," Cardinal Grielle said. "I realize that now."

"Is he?" she snapped back. "Do you realize that I never accepted that fact since becoming a nun? I've been so focused on wanting to do good, to be a good nun, and to be a good person so that God would accept me, but I never considered the foundation or reality of my beliefs. I had some friends who were Franciscan Nuns, and their beliefs were God wants people happy, to live and love in the light of the sun. I, in many ways, thought the same.

"My beliefs should be more than a ritual of doing good or feeling good, but a deeper faith in God and his son. I believe that you, Cardinal Millhouse, or the Church hadn't adequately accomplished that in mentoring me."

Cardinal Grielle cast his head downward. He stared at the dark-stained hardwood floor unable to find any words to say.

Sister Justine continued. "If I didn't know any better, there are those who seem to be worshipping the child, and learning the things since all of this started, I..." Sister Justine was unable to finish.

Cardinal Grielle took advantage of the uncomfortable lull in the conversation. "Father Hernandez has had several discussions with me that you and Mr. Saunders aren't aware of, but he's come to the same realization. Isn't it worth to make a change from the inside? He's dedicated with wanting to do that. Stay in the church, let him mentor you. You two can be a definite change for good."

349

"I don't want to be naïve about this. I feel I need to take a stand, Your Eminence," Sister Justine said, wanting to add to her comments that the Cardinal should be taking a stand but didn't want to come of sounding disrespectful or judgmental. This was one of those times she wished she was more like Michael. "I cannot be part of an organization or institution I don't agree with anymore."

Cardinal Grielle leaned in forward towards Sister Justine. "And how do your companions feel about your decision?"

"I didn't talk them about this yet. I know that Father Hernandez would try to talk me out of it, and Michael would encourage me to leave. Either way, it would be for the wrong reasons. I'm doing this for myself."

"Sister, please reconsider, you've been such a blessing in working with the Women's Center and moving to a position of leadership. I see you as a Mother Superior one day."

"Thank you for the kind words, but I've thought this through, and I forgave you and the Church. Now I need to find myself. After we're done here in Rome, consider this my resignation effective once I return to Los Angeles. And please don't tell the father or Michael."

"But..."

Sister Justine removed the wedding ring from her finger. She placed it on the table top with gentle care, got up and departed from the room not wanting to hear any persuasion attempts.

# Chapter 35 – Holy Conclave

The call for the College of Cardinals suggested to the congregants that the high Bishop of Rome position would soon become vacant after declaration of the Pope's resigning. Including the Cardinals across all the Dioceses worldwide, the Holy See had lodged all local Cardinals who lived outside of Vatican City in the Domus Sanctae Marthae (Saint Martha's) House to sequester them from the media. Since this was mandatory during a papal selection conclave, it reinforced the idea of a papal transition. Once checked in, the reception staff presented each arrival a preliminary press package stating the assembly's focus was to prepare for a special message to the College, and a Papal audience to the world.

Most of the Cardinals speculated that the Holy Father would announce he would either step down or retire due to reported health issues. The Holy See had suspended his travel plans to various Dioceses the preceding year. The verbiage in the cancellation communiques implied an indefinite cessation of public appearances. The news of purported angelic visits in Vatican City, more importantly, within the papal residences, increased legitimacy to the rumors of his ill-health.

9 A.M., the last of the attending Cardinals sat in their assigned seats facing a temporary stage erected in front of

the baldachin - the multi-story high Baroque sculpted bronze canopy Papal altar under the dome in St. Peter's Basilica. Gold-trimmed white bunting draped the base of the erected dais, and a multitude of potted plants sat atop the flooring bordering the edge. Scaffolding erected fifteen feet high at each side of the platform supported a large Chi-Rho crest and public address speakers. Most of the Cardinals noticed the ring of armed Vatican City Gendarme and Italian security specialists wearing black tactical outfits posted along the walls. Several senior Swiss Guard Gendarme officers wearing dark purple suits stood near the seated clergy and next to the stage.

The Holy Father had desired to host the Papal Audience in the Sistine Chapel. The child recommended the Basilica. The attendant to the Holy Father briefed that the Camerlengo, Jude, along with his contingent of two security members from the Swiss Guard, and Gary Applethorpe departed their quarters and were walking over to the Chapel Santa Maria Regina Famiglia for a final check of the artwork. They should then arrive to the conclave in a matter of minutes afterwards. The Holy Father was confused why they would need to visit the chapel. They had dedicated and anointed the commissioned pieces the previous day.

All the Cardinals, apart from the ones assigned to the Vatican and who worked with the Holy Father, didn't expect him to spryly move about as he approached the podium. After delivering the opening prayer, he started his speech, beginning with a welcome and introductions of the Curia in attendance. With Cardinal Tullono's seat being empty, he bypassed the name.

After several minutes of formal oration, the Holy Father transitioned to the theme of his speech. "So why

352

are you here many of you are asking. We know the information in your press packages wasn't very clear. I will tell you directly, there are child prodigies so advanced, they graduate college, some as early as the age of eleven or twelve. They are super-intelligent in their fields of study and excel in their discipline of learning well before becoming a young adult. There is one child who exceeds all of that, and not with the secular knowledge of men, but has a deep knowledge of religious doctrine and church history."

"Just as with our Lord Jesus Christ two thousand years ago, our father has seen fit to grace us with another blessing, another child, who is now the age of thirteen. The child is both intelligent and wise. He has learned and mastered Latin, Greek, Hebrew, and understands Aramaic, not simply memorizing phrases, words, or the alphabet, but having full grammatical understanding of the languages.

"I will say this – whereas conceived by a marriage of science and the divine, he is blessed and has performed numerous supernatural deeds. Many of you were aware that my health had been failing, yet he demonstrated the ability to perform the miraculous, restoring me unto improved health in his own time. He has also healed the hearing of a Sister here on these sacred grounds. He is one divinely inspired, supernaturally conceived, and unique in his being. A special destiny awaits him."

A loud discourteous murmuring budded amongst most of the Cardinals.

The Holy Father continued. "I have been, and will continue to mentor, along with angelic majesties, this child for as long as our father in heaven sees fit, and as such until that day, I will step down to the position of

353

Pope Emeritus and the child shall one day become my successor..."

"Heresy, heresy", "sacrilege", "this is not doctrinal", or similar outbursts spewed out from most of the Cardinals in the audience, all boisterous with their disapproval. The other Cardinals attempted to ask a volley of questions or engaged in side conversations with one another.

The Holy Father continued. "...at this time, I am convinced he could assume my duties, blessed by Heaven, as his nature is blessed. There is no one more worthy."

The acoustics in the cavernous basilica caused the echoes from the increasing roar of angry jeers, verbal consternations, and one on one side discussions difficult for anyone to hear, or for the Holy Father to continue.

"My brethren, please calm down," the Holy Father said, exerting forcefulness with his aged and gravelly voice into the microphone, and as he pounded his hand on the podium top. The request blaring from the speakers caused the spirited disagreements and side discussions to subside.

The Holy Father continued. "This should not be a surprise to most of you. The angelic majesties themselves have proclaimed the child's advent, with the world unsure of the meaning at the time. We now see that it was to herald the fulfillment of that announcement. The child is blessed greater than any holy saint in church history."

The Cardinals' roaring vocal discontentment amplified again competing with the audio emitted from the temporarily installed speakers. Suddenly, an unnatural rumbling reverberated throughout the basilica, sounding as if thunderous horses raced upon the vaulted and gold painted ceiling domes. The continuous blare of muffled trumpet playing echoed in the grand hall. The gathered Cardinals quieted, all craning their necks attempting to determine the source of the mysterious sounds.

## Chapter 36 – Chapel of Santa Maria Regina

Father Hernandez, Michael, and Sister Justine each ate breakfast at their respective residences, deciding to meet at the entrance of the Chapel of Santa Maria Regina della Famiglia. The Gendarme guards were accommodating, with one holding open the door. After entering, the beautiful interior mesmerized the three. A score of dark cherry wood pew rows lined up in two columns, separated by a center aisle and elaborate designed Baroque style pillars spaced every three rows, lined on the outside aisles. This created an interior colonnade between the pews and vibrant alabaster white walls. The expanse of the nave at the points where the lower ceiling from the walls met the pillars, spanned upward to the intricate inlay designed in the ceiling vault floating above the pews. The floor was composed of square shaped amber and white marble slabs laid in a diamond pattern.

They wandered down the center aisle finding traditional Renaissance era religious themed paintings hanging on the side walls, unable to identify any out of the ordinary artwork Cardinal Tullono urged for them to find. Once they passed through the gloss-varnished wood pews, approaching the front transept crossing, they became aware of two four-foot-tall paintings on easels resting behind a marble table that sat in the middle of the dais. The artwork sat in front of a Madonna enthroned with the child between two saints wall mural. They wondered how they missed the two oversized works after entering the chapel.

The oil painted image on the right canvas was the child recognized as the one they had met earlier back in Los Angeles, now portrayed as having the mature face of an older adolescent teen. The vibrant use of colors with the use of light and shadow gave a realistic depiction to his face. His entire body displayed a subdued aura as he stood amongst a throng of angels shown upon their knees with their heads bowed.

The image on the left canvas was another portraying the child. A black and gray impressionistic and abstract background blended with varying shades of white and silver mixed with short streaks of matte gold. Areas surrounding the subject painted with broad strokes of light gray formed a drop shadow adding depth to the image.

"You know who the paintings look like?" Sister Justine asked.

"I think we're all thinking the same thing," Michael replied.

"There's something about this one picture," Sister Justine said as she stepped back from the painting on the left. The obscure background evoked an obfuscated silhouette of a tall figure standing next to the foremost image of the child. When she shifted slightly to one side affecting how the light fell upon the painting, ambiguous facial features, torso, appendages, and the shape of wings emerged as part of the background.

"Do you see that?" Sister Justine squealed.

"See what?" both men answered.

"It's as if the picture has a 3-D effect and there's another figure painted as part of the background." Sister Justine caught herself; the perceived image distortion disappeared and faded into a muddled mix of earth-toned colors. "That's weird, I could've sworn...the background...it looked like..." Her words trailed off.

Father Hernandez and Michael stared at the portraiture unable to find anything unique or distinguishable.

"It's odd," she said.

They were about to step up onto the altar dais to get a closer look at the paintings, when the click of an unlatching mechanism came from the entranceway leading into the hallway connecting the chapel with the Pontifical Governate offices. The door swung open. Cardinal Picoli, two clergy members, Gary, Jude the child, and a Gendarmerie contingent of four men filed through.

"Who are you and what are you doing in here?" Cardinal Picoli demanded, irate to see three strangers in the chapel.

"What the hell are you doing here?" Gary roared. "Gendarme, take these three pains in the asses out of here."

"You know these three Gary?" Cardinal Picoli asked, also crossed at his use of an expletive.

"No, let them stay," the child said.

Gary snapped his head around towards Jude, displaying a smirk of confusion. "What? My prince, you don't know how much trouble these three have been."

"On the contrary, I know more than you realize," the child said. "They should stay. I'm impressed that their investigation and research led them here."

Father Hernandez took a step forward. "Prince? How is this child a prince when he's a clone?"

"The child's name is Jude," Cardinal Picoli said, interrupting, uncomfortable with the father about to discuss the child's background in the open. "And who are you?" the Cardinal asked, intrigued that Jude had requested for the three to remain.

"They're a pain in the rear, that's what they are," Gary said, interjecting into the conversation. "And they're a long way from home. What are you three doing here?"

"We were tasked to investigate what happened after Cardinal Millhouse was murdered. We believe an angel killed the two mysterious men who killed the Cardinal and it led us to here."

Gary trembled hearing the revelation, but pretended as if it didn't bother him. If the investigation into Cardinal Millhouse's death led the three to Vatican City, would those interested in finding him know of his location?

"You're the ones involved with that investigation initiated by Cardinal Grielle?" Cardinal Picoli asked.

"Yes," Father Hernandez answered. "Even back to when Cardinal Millhouse and Cardinal Grielle had us find out what happened at the Thomson and Thomson incident in Los Angeles. Along the way we learned about your biological project and the child."

Cardinal Picoli flaunted a wry smile. "Then you understand how special Jude is. We would've liked for the biological component to be successful, but even so, we are more blessed than you can imagine."

"He's still a child," Father Hernandez responded, "regardless of his inception."

"You don't understand, Father, even angels bow down before him. If angels who are greater than us bow down to him, how much more we as simple men should as well? What he's been imbued with is nothing short of miraculous." Gary said puffing his chest out like a proud father. No one missed his haughtiness as he made the comment.

"How is it you could worship someone who is still a mere man nonetheless?" Father Hernandez asked. He purposefully dismissed the alleged angelic portion of the child's biological makeup.

"You don't notice what's here before you, do you three?" Gary said. "He's more than a mere man."

"What are you talking about?" Father Hernandez asked.

"Look around."

"We saw the pictures already," Father Hernandez responded.

"Look again."

Father Hernandez, Sister Justine, and Michael reluctantly followed Gary's recommendation. They scanned the front area and observed a statue crafted with intricate detail emulating the Madonna and young child walking hand in hand, erected in the transept against the wall opposite the door to the Governate offices. The more they surveyed and scrutinized the features of what they first thought to be a representation of the Madonna, turned out was an angel, its wings indiscernible and chiseled to display them as if tucked in. The life-like facial features of the child resembled Jude.

"What the..." Father Hernandez said, moving closer to the statue. "That's not a representation of the Holy Mother and Child." Father Hernandez took a closer look at the child's face on the statue. He was confident it was that of Jude. "Is that an image of the angel Aurora and the Child?"

"How did we miss that?" Michael whispered. "It was right here in front of us."

"It represents the embodiment of the angel who is the glory and beauty of Aurora," Cardinal Picoli said.

"And this beautiful piece of artwork was commissioned by Jude," Gary said.

"He commissioned it?" Father Hernandez asked.

"This is another wonderful representation of who he is," Cardinal Picoli said. "This is why angels bow before him. That's why I now know that men will bow before him. He is the miraculous union of man and angel, an angel of the Lord that science and the heavens have helped to conceive. Recall the scriptures say that man shall be greater than the angels. Jude is the one."

Cardinal Tullono, entering from the right transept hallway door, wanting to follow up with Father Hernandez, Michael, and Sister Justine's opinion on the artwork, came upon the group engaged in discussion. He hadn't anticipated anyone other than the three to be in the chapel. "What's going on here?" he asked.

Cardinal Picoli's bushy gray-haired unibrow crinkled rising in the center, and a corner of his lip pursed as his peer approached.

"No, no, no, no, no, no, this is all wrong," Father Hernandez said, ignoring Cardinal Tullono's question as he moved back to the group away from the statue. "He is not an angel of the Lord."

"All angels are of God," Cardinal Picoli said, in a rebuking tone.

Michael interjected. "But not all of good standing, you have the fallen."

"Now you have an accomplice getting into one of your religious beat downs, Father," Gary interjected. "Because if you are, I'm going to have the Gendarmerie take you out of here, regardless of Jude's request."

"Don't you understand, Gary, all of this is about religion," Father Hernandez replied.

"First off, you're not on a first name basis with me, and secondly, everything in this world isn't about religion."

Father Hernandez had hoped by addressing Gary by his first name it would allow their conversation to become more personable. He pressed on with a different point to counter Gary's point of view. "You've been doing this for the church and your beliefs all along. What do you think all of this has been about anyway?"

Cardinal Picoli, still tense, his unibrow furled and eyes glaring towards Father Hernandez clenched his hands to control his anger. "Pieter, are you aware of these troublemakers?" he asked, his voice throaty and guttural.

"Yes, I'm sponsoring them on behalf of Cardinal Grielle of the Los Angeles Diocese to investigate the spiritual motives of why Cardinal Millhouse was killed."

"You're sponsoring them? How come I wasn't made aware of this?" Cardinal Picoli asked.

"We know about the Council of Rome and Pisa II, and the official plans for the virus and the child," Father Hernandez said.

"Dude," Michael said in a whisper, "have you ever played poker?"

Cardinal Tullono, his facial expression displaying the same emotions as Michael, turned towards Father Hernandez giving him a disapproving glance, wishing he hadn't disclosed the information.

Cardinal Picoli smirked. "So, you know about the Council of Pisa II? Then you know that the Council acknowledged that the current Holy Father would abdicate his role to that of Emeritus. All the while the real prize was the child who would then become the unifying progenitor of reconciliation for the Church and nations? Through him universal peace is possible."

"We faced many setbacks," Gary added. "But towards the end, many of us working the projects began to realize that the virus wasn't the real prize. It was the child, the future of the Church, that was the focus of Aurora, and something we were willing to risk."

"This isn't the path the Church should be taking," Father Hernandez said. "We'll find a way to bring the truth out."

"What truth is there to bring out?" Cardinal Picoli said, in a snarky tone. "This is part of the divine plan through the angel Aurora. How can they reject the child upon the appointed time when in many ways, he and the Holy Father are one in the same. And what are you three to do, a simple nobody priest, formerly carnal nun, and disrespectful substandard college professor at a second-rate school? I know of you three and your ungodly works and conclusions in your investigation sent by Cardinal Millhouse."

"Screw you," Michael said.

Sister Justine wanted to chastise Michael and downplay his offense, but understood his outburst.

"Michael, calm down," Father Hernandez said.

"It's better than what I really wanted to say," Michael replied, hardening his stare towards Cardinal Picoli. "I'm not gonna stand here and let you insult the three of us. I respect these two more than any other persons I know. Sister Justine and Father Hernandez present more of a godly life I bet than you as a pompous and religious gas bag wanting to worship a bastardized human chimera."

Cardinal Picoli's capillaries in his forehead, cheeks, and jaw had swollen reddening his face. "Cardinal Millhouse was correct about your obstinacy. You should be paying homage to the future Bishop of Rome."

"How could he become the next future Pope?" Michael asked. "He's not a Cardinal, or even clergy for that matter."

"You don't have to be a Cardinal to be elected Pope by the College of Cardinals," Cardinal Tullono answered. His voice trembled with foreboding from his self-revelation. "There are only two requirements for becoming pope, being male and being baptized into the Catholic Church."

"Correct, Pieter," Cardinal Picoli said.

"So why would he be considered?" Father Hernandez asked. "Being a clone of the Holy Father wouldn't make him eligible."

"He's eligible due to his divine nature," Cardinal Picoli said.

"What do you mean by his divine nature?" Father Hernandez asked, as he recalled the images of Doctor Cochrane's room and discussion with Ashere. "Are you saying that because he's part angel?"

Cardinal Tullono was also interested in the response.

Cardinal Picoli grinned with a sly confidence. "Jude fulfilling the position is not one as an apostolic succession

364

heir, or due to his human genetic lineage, but his possessing the supernatural succession by miraculous conception. He's the child of genetically engineered perfect humanity and divinity – Aurora, the angel of dawn for the morning star, God's representative and more qualified than any Cardinal. The miracles he's accomplished, and will accomplish validate his standing."

"Aurora as the angel of the dawn?" Cardinal Tullono questioned, concerned regarding the direction of the conversation. "There is solely one true morning star and the other is..."

An attending priest rushed into the chapel interrupting the conversation and proceeding over to Cardinal Picoli. "Your Eminence, the Holy Father has begun his audience with the College of Cardinals. They've convened in the Basilica and want to make sure the child is in place for his entry at the proper time."

Cardinal Picoli turned his attention to Cardinal Tullono. "We must go," he said. "And Pieter, make sure to dismiss these three reprobates from the city proper. We're about to proclaim and announce Jude to the College of Cardinals. I'll see you over in the Basilica." Cardinal Picoli directed his attention to the Gendarme. "Ensure this room remains secured for the press discussion and art unveiling after the Holy Father's announcement to the Cardinals."

The entourage with the child began to leave with Cardinal Picoli placing his hand on Gary's shoulder gesturing for him to remain. "I'm sorry, Gary, but only clergy can attend the Conclave during this first official introduction of the child to the entire College. Please wait with the press in the reception room down the hall."

Disappointed, Gary compressed his lips and maintained his composure not being able to accompany Jude and Cardinal Picoli to St. Peter's Basilica.

"Don't worry, Mr. Applethorpe," Jude said. "Today you'll attain the fruits of your efforts."

After the entourage exited the chapel, two Gendarmes remained standing by the hallway door. A priest and nun promenaded into the chapel carrying three folded creamy-white cotton linen sheets embroidered with the Chi-Rho symbol in scarlet, and began to drape the new paintings and statue.

* * * *

A junior priest assigned as an escort, marshalled a group of reporters, photographers, and videographers into a chamber meeting room down the atrium hallway leading to the Chapel of Santa Maria Regina. The press corps consisted of members from varying ethnic backgrounds, each wearing a lanyard or temporary badge that displayed Stampa/Press. Many carried professional grade SLR cameras, small professional video cameras, tablets, or other personal assistant devices, note pads and pens to report on a special Papal event. Several carried a camera or video cases containing additional lenses and support equipment.

"Please wait here for your official escort to the Chapel for a special unveiling and press announcement having major implications for the Church and all religions across the world," the junior priest said.

Gary strutted into the meeting chamber room capturing the attention of Xavier and Ben. The Vatican Press office had approved both as members of the press corps and cleared their access onto the city-state. They assumed this would be an exploratory run and they would need to find a way to sneak away from the group to reconnoiter the grounds. They would pretend to be lost if questioned during the attempt to talk to someone who would know of Gary and the child's location.

Xavier leaned to Ben. "Thank goodness we brought the special travel kit. You need to prepare your gear in case we get a chance for a one on one interview," he whispered, keeping an inconspicuous eye on Gary.

Ben reached into his camera case and in less than ninety seconds assembled a carbon fiber handgun with a silencer fashioned from the disassembled parts of a mini-tripod, false battery pack, false high-end flash unit, and the components from a small video camera. He extracted bullets concealed in modified fake Lithium battery packs, loaded them in a magazine, then inserted the magazine into the fabricated weapon and chambered a round. When Ben finished, he pulled out a functional small video camera also in the bag and pretended to complete an equipment check. His actions mirrored those of the other press members preparing their gear.

Minutes later, a young Bangladesh priest having thin eyes, bronzed skin tone, and straight black hair walked into the room. "Ladies and gentlemen of the press," he said in English laced with a thick accent. "Sorry for short delay, we needed to ensure Chapel prepared for arrival of special guest and presentation. Please follow me."

* * * *

"I think that went well," Michael said.

Cardinal Tullono, Father Hernandez, and Sister Justine stared at Michael, baffled by his comment.

"Really?" Father Hernandez responded with skepticism.

"Wow, you three are way too serious," Michael replied.

"We need to head back to my office and regroup," Cardinal Tullono said as he led Father Hernandez, Sister Justine, and Michael to the hallway atrium entrance, waiting a minute after the entourage of Cardinal Picoli, Garry Applethorpe, and Jude had departed.

"You're not going to the Conclave?" Father Hernandez asked.

Cardinal Tullono smirked. "Not now, especially with what we discussed. I don't want to be involved with that blasphemous child."

The stockier of the two Gendarmes guarding the hallway entrance leading into the Pontifical Governate offices sidestepped in front of the door blocking its access. He made a comment in Italian, followed by an incensed response in Italian by Cardinal Tullono.

The Gendarme stepped to the side. "Mie scuse'."

"What was that about," Michael asked as they proceeded down the hallway towards the main Pontifical Governate offices.

"He said this area is off limits due to a press group coming through and directed us to walk around outside. I had to remind him that I'm in charge of the offices and hallways in this building, and I'm not walking around," Cardinal Tullono said as they approached a set of double doors to the side with a sign above that displayed "Meeting Chambers." A young Asian priest guided a small pack of men and women who flowed into the corridor from the chambers towards the chapel.

The four moved to the side of the hallway and waited to allow the migrating swarm of press personnel to pass. One of the men, tall, thin, short afro, sable skin

368

complexion, and black and tan leopard-patterned glasses, caught Michael's attention. The gaze of Xavier's light brown eyes engaged with Michael's. He promptly turned away. Sister Justine noticing Ben, who looked familiar, was walking next to Xavier. Gary, accompanied by an attending priest, followed in the rear. He stopped for a few seconds; his eyes unblinking – his face soured in disgust and neck vein popped out as he stared down Father Hernandez, Michael, and Sister Justine.

Michael had wanted to flip his middle finger, but constrained himself. The three trailed behind Cardinal Tullono who continued down the hallway.

"What's with all these people?" Sister Justine asked, after she and her companions turned into the main corridor of the building, not having observed the badges and identification credentials most of the individuals wore.

"That's the secondary press corps I had mentioned for the circus centered on the child," Cardinal Tullono answered. "That group is primarily those from the smaller publications or press houses. The major press services are in the Conference Hall of the Holy See Press Office receiving a major briefing, and then heading over later."

"One of them looked familiar," Sister Justine said.

"Funny you say that," Michael exclaimed. "I was thinking the same thing. It seemed like I saw one of those guys before – I don't remember where though."

Michael stopped, holding up his companions as he paced in a small circle determined to recall where he had seen the man, he made eye contact with.

"Let's go," Father Hernandez said. "If you think about something too hard, it'll never come to you."

"It seems too weird."

"Don't think about it, it'll come to you when you least expect it as you get your train of thought back."

Michael's eyes widened. "That's it, the train."

"What do you mean the train?" Sister Justine asked.

"I think he was the one on the train when we started our trip from Pisa, but his hair was blond then. Now it isn't, and I think he's wearing glasses too."

"There you have it, he's more than likely a reporter, simply a coincidence," Father Hernandez said.

"Maybe, but why change his appearance?"

"Like Father Hernandez said," Cardinal Tullono said, "it's probably a coincidence."

Cardinal Tullono resumed walking to his office, indicating for his guests to follow. Father Hernandez and Sister Justine heeded the Cardinal's gesture, with Michael deciding to keep up with his colleagues. As they approached the stairwell to proceed upstairs, the Public Affairs administrative officer who processed the last-minute press permits for Cardinal Tullono rushed up to the four carrying a sheet of paper. Breathing heavy, a panic-stricken appearance distorted his face. "Your Eminence, I need to talk to you about those two last minute requests you submitted for press credentials."

"Yes, what about them?"

The Public Affairs administrative assistant handed Cardinal Tullono the sheet of paper. "Since they were American and after their initial checks came back valid as reporters, the Interpol security attaché assigned to us decided to submit the information to the FBI International office in Rome when he noticed a small timeline discrepancy in their work history. The facial recognition for the white male came back as a person of interest associated with two men involved with the death of the Cardinal for the Los Angeles Diocese."

"Cardinal Millhouse?" Father Hernandez and Sister Justine asked in unison.

"Yes," the Public Affairs administrative assistant said, his eyes widening as he stared at Father Hernandez and Sister Justine. "How did you know that?"

Father Hernandez, Michael, and Sister Justine encircled the Public Affairs officer to view the image of the man. Cardinal Tullono trembled with sweat forming on his forehead and temples.

"The Women's Center!" Sister Justine said. "That's the same man."

Father Hernandez and Michael glanced at each other for a quick instant, both having the same thought. They rushed back down the hallway towards the chapel.

"Father, Mr. Saunders, get back here, we should find out what's going on and contact the Gendarmes and Interpol," Cardinal Tullono commanded.

Both men ignored the Cardinal, Sister Justine decided to follow her two companions.

"Sister!" the Cardinal said. He trailed and caught up with the three.

They arrived back at the chapel entrance from the hallway. "Wait here," Cardinal Tullono directed as he signaled for the Gendarme they had previously encountered to step over. He presented and explained the printout from the Public Affairs office.

Father Hernandez, Michael, and Sister Justine shifted further into the chapel past the doorway attempting to look non-conspicuous. Press members stood or sat scattered among the pews. The three spotted Ben, who sat next to Xavier three-fourths of the way back in the set of

371

pews on their left. Gary was the focus of the two men's attention. Father Hernandez, Michael, and Sister Justine stepped back to the chapel entrance and conveyed the location of the suspicious men to Cardinal Tullono. The Cardinal and Gendarme conversed in Italian and moved next to the chapel entrance. The Gendarme guard signaled for his partner to join them. The Cardinal whispered into the ear of the newly arrived guard, who then returned into the chapel. He skulked down the outer aisle towards the back with slow methodical steps. The Cardinal, Father Hernandez, Michael, and Sister Justine stepped inside of the chapel moving near the center of the front pew attempting to act casual, huddling with one another and engaged in a fake conversation.

Across from the side chapel entrance, Gary worked with the priest and nun who draped the statue and pictures, making incessant last-minute adjustments to the linen shrouds embroidered with the Chi-Rho symbol. He wanted to ensure each was to his liking. Gary was initially unaware of the commotion at the side entrance. He observed the interaction between Father Hernandez, Michael, Sister Justine, Cardinal Tullono, and the Gendarme guard. Irritated to see the three again, he strode over curious as to their return.

Xavier and Ben occupied with tracking Gary, now observed the activity up front and a Gendarme moving along the side aisle next to the wall, his gaze fixed in their direction. One of the columns temporarily blocked his view as he moved closer. Xavier glanced to the front to see Michael and Father Hernandez now staring at him. Sister Justine focused her stare on his partner. Gary approaching the group momentarily distracted their attention. The next column blocked the sight of the

Gendarme as he inched closer to where Xavier and his partner sat. Ben reached into his gear bag resting on the pew seat and retrieved his assembled weapon. The guard stepped into view. With speed and dexterity, Ben aimed and fired striking his target in the upper torso. Unarmed, Xavier dropped down to one knee taking cover behind the pew to minimize his exposure.

The silencer on Ben's weapon was effective. Before any of the nearby press members realized what happened as the fatally wounded Gendarme fell, Ben aimed forward and zeroed in on Gary's tall thin frame as he stood next to Father Hernandez, Michael, Sister Justine, and Cardinal Tullono. He fired two shots striking their mark. Ben next took aim at Sister Justine. Michael initially paralyzed watching the gunplay and weapon pointed in their direction, swung around between her and the shooter, then commenced to grapple her to the floor. Ben fired two rounds. Michael sensed two sharp stinging pains, one in his side, one in the back. He collapsed.

Panic erupted upon the small group of reporters and photographers in the chapel, many now screaming after witnessing Ben's drawn weapon and comprehending the muffled sounds of fired shots. Several cowered down to the floor or rushed for the entrance in the rear.

The Gendarme up front reached into his concealed holster and pulled out his weapon after observing Ben pull out a handgun and fire, witnessing his partner, Gary, and Michael falling to the floor in a matter of seconds. He grabbed Cardinal Tullono with his free hand, shoving him towards the hallway while attempting to aim his weapon at the assailant, unable to get a clear shot due to a photographer in one of the front pews who ran to the side of the room instead of dropping to the floor.

Two Gendarmes posted outside the main door rushed in to determine why the frenzied exodus of press members scurrying from the chapel. A Gendarme's voice shouted, "Drop the gun" in Italian from behind Ben after observing a weapon in his hand. Ben swung around and fired striking the Gendarme on the right. Both guards were able to return fire. Ben fell to the floor struck by two rounds. Xavier reached over his fallen partner in the pew and grabbed his weapon. The Gendarme still standing and observing only one shooter was confident he neutralized the threat. He stepped around the rear pew into the aisle, slowly moving forward with his weapon pointing upwards, not wanting to shoot any innocent bystanders. Xavier sprung up and fired twice at the unsuspecting guard. The first shot found its target, the second pull of the trigger – click, the specialty weapon was empty. Xavier rushed out from the pew into the aisle, finding the guard he struck wounded and unconscious, and snatched the Glock from the Gendarme's hand. Xavier then strode out of the main entrance concealing the pilfered handgun under his jacket, while keeping his head down hoping to minimize distinguishability of his face from the security video cameras on the grounds.

Outside was clear, with bystanders seeking cover or hiding after hearing the gunshots inside of the chapel. Xavier, checking over his shoulder making sure no one had observed or followed him, subtly traversed down the pathway. Once far away enough from the small cathedral, he picked up his pace blending in with a tour group leaving the city. After he stepped through the exit turn style into Rome proper from Vatican City, the security teams secured the gates receiving word of a serious incident on the grounds.

A warbling klaxon alarm sounded in the Pontifical Governate offices. In the hallway connecting the chapel and throughout the building corridors, an announcement in Italian blared over the public-address system, followed by "Active Shooter, Active Shooter," in English, French and Spanish.

Cardinal Tullono wanted to reenter the chapel against the wishes of the Gendarmes and recent reinforcements arriving from inside the building. They considered the area unsafe with the situation not yet under control. The Cardinal continued his insistence. The guards yielded and preceded him with weapons drawn. An estimated eight persons cowered by the doorway on the marble floor next to the baseboard, two of them sobbing. In front of the altar dais on the floor, Gary lay lifeless with his eyes frozen open, unmoving as if staring at the ornate detail of the ceiling. The attending priest began to administer last rites after checking the neck artery and determining there was no pulse.

Crying, Sister Justine knelt over Michael as she attempted to deliver first aid. Blood oozing from his motionless body pooled on the floor. "Michael, you come back, you're not leaving me, you hear me, you're not leaving me."

Father Hernandez, kneeling opposite of Sister Justine, checked Michael's vitals, not able to find a pulse or any indication that he was breathing. The Father's eyes shrouded with tears as he began to deliver the last rites as a precaution.

"He's not dead!" Sister Justine hollered as tears poured from her eyes.

Father Hernandez replied in a soft tone. "Sister, he's gone."

"No!" Justine interrupted, as she grasped the side of Michael's face and put her forehead against his. "You can't die." She gasped for air between words. "You have to know that I'm leaving the church," she wept before gulping for air again. "There could be an us again." Her tears clouded her vision as she laid her head on Michael's chest. "You come back to me."

Father Hernandez sat back on the floor not anticipating Sister Justine's revelation.

"Michael," Sister Justine continued, still crying. "I…still…love…you." She kissed Michael's forehead.

The medical response teams arrived. The first set attempted to revive Michael and Gary, as the others rushed over and attended to the fallen Gendarmes. Additional security personnel with unsheathed weapons arrived and dispersed throughout the chapel, interrogating the cowering press members, searching each and requesting identification.

Cardinal Tullono sat in the first row of pews by the hall entrance bent over forward with his head in the palms of his hands, not wanting to move to his office upstairs under the recommendation of the security teams. *My God, what have I done?*

# Chapter 37 – Presentation

A shimmering ethereal light originating from behind the seated Cardinals prompted them to turn around. Entering from the rear of St. Peter's Basilica, Jude, accompanied by the Camerlengo and two plains clothed Swiss Guard members dressed in their traditional purple suits, approached the installed rows of chairs from the rear and strolled down the center aisle up to the temporary platform. The sweetest and fragrant smell of spices and flowers wafted in the air. A veiled, muscular angel with four wings, donning bright white linen-like garments, a purple sash, and leather sandals with straps crisscrossing up its calves, manifested and hovered several feet in the air before drifting down with its feet touching down upon the floor behind Cardinal Picoli and Jude. The angel raised its hand directing the two Swiss Guardsmen to hold fast – they trembled and remained still. The angel removed its veil to display the head of a human – bird hybrid. It glided across the floor behind Jude and the Camerlengo, watching the audience of Cardinals with a piercing stare.

"I present to you the blessed child, Jude Ignatius," the Holy Father announced. "Through him, the church will become the center of the church universal for all those involved with the Council of Churches and all religions,

377

and you my brothers will help to take the message of his arrival across the world."

Two additional angels materialized, one on each side of the temporary stage. Many of the Cardinals knelt and began to recite the rosary or articulated personal prayers. Others stood and performed the gesture of the cross.

The first angel turned and faced the congregation of Cardinals once he arrived at the stage. "Behold, we give unto you the presentation of the child who is worthy." Its voice bore a bassoon-like baritone quality and spoke with authority.

The angel turned to the child, kneeled, and bowed its head. The other two angels did the same. The Holy Father knelt and bowed towards the child. Many of the awestruck Cardinals not already kneeling followed suit.

"Holy is the child," the first angel said.

"Holy is the child," the other two angels mirrored.

The tonal quality of the three angels resembled that of a perfect in-tune acapella group.

A fourth of the conclave stood up from their seats and flowed out of the temporary pews from the sides, not wanting to participate with what they considered sacrilege. Several nudged their peers out of the way to make room while attempting to leave, without rendering an apology.

Jude stepped up to the microphone. "Where do you go Cardinal Rajesh from the Archdiocese of Dhaka, Cardinal Abernathy from the Archdiocese of London, Cardinal Jurilla from the Archdiocese of Cebu, Cardinal Grielle from the Archdiocese of Los Angeles, Cardinal Demetrius..." he asked as he continued through the litany of names of those who were attempting to leave, wanting to renounce the ceremony by their departure. Jude impressed only a few of those he called that he knew their names. They knelt in place to show homage. The remaining Cardinals, including Cardinal Grielle, continued to funnel out from the gathering as Jude finished the announcement of names.

Members of the Swiss Guard and Gendarme stationed on the periphery of the basilica interior raced over and encircled the Cardinals, all brandishing their submachine guns outward, with several of the senior officers unholstering their Glock handguns, interrupting Jude's call out of those attempting to leave. Four members of the Swiss Guard plainclothesmen wearing the dark purple suits rushed onto the stage, two pressing the tiny voice activated transceiver earpiece in their ear to prevent it from falling out. The commandant of the Swiss Guard darted up next to the Holy Father to escort him to safety. The two guards assigned to Jude attempted to direct him off stage.

"What's going on?" the Holy Father asked, complying with reluctance to the commandant's request.

"We need to get you to your residence for your protection. We received a transmission that there's been a shooting incident in the Santa Maria Regina Chapel," he whispered, loudly enough for the Holy Father to hear while directing him over to the stairs of the platform. The guards began to guide Jude in the opposite direction.

"Hold fast," Jude said, stepping away from his security team. "We're fine here, don't you see the host of angels and men around us." He walked up to the microphone. "Cardinals of whom I have the greatest admiration and respect, there is an incident that has occurred over in the Chapel Santa Maria Regina. You'll find that we are quite safe here. Although we had planned for a special walkthrough and reveal after our meeting today, let not your hearts be heavy. All plans will come to their fruition. First and foremost, I am the one of whom the Sons of God have heralded, I am the one, I am the child."

Jude spoke with authority impressing most of the Cardinals as he described his inception, unique birth, and education.

# Chapter 38 – Papal Announcement

Interest intensified throughout the Holy See and the public with the mysterious events occurring outside St. Peter's Basilica, and reports of a shooting on the grounds of the city-state. News stories stated the wounding of one Gendarme, and two who died protecting a high-ranking Cardinal assigned to the Roman Curia. Press releases flowed from Vatican City stating that the Holy Father delayed the scheduled Papal audience by forty-eight hours, where he was to make a monumental announcement in Saint Peter's square.

Two days later, the rescheduled time arrived. The Holy Father appeared onto the small terrace by his residence used to address the crowd, stepping up to the clear Plexiglas podium with attached microphone. Angels materialized and floated above the square encircling the throng of spectators. The awestruck multitude silenced and gazed in wonderment. The Holy Father began his speech.

\* \* \* \*

The announcer proclaimed a throng of angels arrived and appeared as if floating above St. Peter's Square. Television screens and monitors across the world displayed vague and indistinguishable light distortions.

Cardinal Tullono turned off his office's flat screen television receiving the closed-circuit transmission of the Holy Father's speech presented from his residence's balcony in the square. Cardinal Grielle and Father Hernandez, visiting Cardinal Tullono, were appreciative with him not wanting to watch the remainder of the broadcast.

"Father, how's Sister Justine doing?" Cardinal Grielle asked. "It's been a couple of days now."

"She's still in mourning at the convent getting some rest. She does want to join us on the flight in transporting Mr. Saunders remains back to the states." Father Hernandez didn't want to mention that Sister Justine was mad at him, believing he didn't try hard enough in trying to save Michael's life.

"I have no problems with that, "Cardinal Grielle said. "And I'm glad you're able to help counsel her. We do need to put all of this behind us and move forward."

"Move forward?" Father Hernandez said, standing up and beginning to pace back and forth in the office. "Your Eminence, we now have a greater purpose ahead of us, we have to prevent the child from ascending to whatever they have planned,"

Cardinal Tullono returned to his chair and sat. "Just what is it you think we can do about that arrogant snit?"

"That's just it, have you noticed how prideful he is? I don't think there's an ounce of humility within him," Father Hernandez said, as he focused his attention towards Cardinal Tullono. "And if there was, it's a false humility. Remember how he commissioned artwork to magnify himself."

"None of this is my concern now," Cardinal Tullono said. "I must be prepared to accept responsibility for what's happened to Mr. Saunders."

"I don't get it?" Cardinal Grielle said. "Why do you think you're involved with any of what's going on?"

Father Hernandez himself was confused and stopped pacing.

Cardinal Tullono hesitated before answering. "The Gendarmerie Corps detectives are working their investigation into what happened in the chapel, and I've had to admit to my unknowing involvement. I approved for those two men pretending they were members of the press to have access onto the grounds. I didn't know about their backgrounds, or their association with those involved with the death of Cardinal Millhouse. I assumed I was doing an acquaintance a favor, someone who turned out not to be who I thought they were."

Father Hernandez shuddered with disbelief. "Why? What?"

"I should've told you sooner, but I can't explain it all to you. I was told yesterday afternoon to expect for the Holy Father to censure me and submit my resignation. If I wasn't so concerned about my past, none of this would've happened. That's all I'm going to say. Cardinal Grielle is correct, we need to put all of this behind us and let God handle it from this point on."

"You're still looking at everything that's happened since we began this undertaking through the eyes of the world," Father Hernandez said. "I'm trying to look at it all through the eyes of God. As such, I believe the child will be more of a spiritual wolf in sheep's clothing. There is nothing biblical regarding any of this, in his conception, if

383

you call it that, his advent, his presentation…nothing. He must be stopped."

"Listen to you, Father, one could say the same about you becoming so arrogant as to think you're the one to stop all of this," Cardinal Tullono rebuked. "And you're talking about squaring up against a child,"

"You've seen him, is he really a child. Think about what or who he is," Father Hernandez responded. "The short time when I, Sister Justine, and Michael Saunders talked to him back in Los Angeles, his knowledge and demeanor was anything but."

"Father, listen to yourself," Cardinal Grielle said. "You lost a friend and haven't mentioned anything about it in the last two days. I know Mr. Saunders may have been difficult, but he was straightforward and direct. You lost a friend."

"And do you know who Aurora is?" Father Hernandez said, ignoring Cardinal Grielle's comment not wanting to focus on Michael's passing. Being angry helped to distract him and displace the sorrow on the loss of his friend. "I think I realize now, it is a subordinate to the glorious angel of the dawn, the bright shining one who presented the message of the child those years ago, the nameless one with many names."

"What are you saying," Cardinal Tullono asked.

"We've been circling around this all along and didn't realize it. The child is an unholy hybrid of fallen man and the first fallen angel."

"Are you saying what I think you're saying?" Cardinal Grielle asked.

"I believe we're witnessing the rise of the Antichrist, an imitation to the perfect humanity of Christ. It was so simple I didn't even recognize it."

"Whether the child is or not, that's not important at this time," Cardinal Grielle said in a soft voice as he got up and walked over to Father Hernandez, placing his hands on the father's shoulder. "You lost a friend, don't run away from that."

\* \* \* \*

In St. Peter's Square, the Holy Father finished his speech and introduction of Jude to the world. The arrival of angels, along with their singing at the time of the presentation validated the child's prominence in the eyes of most everyone watching, with the crowd chanting "Hail Jude Ignatius, Hail Jude Ignatius." After several minutes, the Holy Father and Jude stepped inside from the balcony into the residence. One of the attending priests closed the door to the terrace dampening the noise from the thunderous shouts of cheers and ovations.

Cardinal Picoli worried observing the complexion of the Holy Father had become pale. "Your Holiness, are you all right?"

"I don't feel well," the Holy Father said, as he walked over to the bed, laid down and closed his eyes.

\* \* \* \*

Cardinal Tullono, Cardinal Grielle, and Father Hernandez all sat in Cardinal Tullono's office for fifteen minutes not finding anything to say.

Father Hernandez forced himself not to cry, suppressing an onslaught of tears as he reflected on Michael. A question entered his mind concerning Sister Justine. "So, did you know about Sister Justine's intention to leave the Church?"

Cardinal Grielle knew Father Hernandez directed the question to himself. He held off from answering right away. Father Hernandez's harsh stare exposed he anticipated a response.

"I did. She told me the night before the Chapel incident but wanted me to keep quiet about it."

There was a gentle knock on the door.

"Enter," Cardinal Tullono said.

The Cardinal's attending priest stepped in, his eye deluged in tears.

"What is it, Father? Why are you crying?"

"The Holy Father has died."

## Chapter 39 – Return

Xavier emailed an encrypted message to Angelo.

*As you're aware, team member was successful in reconciling the deception against your sponsors. Reports have confirmed that the expiry of our primary goal was successful. There was no opportunity to accomplish actions against the secondary objective. Currently taking up residence at predetermined safe house outside Paris in Boulogne-Billancourt. Request exit protocols.*

Angelo's response followed an hour later.

*With the death of the Pope, the Camerlengo will be Pope Emeritus until an official vote for the ascension of the child, and the fulfillment for the tradition of white smoke. Some reports state the delay of the vote will be eight to ten years. Another Vatican City source divulged that there is great divide as to if the Church would follow these wishes of the Holy Father. We may soon be able to take advantage of the rift. At this time, the leadership in Vatican City forced the primary source that helped with your access into the city to retire, thus we will need to cultivate another operative.*

*The alliance of sponsor nations that formed since the Council of Rome has fractured. We learned that the angels helping to direct our endeavors have been misdirecting not only the leaders of Nadia's government, but several of our other employer's governments over the years, who are now disavowing all your activities.*

*After the supernatural events that occurred while you were in Vatican City, many across the world are not quite ready to accept the related religious announcement. Yet, half of our sponsor nations are turning to support the child. They are impressed with his intelligence and abilities which they consider genius and supernatural. Under the Vatican's authority, he released a twenty-year plan to support his concepts and ideas for the consolidation of banking, trade, economies, and security amongst the nations. Some analyze this as possible aspirations for secular governance as well. If you had been successful with the secondary target, none of this would be an issue.*

*With the falling away of support for our contracts, and the rift growing between the nations, effectively nullifying our earlier work, we will not be able to establish an exit corridor. Several nations have labeled you and your team terrorists. You will need to work your own exit strategies out of Europe.*

\* \* \* \*

Father Hernandez read the following excerpt from a newspaper article concerning the recent events in Rome while waiting to board his plane in Rome for the return home.

> *Thanks to an anonymous tip, police tracked one of the two terrorists responsible for the attack in a smaller chapel on the grounds of Vatican City four days ago to an apartment in a suburb outside of Paris. Police killed the man during the confrontation as he attempted to resist arrest. It's reported the two men involved in the shooting had acted alone.*

*       *       *       *

Father Hernandez presided over the short and terse graveside funeral mass. Those in attendance were remnants of Michael's family, Justine, Stephen Williams, Alder Dennison, the Dean of Michael's department, along with several of Michael's peers and students from the university, and Alicia. Cardinal Grielle commissioned for a large wreath of white roses upon an easel delivered to the service. Father Carson attended in his place.

The benediction signaled for the mortuary attendant to lay Michael to rest by activating the casket lowering device. As the coffin descended into the ground, Alicia brandished furled eyebrows focusing a harsh stare towards Justine. Justine ignored her.

After the service as the mourners returned to their vehicles, Father Hernandez, Justine, and Stephen walking together breathed in a dense scent of flowers, cinnamon, spices, and fresh rain water. The aroma was familiar. Father Hernandez and Justine then felt as if someone had tapped them from behind on the shoulder. They turned around. Stephen noticing his two companions did the same. Ashere had walked up to the gravesite wearing a well-tailored black skirt suit, natural tone stockings, and conservative black pumps. Her long black hair radiated a clean and glossy sheen.

It took a moment for the father and Justine to recognize her.

"Who's that?" Stephen asked. He didn't recognize her as the same woman who had stood at his bedside when he awoke from his coma, or as the one escorted by an angel, who surprised him by his car when he had visited Cardinal Millhouse back at the Los Angeles Cathedral months prior.

"Someone who can probably answer a lot of questions I have," Father Hernandez replied.

As they strolled back up the small knoll, an angel appeared behind Ashere. Stephen recognized the ethereal individual in vibrant white linen wearing a golden sash and leather sandals with straps crisscrossing up its calves. Broad snow-white wings emerged from the rear shoulder blade region. It was as Abriel. Stephen's two companions seemed oblivious to the new arrival. He was about to acknowledge the angel's presence, when Abriel shook his head while putting his index finger pointing upward to his closed mouth gesturing for him to hush. Stephen kept quiet and then remembered the woman as Ashere.

"Ashere, we weren't sure if you would show up or not," Father Hernandez said, surprised she was well dressed and groomed. "Aren't you afraid for your safety?"

"Why did this happen?" Justine asked.

Ashere's eyes saturated with tears. "Everything that's happened is beyond us now, as God said it would be." She wiped her cheeks to remove evidence of crying.

"God allowed this happen, for Michael to die?" Justine said, with scorn. Her small petite face framed puffy blue eyes and flushed cheeks.

"I'm saying we don't control who lives and who dies."

"You're saying there's a reason for Michael to die," Justine said, while sniffling. "He may have been difficult, but that's no reason for him to die, he was a good man."

"You, more than most, know better, there's no reason for any men to die, but why do we? All men die, and that's why we have a need for a savior. It's not based on how good we are."

"So now you're gonna lecture us on theology?" Father Hernandez said, jumping into the conversation. "The savior was the ideal on how men should live."

Father Hernandez recalled how Michael would berate him for bringing religion into their conversations. Here it is now he was doing the same with Ashere.

"Think about this, Michael died so that Justine may live," Ashere said. "Before the disappearance of millions across the world, I considered myself a good person, but never knew God. I believed that I was doing his work at Everest, until Doctor Cochrane showed me some verses in the bible. I became conflicted, but after what happened to me at the funeral in Aguascalientes, and during the eulogy of angels all those years after the world wide disappearance, my path began to change and an angel ministered unto me. You, Father, I suspect know who the child is – the Antichrist. And is he real, the embodiment of arrogance? On the other side of the scale, the true Christ, do any of us here truly know who he is? We know him and his finished work on the cross for our sins to be

391

real, and not a mere archetype. Do any of you believe and accept that?"

Ashere turned and walked away.

\* \* \* \*

Later in the evening, after prayer and spiritual deliberation, Father Hernandez typed a letter of resignation as a priest in the Holy Roman Church.

Ω Ω Ω Ω

You can find bonus information "The Writings of Michael Saunders" at

https://jjkr-writings.info/angelsbackground

# *Acknowledgments*

I want to first thank the reader for taking the journey through the series, and hope you enjoyed the story. Unbelievably, I referenced much of the science in the story from current day science news. I find it interesting how science could crossover with religion, grounding our beliefs.

Hilda, Matt, Debbie, Mark, Darlene, and Bobby, thank you for making each Sunday worth the drive down to church. You continue to be a blessing.

I also want to thank the wonderful efforts of the editorial team and beta readers who worked on this project.

# About the Author

Jerry Rogers retired as career airman and civilian technician working both in the United States Air Force and in the California Air National Guard. He has over thirty-one years' experience working in technology supporting legacy and state-of-the-art telecommunication and data-communication systems. He also worked for nearly seven years at two post-production film companies working in Information Technology. One of Jerry's greatest joys is being able to teach at a small church in Orange County, researching biblical history, and unique science facts. He's traveled across the vast country to each of the contiguous forty-eight states and the world to both Southwest Asia and Europe.

Ever since he was a teenager, Jerry's has had a fascination with Religion and Science Fiction and has enjoyed writing, starting with writing short stories over the years. He took the next step and wrote a humorous novella called "The Legend of the Salad Traveler." He later began working on his first novel, the Fallen and the Elect in 2011 developing the concept after months of research, building notes, and jotting down ideas. The story has now blossomed into a full supernatural mystery and religious surrealism story blending both religion and a sprinkling of Science Fiction.

See what else is brewing at his website at http://www.jjkr-writings.info.

# *Other Works*

*I will bless those who bless you, and whoever curses you I will curse; and all peoples on earth will be blessed through you.* Genesis 12:3

*How you have fallen from heaven, morning star, son of the dawn!* Isaiah 14:12(a)

*I have come in My Father's name, and you do not receive Me; if another comes in his own name, you will receive him.* John 5:43

Made in the USA
Middletown, DE
07 August 2020

14728462R00225